Ahasuerus

Ahasuerus

by
Edgar Quinet

translated, annotated and introduced by
Brian Stableford

A Black Coat Press Book

Visit our website at www.blackcoatpress.com

ISBN 978-1-61227-214-6. First Printing. September 2013. Published by Black Coat Press, an imprint of Hollywood Comics.com, LLC, P.O. Box 17270, Encino, CA 91416. All rights reserved. Except for review purposes, no part of this book may be reproduced or transmitted in any form or by any means, electronic or mechanical, including photocopying, recording, or by any information storage and retrieval system, without permission in writing from the publisher. The stories and characters depicted in this novel are entirely fictional. Printed in the United States of America.

Introduction

Ahasvérus by Edgar Quinet, here translated as *Ahasuerus*, was first published in 1834 by the Bureau de la Revue des Deux Mondes. The *Revue des Deux Mondes* was the periodical for which Quinet was then working; founded in 1829; the editor who had taken it over in 1831, its editor François Buloz, had rapidly made it one of the chief focal points for the activity of the French Romantic Movement, featuring the literary work of Victor Hugo, George Sand, Honoré de Balzac, Alfred de Vigny and Alfred de Musset, among others, although it differed from the movement's other chief organ, the *Revue de Paris*, in adopting a much broader remit in its articles on cultural, political and economic affairs. Quinet, a historian of a new breed, interested in human history in its broadest sense, seen primarily as the history of ideas, and intent on developing a theoretical account of the progressive evolution of those ideas, was an important contributor in helping to shape and develop that agenda.

Excerpts from *Ahasvérus* had been published in the *Revue des Deux Mondes* in the year before its release in book form, and it had been represented in advance as a work of an entirely new kind: an epic drama, in prose rather than verse, which would encapsulate the theory of history that Quinet was trying to develop in its broadest possible sense, in a quasi-allegorical fashion. It would place the history of humankind within a context derived from the principal means by which the ancestors of the people of Quinet's era and culture had tried to interpret their own identity and history, and thus further their development: the Christian religion. Rather than dealing with the evolution of the religion as a historical phenomenon, as he had already done and was to do much more elaborately in his non-fiction, Quintet set out in *Ahasvérus* to turn that process inside out, using the ideas of the religion as a mythological container and framework for the phenomena of history.

The story told in *Ahasvérus* thus begins with the Creation of the world—preceded by a prelude in which God, his angels and saints are imagined to be conducting a critical review of his work—and, with only a handful of brief pauses for detailed examination, moves rapidly to its supposed future terminus: the Last Judgment. Because it is a critical analysis rather than a dramatization, however, the "plot" does not conclude with the Last Judgment, as previous literary visions of the Apocalypse had done, but goes beyond it, in order to pass judgment on the verdict. In this epic, therefore—uniquely, at the time—the Last Judgment is not only appealed but set aside, re-weighed in a supposedly-superior balance and found wanting.

The verdict passed on the human race by the Eternal Father is supplemented by a very different individual judgment delivered by Christ of a particular individual that he had cursed to be a witness to the unfolding of human history—Ahasvérus, the Wandering Jew of legend—but even that is not the end of the story. Having overturned the traditional Last Judgment and substituted one more in keeping with modern ideas, the author continues his narrative to provide a further vision, which passes judgment not on humankind but on God himself—or, strictly speaking, on the idea of God—in a curious and strangely poignant coda.

That tripartite climax went far beyond all previous literary ambition, and deliberately so. The work was planned from the outset as something uniquely far-reaching, and, by virtue of the manner of its publication, was loudly trumpeted as such. The novel's publication date is sometimes given in bibliographies as 1833, not so much because of the appearance of excerpts in the *Revue des Deux Mondes* in that year, but because the periodical published a long review-essay of the complete text in December 1833 by the critic Charles Magnin, "*Ahasvérus* et de la nature du génie poétique," [*Ahasvérus* and the Nature of Poetic Genius] which—as its title indicates—

proclaimed the work's virtues in no uncertain terms. Magnin's essay was reprinted as a preface in the second edition of *Ahasvérus*, issued in 1843, and again in the version included in Quinet's *Oeuvres complètes* in 1858, and has thus remained firmly associated with it ever since, ensuring that the text has always been accompanied by a certification, not merely of its ambition, but of its genius.

The notion of the work's literary genius was not endorsed by all the work's contemporary critics, and the tripartite climax provided a challenge to religious believers, which was bound to make the work seem dangerously heretical to some. Its sheer peculiarity meant that many readers simply did not know what to think about it, finding it too alien for comfortable analysis, there being nothing else in the literary canon at the time—and precious little since—with which it might be juxtaposed for the purpose of comparison. Whether it is a work of genius or not, however, it is certainly an extraordinarily exceptional work, whose uniqueness recommends it for attention and admiration.

Even if it is considered to be merely bizarre, the extremity of *Ahasvérus*' bizarrerie establishes it as a literary landmark; whether or not one disagrees with the import of its philosophy, there is no doubt that it does have sufficient ingenuity and philosophical profundity to make it worthy of serious contemplation and consideration. It is astonishing that it has not been translated into English previously; had it been translated in the 1830s, it might well have risked prosecution under English law on a charge of "blasphemous libel"—the charge that suppressed the full version of Percy Shelley's "Queen Mab," one of the few works with which *Ahasvérus* bears some slight comparison—but that does not explain why no one undertook the task when that danger receded.

Edgar Quinet was born in 17 February 1803 at Bourg-en-Bresse in the Ain. His mother's family was Protestant, his father's Catholic; although Quinet was received into the Catholic Church, taking his first communion there, his personal beliefs seem to have been in conflict even then, and to have remained conflicted throughout his life. His father was a fervent republican who had resigned his commission in the army after Napoléon's coup in order to devote himself to scientific studies. In spite of his own resignation, and although he had left Edgar almost entire to the care of his mother previously, Jérôme Quinet wanted his son to go into the army after finishing his studies in Bourg and the Collège de Lyon, but Edgar wanted to go his own way, and was already nursing literary ambitions at the age of seventeen. The subsequent dispute soured his relationship with his father permanently, and made Edgar's close relationship with his mother increasingly awkward.

Jérôme Quinet initially accompanied his son to Paris in 1820 in order to enroll him in the École Polytechnique, but was persuaded to compromise and allow him to study law instead. As soon as he was left to his own devices, however, Edgar began to neglect the narrow curriculum prescribed for law students in order to develop much wider scholarly interests and attempt to develop his literary talents. His first publication, in 1823, was *Tablettes du juif errant* [Pages from the Wandering Jew's Notebook], which was planned as an extensive work but eventually materialized—when he could not interest a publisher in a fuller version of the envisaged project—as a relatively brief piece, little more than a short story.

When Quinet reprinted *Ahasvérus* in volume VII of his *Oeuvres complètes* in 1858, he accepted the inevitability of appending *Tablettes du juif errant* to it, but took care to emphasize in his preface not only that it was an item of juvenilia, really unworthy of preservation, but that it was so completely different from the later work as to qualify as its "opposite" rather than a preliminary sketch. The difference is not quite as extreme as he suggested, however; *Tablettes* is a first-person narrative in which the Wandering Jew offers a few flippant anecdotes excerpted from the long catalogue of his memories, but the sum of those anecdotes does provide a synoptic account of a theory of history, in which the evolution of the

Christian religion inevitably plays a central role. In consequence, it does share a certain degree of common consciousness with the late work, which is not so much an opposite as an inversion of it.

Quinet became something of a wanderer himself after 1823—a circumstance whose irony, in the context of his two accounts of the Wandering Jew, did not escape him. He suggested in the preface to the serialized excerpts that he had been working on the longer work throughout that interim, although other evidence makes it clear that he did not actually set out to compose *Ahasvérus* until 1831. What he evidently meant was that he had continued his experimental literary endeavors during his various travels, thus laying useful groundwork for his major endeavor; given the patchwork nature of *Ahasvérus*, it is by no means improbable that some of the individual "monologues" or "prose poems" making up its substance had been written long before he began to conceived the overall plan of the epic and began to organize it as a focused and coherent endeavor.

Quinet's original intention in setting out on his travels was to go to America, and he initially went to England with the plan of obtaining a passage from there to New York after a relatively brief sojourn, but he was summoned back to France when his sister fell dangerously ill; although he subsequently returned to England, he then changed direction and went to Germany instead of America, where he spent a good deal of time in the late 1820s. That change of agenda was inspired by the fact that while he was in England, attempting to master the language fully before going on to New York, he read an English translation of Johann Gottfried Herder's *Indeen zur Philosophie der Geschichte de Mensscheit* [Outlines of the Philosophy of the History of Humankind], which struck him with the force of a revelation, perhaps all the more so because Herder had died (in 1803) leaving it incomplete, crying out for further elaboration and proper conclusion. Quinet began work almost immediately on a French translation, although he had to learn German in order to do that, and he went to Germany partly to secure that education and partly to track Herder's work, as it were, to its source in German idealistic philosophy and the German Romantic Movement—or, as it was represented in Herder's day, as the *Sturm und Drang* [Storm and Stress] movement.

Herder, born in 1744, had been a student of Immanuel Kant at the University of Königsberg, but had become a protégé of Kant's less famous colleague Johann Hamann, whose inclinations were far more mystical, and who was more interested in the emotions than the "pure" and "practical" reasoning of which Kant produced his two epoch-making analyses. Herder did, however, retain enough Kantian influence to import a strong element of rational pretention into his analyses, whose initial target was German literature and its history. It was that interest which brought him into contact with J. W. Goethe in 1770, and it was his crucial influence on Goethe's literary endeavors that founded the *Sturm und Drang* movement and gave birth to German Romanticism, helping to ensure the strong influence thereon of idealistic philosophy and a marked interest in national folklore as a key to the evolution of national identity.

Although Herder insisted in the book that made such a deep impact on Quinet that history ought to be and could be a science, he was also insistent that it was essentially the history of ideas rather than mere events, and that ideas were the true actors in history, while human collectives were the embodiments of those ideas and individual humans merely microcosms reflecting the macrocosmic ideas of their religions and nations.

That approach to history was crucial to Quinet's conceptualization of *Ahasvérus* and is essential to the understanding of it; the "characters" in the epic are ideas, which have their own evolutionary dynamic, and the material entities featured therein—which include cities and natural phenomena as well as individuals, such as Ahasvérus, the Christ who curses him and the fallen angel who loves him—are essentially symbolic expressions or representations of those ideas. Such eccentrically-loquacious voices as the various cities, the Ocean, Strasbourg Cathedral and personalized Death, here conceived as an old crone named Mob, can all meet and converse on more-or-less equal terms within the framework of the drama, which is set in a hypothetical "mindspace" rather than scenes sketched in the backcloths of an imagined stage.

Although Herder and Quinet were not as extreme in their philosophical idealism as Johann Gottlieb Fichte, who argued that Kant's notion of a "noumenal" world of things-in-themselves ought to be rejected, in accordance with the recognition that consciousness can have no reliable grounding outside its own contents (solipsism), there is a sense in which *Ahasvérus* is a thoroughly solipsistic work, set entirely within the consciousness of its author or reader, not merely in the inevitable and trivial sense that all literary works are essentially immaterial, but in a deliberate and methodical manner.

Because literary endeavor is a kind of "secondary creation" (as the German idealistic philosopher Alexander Baumgarten put it) no literary work can contain a "real world" and "God" can never be any more, in any literary work, than a character enslaved to the author's notion of him, but most authors nevertheless insist on maintaining the pretence that they are writing about an external "primary creation," which they are doing their utmost to represent accurately. *Ahasvérus* makes no such pretence; within Quinet's work, the secondary world of his fiction is simply and manifestly a nexus of ideas, and God, like Ahasvérus, the sea and the stones in the road, is simply an idea within it, operating purely in relationship to other ideas. The question of God's possible real existence outside the text is simply not an issue, any more than the question of whether there ever really was a Wandering Jew. The reader who cannot appreciate that has little chance of understanding the grounds on which the novel's Last Judgment is appealed, and the reason why the story then extends further than the revised judgment to the magnificently peculiar third element of its tripartite climax.

Quinet's translation of Herder was brought to the attention, in advance of its publication, of the French realist philosopher Victor Cousin (1792-1867), who was also famous as a great orator and educationalist. Although Cousin had by then rejected the idealistic philosophy that had once fascinated him, he had retained a strong scholarly interest in it, and he saw Quinet's philosophical pilgrimage to Germany—which had included meetings with Goethe, Ludwig Tieck and other contemporary stars of the Romantic Movement—as the echo of one he had made himself, in order to meet G. W. F. Hegel and Friedrich Schelling. Cousin immediately took Quinet under his wing, and introduced him to other members of his intellectual circle.

The most important contact Quinet made via Cousin's patronage was another ambitious young historian, Jules Michelet, with whom he formed a lifelong friendship of great importance to both writers, but Cousin also introduced him to the famous salon-keeper Madame Récamier and her great friend René Chateaubriand, hailed by the members of the French Romantic Movement as their founding father, and author of the influential *Génie du Christianisme* (1802; tr. as *The Genius of Christianity*), another work that Quinet had found inspiring, and on whose intellectual legacy he tried to build.

Cousin also brought Quinet into contact with Pierre-Simon Ballanche, another unorthodox historian attempting to develop a theoretical overview of human evolution. In that quest, Ballanche had given a crucial role to the notion of "palingenesis," or successive regeneration, by means of which he tried to combine two theses then generally seen as competing rivals: the assertion that all civilizations went through a kind of life-cycle in which they were doomed to decadence once they had passed their peak, and the notions of continual social progress based on technological and scientific advancement.

Like Herder, Ballanche did not live long enough to finished his intended masterwork explaining the palingenetic history of humankind, but he did contrive to produce a sketch of it in literary form, *La Vision d'Hébal* (1931)[1], with which Quinet must have been familiar, and which might well have helped to prompt him to plan his own literary sketch of his very different thesis. Like *Ahasvérus*, *La Vision d'Hébal* begins with the Creation and proceeds to a futuristic Last Judgment, but the devout Ballanche's last judgment really is final, providing an justificatory "explanation" of the vicissitudes of human history, in which the continual rise and fall of civilizations is explained as a necessary epicycle with a progressive pattern that ultimately leads to a triumphant Christ-assisted redemption. There is a sense in which the argument of *Ahasvérus* is a flat contradiction of Ballanche's thesis; in Quinet's skeptical thinking, humankind does not stand in need of moral redemption but in need of imaginative liberation; in the final analysis, the idea of a divine judgment, however well-intentioned and useful it might once have been as a moral spur, is a shackle better cast off and left behind.

Victor Cousin also used his social influence to further Quinet's travels, by obtaining an appointment for him in 1829 to accompany a government mission to Greece, then attempting to obtain independence from the Ottoman Empire. With that experience behind him, Quinet hoped to obtain a government post in France after the "July Revolution" of 1830, but the outcome of that upheaval—which replaced the superannuated Bourbon dynasty with the more liberal monarchy of Louis-Philippe—proved disappointingly slight to the staunchly republican Quinet, and his views were apparently considered far too radical for him to be given any further political appointment. He joined the staff of the *Revue des Deux Mondes* instead, immediately beginning to contribute substantial articles on various historical and political topics, including "De l'avenir des religions [On the Future of Religions] (1831) and "L'Avenir de l'art" [The Future of Art] (1832). He had already followed up his Herder translation with a book researched

---

[1] tr. as "Hébal's Vision" and included in *Investigations of the Future*, Black Coat Press, ISBN 9781612271064.

13

during his excursion to Greece, *De la Grèce moderne, et ses rapports avec l'antiquité* [On Modern Greece and its relationship with Antiquity] (1830) and he also produced *De l'Allemagne et de la Révolution* [On Germany and Revolution] (1832) before completing *Ahasvérus*.

Shortly after publishing *Ahasvérus* in 1834, Quinet married Minna Moré, whom he had first glimpsed at a concert in Germany some years before and with whom he had fallen in love at first sight, although their subsequent relationship had proved direly difficult because of parental opposition on both sides, partly occasioned by the fact that he was notionally a Catholic while her family was Protestant (they were eventually married in a Protestant ceremony).

Given the solipsistic quality of the project, it is entirely natural that Quinet's relationship with Minna, and the problems surrounding it, should have had just as much influence on the drama's contents as any of the historical and philosophical issues developed therein, and it is a much stronger work in consequence. The intensity of the relationship between Ahasvérus and Rachel, clearly reproducing essential sentimental elements of the relationship between Quinet and Minna, as he perceived it in 1831-33, is not merely a supplement to Quinet's philosophical considerations regarding the pattern of human social evolution and the motor of history but is inextricably bound up with them.

It is important to bear in mind, while reading *Ahasvérus*—especially the scene in which Mob takes Ahasvérus and Rachel to Strasbourg to be married—that when Quinet wrote it, he did not know that he would eventually be able to marry Minna, and undoubtedly suspected and dreaded that he might not. The interlude between the third and fourth days, when Quinet appears in the text as "The Poet" is a frank expression of despair that he would ever be able to attain that goal.

It is worth noting, in this context, that the first edition of the text has a dedication that reads, in translation: "To Madame Sophie D., testimony of a pious respect. This book is dedicated to you. When it is forgotten, you alone will remember the man who wrote it." Subsequent scholars contrived to expand the surname of the dedicatee as "Duvant," crediting it to a young woman with whom, according to Albert Valès, Quinet had a brief "pure but dolorous" love affair in the late 1820s, although a more recent study by Willy Aeschimann claims that her surname was actually Duvault. The uncertainty is revealing in itself, as is the fact that the dedication was removed from all future editions.

Whatever the significance of that dedication was (and it might be deliberately misleading), it still needs to be remembered, in reading *Ahasvérus*, that when Quinet wrote the book he was deeply unhappy, and far from any confidence that he would eventually be cured of that unhappiness—as, in fact, he was, by his subsequent marriage—although the last phase of the narrative clearly expresses the hope that he might be. The epic quality of *Ahasvérus* inevitably invites comparison with Goethe's epic drama of *Faust*, but there are also marked echoes in its more personal episodes of Goethe's other Sturm und Drang classic, the maudlin sentimental melodrama *Die Lieden des jungen Werthers* (1774; tr. as *The Sorrows of Young Werther*).

Because the limited time Quinet spent in France during the late 1820s was largely absorbed by his family and the social contacts he made via Victor Cousin, his communication with the other literary figures who came to constitute the Romantic Movement in that period was limited. The one he knew best was Jules Janin, the pioneer of *roman frénétique* [frantic fiction], of whom he had twice been a schoolfellow, once at school in Lyon and then again while studying law in Paris. Quinet's various biographers report that when Janin heard in 1831 that Quinet intended to begin work of a work of imaginative fiction he immediately volunteered to collaborate on it, but that Quinet refused.

By that time Quinet was certainly acquainted with Victor Hugo, with whose political ideas he had a good deal in common, but he does not seem to have attended the *cénacle* that Hugo hosted, at least not on a regular basis. Information is, however, a trifle sparse; when Quinet eventually began to write the autobiography on which most of his subsequent biographers relied for information—which he never finished, although he thought that he ought to include it in his *Oeuvres complètes* regardless, and which stops short of 1831 in its internal chronology—he titled it, perhaps inevitably, *Histoire de mes idées* [The History of my Ideas], concentrating entirely on his intellectual development and the influence thereon on his father, his mother and the books he read, and giving no details at all of his social life, beyond recording his debt to Cousin and Michelet, and none of his personal life, making only slight passing references to Minna. Although some further personal details were added to the record by two belated memoirs written by his second wife, Hermione Asachi, whom he married after Minna's death in the 1860s, they are inevitably scant and skewed in their perspective.

In spite of the lack of any close social relationship, however, Quinet can certainly be seen as a key member of the Romantic Movement as it took wing in the early 1830s, and was certainly seen as such at the time, by virtue of his association with the *Revue des Deux Mondes*. Quinet and Michelet can be considered to have formed the hard core of the "historical wing" of the movement, along with Hugo's close friend Paul Lacroix, who signed his most of his books "P. L. Jacob, Bibliophile."

Although there was probably little direct communication between the writers during the process of composition, it is of some significance that, as well as following on the heels of Ballanche's *Vision d'Hébal*, *Ahasvérus* was closely contemporary with Hugo's *Notre-Dame de Paris—1482* (1832) and Lacroix's *Danse macabre* (1833)[2], and has echoes of both of them, especially in the scene in which Strasbourg Cathedral

---

[2] Available in a Black Coat Press edition, ISBN 9781612272054.

becomes a key symbolic location, playing host to a dance of the dead. As an item of Romantic prose, *Ahasvérus* was a key contribution to the sudden and spectacular flowering of activity in that regard, outstripping the rest in narrative bizarrerie as well as philosophical ambition.

Although he was not unsympathetic to the historical role played by religions, which he considered to be vitally important to social evolution, Quinet's hostility to certain aspects of Catholic faith won him even more enemies than his political radicalism; *Ahasvérus* can easily be read as an atheistic and explicitly anti-Christian work, although that is probably not the right way to read it, and the apologetic ambiguity with which it is carefully dressed is genuinely representative of a theological uncertainty on Quinet's part. Anyone inclined to suspect the work of anti-Christian inclinations would not, however, have been reassured by the author's subsequent exploits as a polemicist, and there must have been a temptation to tar him with the same brush as Alphonse de Lamartine and Victor Hugo, both of whom eventually took skepticism to the extreme of producing literary works explicitly sympathetic to Satan's rebellion against divine authority, in *La Chute d'un ange* [The Fall of an Angel] (1838) and *La Fin de Satan* [The End of Satan] (incomplete; written 1854-62; published 1886) respectively.

That temptation must have been greatly increased by the obvious debt owed by Quinet's characterization of the fallen angel Rachel to Alfred de Musset's classic sympathetic depiction of a female fallen angel in the long poem "Eloa" (1824). It is, however, worth noting that one symbolic character conspicuous by his absence from the ideative schema of *Ahasvérus* is Satan. Although one of the interludes—all of which are extraneous to the narrative—features a devils' dance in which Lucifer takes part, he remains outside the story, confined to an insignificant annex; he comments dismissively on the plot from without, but is not involved in it. Hell is peripherally featured, and has one crucial line in a brief and terse dialogue with Heaven, but this imaginary history pays no attention to any War in Heaven and Lucifer does not assume the role of God's adversary.

Unlike Eloa, and the many other fallen angels featured in Romantic literature, Rachel does not fall from Haven out of mistaken sympathy for a handsome rebel angel, but by innocent sympathy for a wretched human being, and she is entirely unique. Quinet's theology is, in fact, radically un-Christian is ignoring the entire facet of Christian mythology related to active diabolism; it contains not the slightest hint of Manicheism. The belated Christian insertion of Satan into the story told in Genesis is flatly ignored, and although the account of the Creation features a symbolic Serpent, it is a serpent, not a devil in disguise; humans sins, in this schema, are purely human, not occasioned by any deliberate external temptation, and not to be subject to any demonic punishment.

This move not only separates *Ahasvérus* from the mainstream of the Romantic Movement as it was to continue in such masterworks of literary satanism as Gustave Flaubert's *La Tentation de saint Antoine* (1874; tr. as *The Temptation of Saint Anthony*) and Anatole France's *La Révolte des anges* (1914; tr. as *The Revolt of the Angels*), but from the entire Christian epic tradition prior to the evolution of the movement, extending from Dante's *Divina Comedia* (written c.1308-1321) through Joost van den Vondel's *Lucifer* (1654), John Milton's *Paradise Lost* (1667) and Friedrich Klopstock's *Der Messias* (1748-73) to Goethe's *Faust* (Part I 1806; Part II 1832). It is essential to the work that Ahasvérus is not an adversary but a victim, and that the historical schema of which he is an element features no active evil, but only a failure to live up to the highest standards of good—a failure of which Christ is arguably just as guilty as the man he curses, and for which even God may be judged when his own Judgment is called into question. That uniqueness is sufficient in itself to entitle the work to a special interest, from readers, literary historians and philosophers alike.

Quinet's reputation, and that of *Ahasvérus*, were considerably affected in his own lifetime by his subsequent exploits. Although he continued to devote the bulk of his effort to his non-fiction, he did try to follow up the literary debut he had made in *Ahasvérus*, writing two more epics in a more orthodox poetic form: *Napoléon* (1835) and *Prométhée* [Prometheus] (1838). Their reception was, however, muted, and they failed to confirm the reputation for "poetic genius" that Charles Magnin had claimed for him. The former, dealing with real events and personalities, inevitably relegating ideas to a background role, proved less conducive to the particular character of Quinet's thought, and although the second restored a mythological framework, employing Greek theodicy as a kind of stand-in for Christian theology, much as Percy Shelley had done in *Prometheus Unbound* (1820), the exercise was bound to seem more limited as well as a trifle secondhand. It is worth remembering in this context that, having married Minna, he no longer had the well of lachrymose desperation on which to draw that had provided so much sentimental fuel for the poignant heart of *Ahasvérus*.

After the relative failure of *Prométhée*, Quinet made the decision to concentrate entirely on his scholarly endeavors. In 1839 he obtained a professorship of foreign literature at the Université de Lyon, which he was able to relocate two years later to the College de France, thus moving back to Paris and the heart of French culture. He found it impossible to confine his interests and concerns to the specific subject he was supposed to be teaching, however, and used his lecture courses as a pulpit for the oratorical development of his ideas regarding history in general, French history in particular, and the specific role therein played by the Christian religion and the Catholic Church.

Partly by virtue of his close association with Jules Michelet, who was by then ten years into the monumental history of France that would eventually take him thirty years to complete, Quinet became interested and incensed by the role played in the history of Christendom by the Jesuits, which he began to criticize scathingly in a very public manner. The substance of his lectures on the subject was eventually integrated into a book co-signed with Michelet, *Des Jésuites*, published 1843, which caused such a fierce reaction that he was eventually sacked from his professorship in 1846. That simply relegated his polemicizing from the academic context to a more general political arena, and, like Victor Hugo and Alphonse de Lamartine, Quinet became an active revolutionary endeavoring to put an end to Louis-Philippe's monarchy and institute a new republic.

That endeavor helped to bring about the 1848 Revolution, and Quinet, like Hugo and Lamartine, was appointed to an office in the short-lived Second Republic, to which Louis-Napoléon's 1851 coup put an abrupt end. Like Hugo and many other prominent Republicans, Quinet went into exile, initially in Brussels and then in Switzerland. He continued to write copiously, and it was while in Switzerland that he organized the publication of the first version of his *Oeuvres complètes* in the late 1850s, although the set subsequently had to be increased by several more volumes to accommodate, among other works, his fourth major literary endeavor, the long philosophical Arthurian romance *Merlin l'enchanteur* [The Enchanter Merlin] (1862). Some commentators also place *La Création* (1870), which attempted to set the 19th century revolution in "natural history" in the more general context of the history of the human mind, in the category of literary works because of the ambition and eccentricity of its attempt to reconstitute a narrative prehistory of the Earth, and the human species, on the basis of paleontological and anthropological evidence that inevitably seems woefully thin today's standards, but it is better regarded as an offbeat exercise in popular science.

Like Hugo, Quinet refused to take advantage of the amnesty offered by the new emperor that allowed a number of other prominent writers, including Alexandre Dumas, to return to Paris and resume their careers there; he insisted on delaying his return to France until the collapse of the Second Empire in the Franco-Prussian War of 1870. He was, however, prompt in returning after the Battle of Sedan, arriving in time to play an active role in the subsequent siege of Paris, about which he published a book in 1871. His academic position was then returned to him, but he was no longer the firebrand he had been twenty years earlier, and the remainder of his career was relatively quiet and sedate. He died in Versailles in 1875.

It is probably appropriate to add to this introduction a brief account of the legend on which the eponymous hero of is based, and its previous literary uses. According to

George K. Anderson's admirably comprehensive account of *The Legend of the Wandering Jew* (Brown University Press, 1965) the story was first written down in the 13th century; as to how long it had flourished as an item of oral tradition before then we can only guess. It is a Christian adaptation of a much older idea; eternal restlessness is inflicted as a punishment for offences, in various Classical myths, and examples of accursed wanderers appear in both Judaic and Islamic mythology. Cain is sent into exile in the fourth chapter of *Genesis*, while the twentieth chapter of the Quran, parallel to the thirty-second chapter of *Exodus*, relates that Al-Sameri, the maker of the golden calf that lured the followers of Moses to apostasy was similarly cursed. In neither of those cases is it explicitly stated that the sinners are made immortal in order to suffer longer than a normal lifetime would permit, but it would have been easy enough for anyone familiar with the eternally tedious punishments inflicted in the Greek Underworld to add that inference.

The gospels of the New Testament are more preoccupied with the idea of immortality than the older writings they set out to overlay with a new faith, and there are passages in them that can construed as implying that Jesus decreed that certain individuals would not die until he returned. In *Matthew* 16:28 Jesus says to his disciples: "Verily I say unto you, There be some standing here, which shall not taste of death, till they see the Son of man coming in his kingdom" and in *John* 21:20-22,

21

Jesus replies to a question by Peter with words similar to those he was later credited with addressing to the accursed wanderer: "If I will that he tarry till I come, what is that to thee?" It is not entirely clear from the text whether Jesus is referring to John or to Judas, and some accounts of the Wandering Jew assume that he is, indeed, Judas.

The first surviving record of the legend as it became familiar dates from 1223 and appears in a Latin chronicle from Bologna; it tells of a Jew encountered by pilgrims in Armenia, who had taunted Jesus as he was going to his martyrdom and was told "I shall go, but you shall await me until I come again." It is alleged that ever since, the man in question had been rejuvenated to the apparent age of thirty at hundred year intervals. In referring to waiting rather than moving—thus echoing the passage from *John*—this version stresses the immortality of the Jew rather than his restlessness, an emphasis that was to cause some later writers to wonder whether his punishment was really so terrible. This doubt was reemphasized five years later by a more extensive account of the same story, recorded at St. Albans by the English monk Roger of Wendover.

Roger claims that St. Albans had been recently visited by an Armenian archbishop, who was questioned on the subject of rumors about an immortal man named Joseph. The archbishop replied that he had actually met the man in question, who had been a hall-porter in the service of Pontius Pilate, named Cartaphilus. This Cartaphilus had slapped Jesus on the back as he was being removed to be crucified, urging him to move faster, whereupon the fateful words—again referring to waiting rather than walking—were spoken to him. The report further adds that Cartaphilus was later baptized by the same man who baptized St. Paul, and had become a penitent ascetic.

Roger of Wendover's account was reproduced by his successor as chronicler at St. Albans, Matthew Paris. In later versions of the chronicle Matthew supplemented the story with endorsements by other supposed witnesses who had visited or come from Armenia. Various version of the St. Albans chronicle were copied and distributed abroad, Matthew Paris's ultimate version being widely circulated and translated. Its distribution was, however, subject to the limitations of the manuscript medium; the next important stage in the popularization of the legend came, inevitably, after the advent of printing—a technology whose destruction of the Church's virtual monopoly on the reproduction of ideas became part and parcel of the Reformation and the subsequent wars of religion.

The St. Albans chronicle was translated into German for a printed version in the 1580s; in 1602, about fifteen years after publication of the pamphlet that popularized the legend of Faust, a pamphlet printed in German appeared entitled *Kurtze Beschreibung von einem Juden mit Namen Ahasverus*. The story it tells is attributed to Paul von Eitzen, Bishop of Schleswig, who is said to have encountered "a very tall person" in a church in Hamburg in 1542, and to have learned from him that his name was Ahasuerus. Ahasuerus had been a shoemaker in Jerusalem and had cried out in anger when Jesus, carrying his cross, had stopped for a moment to rest against the wall of his house—whereupon Jesus replied: "I shall stand here and rest, but you must walk." After this, Ahasuerus was compelled to follow Jesus and witness his execution, and then to leave Jerusalem and wander about the world unceasingly, miserably but reverently certain of the truth of Christ's power and teaching. The pamphlet adds that Ahasuerus had been seen in Danzig as recently as the year 1599.

As with the legend of Faust, the contents of the German pamphlet were widely reprinted in new editions, translations and paraphrases; they were almost certainly re-appropriated into oral tradition, where they were amalgamated with other items of folklore. The story was exported to all of the major European languages; while it was told and retold it was presumably continually bolstered, after the manner of modern urban folktales, with news of more recent and local sightings of the immortal wanderer. Such embellishments helped to maintain the immediacy of the tale, and each new addition contributed more apparent substance to the weight of hearsay evidence. The 1602 pamphlet is as near to a "definitive" version of the story of the Wandering Jew as there is; it is the basis of most subsequent transfigurations.

Once the legend had become commonplace it invited both literary recycling and scholarly analysis. The symbolic significance of the accursed wanderer was extensively discussed by Johann Jacob Schudt's *Jüdische Merckwürdigkeiten* (1714-18), which concluded that Ahasuerus ought not to be imagined as a single person, but the entire Jewish people. Schudt's thesis was reiterated by others, sometimes broadened to make the wanderer a symbol of the existential predicament of the entire human race, and became a kind of standard interpretation, echoed in many literary transfigurations. The most significant use of the figure in 18th century French literature was in Simon Tyssot de Patot's utopian romance *La Vie, les aventures et le voyage au Groenland du Révérend Père Cordelier Pierre de Mésange* (1720).

The German pamphlet had first been translated into French in 1605 as *Discours véritable d'un Juif errant*, and one of its early reprints, in 1609, was supplemented by a *complainte*—a lyric lament—in which the wanderer makes much of the quality of his suffering, emphasizing that immortality is no boon in combination with eternal restlessness. The *complainte* remained associated with the story in many subsequent versions, and similar lyrics became at least as important in maintaining the currency of the legend in France as prose versions. The most important item of that kind appeared towards the end of the eighteenth century, relating to an alleged sighting of Ahasuerus in Brussels on 22 April 1774, celebrated in a Belgian *complainte* that came to be known as the Brabantine ballad, which was spread far and wide throughout France by virtue of an *image d'Épinal*: a pictorial print illustrating the Jew's confrontation with the burghers of Brussels, which sold in vast quantities through a distribution network of *colporteurs*.

24

The Brabantine ballad stimulated many imitations in France, the best-known derivative being an 1831 lyric by Pierre de Béranger, which was intended to be sung to a familiar tune, although new music was eventually provided for it by Charles Gounod. Quinet undoubtedly heard the original version, which might well have played some part in promoting him to begin work on *Ahasvérus*, and certainly added to the continuing popularity of the *image d'Épinal* in maintaining the currency of the legend and making the reference immediately comprehensible to Quinet's audience.

Quinet was by no means the first writer associated with the Romantic Movement to take an interest in the legend, and was undoubtedly familiar with at least one of several poems by German Romantic writers. The most famous was Christian Schubart's "Der Ewige Jude" [The Eternal Jew] (1783), an English translation of which prompted Percy Shelley to make use of the figure in "Queen Mab" and two other poems. There was, however, an English ballad, presumably adapted from the French *complaintes* and reproduced in Thomas Percy's *Reliques of Ancient English Poetry* (1765), which presumably had a similar influence, and was probably responsible for uses of the motif in various Gothic novels, most notably Matthew Gregory Lewis' *The Monk* (1796) and William Godwin's *St. Leon* (1799). Although the only English Romantic to whom specific mention is made in *Ahasvérus* is Byron, it is not improbable that Quinet was familiar with other English examples.

Ahasvérus was undoubtedly influential, in its turn, on subsequent works, most obviously in France, although it might also have helped to stimulate the German Romantic Julius Mosen to produce his own epic *Ahasvar* (1838). By far the most famous subsequent French version was Eugène Sue's extraordinarily elaborate *Le Juif errant* (1844; tr. as *The Wandering Jew*)—in which Ahasuerus plays a purely symbolic role—produced at the height of the newspaper circulation war conducted by means of feuilleton serials, in which it ran head-to-head on a daily basis with Alexandre Dumas' *Le Comte de Monte Cristo.*

Sue took up the thesis of Quinet and Michelet's *Des Jésuites* in order to make the Society of Jesus the villains of his melodrama. Dumas subsequently set out to write his own far more explicit Wandering Jew epic in *Isaac Laquedem* (1852-53), which he intended to be his masterpiece, but it ran into trouble with the Second Empire's censors and Dumas abandoned it in disgust, although that did not stop him making the most of the adumbrated text.

Although neither Sue nor Dumas copies anything directly from Quinet's particular version of the legend, there can be little doubt that both writers had its symbolism and its radicalism in mind in planning their own alternative versions. The third member of the great triumvirate of mid-century *feuilletonists*, Paul Féval, added his own version to the canon in "La Fille du juif errant" (1864)[3], and although he did not copy anything directly from Quinet either, he too was aware of his work—he was later to pen a fervent rebuttal of Quinet and Michelet's *Des Jésuites*—and probably intended his own repentant version of the accursed wanderer partly as an ideological reply to Quinet.

The influence of *Ahasvérus* undoubtedly waned once the Romantic Movement passed into history and it joined the vast ranks of books that are no longer widely read, but that is partly because its innovative work was done and its prophetic element had worked out. There are still people in the world looking forward to a literal Last Judgment, who can see no reason to anticipate the need to appeal it, but in the main, the idea of such a Judgment has faded into oblivion, for precisely the reasons anticipated by Quinet, and although the third element of his tripartite conclusion still has a way to go before it can be declared fully justified, the signposts do point in that direction—and whether one agrees with that particular post-

---

[3] tr. as *The Wandering Jew's Daughter,* Black Coat Press, ISBN 9781932983302.

apocalyptic judgment or not, there is no doubt that the argument supporting it still provides nutritious food for thought.

This translation was made from the version of the "new edition" of *Ahasvérus* published in 1843 "Au Comptoir des Imprimeurs Unis," with occasional assistance from the London Library's copy of the same edition. Although I have anglicized the name of the central character and most of the others employed in the text, I have reproduced Quinet's idiosyncratic spelling of several names for which he deliberately does not use the conventional French spelling, and have occasionally retained French spellings for reasons indicated in the footnotes.

Brian Stableford

PROLOGUE

VOICES IN THE SKY
Hosannah! Hosannah!

GABRIEL
Silence! The Lord is going to speak.

THE ETERNAL FATHER
Listen, Saint Michael, Thomas, Bonaventure, great Saint Hubert who was archbishop at Liège, and you, Pythagoras, Joseph the Just and Marcus Tullius.[4] For a thousand years and more your ordeals have been complete and your souls have risen from limbo to the highest seats in paradise, as the dew of the marsh reeds once did, when the sun brought it to my feet. You know that time is complete, after three thousand five hundred years, and the last judgment will soon take place in Jehosophat.

Look! In the depths of the skies, the earth is still trembling; bewildered, it rolls through space, no longer knowing where it is going. Consider whether a leaf fallen from a birch tree in the Ardennes, on the feast of the dead, has ever blown over more mountains and more paths, traveling without knowing where before being engulfed in my well of wrath. You remember. When the hawk of Germany or Judea rose up from the heather, in the early morning, every bird in the fields and every bird in the towns went to hide its head under a twig and suppressed its voice. Consider whether all the worlds that

---

[4] The inclusion of Pythagoras and Marcus Tullius (Cicero) with the saints serves to emphasize the eclectic quality of the heavenly company that the Eternal Father likes to keep while preparing for his post-apocalyptic new world, whose planning and population are more elaborately described in the account of "The Fourth Day."

powder the abyss would not like to cower beneath a wisp of thatch, beneath the grass of a spring or the cloak of a man, while I deploy my extended wings over their hiding-places in an eternal circle.

The silence is profound. Do you hear, from the heights of the Empyrean, that sun which is humming so far away that the news has not yet reached it, and the Hosannah of the Cherubim that falls from one world to the other, more monotonous than raindrops into the lake of a grotto? That's enough rest. Another hundred years would be too many. If the World is weary of its first day, by touching it with a wing, my angel Gabriel, you shall reawaken the worker in my vineyard. I have said to you: the earth is bad, I shall create another tomorrow.

This time, I will make humankind from a better clay, and knead it better. The trees will have more shade, the mountains will be higher. Neither your cope, Saint Hubert, nor your lance, nor your azured shield, nor your diamond-studded miter will shine as brightly as tomorrow's light on a golden sea. The days will be longer, and your experience will save that world more effectively from all temptation than the Cherubim and Seraphim were able to do of old, in emerging candidly from the cradle of nothingness.

But whatever the state will be into which the world that is about to be born shall eventually fall, in order to prepare yourself better to hold it in your charge, I want the good, the bad and all the deeds and destinies accomplished in the world where you have lived to be retraced now, in eternal figures. I want the secrets that I hid, with my hand, in the hollows of rocks and the shimmering sky of lakes to be revealed. I want you to be shown the earth since it escaped my hand like the grain of the sower to produce its tares, until the day when I reaped them, all dry and withered, in the valley of Jehosophat.

The adulterous woman that I stoned on the edge of the road the day before yesterday, you shall see in veils, beneath the girdle of seas, valleys and forests that she untied on the evening of her eternal night. You shall see by what long sunlit days and arid nights the cup from which my name and my life overflowed gradually emptied, only retaining the lees and the universe in its depths.

SAINT BONAVENTURE
Lord, when a swallow is about to depart for Africa or Asia, its little ones are already fluttering their wings in advance over the roofs of Florence the beautiful. Thus we make haste, divine swallows, to follow you forever into the future worlds that are dormant within you, which you will create. Will this world, Lord, be another world of Calabria, with monasteries and diamond cells? Will there be cypresses with a sea asleep beneath their ivory foliage, boats on the bottomless waves with sails of light, and brothers with their aureoles sitting among hives and golden bees?

SAINT HUBERT
Will there not, Lord, be massive gold cathedrals, thick vaults in stone, stained glass windows made from a flap of your robe? Will there not be, in the surroundings, silver birches and ash-trees, and marble balconies overlooking a river six times as wide as the Rhine in Cologne?

SAINT BERTHE[5]
Will there not, Lord, be children fast asleep, whom you will rock endlessly in your arms above the clouds? Will there not be souls in ivory cities, in which the tears of a rose will live for a hundred years?

THE ETERNAL FATHER
I have already told you that before creating another star, I want to make known and explain to you the mystery of the

---

[5] The reference is probably to Berthe d'Avenay rather than Berthe de Blangy or Berthe de Bingen, but it make little or no difference. I have not Anglicized the name because "Saint Bertha" is often used to refer to the Kentish Saint Aldeberge, who is surely not the person intended.

world whence you have come. You have lived there without knowing what it is. Some have seen it in the Holy Land, others in Brabant, some for ten years, others a hundred; but not one of you has held the fruit fallen from my branch in your hand to seek the gnawing worm; not one has lifted the seal of the seas and the ruined cities and the tombs of peoples that I always heap up to hide my treasures; not one has bent down to see the seed of my new crops verdant in the abyss, beneath the cloud of the earth.

SAINT HUBERT

Lord, I traveled in Europe and Africa a long time ago, where I've seen orange-trees higher than great oaks; around monasteries, waves bluer than your only son's tunic; on the road to Jericho, spangles and silver sands; on the trees of the desert, gum and the incense of the mage-kings; and in the roses of Joppa, crystal tears. Is it possible, divine Creator, that beneath those myrtle woods, those transparent rivers and streams, you had put more marvels and magical treasures than any man has seen or touched?

THE ETERNAL FATHER

It's a long story, which oppresses me. My Seraphim will celebrate the terrible mystery before you; everything will have its place therein; every time, every century that I shook, one after the other from the folds of my cloak, will be explained by them in its own language. Mountains and plains will open like flowers; find a voice to speak the secret that that you have kept so well in the depths of your calices. Dead and newborn children, repeat here, in their mothers' bosoms, your dormant thoughts, your embalmed dreams. Earth, open up to display your genius. The choir of angels will repeat your words with to the sounds of trumpets. Let the stars shine like a night-lamp full of oil. Come, troop of the elect, like mown grass, to pile up around me; lean over without fear from your every cloud, look into the abyss and be attentive; the spectacle will last approximately six thousand years.

THE FIRST DAY OF CREATION

I.

THE OCEAN

Thank you Lord, enough accumulated waves; your urn is full, it is overflowing drop by drop as it emerges from the spring. The trough is full; when will the herds come to drink? Your breath is exhausting me; you are whipping my flanks and tearing my rump; I cannot run any faster, nor bound to lick the fleeing sky with my waves more often under the spur of your whip. I cannot span the abyss any better with my streaming feet, nor shake my mane of foam and further, nor roll my breast and my flanks any harder. Where are you going, Lord? For a long time I have been driving and heaping up my waves, without ever arriving; still I hear nothing but my waves whinnying; still I see nothing but myself in my immensity. Yesterday, when a nascent ray of moonlight chanced to skim the summits of my waves, that was a cause for celebration: I thought that your hand was caressing my breast and wanted to tie me down with a golden thread, or that a wing of flame was passing through my tangled mane; but as soon as it had touched me, the ray trickled like a spring and erupted in foam. Oh, if I ever found a shore, a world other than me, I would make myself a bed there of white foam, the dust of pearls, coral crystals, algal roots and red seashells; my waters would be suspended there, Lord, like the blade from your belt. All night long I would kiss the sand on my shores; my panting waves would swell up without a murmur; there is only you who could say: It is there that they sleep.

LEVIATHAN
launching waters over firm ground

Who has hurled me out of the gulf? Who has given me my polished scales, my gaping jaws, my tail the color of the vegetation of the strand? Water is crawling over the beach, islands are crouching in the mist, the abyss is opening its maw, the wind is mewling in the rocks, the waves are swelling into teats, the wavelets are jostling like a litter of crocodiles hanging on to their mother; the crests of mountains are shining like scales crunched between the teeth of Leviathan.

THE VINATEYNA BIRD[6]

Lower, Ocean, transparent sea, much lower; fold up your vast waters as I fold my wings when I want to stop; more, more! Let me see all the way to the depths of your bed how beautiful my golden feet, my golden beak and my twenty-cubit wingspan are; you, who know everything, tell me where I am this morning. Have I, then, curled my neck beneath my wing on the edge of chaos, or was I sleeping in my down on a silver rock? Tell me who has come to take me from my nest, who has set me on a cloud; since that time I have been flying, flying without rest; look, it is from my beak that the seeds of life are falling, one by one, that will make plants and forests; I let the water-lily fall into the valleys, the tamala on to the mud, the baobab into the plains, the vine-flower into the hollows in the rocks, the willow-flower at the edges of springs, the heather on mountain-tops. The leaves quiver, the reeds rattle, already the stars are flying like a flock of birds with golden wings setting out for distant lands.

THE SERPENT

Oh, if I had wings like you, before speaking, I would climb up to the highest cloud, I would find out what is around us; since it is necessary, it will be me who will rear up from the mire to see whether the universe has been born; behind the

---

[6] This was the name given to the giant bird that carries Vishnu, the god responsible for maintaining cosmic order, in the French translation of the Bhagavad-gita published in 1787. Most English translations refer to it as the Garuda bird, garuda being Sanskrit for eagle.

tree of the world, I shall climb around its trunk, knot myself around its branches. Look! My tail is touching the earth, my thousand heads are standing at its summit; above its foliage my tongues dart their venom at the four winds; who wants to pick those bloody flowers? But truly, I see nothing but mountains folding up their coils, nothing but rivers sliding like grass-snakes through the forests, nothing but the horse Séméhé[7] racing without ever stopping under the claws of djinn; he is sweating blood, the wind is shaking his silver tail; in his breast two eyes are blazing; at every moment his color changes; he is pale he is black, he is as blue as the sky, bruised like the venom that falls from my mouth. Oh, it's a pity!

LEVIATHAN
Look toward the sea again.

THE SERPENT
There too I see nothing but the fish Macar,[8] who has stolen his trunk from Behemoth; if I had fins bound to my coils, I would know what is growling in the depths of the sea before you had taken a single step.

LEVIATHAN
So, you see nothing that is greater than us; we are still the masters; creation has stopped at us. Oh, I shivered for a long time in the fear that the rocks, in rising above us, might vomit up a master with scales of stone, and that he would force me to go back into the abyss from which I have emerged. But you—you have seen nothing?

---

[7] The horse Séméhé is an invention of Quinet's; its addition to the legend of the Wandering Jew seems distinctly anomalous, and the logic of its inclusion is as obscure as the name's etymology.
[8] The Macar fish is another derivative of Indian folklore.

THE VINATEYNA BIRD

I have gone up as far as the highest branch of the world-tree; I have followed in its flight the most rapid of stars; I have descended into valleys to depths where the rain does not fall; I have found nothing anywhere but the morning lark, the djinn with black wings; the loriot that hangs two threads of silk from her nest and rocks her fledglings above the nascent world.

LEVIATHAN

And you, tell us what you have seen at the in the watery deeps.

THE MACAR FISH

With my trunk I have sounded the whirlpools of foam. To the utmost depths I have plunged into the gulf of the sea; there is nothing to be heard but the roaring water, nothing to be seen but the waves painting palaces of coral green.

LEVIATHAN

So we are alone. Neither here, nor there, nor on high, now down below, is there anyone but us. The mud has been formed so that I might leave my footprint at every step. The world has unfurled so that the serpent might envelop it with his coils. Now that the eternal vulture is carrying it away in its claws, fleeing with its prey at full tilt, everywhere, in all the heavens, we are the gods.

ALL

Yes, Leviathan, you have said it; we are the gods.

THE OCEAN

Search, continue searching. Life the branches of the forests; divide the waters of the springs more carefully. Dig deeper, ever deeper, into the mud. Who has rummaged in that marble crack? Who has shaken the fold of that cloud? It is there that he has hidden himself in order to listen to you. When you came, I was talking to him. Leviathan, there is a blade that rings truer than all your scales; bird with the golden beak, there are wings more capacious than yours; serpent with a thousand heads, there are bites more venomous than those of your mouth. Before the daylight, all through the night, he drives my waves before him as the sea-lion drives his cubs. He woke me up when everything was asleep; he disappeared as soon as the sun began to shine.

ALL

Liar! A curse on your waves, greener than the venom of vipers. May the djinn dip their wings in our foam! May the Tchinevad Bridge[9] collapse over your waters. Let us mingle together all our cries: the rubbing of scales, the flapping of wings, the sliding of coils. Let the talon be sharpened on the trunk, the beak on the branch, the ivory on the granite; let the hoof resonate on the sand, the fin on the waves, the tail around the flanks. Murmurs of leaves and savannahs, burning nostrils, bounding manes, screeches, whistles, howls, let the noise grow louder and be prolonged, let the rock quake, the avalanche slide. Tell us, old Ocean, if his voice is more powerful than ours. The devas[10] are circling in the air; the gryphon is hollowing out the crests of the clouds with its horn; eternity is putting its crown on the head of lions. Life is swarming, life is buzzing, life is streaming; rumps are bounding, sweat is pouring from nostrils like light from the nostrils of the sun. More manes are fluttering in the wind than there are lianas in the woods; variegated feathers, crawling pearls, gazes falling from the clouds on to the shadow of a leaf, thirsty for life, thirsty for

---

[9] The bridge of Tchinevad above the gulf of Hell separates the earth from the heavens in the Zend-Avesta, the central scriptural text of the Zoroastrian religion; souls are judged when they pass over it.

[10] This terms has slightly different meanings in Hindu theology, where it can refer to any deity, and the Zend-Avestra, where it refers to evil spirits, akin to the Arabic djinn to which reference is also made in this section of the text.

death; tell us, Ocean, whether that is not enough to be a God. Days will come, time will accumulate, but a time will never come that will see our claws worn down, nor the tips of our wings soiled with mud, nor their colors washed out by the rain. After a thousand years, the drying spring will reflect, as today, our nascent feathers, our down that had molted. We shall always pass by the same route without ever tiring; we shall always extend our wings in the clouds without ever furling them; we shall always be setting forth on the same voyage. Let the birds begin to form a point to cleave the wind; let the lightest take flight. Three days and three nights let him fly straight through the sky; let him cry to the four winds: "Where is the king of worlds?" And Leviathan will descend crawling into the marshes, and reply from the gulfs of the earth: "We are the gods."

II.

CHORUS OF GIANTS AND TITANS

Brothers the hour has come; let us emerge from our caverns. Our slumber has been long, longer than the dreams that weighed upon our breasts in that immense night. Before being, the universe, like a dream fading away, always to be remade, has passed through our souls and made us shiver on our rocky beds. What monstrous shadows, which will never be weighed, in spirit, on our breathless bosoms! Brothers, do you remember the endless expectation that slept within us, those half-born worlds that crawled relentlessly over our thoughts of yesterday, that speech on our lips for a thousand years, that thirst for life, the shadow of Ocean that dried up at our bedsides, the phantom of God that poured out dreams, filling us to the brim, the tongues of light that were neither life nor death, neither day nor night, and the serpents that brooded beneath their fetid wings the specter of the universe hatching in our dreams?

A GIANT

Do you also remember a confused sigh that emerged from abysms, which every being repeated? Do you remember a drop of blood that hung from the vault, and moaned as it fell into an invisible lake? That dream presaged for our wakefulness an eternal dolor. May it please God that we can go back to sleep, and never again pass its threshold!

CHORUS OF GIANTS AND TITANS

Courage, companions; let us all set to work; let us fashion subterranean cities. While the mud is moist, let us knead the rocks in the depths of their beds. Let us trample underfoot the ferns taller than palm trees; let us crush beneath our tread the hundred-cubit crocodiles wallowing beneath the forests of reeds. Let us mingle with the clay of marble the flowers of ferns, with the bark of the palm-tree, with the palm-tree the jaw of the serpent, the beak of the eagle, the scale of the fish and the teeth of the elephant. Let us crush the clay between our hands, let us lay the slate in its bed. Courage, the work rises up like a wall. On the trunks of forests are amassed the carcasses of monsters run around on the shore. Let our giant thoughts rise up with the rock and be inscribed on its flanks; let runes, hieroglyphs, letters of porphyry, variegated jasper and granite, conserve forever the language and history of the giants. Let us bend down and roll up the vaults of caverns as easily as a mat. The giant tree of the universe is already shivering in the breath of the morning. Beneath its shade, the well of past time is being hollowed out; eternity is wrinkling at its edges. Our centuries of life will commence, bushier than its foliage; our empire will be more durable than the bark of its trunk, stronger than the claw of the vulture that has built its nest therein. See our God already rising from his seat; he has the firmament for a skull, the lianas of the woods for hair; for a belt, he has the Ocean knotted around his waist; for a sword, he has the light, every spark of which is a star.

A GIANT
Malediction! It is against us that he is rising.
(*The island sinks*.)

III.

THE ETERNAL FATHER *to the Ocean*
Like a word poorly written in my book, go efface the earth.

THE OCEAN
I shall make haste. Already, nothing remains of the summit of the world but the tower of a king, who is eating a banquet from silver plates. My deluge will enter the hall within the hour.

THE KING, *at table among his princes*
The deluge, like a lake, is drowning the low-lying areas; it is filling the troughs of slaves. Let the Ocean growl, if it wishes; it will not come as far as this; my guards will halt it at the limit of my kingdom.

FIRST SATRAP
If it comes, king of kings, it will be to lick the soles of your feet.

SECOND SATRAP
Or to bring you a diadem of its pearls.

THE KING
1.
A thousand kings are sitting at my table. All the grandeurs of the earth have climbed my stairway this morning. A hundred nimble dromedaries have brought wine on their backs to slake thirst, and a hundred racing camels bread for hunger.

2.
The wine will be drunk and the bread eaten. Before dusk, the stars will have finished their banquet of light, and the

Ocean will have poured the last drop from its gourd into its cup. But our lives of patriarchs will never end, not tonight, nor tomorrow...

Silence! What is that noise? I believe I heard an approaching wave.

FIRST SATRAP
It's nothing; it's your people sighing.

THE KING
The noise is getting louder.

SECOND SATRAP
It's your empire sobbing.

THE KING
1.
Let us begin again, then, to sing until midnight. The rain is falling, the lightning flashing. Before our eyes, the ship of the world is being wrecked for our amusement. In dying, the Universe, at our feet, only requests a smile from our royal lips; let us whistle over its ruin.

2.
Ocean, distant sea, have you counted accurately I advance the steps of my tower? There are more than a hundred of marble and bronze. Take care, poor angry child, that your foot does not slip on my floor-tiles and your saliva does not moisten my banister. Before having climbed half of my steps, ashamed and breathless, veiling yourself in your foam, you will have gone home, thinking: *I am weary.*

3.
In the caverns, in the lairs, in the grottoes where you pass, tremulously, the lion encounters its trembling prey; the serpent hides beneath the woman's foot, and cities of giants

wait, mute, with one foot in your mire and the other plunged therein up to the knee.

4.

The hawk and the sea-eagle flee before you; feet dragging, they climb their rock to take shelter against you, their brood beneath their breast; with beak, wing and blazing eye bristling, they are afraid of your wave. Pursue the hawk and the sea-eagle, if you want to take their down-clad chicks in the egg.

5.

Here, in my imperial aerie, there is nothing but nestling kings coiffed with rubies, risen to the utmost height of their glory; how can your waves upon waves ever rise as high? From our feast, we will throw you a crumb; go, be on your way.

FIRST SATRAP
Someone's knocking at the door.

THE KING
Help me.

SECOND SATRAP
It's your heir; I don't know you anymore.

THE KING
Who's there?

THE OCEAN
Open up; let me in.

THE KING
Mercy! Sea of islands, Ocean of foam, what do you want at my door? If you're asking for my cloak, here it is.

THE OCEAN
Your cloak, good sir, is too small for my shoulders.

THE KING
If you want my golden cup, full of wine to intoxicate you, take it in your wave.

THE OCEAN
That your cup, on my lips, might slake my thirst…that's a joke, my master.

THE KING
 Well then, here's my crown; put it on your head.

THE OCEAN
Away with your crown! As a headband, I prefer my dust of foam.

THE KING
What do you want, then?

THE OCEAN
To sit down there, at your table, in your place. Go and reign over my grains of sand. One more step, and I'll be on your throne. Here I am—it's very comfortable! Here, where there was a world, there's a fleck of foam; in my turn, therefore, I shall be king. I want to play with the scepter, with the odorous tiara, with the mud of the banquet; I'm licking the guests' cups to the dregs. This royal wine is inebriating me; my waves, which are staggering, are my subjects. There—let them bow down to the ground! Now they're sighing; now they've fallen silent; now they're sobbing. My rivers, digging out the vine-branches of their banks like grape-growers, are my cup-bearers, bringing me something to drink. This wave is too bitter; let it return to its source! Another, another, and then a hundred, and then a thousand. Everything bends the knee at my caprice! With a breath, I make and unmake my roaring

cities; my walls, to defend me from thieves, cost me nothing more, to build up to the clouds, than a breath. My kingdom has no borders, nor exit-gates. The fletched arrow can do nothing against me; the sword that strikes me rusts in my breast. Near or far, there is no neighbor who can think of dethroning me. If I soil myself, I have what is needed to wash away the stain; and nothing leaves any trace behind me but my cloak, when the sun dyes it red.

THE ETERNAL FATHER

Enough, majesty of foam, drop of water in your turn, already too inebriated. Here, for your trouble, is some uprooted grass, with a little moss, to gnaw on my shore.

IV

Human Tribes Assembled on the Summit of the Himalaya

A CHILD

Father, look out there, far away, in the middle of the sea, the water covered in foam! Oh, tell me, is that a great eagle that has touched it with its white wing? Is it nor rather a baby swallow, which was unable to get back to its nest, and has drowned in the sea?

ANOTHER CHILD

No, it's the date-flower that I floated in the stream, and which fled of its own accord from wave to wave, from bank to bank, far away, to where there is no longer any branch to rock it like a baby asleep in its cradle.

AN OLD MAN

No, it's not a baby swallow that has drowned in the sea; no, it's not a date-flower whitening like the foam. Can't you hear a plaint emerging from every wave, a murmur that finishes up on the sea-bed? Neither the plaint of the waves nor the murmur of the sea could rise any higher if the whole world had been swallowed up. I seem to hear a thousand voices dying away, a thousand secrets of times past crouching down and gradually falling asleep, like white-haired old men, beneath the sands and the sea-shells.

CHORUS OF YOUNG WOMEN

Oh, Father, don't look out to sea for so long. The quivering is that of lotus leaves rejoicing in being born. The murmur is that of springs seeking their path and asking the banana-trees and flowers they encounter: Banana-tree with the green shade, a diamond sparkling in the sun, little bird that has just drunk my water, tell me, what path should I take to descend into the bottom of the valley?

"Yesterday's fresh spring, where I bathe the tip of my wing, over which my branches incline, in which my azure neck is reflected, pass beneath my shade. Spread out over your steps, follow my light feet as you go, and you will find the Ocean at the bottom of the valley, waiting for you. It is waiting for you on gilded sand, with blue waves the color of the sky."

Oh, my Father, don't look any longer out to sea; that is where the voices are that you can hear babbling around us.

CHORUS OF TRIBES

Greetings, day! Greetings, night, daughter of day! Greetings, sea, rivers, mountains! As the dew of the first day of the world swells the flower of the tamala before the sun has drunk, as the water leaps in its source before having crossed its bounds, as the chicks of hawks and Malayan vultures frolic in their nests of foliage before knowing the summit or the plain that extend over their downy heads, so our tribes, newly-hatched today, jostle in the aerie, and remain suspended over the world. The leaf of the palm-tree quivers in the forest, the water of the lake ripples at its spring, the soul quakes in our bosom.

Oh, who can tell the soul in or bosom, the leaf of the palm-tree the water of the spring, who has made the daylight so bright, the night so dark and the wind so swift? Who can tell the mountain who has made the waves so blue to bathe it; the sea, the star to plunged into it; the horse's main, the wind to stir it; the pebble, the bed along which it rolls?

Blue wave, covered in foam, I will make you a bed of seashells and gold, if you tell me who drove you over my feet. Sycamore with a hundred branches, I will wash you with the water of a new-born spring if you tell me who gave you your tresses of leaves; serpent, handsome serpent all dappled with colors, I will make you a road of sand on which to slither, if you tell me where the person is who gave you the blue of the firmament and the gold of the mountains to paint your scales. Rocks, call to me to show me where he has marked his hundred-cubit feet; I will follow him all the way to the mountain of gold. If he descends into the valley, I shall descend. The wood-pigeon chick, when it flaps its wings, has its father to guide it out of the nest, but me, where is my father to show me my path?

THE VOICE OF WOMEN
Is it necessary to go already?

CHORUS OF TRIBES
Oh, yes, it's necessary to go. Can't you see the swallows already taking flight over the sea? My heart rises up in my bosom, like the stork in its nest, when the day of the departure comes. Are not the clouds gathering on the horizon, like travelers beneath flaxen tents? Is not the river hurrying, for fear of arriving an hour too late? Are not the islands passing into the mist like teals? The wind is sweeping the sea-hawks away, shaking the manes of the wild horses; where, then, are they all going? Is it not us alone who are not crossing our threshold?— we who got up in the night, like the spring of the earth that does not know where it will spend the evening. Since everything is in turmoil, let's go, let's follow the crowd.

VOICES IN THE UNIVERSE
Come, come.

V.

FIRST TRIBE
I choose, to guide me, the great river Ganges; it is the one that has the widest banks, and waves as profound as the sky.

SECOND TRIBE
I know what my guide will be: it is the gryphon. It is as strong as the lion, as swift as the eagle and it has a crown on its head; when it stops in the desert, all the lions fall silent.

THIRD TRIBE
I know a guide that runs faster than the river and is more knowledgeable than the gryphon: it is the ibis with the golden beak and feet of silver. When it is at rest under the palm-trees it foretells the future; when it is moving over a rock it recalls the past.

(*They leave.*)

FIRST TRIBE
River Ganges, you run faster than a gazelle. Halt your waves momentarily so that we might slake or thirst therein.

THE RIVER
Not yet, not yet; we are still far from the bank where you shall rest. With the current that follows me I am towing a white lily like as vase; in the white lily is the beverage of Amrita, which gives immortality. You can put your lips to it when we have arrived.

FIRST TRIBE
Tell us, at least, with your murmuring isles, tell us with your white foam, what the bank where we shall halt is like.

THE RIVER

Beneath the fig-trees and grapefruit-trees of India I have already hollowed out my valley in order for you to spread your waves there. As I fill it every day with the water of my source, you, in your turn, shall fill it with tears, sweat, hymns and tombs. Your name shall germinate in the centuries as the lotus germinates in my mud. Your gods shall be amassed around you like the shells on my banks. They shall spread out in your dreams like the fruit of the amla-tree on an autumn night.

FIRST TRIBE

Oh, how slowly your waves at moving at present beneath the vaults of savannahs! The branches of palms cover them with perfumed shade. In the crystalline dream that cradles you night and day, your weak and somnolent flux only rises up on occasion to say to you: "Carry me, carry me with your bank to where you are going."

THE RIVER

Thus your days and your centuries shall pass, without being able to move away from our banks. Thus your future empires shall fall asleep in the shadow of your dreams.

FIRST TRIBE

Stop, river Ganges; do you not see the Ocean before you? It is immense; it is boundless. Go back, go back into your valley; you will be lost, lost forever with your waves the color of an antelope's eye, in the sea that is spreading out before you.

THE RIVER

Thus you shall be lost one day with your tribes, you pearl necklaces, your embalmed centuries, your gods, your murmurs, your cities, in your ocean and your eternity.

SECOND TRIBE
A CHILD
Mother, Mother, this road is full of stones; a thorn has pierced my foot. Is this the land of Iran to which the gryphon is leading us?

THE MOTHER
Not yet—be brave! We'll arrive soon.

THE CHILD
I can't walk any further; the gryphon's still racing; when its feet are weary, it uses its wings.

THE MOTHER
If you stop on the road, when everyone else has gone past, the black devas will carry you away into the sky where they hold their dances.

THE CHILD
I don't want to be carried away by the devas, but my feet are bleeding. (*He weeps*). Am I going to die?

A PERI
Come, Ferdoun, suspend yourself from my neck; hide your feet in my long hair; I will carry you all the way to the land of Iran. You shall find crystal springs for your thirst, fountains of naphtha to warm you, fresh figs, dates in the leafy woods, coconuts and golden oranges for your hunger.

THE CHILD
Truly—golden oranges too?

THE PERI
You shall encounter, as you pass by, streaming with foam, on the shores of bays, avatars with the bodies of women who will beckon and call to you in order to cradle you in the watery depths. The rivers run over their sands there more rap-

idly than archers on horseback when they cause their quivers to resonate. The desert extends around with its perfume of myrrh, better than the linen girdle that your mother extends beside her by night. Snow whitens the mountain-tops there, better than miters on the heads of priests. For the thousand years, the lakes have been suspended there in their valleys, like kings dreaming their royal dreams beneath azure tents.

THE CHILD

Peri, good Peri, I want, on arrival, to awaken the lakes in their beds; I want to hear the quivers of the rivers resonating, to touch the snow whiter than miters, learn the song of the avatars.

THE PERI

How many cities shall be born of your caprice, in which you might rest at your ease! Babylon will bend down behind you like a thirsty lioness that has not found a spring all day. On the banks of the Euphrates, Bactra will flee over the mountain like a unicorn on its rock. Have you seen the reeds in the marshes? Marble columns will rise up like them in the marshes of Persepolis. Have you seen the colors of the rainbow in the rising sun? Ecbatana will gild its walls in order that you might count them as you pass through its gates. Gods, born yesterday like you, will salute you on your road; the young peris of Chaldea will read your horoscope in the stars of your age. Are there not already, in your dreams, phantoms crowned with miters, kings suspended from your name as that pearl necklace is suspended round your neck, centuries and perfumed cities that extend their carpets into the future beneath your feet, and birds with silver plumage that greet you beneath the palm-trees as you pass by?

THE CHILD

You're carrying me too rapidly; I can only see the tops of the trees swayed by the wind, the glistening water of the lakes, the nests of the little birds shaking on the branches. Is Ecbatana or Babylon already there?

THIRD TRIBE

Look at the sinister shadow the ibis is casting on the sand; it is a bad omen; I wish that we had chosen a different guide.

A WOMAN

It has never stopped under the incense-trees, nor the gum-trees. Why did it not leave us in Arabia? Why did it not leave us on the grass of the oases? It has strewn us now beside the Nile, like ostrich eggs, on a muddy bank where the first tempest will break us. The river drags livid specters in its depths; the valley is hollowed out beneath our feet like a tomb; the ibis is folding its head beneath its neck and falling asleep on the summit like a hieroglyph of death. This land is full of funereal presentiments.

THE IBIS

If you had known where your long route leads, rather than setting forth, you would have stopped on its threshold. Born yesterday, are you not afraid of surrendering life too soon?

THIRD TRIBE

Yes, we are already weary of our task. A single day of life is enough for us. As we emerge from nothingness, the sun of the Orient dazzles and exhausts us. Like night-birds suddenly surprised by broad daylight, staggering and bewildered, we hesitate to follow you. Rather than pass the threshold of our life, let us return to the obscurity from which we came. Oh, give us, give us your wings, in order to return more rapidly to the eternal night.

THE IBIS

First, build pyramidal tombs to enclose you all, like the worm in its shell; you shall fall asleep in their shadow; I shall set myself at the apex, as the owl perches by night on the Arab's tent. I shall wake you up when it is time to enter, people of Egypt. The desert lies motionless. Already your stone sphinxes are producing their litters in the sand. On your obelisks the hawk of the mountains is closing eyes of granite. And you too, hawk of the Egyptian valley, fold your head beneath your wing until the time comes. Your centuries shall pass, one after another, with less noise than the breath of a drowsy sphinx. People of yesterday, crouch down on the threshold of the void from which you came, like the lions at the gates of your cities. In your vicinity, everything shall fall silent. Babylon and Niniveh will get up barefoot in the darkness, for fear of awakening you, and the mist of the nascent universe will envelop you in its shroud.

VI.

An Oriental Night

CHORUS OF STARS
The gryphon and the ibis have led the tribes through the valleys into the lands of their heritage. And a guide leads us, also, through the mountains and valleys of the firmament, over the cloud where we must sleep by night.

THE MOON
The patriarch of Chaldea, sitting before his tent, watches his flocks graze around him on the mountain-side. Graze too, my flocks of stars, bounding around my silver tent, which I have pitched on a spring cloud.

A STAR
Each tribe is asleep in its marble city, each star in its silvery robe. My rays dangle confusedly from the columns of Persepolis. Nineveh has crenellated towers, where they lean out of windows. But best of all I like the walls of Babylon; on its roofs they are amassed and quietly become drowsy, like snowflakes on mountain-tops.

ANOTHER STAR
Perhaps, my sisters, we are making the same voyage as the human tribes. As they wander, I would like to converse with them. I would gladly send them dreams with my golden rays. I would give my words to the wind, the wind would carry them to the flower of the desert, the flower to the river, and the river would repeat them as it passes through cities.

ALL
Yes, that is what we ought to do.

A FLOWER OF THE SYRIAN DESERT

My head bows down beneath the light of the stars; my calyx inflates with dew, as a heart fills with a secret that it would like to repeat. In the night, my flower has reddened with patches the color of blood, like the robe of a Levite on the day of sacrifice; the murmur of the stars has descended into my calyx and mingled with my perfume. I bear a secret in my calyx; I have the secret of the universe, which has escaped it in a dream during the night, and no voice with which to repeat it. Oh, tell me which is the nearest city. Is it Jerusalem or is it Babylon? Let passers-by come to collect the mystery that is charging my crown and causing me to lower my head.

THE EUPHRATES

Flower of the desert, curb your head a little further over my bed, that I might hear your murmur better; from wave to wave, endlessly bounding, I shall bear it to the walls of Babylon; tell me your secret; I shall deposit it on the silvery waves at the foot of the towers of the Chaldeans,

INHABITANTS OF BABYLON ON THEIR ROOFS

See how the Euphrates shines this evening beneath the willows, like the blade of a dagger fallen from a table at a feast. Its murmurs could not be softer if it were rolling sacred vessels of gold and silver along its bed.

A SLAVE

Or if an entire people leaning over its bank were letting tears fall into it one by one.

A KING

Or if an empire with the tiaras of its priests, the robes of its kings and its glittering gods had been swallowed up a thousand years ago by its gravel bed like a water-flower.

CHORUS OF PRIESTS

The light of the night illuminates the inscriptions of Semiramis engraved on the rock of the mountain of Assur. Every word shines here as if a fiery blade were writing the language of the firmament on the stone. As the lyre responds to the lyre, let the voices of the stars allow their mute will to burst forth among us with the voices of peoples and echoes that will last for a century.

The Orient has extended its peoples and its empires around it, as the night extends its robe embroidered with stars, in order that the gods might dress therein some day. But the universal dawn has only just broken, and the one who has warmed it with his breath holds it as a child holds a twig in his hand. While the footsteps of the God of gods pass over the grass of Eden and Kashmir, let us take note of his footprints on the mountain-tops. Neither the sun nor the human heart has drunk his breath as yet.

As the Arab gets up in the night to lick the dew of the desert before the daylight spreads, thus we get up in the first days of the universe to draw the thought of the Eternal from our urns, before its source dries up. Drop by drop, it falls from the stars and the vaults of heaven, and from every leaf of the palm-tree; let us intoxicate ourselves with its liquor, like a resinous wine.

O peoples of India, Chaldea and Egypt, in your turn, take up and drink from the cup of the Eternal, which he has left full in leaving his banquet. Let all the nascent peoples bear to their lips, without delay, the vessel in which infinity is fermenting to the brim, and after us our sphinxes, and after them our idols of granite and bronze. If the universe vacillates before our eyes, if it is divided into a thousand various gods, birds with human heads, serpents with women's bodies, crowned unicorns, it is as it is at our feasts, when the heart is gorged with wines of Idumea, and every guest, with his pantler, sees the golden vessels totter, collide and shatter in his mind on a table of porphyry.

57

From India to Arabia, let us hasten; who knows whether the time will come when the universe, centuries hence, will be like a faded, withered flower in the evening of the Arabian sun, and whether human lips might not press in vain upon the cup from which we drink, and there will then be no more perfume, nor any eternal beverage.

VII

CHORUS OF SPHINXES
1.

By Memnon, how good it is to lie down, all together, beneath the portico of Luxor, to catch our breath, to bend our knees beneath our breasts. In order to rest better, let us curl up, let us gather in our rocky rumps. Let us unwind our feminine necklaces and expose them to the four winds. With our claws, let us loosen the bandlets over our sibylline faces.

2.

Until now, disheveled, we have run without being able to find shelter. Eternity has employed us since its birth as messengers: Hola! handsome messenger with a woman's breasts, take this news to the ends of my kingdom, without pausing.

"The ends of your kingdom are far away; one finds on the road neither shade nor posture, nor a fragment of wall on which to sit; what will you give me?"

For an awning over your head, my empty sky; beneath your claw, my chaos; for a lair, my black abyss.

3.

But Thebes, which has encountered me, has built me a temple roof, and has made my lair in the rock of Karnak. Every hundred years, if I am hungry, I chew the acanthus leaves, dates and pomegranates that she has carved for me on the capitals of her columns; if I am thirsty, I lick the sacrificial platter; the storm pursues me, I crawl into my stable in the great pyramid of Giza.

4.

In order to avoid boredom, we teach our little ones, while still at the breast, to read, while roaring, the hieroglyphs on our walls. By the apex of the obelisk, by the beak of the ibis, by the wing of the flying serpent, by the antenna of the scarab, by the two sculpted bowls in which souls are weighed, by the hawk sitting on the prow of the boat of the dead, yes, by the sign of the flail, by the sign of the owl and by the sign of the voracious crocodile, our wisdom is greater than the wisdom of the Queen of Sheba.

A SPHINX

How quickly the days pass when one is eternal! A thousand years have already gone by while we've been talking. Every word from our mouths takes a century to fall; every breath is a year. To tighten our bands around our foreheads we take the entire lifetime of a patriarch; to lie down on our lioness rumps we take the lifetime of an empire; and when the sands of the deluge cover us breast-deep, we shake them from our shoulders while shivering.

CHORUS OF SPHINXES
1.

Pass, pass before me without fear, centuries, ages of patriarchs, thousand-year days, times of gods, times of mysteries. Young years, which want to stay hidden with your ground-length veils, let me look at you all alone; walk barefoot over my steps; with my monstrous claws, let me attach your girdle of darkness to your robe. Pass too, chariots of war, which do not want to make any noise with your wheels. Armies, handsome horsemen, I shall shed my tresses of sand over your clothes. Pass without trumpets, nor heralds nor sandals, tribes, peoples, empires, mitered races who never fell me your names or where you are going. Pass, towers, old Babels, magical cities that hold your breath beneath our gates in order that the shepherd will not hear you. Pass, unknown kings who cover yourselves to the knees with your beards. Gods who veil yourselves in my shadow, write your mystery on my wrinkle-free forehead; I alone know whence you came, what your age is; but my lips shall not be unsealed, my mouth shall not name you. When a traveler asks me, have you seen them pass? I shall say: "Yes, your whinnying mares have gone to the field."

2.

A thousand years, another thousand years, and as many days and nights have gone by. No, not yet; don't awaken in their beds the cities that we guard. Let the kings sleep beneath their crowns, the gods beneath their palanquins. Look! All goes well. The rivers go forth, without murmuring in their valleys; the diligent stars light their lamps at dusk, on their tables, to thread their golden robes; the desert, without finding its road too long, only waits, in order to drive its sands, for us to bark around it; the Ocean, obediently, flows toward its shores without our having any need to bite its foamy breast. Let us rest; let us chew, let us ruminate our acanthus leaves and our pomegranates, ripened under our portico of Luxor.

3.

Like a shepherd's dog, let us remain lying down, to watch, here, at the gate of the world. Let us listen to everything that surrounds us. If some rumor happens to reach us of a city's collapse, a new god or a people in revolt, we shall howl, all together, with our mouths of stone and our voices of granite: Hola! Hola! Shepherd of the sky, come out of the fold; someone's coming.

THEBES
My beautiful hundred-cubit sphinx, what is causing you to bark so loudly? Has a messenger come from Sheba or Taurus?

THE SPHINX
Neither messenger nor groom. Go back to sleep.

THEBES
During my long night I had a bad dream on my bolster, as if I had forgotten a god in my great temple.

61

THE SPHINX

Don't think about your god any longer; have you not made a roof for the eternity that bears the firmament in his arms, as a woman bears her child?

THEBES

Yes, a roof of granite. To clothe him, I have carved a loincloth in the rock; in order that he might sit down, a fine black marble bench.

THE SPHINX
That's enough. No other gods have come for a long time.

THEBES
What news is there?

THE SPHINX

Of your date-palm, which is verdant; your camel, which is ruminating; your hawk, which is shrieking; and your desert, which is thirsty.

THEBES
Are you sure of that?

THE SPHINX

I have not quit your threshold. Go, sleep for another thousand years.

VIII.

THEBES

The sphinx's thousand years have passed; my granite eyelid is heavy to raise; my bed is hard. Still I dream of hawks with human bodies, owls that carry spheres on their backs. I get bored alone in my temple, when I have lit my lamp. If I dared, I would rather go up on my terrace to call to my sisters. Where have they gone, since the day when the ibises and the gryphons led us here, each by a different path?

BABYLON

Is that you whispering, my sister? Is that you, Thebes, wearing those bandlets on your head? Is it you to whom a reaper has given these baskets of sculpted acanthus leaves that sphinxes will browse? If it is you, go up to the highest of your towers with your sisters. Speak to me, all of you, with the noise of the chariot, with the noise of ruin, with the tip of the blade, with the murmur of the crowd, with the footsteps of armies beneath your gates, with your crumbling columns, with the zithers in your temples, with the scepter of the king who falls, with the whistle of the arrow in battle, with the oar of the galley in the river; speak to me more loudly, so that I can hear your voice on my terrace.

NINEVEH

I reside close to you, but I am too old to go up to my terrace. My staircase is crumbling underfoot. Neither golden zithers nor people in my streets any longer swell my voice. In my palace, I no longer have anything to reply to you but the murmur of nettles and grasses, which is now my song.

PERSEPOLIS

My land is in Iran. When you called, I was leading my herd of gryphons to drink at my naphtha well. In the morning, in my tower, I spin a robe for my peris; in the evening, I light my fire in my ashes in order to lend a brand to a star that is going out. Can you hear me? I have screeched with the chariot's axle, whined with the mare, whistled with the arrow, resounded with the sword against the buckler, shivered with the battle on the Granicus.[11]

SHEBA

My land is further away. Neither astrologers nor diviners can tell you where it is. Spirits built my tower; peris built my walls; enchantresses dwell therein. My queen is always the wisest. Enigmas or hieroglyphs, she can read the books of stone without moving her lips. Her throne is made of coral, her wand is magic, the road to her pagoda is sprinkled with golden sand.

BACTRA

My fiancé brought me to the mountain of Media. I climbed up after him by a rugged path; he gave me amulets to make a necklace, three arrows to defend myself, three towers to climb, three gods to adore. Now a Chaldean diviner is telling my fortune at my door.

PALMYRA

Yesterday, all alone, I went into the desert to pick dates. Oh, how sad the desert is! My column is weary of seeing nothing but sand, the hinges of my gate cry: Let's go away! No one passes here, neither merchant nor shepherd, and I am afraid that the unicorns might come to gnaw my steps and dragons to slither beneath my marble sandals. This time, my sister, have you heard me? I have spoken with the voice of a people; I have spoken with the hoof-beats of horsemen in my courtyards, with the whips of grooms, with the clash of lances,

---

[11] The river where Alexander won a crucial battle against the forces of Darius' Persian Empire in 334 B.C., beginning his world-conquering exploits.

with the litanies of priests, with walls crumbling in my halls, with crowns falling from the heads of my kings.

BABYLON

Yes, I hear you; your crowd is rumbling. To make more noise, you strike in cadence people against people, empire against empire, kings against kings, Asia against Asia, cymbals against cymbals, ruins against ruins and shield against shield. I hear you, but I cannot see you yet through the cracks in my walls. I am bent too low beneath my burden of gods. My head is so laden with their amulets that it has slumped on to my knees, like that of a sleeping woman. Their names are so numerous that my tongue is exceedingly thick from having spoken them without making a mistake. Listen to me, my sisters, since you are gathered together, what would you think if, out of all of our gods heaped one atop another, we were to make just one God. Like a founder stirring his crucible, what would you say to throwing all our idols, bronze rams, hawks' beaks, copper amulets and golden serpents pell-mell into a divine melting-pot, in order to make a single idol that would have but one name? We would no longer have to carry so many little penates in our arms, which we lose on the way. One boundless colossus, as great as the universe, we could follow everywhere, as one man; at a single stride, he would encompass our seas and our years.

THE CITIES

You are the oldest of us; you are the greatest; tell us what we need to do

BABYLON

Harness your unicorns; each of you mount your resounding chariots; form an enchanted round around my furnace. Hurry, Bactra, throw your bronze centaur into my melting-pot as you pass by; Persepolis, throw me the gilded feet of the dragons of Iran; Memphis, collect the scales of your crocodiles on your stairways; Thebes, cut the flattened tresses of your goddess with your scissors; Nineveh, bring me the scintillating stars that your priests have attached to your miter; Sheba, send me, on an Indian elephant, the God with a thousand ivory heads lying in your pagoda. Pass by, turn your chariots rapidly around my magic fire, cities of the Orient. I shall mix and crush heavens and earth with my diviners.

THE CITIES
We shall do as you say. Will you soon be finished? Here are our gods of brass, and also those of bronze.

BABYLON
Look, and behold the great idol that is appearing; it is boiling in the crucible of the world, like a rumor growing within our walls; look, it has neither beaks, nor gryphon's claws, nor wings to fly, nor serpents' coils to crawl. Behold one who stands on his feet like a human being. Truly, one might think him an old man from Chaldea who has been alive forever, but who is leaving his abode for the first time. What shall we call him? Allah? Elohim? Jehovah? Who knows?

JERUSALEM
Me?

BABYLON
Who's that?

JERUSALEM
Your sister Jerusalem? Wait for me; I'm coming; leave your work there.

BABYLON
Where are you?

JERUSALEM
In the direction of Joppa. I have cried with the army that besieged me, with the herald's trumpet, with the rasp that eats

me away, with the soldier that whips me, with my crumbling roof.

BABYLON

Oh, it's you, my sister. Where did you come from? You haven't brought your share either of amulets or relics from your neck; all you have in your temple is a worn piece of cloth with which to swathe an idol. Have you come once again as a beggar, to borrow my gods without a pledge?

JERUSALEM

I'm bringing you a better one than all of yours.

BABYLON

Keep your ancient god, sister; what use is he to us? He has neither linen nor a scrap of clothing in which to dress himself; he is as naked in his abyss as you are beneath your roof. He is wandering through his empty eternity as you do on our roads. When night comes, there are no temples to enclose him; when rain falls, no cloak to keep him dry. At his age, old in years, he goes forth alone in exile to the utmost depths of the universe, beaten by the wind and the rain, without ever resting, like you, poor captive, traversing the desert under the rods of our archers.

JERUSALEM

Listen to me; I bring news.

THE CITIES

What news?

JERUSALEM

I have traveled far, farther than you, to the edge of the sea of Joppa to bathe my feet and gaze where the world finishes. My prophets climbed up to my highest tower. That night, before daybreak, they summoned me to see, in Bethlehem, a God hidden in a stable manger. Look, look, Jerusalem; he has an aureole around his head; he is a tiny infant. The shepherds are playing their pipes to amuse him.

THEBES
Why have we not found him before you? Have you already taken him on to your knees to rock him and offer him the teat?

JERUSALEM
To rock him there is a Galilean virgin, clad in linen, whom he loves more than me.

MEMPHIS
Does he wear broad bandlets on his temples, like those worn by my kings in their tombs near Aleppo?

JERUSALEM
No, his hair is as radiant as the sun in a dusty haze.

BABYLON
Does he not have a robe the color of the sky, which diviners have embroidered with the stars of the night?

JERUSALEM
When I saw him, the cold wind was making him a tunic and the warm wind sowing him a cloak.

PERSEPOLIS
I know him. At his door he has two gryphons whose claws make naphtha wells spring forth from the earth.

JERUSALEM
No, the one I saw had two angels on his threshold, carrying a palm-leaf.

BABYLON

We'll finish the work we've begun another time. Let's go see the new god.

THEBES

I already know what place I shall make for him in my great temple of Luxor. I want to hang his cradle from my portico, so that my sphinxes can rock him without getting up, day and night.

PERSEPOLIS

I shall have him suckled by a unicorn, in my desert.

BABYLON

And I shall carry him in my arms on my terrace, in order that he might learn to count the stars by night.

THE CITIES

Jerusalem, our sister, climb your staircases in order to see him at closer range. Tell him that tomorrow, before daybreak, we shall send him three royal mages as messengers. We shall choose the oldest and the wisest, the kings of Sheba, Persia and Babylon; each will bring him presents under his cloak—truly rich presents, from the mountain and the plain, amulets and enchanted stones, as many as he pleases.

Tell him, on our behalf, that although he is still a little child, and our towers are high, we shall take him up to our summit; that our gates are very heavy, but that he shall make them screech merely by touching them; that our chariots are fast, but that he shall hold the reins of our unbroken mares on his own, for his amusement; that our royal crowns are heavy on the heads of men, but that we shall coif him with them in his cradle, that he might play with them; that our voices are the great resounding voices of empires, but that we shall sing him softly to sleep with young women's canticles. Tell him that we are very old within our old walls, but that if he wishes, he shall take up in the palm of his hands with all our towers and bastions, like a little woodland bird in its nest of ferns.

Also salute by name, on our behalf, the virgin dressed in linen who loves him, and the two angels bearing palm-leaves.

IX.

The Mage Kings

THE KING OF SHEBA

Adieu, Queen of Sheba, don't cry. I'm departing as a messenger with my brethren, the mage kings. If I should happen to die on the journey, embalm me with Syrian balm; put me, fully dressed, in a pyramid of emeralds as high as the pyramids of Memphis. In the meantime, devote yourself to what justice demands of you. Listen to the two parties without differentiating between them; let fortune and misfortune be as one to you, and know that a single loyal archer is worth more than a hundred felonious cavalrymen. Teach your two daughters to spin cotton and wash linen. If you marry them off, make sure that our son-in-law does not command where I am master. Build a pagoda full of amulets. Look after my chariots, my elephant towers, my brave men of war and my squire, in order that I might find, when I return, my kingdom as increased in power as you are in wisdom.

THE QUEEN OF SHEBA

Come back soon, my lord. I shall not be able to sleep without you, my love.

MELCHIOR, KING OF PERSIA

Remain behind, my gryphons, to close the gates of my city when I am no longer here. If a king comes to lay siege to it, light a fire of heather on the mountain to send me a signal. Every morning and evening, let my wives sing a prayer for me with their jasmine lips, before dawn and before dusk, before taking a bath and before tying or taking off their turbans; and let their veils trail on the ground, so that their amorous ankles are unseen. Have my history written with a chisel on a rock polished by the sirocco, in five-cubit letters, and, so that the

71

lions can read them if they wish when they pass by. Sit down, to wait for me, at the place where my kingdom ends; and if my people ask after me, gather them, like the sand, to raise a mosque in Iran as large s their shadow.

THE GRYPHONS
To remain at the gate of your city my wings are too rapid. A divine breath has brushed my mane and I have heard the night of Eternity whinnying in the direction of Bethlehem. Since then, my claw has been digging an abyss in the desire to leave. My nostrils are sniffing the air. Let me run before you like a dog before its master.

THE KING OF PERSIA
Who, then, would watch over my walls?

THE GRYPHONS
The desert.

BALTHAZAR, KING OF BABYLON
My presents are the most beautiful. I have a hundred castles, and as many cities; every city has sent a hundred camels laden with silk, myrrh and vessels, every castle a hundred racehorses with Moors to guide them. My ivory baldaquin is carried by four Ethiopian kings, all the color of ebony wood, my cloak by four Mesopotamian kings, all armed with golden arrows. Damascened sabers, silver baldrics, diamond-encrusted miters, lighted candelabras, cassolettes of smoking incense and turbans embroidered by my wives fill my courtyard; mules are prancing on the paving-stones. The camels kneel and get up by themselves; the falcons and merlins are growing bored on the wrists of the squires; the carts are screeching on their axles; so you, beautiful Morning Star, rise in your turn to guide us.

THE STAR

Carts and chariots filled with myrrh, it is me who has been waiting for you since the middle of the night; do not lost the track of my wheels.

THE CARTS

Our wheels are heavier than yours, our road is rougher; but we shall whip the rumps of our mares with our hard shafts and give them the sweat of their manes to drink.

THE STAR
Follow me.

THE CARTS
We're leaving.

THE STAR
Where are you?

THE CARTS
Here we are.

THE STAR
Are you coming?

THE CARTS
In your dust.

THE MAGE-KINGS

Beautiful star, our kingdoms are already far away; soon we shall no longer be able to see them. We are traversing many lands and many cities without stopping there. Our massive golden scepters are our traveling staffs and our diamond-encrusted crowns shelter us by night. Never, at our festivals, have so many people kissed our robes. We pass before caravanserais without sitting down at table. At the crossroads, lions bring us dates and figs for our meals, and eagles come to fill our ruby cups from the springs they know. Impatiently, the rivers in which our diadems are mirrored set out to follow us; in their nests, the little storks stand up, beating their wings, when they discover where we are going; and the sea breeze, which can never quit the shore, says to us, wherever we encounter it: "Take me with you, great kings, in the flaps of your clothing."

THE STAR
Neither here nor there, do not stop your mules with the bridle. A cloud draws my axle and the wind drives my wheels. In my hand I carry the presents of the firmament: an aureole of light that does not go out by day or by night; a mantle of azure that I have sown with my golden needle; and a cassolette full of the scent of the sky. Everywhere I have gone I have found my drink of dew prepared. The stars are taking their festival dawns from the vault, and the void is rising up with a start, propping itself up, in order to try to follow me to where I am leading you.

THE MAGE-KINGS
In the direction of the plain we can see seven pyramids emerging, which touch the sky. The smallest bows down and picks up the shadow of the largest, in order to veil itself, as a child does the hem of his mother's cloak. Around it, obelisks, columns and colonnades, temples and frontons, are lying on the ground, like the booty of a god's caravan that has unloaded its camels for the night beneath a grove of sycamores. At their feet, the desert has lain down to like their stairways. Is that not the dwelling of the king's son to whom we are taking our presents?

THE STAR
No, he is not there.

THE MAGE-KINGS

Now, here is a noisy city that has painted walls like a sash around its hips. Its columns are less weighty to bear than our scepters in our hands. Seated on multicolored horse-coats, agas and sheikhs are riding out of the gates with a pack of greyhounds. Its guards are signaling to us with silver pikes. To salute us on their thresholds, its women stand up straight, more lavishly perfumed than the lemon-trees in the hedge. The keys to the gate are brought to us by two cup-bearers, on a silver plate. Toward sunset, a date-palm planted there donates its sheet of shadow; a wood-pigeon nourished there brings its messages of war around its neck. Without saying anything, the amorous sea has rolled under its windows during the night, to cradle it while it sleeps, with its rumbling walls, its panting people and its towers drawing breath, in its giant arms. Is the palace we seek not there, we wonder?

THE STAR

Not yet.

THE MAGE-KINGS

Now we are entering the gate of Herod's kingdom. Over there, in the distance, is his city, which has climbed on to its hill in order to see us coming from further away. It has climbed up its highest stairway like a messenger in search of news. Like a diviner tearing his cloak, it has shredded its walls. Its towers and ruined turrets are lying on their sides and will not get up again. Absinthe has climbed through its windows in order to discover its secret: the crane has alighted on its roof to ask for news, and the evening wind is crying through the gap under its door: "Come on, Jerusalem; prophesy for me!"

THE STAR

Pass by quickly. He is not here.

THE MAGE-KINGS

It's at the end of the earth, then, that the castle of this king's son is built? The cities and villages of Moors and Indians, the columns and the colonnades, the pyramids and the minarets, the tombs of kings under the palm trees, and the peoples in the sand are the porticos that lead to his pagoda; the gods on the road are his messengers; the temples of granite and African stone are for his squires, and those of polished marble in the isle of Candia are good for his cupbearers; he desires only ever to sleep beneath a roof of rubies.

THE STAR

Whip your mules; we're nearly there.

THE MAGE-KINGS

Beautiful star, what are you thinking? Have you gone astray? The palaces and cities are far away. The path is damaging our wheels. No more women in the doorways, no more silver pikes, no more baldaquins or caravanserais, no more guitar-players or zither-players in the streets, no more carpet beneath our mules' hooves. There is nothing to be seen but a thatched cottage with little birds on the roof. The staircase is crumbling, the rail worn; shepherds tremble as they go up it. Let's go back; truly, this is not a road of kings.

THE STAR

Kneel, kings. Here it is.

X

THE LITTLE BIRDS ON THE ROOF, *to Christ*
1.

Wake up, beautiful little infant. We are the same age as you. Our down-feathers serve as an aureole over our heads. Our father and mother have brought us to you. How high the sky is! Oh, how large the earth is! Oh, how well-built the cities are! Truly, our bed of moss and white linen washed in the spring was nothing compared to their walls. Open your eyelids, beautiful little infant; wake up. It is for you that we are singing our song. Come and see, at your door, how the sun is rising, and how beautiful the world is becoming! Come and see how green the olives are, when they ripen in the Garden of Olives, how Calvary smiles in looking down at you from the height of its summit!

2.

Kings! Kings! Come and see! Here are three mage-kings on their knees, taking off their golden spurs! All in silver robes! All in scarlet cloaks! All in multicolored turbans! Their carts travel as rapidly on their wheels as we do on our wings. Their diadems weigh them down as much as our crests of dew. Oh, how far away their kingdoms are, how great their age and their wisdom too! Never has our father, when he has returned from the fields, brought diamonds back on the blades of morning grass as shiny as the gifts that they have brought you in their cassolettes.

CHORUS OF SHEPHERDS

If it's us you're talking about, we're not mages and we're not kings. The presents we've brought are an otter-fur, a cord necklace, a hazel-wood cross and a clasp of carved wood. Our coffers are empty, our slave-wages haven't been paid; we haven't been able to buy silk or jewelry in the city.

There, good laborer on your bed of straw; come to labor in our glebe.

Gentle harvester, get up to carry away your sheaf of peoples on your back.

Little vine-grower asleep in your manger, get dressed quickly to gather from your vines the grapes of the world, which the sun has ripened.

Handsome cowherd, in your stable, take your bagpipe from your neck and your cattle-prod, to drive before you the stars and the idle kings who dawdle on the road.

THE ANGEL RACHEL

1.

My viol, which you father has given me, has three silver strings. The first is for him, in the clouds, the second is for your mother, beneath her veil, the third is to sing you a carol in your manger. Dream your dream while listening to my viol; dream sweetly that your stable is a golden ship, that your manger is made of diamond, that your roof is built with the stones of the sky. Don't weep, God of the earth! If the wind blows, if the rain falls, I have opened above your head my two wings, which the winter wind cannot dampen.

2.

To whom is your mother married, that you are so poor? Is he a weaver without work, a spinner of yarn without a distaff, or a maker of footstools? To earn his living, his weaver has woven over his work the cloth of the firmament; his spinner has spun the rays of the sun with his spindle; his maker of footstools has carved Golgotha beneath his awning. Don't weep, God of the earth; the falcon had gone to seek spring water for you to drink, on his highest summit; the bee has flown up into heaven from her hive to gather golden honey for your meal; and the lion of Judea is lashing himself with his tail as he runs, in order to bring you blessed figs in his claws more rapidly.

3.

A diviner I have found has told me your good fortune, and a very young prophetess has read your fate in the palm of your hand. When you are grown up, the sons of princes will say to you: "Let us exchange cloaks;" the sons of kings: "Let us exchange crowns;" the rosemary, when it is born, will say to you: "Will you give me the scent of your hair?" the swan, when it hatches: "Let us exchange down;" and the star, when it appears: "Let us exchange aureoles." Don't weep, God of the earth; I have made you a robe, a scarlet robe. The firmament has spun you, a long time ago, a girdle of azure, and the desert has sown you, without receiving any wage, an entirely white tunic.

THE VIRGIN MARY

1.

Angel Rachel, is your father not coming? Is it true that he has abandoned me for a better-adorned virgin in a spring star? Tomorrow I want to go to look for him, to sit down with my veil on the benches of fisherman's boats, in the carved bow of sailing ships, at crossroads, under the lamp in hostelries. I shall go sit down beneath a soldier's shield, in a hermit's tower, at the door of churches, without roof or awning on the boundary-markers of streets. I want to climb up the highest stairway in a cathedral, to an open niche, in order to cry to the four winds: "Father, we are hungry and thirsty, and I have no more milk: bring your infant what he needs to live until tomorrow."

2.

I'm not asking for the golden veil or girdle of a newly-wed. I'm not asking for the two bracelets or the glass necklace that virgins wear when they go to a fête. I'm asking for a sheet of cloth for the greatest king of kings. If he dies in my arms so young, who will make me mourning-dress in order to weep? The night, in winter, will not be dark enough; the snow, at Yule, would not be white enough; to make my tower, ebony would not be black enough; to make my veil, the firmament would not be long enough.

3.

Go away, nightingales, don't sing so early; little storks, don't get up so soon. I'm the one who has put me lord to sleep; I'm the one who wants to wake him up. You have nothing to carry but your crests of dew; he, so small, must carry, without flinching, his divine crown. Let him sleep, let him continue sleeping! I've sown basil in his garden, but I'm afraid that he will gather nothing but tears when he gets up.

CHRIST, *waking up*
Mother, take me in your arms. The nightingales are already singing, the little storks are already flapping their wings.

THE VIRGIN MARY
I will rock you on my shoulder while the dew is born, when the sun rises.

CHRIST
Mother, are you alone? Where has my father gone? I have not seen him yet.

THE VIRGIN MARY
Your father lives a long way from here.

CHRIST
What will we do, if he doesn't come?

THE VIRGIN MARY
He has a burden to bear as heavy as the world.

CHRIST
Is it necessary to walk for a long time to reach the city where he dwells?

THE VIRGIN MARY
Longer than your feet can carry you.

CHRIST
As soon as his work is done, he'll come back to us.

THE VIRGIN MARY
His work is never done; we're the ones who must leave in order to discover where he is.

CHRIST
Don't weep, Mother; when I'm older, I'll go in search of him on my own.

THE VIRGIN MARY
You'll take me with you.

CHRIST
Tell me, Mother, has he, like you, an aureole around his head?

THE VIRGIN MARY
His aureole is the clouds, and the clasp of his mantle is a star.

CHRIST
And his house is larger than yours?

THE VIRGIN MARY
You shall see his house. His roof is the azure of the sky; the sun is his workman's lamp; and the haze of the morning is the dust he shakes off at his door.

CHRIST
Since he's so rich, he'll send us fine messengers.

THE VIRGIN MARY
Here come his messengers now.

XI

A CROWNED LION
For a thousand years, I have worn my crowd on my head. Neither the desert wind nor the unicorns of Iran have knocked it down; I have kept it until now, all shiny, in order to lay it in your manger.

CHRIST
I'd also like to touch the mane on your back.

THE LION
My back is dirtied by the sand; my mane is too high. I you want to touch it, I'll lie down on your bed of straw.

A GRYPHON
Neither the claws on my feet nor my equine rump could run fast enough. I took to my silken wings in order to reach your door before the kings. Here is the golden sand that I collected in the Euphrates; here is a piece of Persian linen, with which to make you a tunic.

CHRIST
And you, beautiful eagle, what are you holding in your beak?

THE EAGLE
My cargo of down for your aerie; here, as well, to distract you, is a globe of the world that a Calabrian eaglet brought from its nest in Rome, from the summit of the Capitol.

CHRIST
Lay it at my feet; it's tiring you to move it.

THE MAGE-KINGS

Is that you, king of the abundant skies? When your eyes are open, the stars close their eyelids and their golden lashes. When your mother lets down your hair over your shoulders, you shake the daybreak around you, as a swan shakes off the dew. The sprig of rosemary that saw you first told the road, the road told the river, the river the sea, the sea the mountain, the mountain our scepters, and our scepters repeated it to us; and in order to adore you, we are kneeling down, like the sprig of rosemary. As a present, we have brought you a beautiful silver-plated chalice. All we kings have drunk from it, one after another, and all our gods before us. The most powerful has mixed the tears and sweat of worlds therein, with his finger, like water and wine. Drink from it in your turn; drink for your thirst from this enchanted cup.

THE VIRGIN MARY

Don't take that chalice in your hand, my lord, I beg you; there' bile and absinthe on its rim.

THE MAGE-KINGS

That's not bile, truly, and not absinthe; it's only tears.

CHRIST

My hands are too small to hold that large chalice.

THE MAGE-KINGS

A genius in a hollow mountain has been polishing this ruby crown for a thousand years. Brahma has put it on his head; Memnon wore it after him; but in order to give it to you, we have discrowned him on his seat of oblivion. Try it on your infant's head.

THE VIRGIN MARY

What do I see in the depths of that crown? Blood pouring out, sharp thorns of Judean wood. Don't touch it, my lord.

THE MAGE-KINGS

That's not blood, truly, and those aren't the thorns of bushes or forests; they're golden nails.

CHRIST

The head on my shoulders is still too inexperienced to bear that heavy crown.

THE MAGE-KINGS

Although these presents are too heavy, they will be useful to you later, when you reach our age. We have others yet: amulets to suspend around your neck, hookahs of amber and gum, the silver keys to a hundred cities and as many castles, twenty carts filled with furbished steel broadswords and incense, which the Moors have gathered from the branch, a thousand idols of white ivory with the workmen that have made them, an odorous miter of topaz, for kings the color of night to wash your feet, and four kings the color of bronze to wipe them dry.

A SHEPHERD

Farewell, Master, master vine-grower, who fills your chalice with all the tears of the vine; farewell, Master, master woodcutter, who puts all the thorns of the earth in your crown. After the king of Babylon and the king of Persia, if we showed our presents, we would be scorned, mocked for our mattocks and our carts.

CHORUS OF SHEPHERDS

For our carts and our handcarts, our scythes, our sickles and our ploughshares. Let's go home. Shepherds' wives, open the latch. Pick up your coarse cloaks and put your heavy pitchers, brim-full of your tears, on your heads. Sweep the thorns and lilies-of-the-valley from our thresholds. The child-God, who was to make us richer than mages, has not looked at us. We have nothing to give him in his cradle of straw but the dawn that whitens the morning, nothing but the yellowing thatch, nothing but the gold of the sunlight on our foreheads, nothing but the dew beneath our feet, nothing but the dainty skylark above our heads.

CHRIST

Better than the thousand ivory idols with the workmen who have made them, I like the color of the dew beneath the shepherds' feet.

THE MAGE-KINGS

Back, slaves! Son of a king, come with us to our palaces glistening with precious stones. Our elephants will carry you in silken palanquins. Our peoples will hold parasols over your head. The peris of Persia, clad in diamonds, will rock you lovingly, better than your mother in your stable. From the depths of cisterns, the middle of lakes, avatars with the bodies of virgins will sing you to sleep; and sphinxes crowned with bandlets will tell you tales older than the world every evening, in the desert.

CHORUS OF SHEPHERDS

If you come with us, our rods are hard, harder than our carts. Under our roofs, the snow will fall at your feet, and the robins will eat your bread in your hand while warming themselves by the fireside. For your enjoyment you will have our cloaks hanging on the walls, and our mattocks, wary of the day's work, resting at our doors. Fairies, as big as palm-leaves at the most, scarcely dressed in scraps of cloth, very poor and very old, will beg at your bedside in the evening, and fire-follets will come, at midnight, to try your divine crown on their smoky heads.

THE MAGE-KINGS

In our land, the sun rises like a mage-king going up to his tower; date-palms flourish and lemon-trees too; gum grows on the trees, incense on the branches, amour in the women's tents. There, the stork builds its nest on the roof it likes the best; the sand is golden, the shade scented with myrrh; in the depths of the cisterns the pure sky slakes its thirst by mirroring itself therein all day long. Come to our kingdoms; the sea, which touches them, will bring you pearls to its shore; and you shall caress its green tresses, without making it angry, whenever you wish.

CHORUS OF SHEPHERDS

In our land, the sun sets like a reaper wearied by his day's work; the pine grows verdantly on the mountain, the birch in the forest; there, the clouds are black, the north wind murmurs and the dead leaves sob on our threshold; then the thatched cottage sighs and the grotto weeps; the Ocean brings its unmuzzled flocks to graze in the storm; you will be hungry; you will be thirsty, and there is nothing beside us to protect you but our dogs.

CHRIST

Better than the country of the kings, I like the country where the thatched cottage sighs, where the grotto weeps, where the leaf sobs.

(*The kings go away.*)

XII.

CHORUS
1.

Three falcons have gone to the mountain, weeping. In distress, they have let their prey slips from their talons. Their beaks are bloody all the way to their eyes, their claws all the way to their knees. They have also dropped their golden ring, which the torrent has carried away, which the sea will put on her finger—yes, the distant sea, which the falcons will never see, nor the kites, nor the goshawks, nor the merlins with their emerald eyes.

2.

Three mage-kings have retraced their steps, weeping. Their eyes are streaming with tears all the way to their cheeks, which they wipe with their beards. In distress, they have dropped their scepters into a spring. In despair, they have also dropped their crowns into a river, which the stream will take, which the current will draw away, which the ocean will put on its head—yes, the ocean of islands, which the kings will never see, nor the queen with them, nor the pantlers, nor the squires with their silver-stitched baldrics.

3.

A stork, on its roof, which has seen them, has said to the falcons: "What have you done with your claws, which tear your prey so well, and your wings that fly so rapidly over the edges of storms? Have you made war for three days with the hundred-cubit vulture of Jehosophat, that you are so weary?"

"No, no; it's the chick of a Judean dove who, without emerging from his nest, has mortally wounded all the falcons of Arabia that have gazed upon him."

4.

A well-constructed city, which has seen the, has said to the mage-kings: "Where are your cloaks and your fine clothes? Where are your crowns and your scepters that I had carved? Who has untied your girdles? Who has thrown your amulets on the road, with your miters? You must have made war with the son of a prince who had a hundred horses, all harnessed to his chariot, and a thousand armies to defend him. The slingshot-wielders have torn your robes, the cavalrymen your tunics, and the archers with their arrows have filled your eyes with tears."

"No, no; it is a child off Galilee, with three shepherds, who discrowns all the kings of the Orient, as soon as he encounters them."

THE CARTS

Since the gifts of the mages are worth less than the gifts of slaves, let our wheels no longer follow the kings. Now, the one who shall lead us dwells in Galilee.

THE MULES

Our gilded hooves do not want to walk any further on the paving-stones of the Orient. Now our guardian will set down our litter in another country, where the sun sets, where the shadow is denser.

BALTHAZAR, KING OF BABYLON

Now that it is necessary to travel without carts and mules, what has become of my city with its thousand towers? Ashamed, it has hidden its head in the sand, like an ostrich, and its breast in the brushwood. That child-God has playfully effaced my kingdom with his finger. My people have disappeared without waiting for me, like a knot that he has undone for the sake of amusement. My castles have turned to dust. Hola! Let a lion in this vicinity offer shelter for the night to the king of Babylon in the depths of its lair!

89

MELCHIOR, KING OF PERSIA

An Arab has passed by on a rapid mare to carry away my people on its rump to his tent. My nations, my satraps and my gods can be held today in the palm of my hand. Beautiful infant, what have you done? In your stable, you have overturned the lands of the Orient like a jug of milk.

THE KING OF SHEBA

Let us sit down on the ground to weep. Everything has been erased; our bodies are vanishing; our royalty is turning to ashes in our hands; our majesty is evaporating like a wisp of smoke in a shepherd's fire.

BALTHAZAR, KING OF BABYLON

Look! I am no longer a king, nor the son of a king; my tears have become a stream in which cranes come to drink within the walls of my palace.

MELCHIOR, KING OF PERSIA

I am no more than a murmur in the heather of my halls, which repeats endlessly: "Thorny flower, flower of Asia, your crown has fallen."

THE KING OF SHEBA

And mine, silvered by a ray of moonlight in the darkness, which says to the ruin: "Tower of marble, tower of the Orient, your roof is on the ground."

CHORUS

1.

Yes, weep, falcons in your nest; weep, kings in your brushwood. The lands of the Orient have lost their summer, whose gold and gods ripened on the branch. The world's sun is no longer in its morning, it has gone to seek its stable in other climes. Star of shepherds, will you follow it so far, all the way the lands of the evening, where frost hangs from the trees, where the birch pales, where the moss sighs, and where the stag, with his burden of antlers, bells in the black forests?

2.

Listen! The sphinx has made itself a shroud of sand, up to the neck. Entangled, the cities are going back down their staircases. Trembling, they huddle beneath the ardent heather. The arch is broken, the column bends its knee, the summit of the pyramid asks the stork to hide it beneath its wing.

3.

Pale, the crowd disperses; pale, the crowd vanishes. An entire people fattens a palm tree with its ashes, and an entire empire a flowering aloe. Of Babylon, only a goatherd remains, without a cloak, whistling for his goats; of the Persian armies only a herder of mares, who milks their teats.

4.

High up, on the mountain, the cypress has dressed itself in black to moan; the cistern has dried up. Down below, in the valley, the jackal has paused; he gazes, his hackles raised, and howls at a world that is no more: Awaken! The echo on the mountain, the echo in the valley, the oasis that listens, the sea that is open-mouthed and the desert that advances barefoot reply to it: "Our god Pan is dead."

5.

A God younger than a thousand years has arrived; without jumping, he will overstep the sea in a stride. Grapes of Gaul, ripen beneath your oak; he is the one who will produce your vintage. Figs of Spain, whom no one has planted, he is the one who will pick you.

6.

But you, old Orient, without being able to untie your shores, you shall remain seated on your beach in Byzantium, like a pasha at the prow of his galley; put your turban on your head, fill up your hookah of gum and amber; count the waves that pass by; not one will bring you back the days of summer.

A SPHINX

Passer-by, who sings so well, do you know where there is any more of the wood of Judea in Lebanon, with which to carve a cross?

THE INTERLUDE OF THE FIRST DAY

DANCE OF DEVILS

LUCIFER
As comedies go, the play is good.

ASTAROTH
And the subject quite ridiculous

LUCIFER
The creation, you mean?

ASTAROTH
What else? When the void, ever agape, ever laughing, kisses your hand at your door, it's a pleasant idea, in truth, to exchange it for a weeping world.

LUCIFER
Agreed. I thought, however, that Leviathan and the serpent would amuse you well enough.

ASTAROTH
About them, I've nothing to say; but to round out the sky with his trowel to provide shelter from the storm—for what? A worm? A weed? A thorn, at least; perhaps a mere nothing. No, less than that: a human being! The ending is happy, and merits your affection.

CHORUS OF DEVILS
Peace, now! Listen to Beelzebub.

BEELZEBUB

1.

Angels, dominations, notable masters and doctors in all things, you have heard the first act of our celestial comedy. That act is weak. Our choruses are as lacking in voice as the shades beneath our thongs: the Ocean has remained flat, Babylon has quavered before you, Nineveh has crumbled far too soon. What can be done about it? The fault is in the subject; the Creation is tedious. Neither on high nor down below, neither far away nor nearby, does anyone want it any longer.

2.

If our work is a chaos, is the universe any better? Everyone comes and goes without authorization. Verity, fantasy, what is dream and what is wakefulness? On the road to Antioch I often thought that the stars were about to go out in the firmament like a boatman's lamp, for lack of a little oil, at nightfall; and truly, the earth, leaning sideways, limps away at that hour like a drunkard, along the road that leads to my threshold. So go away then, fine drunken poem, limping cripple, to where the void lurks on your border.

3.

Nature is my passion , and an oriental night has always kept me awake around the trunks of fig-trees; but at present, between ourselves, one can admit it: that light darted over the shores, the indigo of the sea, the black shadow of the mountains, those voices sighing in the branches of forests, those spirits burbling in the springs, and that golden dust thrown in handfuls into the eyes of the universe, are of dubious quality; now, the secret is out. We do as much in our chemical crucibles; for three days, give me the firmament earth, sky, matter, sprit, science, glory, amour and four grains of carbonate in my crucible, and in three days, there will be nothing in the bottom but a fire-follet and a little residue the color of my face.

4.

Anyway, in everything, the commencement is difficult; and the Orient, which opened human life, was the Creator's debut, which merits indulgence. Let's admit it, our divine master's hand was trembling, and searching for ideas while he took thousands of years to knead a nation, and he paused in the dark, in Egypt or in India, for time enough to make four worlds. How many centuries he wasted in heavily planting two or three suntanned peoples in the mid of the Nile, always stammering the same idea, in hieroglyphs, in chiseled stone, in murmuring cities, like a novice angel who stops in mid-verse, counting the syllables one by one on his fingers, with his bow!

5.

And then, one day, when he took all the visages of the religions of the Orient, and said without blinking: "With the hawk of Thebes I screech; with the unicorn of Persia I bound; with the dove of Chaldea I coo; with the crocodile, I lament; with the sphinx I crouch down;" did we not all think, my brothers, that the Eternal, having gone mad, was playing a divine comedy in which he was the only character? A marvelous role, I agree, for an accomplished artist, if he had been less bombastic in Babylon and the land of Egypt.

6.

But to him the real, to us the ideal. It's no lie; on our silken wings, we have raised our subject as high as it could go. Beyond that, one only finds the vault of heaven, where the bird of death roosts, which accompanies each of my words with its chirping. The style has been reviewed and criticized for three centuries; its harmony is as striking as a cherub's viol, and even a trifle hollow, to better reflect our model; for I strongly suspect that those vagabond skies, those vacillating stars, those gods, those immortal souls and that universal sphere are soap-bubbles clad in etheric colors, by means of which the Infinite is amusing himself, with a pipe blown between his fingers, in the cup of the world.

ASTAROTH

Or rather a round that he's making to distract himself, while spitting into the well of the abyss.

LUCIFER

Yes, it's more than probable; this evening, I want to try it in my turn on the pale spring where we drink.

BEELZEBUB

The idea is good; it pleases me entirely, for evil is discovered.

SAINT MADELEINE

I would like to hide my tears beneath my linen robe; when I was sitting by the road to Joppa, when I lowered my eyes to my book of psalms, I heard an exactly similar voice rustling the grass and the daisies of the meadow.

BEELZEBUB

My love, your sensitivity is exaggerated, your imagination is deceiving you; be sure that it's purely an effect of my declamation, and that art pushed to a certain degree produces these illusions. Save the generosity of your heart for the sciences that follow; in any case, I can already hear the fig-trees falling under the apostles' billhooks, and the water of baptism quivering in the Jordan. Those two sensations are equally disagreeable to me, so I shall retire.

THE SECOND DAY

THE PASSION

I

THE DESERT

1.

When a camel-driver passes along my road, singing his song for his herd to follow him, I fall silent in my sand. From morning until evening, I sit down at the entrance to my tent on the strand; I listen, I hold my breath while the caravan emerges from the gate of Damascus or Jerusalem. My voice is the wind of Arabia; walls that it shakes, half-closed doors in which it moans, towers whose crenellations it beats, fig-leaves that it dries out, miters and turbans that it loosens on the heads of priests, manes of horses that it heaps up like a flame in brushwood, listen to my song in your turn.

2.

The mountain adores its shadow; the river adores its mud; the boat adores its shore. I have neither shadow, nor mud to knead to make myself an amulet. Jehovah is the idol that I hang around my neck; he is made like me; like me, he is alone; like me, he marches in his sand without finding a companion; like me, he gazes at his bench, and sees nothing but himself traveling day and night on his beach: his breath effaces his years better than my breath efface the footprints of caravans with resonant bells. Worlds, nations and winged stars rest in passing by his cistern, as the migrating storks stop for a night at the water-holes of my wells. To decorate him, I have no Persian bracelets nor Indian ivory not Chaldean gold; the rays of the midday sun are my entire heritage; I make a flamboyant sword of them; and my immensity, without limits without gates, without springs, without confines, is the only ornament that I can give him.

3.

I had a palm-tree that I loved; its trunk was as slender as a daughter of Damascus, its crown bore its foliage as a Samaritan woman carries a pitcher full of water in returning from the well. Why are you sad, beautiful palm-tress with a thousand flowers the color of fire? If you seek shade, I shall go crawling to request it from my heather; if you seek water, I shall turn back to steep a flap of my girdle in dew.

4.

"Neither the shade of your heather nor the moisture of dew will console me. I want a breath to wither my flowers. I want to hollow out the wrinkles of my young trunk. I want to veil my head with my tangled foliage forever, like a priest in mourning. I am mortally saddened by what I have seen, on climbing to the top of my crown, in the direction of Golgotha."

5.

Do not die, O palm-tree that I love; I have only you for my lips to kiss from daybreak until dusk. Am I not lying at your feet like a faithful dog? Every morning, have I not brought you the dew that I have found? When I wake up in the night, you pour your perfumed tresses over me; my dreams are embalmed when I dream of you. If you sway your crown, I think to myself: *she is calling me*; and I crawl into your shade. Oh, your shade! It is a crowd that lives in me; it is my spring, where I drink; it is my tent, where I go to sleep. You, the lover of my strand, the spouse of my burning sand, now that I love you, what would I become, my God, if the day, in dawning, no longer said to me: "There she is!"

6.

"What, my crown will not fade! How will the pith of my trunk not dry out beneath the bark? I can see, I can see Christ on the path that leads to Golgotha, dragging himself beneath his cross. For an aureole upon his head he has a crown of thorns. Oh, how slowly he is walking! He is looking behind him, to see if the desert might come to his aid. The crowd is muttering in the city like a winter storm. The tribes are climbing like vine-branches to the heights of their terraces; but the eagle is hiding its head beneath its wing. The summit of Horeb in descending in haste into the valley; at the zenith, two giant eyes, which contain more tears than a cistern has rain-water, half-closed beneath their azure lids, allow one of their burning tears to fall on me. If the God who has given me all my flowers is going up to Golgotha like an aloe to the top of its stem, to drink bitter poison from its calyx, I too want to dry myself out at my summit and die like him."

7.

Wait one more hour! If I drive my sands before me, perhaps I shall arrive at the gate of Jerusalem before Christ has climbed Calvary. Tell the storks to give me their wings, the horses of Arabia their rapid stride, the lion his mane, the serpent his coils, in order that I might travel faster than the tribes, than the cross-bearers.

8.

Oh how slowly I creep! Oh, how my saddle is burning my flanks! To cross a river, it takes my more than a year; to trample a city with its obelisks beneath the sole of my foot, I need a century. Before my gaping mouth rises up over the ramparts to drain the cup of that people, will not the cross have been erected? Before I have eaten away the steps of Calvary, will not Christ have drunk his bile and hyssop?

9.

The hour has passed; after the hour, the evening has also passed, and I shall arrive too late. Jehovah no longer has a son; I no longer have a palm tree, or any companion. Jehovah is alone in the firmament; I am alone on my strand; our two deserts come together, and sadden one another. Together we roll on in our immense ennui, without finding any shore therein; we only meet one another, we only hear one another. Our two echoes are similar. Tomorrow, when he passes by, like an Arab in search of his booty, if I ask him: "Where is your son?" he will reply: "And you, where is your shade?"

10.

And me! My voice is the wind of Arabia. Walls that it shakes, half-closed doors in which it moans, towers whose crenellations it beats, fig-leaves it desiccates, miters and turbans it loosens, horses' manes that it heaps up like flames in dry grass, you have heard my song.

Inside the city of Jerusalem, the door of Ahasuerus' house is open.

AHASUERUS' BROTHERS
Come back into the house, Ahasuerus. Let us close the latch on the door; are you not afraid of the wind that is blowing, and the noise that is audible in the city?

AHASUERUS
Go back in, my little brothers, go to sleep on your mats. I want to sit on my bench to watch the crowd go by.

AHASUERUS' BROTHERS
Here it comes! Let's get out of the way.

THE CROWD, *following Christ, carrying the cross*
Hail to the king, the fine king of Judea! Let us take him to the summit of Calvary, in order that he may see the extent of his empire. Has the king of Babylon, Egypt or Persia ever mounted so high a throne? At present, the enclosure of the city is not beautiful enough for him. When our high towers have fallen, when the serpents climb our staircases in our stead, when the desert has sat down at our table, he can come back, if he wishes, with his crown of thorns, his torn robe and his bloody feet, to be king of our ruin.

AHASUERUS
They're coming closer. The sound of footsteps can already be heard; my heart is beating faster in my breast.

THE CROWD
Has Barabbas been given back his sword, his cape, his horse and his quiver full of arrows? Let us give him ten bright

silver deniers in his purse. Let us dress him in red as a messenger; he will ride through the towns and say to the thieves, the net-makers and the slaves turning mill-wheels: "Have you heard the news? Your king is waiting for you on the steps of his tower of Golgotha."

AHASUERUS
The voice of the people intoxicates me like a gourd of Carmel wine. Their anger is surely just.

THE CROWD
Pilate, sage Pilate, have you picked up your golden ewer? Again, again, regard the task of which you have not rid yourself. Rome washes her hands; that innocent virgin, who has only held the spindle in her mother's chamber, does not want to wear a ring of blood on her finger; but we, without delay, will follow the footsteps of our king's son. Truly, is he not better than David? Look, he is weeping, and has neither sword not sling; his cupbearers are two thieves by his side. If he wants to punish us, let him command; perhaps this time he will not send us as far as the willows of Babylon. Will it be necessary to return to return to the desert, hands bound behind our backs, all the way to Egypt? Let's go; we've known the way for a long time—and a short cut by which to come back.

AHASUERUS
They're coming; they're here; they're passing by; they're moving on; their cries fill the street; if that man were a true prophet, the wind that blows from the desert would overturn these terraces along with the towers. He was a false prophet; put him to death!

THE CROWD
If he is a Chaldean magician, he has marble unicorns and winged lions for servants in the desert, beneath the remains of cities, whose manes spirits have sculpted with golden chisels; he has sphinxes for messengers that rest from their running at

the gates of temples in blocks of stone. Let him tell his gryphons to come and form his cortege. But the wings of his gryphons are too heavy, the sleep of his sphinxes too deep. Before
his ensorcelled troop of unicorns and winged lions can bound
around him, before the ibises and stone hawks can descend
from their obelisks to defend him, here come the vultures of
Judea, who will take the crown from his head tomorrow to
carry into the woods to their nest. Oh, don't stop in your nest,
my vulture of Carmel; rise higher than the rocks, rise higher
than the clouds, rise higher than the stars, rise up all the way to
Jehovah: "Do you know what I'm carrying in my beak, O Jehovah? Truly, it isn't a scrap of Joppa cloth; it isn't a sprig of
heather; it's a crown of Judean thorns that I took from Calvary, from the head of your son of Nazareth."

AHASUERUS
As he comes closer, his aureole shines more brightly
than that of a prophet elect; that's another one of his magic
spells.

CHRIST
Is that you, Ahasuerus?

AHASUERUS
I don't know you.

CHRIST
I'm thirsty; give me a little water from your well.

AHASUERUS
My well is empty.

CHRIST
Take your cup to it; you'll find it full.

AHASUERUS
It's broken.

CHRIST
Help me to carry my cross along this hard road.

AHASUERUS
I'm not your cross-bearer; summon a gryphon from the desert.

CHRIST
Let me sit down on your bench at the door of your house.

AHASUERUS
My bench is full; there's no room for anyone.

CHRIST
On your threshold, then?

AHASUERUS
It's empty, and the door is bolted shut.

CHRIST
Touch it with your finger, and you'll be able to go in to fetch a stool.

AHASUERUS
Be on your way.

CHRIST
If you wanted, your bench might become a golden stool at the door of my father's house.

AHASUERUS
Go wherever you wish, blasphemer. You're already withering my vine and my fig-tree. Don't lean on the rail of my stairway; it would crumble on hearing you speak. You want to bewitch me.

CHRIST
I wanted to save you.

AHASUERUS
Get out of my shadow, fortune-teller. Your road is before you. Walk on, walk on.

CHRIST
Why do you say that, Ahasuerus? It's you who will walk, until the last judgment, for more than a thousand years. Go get your sandals and your traveling clothes. Everywhere you pass, people will call you the Wandering Jew. It's you who will find neither a seat on which to sit down nor a mountain spring to slake your thirst. In my stead, you will bear the burden that I shall quit upon the cross. For your thirst, you will drink what I leave in the bottom of my chalice. Others will take my tunic; you will inherit my eternal dolor. Hyssop will sprout on your traveler's staff, absinthe will grow in your water-skin; despair will squeeze your loins in your leather belt. You will be the man who never dies. Your age will be mine. To see you pass, the eagles will perch on the edge of the aerie. The little birds will hide under the crests of rocks. The stars will lean over on their clouds to hear your tears fall, one drop at a time, into the abyss.

I am going to Golgotha; you will walk from one ruin to the next, one kingdom to the next, without ever attaining your Calvary. You will break your stairway under your feet, and you will no longer be able to come back down. The gates of cities will say to you: "Go further, my bench is worn out;" and the river where you want to sit down will say: "Go further, go further on, all the way to the sea; my bank is my own and full of brambles;" and the sea too will say: "Go further, go further on, are you not the eternal voyager who goes from one people to the next, century after century, drinking his tears from his cup, who does not sleep by day or by night, neither on silk nor on stone, and who cannot go back along the path he has followed?"

The gryphons will sit down, the sphinxes will sleep, but you will have neither seat not slumber. It is you who will go to ask for me in one temple after another, without ever encountering me. It's you who will cry: "Where is he?" until the dead show you the way to the last judgment. When you see me again, my eyes will be ablaze; my finger with rise up beneath my robe to summon you to the valley of Jehosophat.

A ROMAN SOLDIER
Did you hear him? While he was speaking my sword was moaning in its scabbard, my spear was sweating blood, and my horse was weeping. I have had my sword and my spear for a long time. On listening to that voice, my heart has been worn away in my bosom. Open the door to me, my wife and my little children, to hide me in my Calabrian hut.

THE CROWD
What do I have to do to rise higher than Calvary? What if he were, by chance, a God of an unknown country, or a son that the Eternal has forgotten in his old age? Before he can recognize us, let us go shut ourselves up in our courtyards. Let us put out our lamps on our tables. Did you see the brazen hand that wrote on Ahasuerus' house: THE WANDERING JEW? Don't let that name remain on the stone! Let the man of the door be the scapegoat of Judah. When he passes by, Babylon, Thebes and the surrounding lands will pick up stones from their ruins to hurl at him. But we, without ever quitting our staircases and our vines, will fill our gourd with our Carmel wine for the Passover.

III.

AHASUERUS, *alone*

1.

Where are they? Where is the crowd? Come back, Jesus of Nazareth and listen to me. Let me speak to you again. My name is Ahasuerus, son of Nathan, of the tribe of Levi. What other name did he give me? Who knows it? Who heard him? Who will remember it? Grass by the roadside, don't tell it to the sole of my foot, if you don't want to be uprooted; stone of my threshold, don't tell it to my sandals, if you don't want to be broken; furrow of my inherited field, don't tell it to my plough, if you don't want to be filled in.

2.

Has he not attached a burning aureole to my head? No, it's the desert wind blowing through my hair. Has he not put a cup full of tears in my hand? No, it's the rain of Carmel that has filled it to the brim. What does the desert have against me? What does Carmel have against me? I shall go back into my house, where the rain doesn't come in; I climb my stairway, which the wind doesn't climb.

3.

Go! Go where? The water of my well is too fresh; my date-palm is too shady. Where else would I find another land of Judah? Tomorrow I shall drown the memory of the cross-bearer in the wine of my vine. With my chisel I shall efface the tracks that his feet left on the pavement. In advance, I see my table full; not one place is empty. No, my guests, go home, all of you. Woe! Isn't my wine murmuring in my cup: "It's the Wandering Jew who is drinking?"

4.

No, truly, I don't want any banquets, or a full table. When the wineskin is empty, joy often remains at the bottom. I want to go up the stairs of my sister Martha; only she can sing me a song while plying her distaff; she'll chase away the brazen voice that is resonating in my ears. Woe! Who do I see on the stairway of my door? It's not my father Nathan, nor my little brothers, nor my sister Martha. It's an angel of death, looking at me; his black wings are hanging down to the ground; his breastplate and coat of mail are shining like a naphtha well. He's holding his pipe in his hand; he's standing up on the black mane of a horse that is sweating blood.

IV.

THE ANGEL SAINT MICHAEL
Is this your name that is written on your door?

AHASUERUS
Efface the fiery name; my name is Ahasuerus.

SAINT MICHAEL
Where are you going?

AHASUERUS
Home.

SAINT MICHAEL
Your door is closed; you shall not pass that way again.

AHASUERUS
I haven't got my sandals, my belt or my traveling cloak.

SAINT MICHAEL
You have no need of them. You shall have for a coat of mail the tissue of your dolors, and for a cloak, the wind, snow and rain of an eternal cloud.

AHASUERUS
I don't know the road out of Palestine and Egypt.

SAINT MICHAEL
You shall follow the storks; you shall walk through the brambles.

AHASUERUS
Tell me what cities I'll find on my route.

SAINT MICHAEL
The cities through which you pass will crumble behind you, and the peoples you leave behind when you get up will not to see another day.

AHASUERUS
How are their walls made?

SAINT MICHAEL
They are still dormant under hedges of hawthorn, like a bird beneath its wing. The stone of their crenellated walls is still in the rock; the beam of their well is still in the forest; the trefoil of their arched windows is still in the meadow.

AHASUERUS
Where does their road lead?

SAINT MICHAEL
Wherever the one who has cursed you has gone.

AHASUERUS
How shall I fare in unknown forests, where there are no paths?

SAINT MICHAEL
You shall go by way of the heather to knock on the door of unknown peoples who are asleep on their elbows around their fires of dry grass. You shall shout at their window that it is time to get up, that their master is awaiting them in Rome, and that they should take down from the vault their clubs, their quivers and their maple-wood arrows.

AHASUERUS
And when I reach the shore of the sea, where there are no boats or fishermen?

SAINT MICHAEL

You shall shout to the shore that it is time to chase away its vessels, as the bird expels its young from the nest when they have grown up, and that it should send them all, laden with catapults and slings, to stone the people of Judea.

AHASUERUS

And in the desert where there is no host?

SAINT MICHAEL

To the shepherds of Arabia, lying down to drink the nocturnal dew, you will shout that they should whet their scimitars, saddle their horses, wind their turbans around their heads, and sharpen their silver spurs in order to carry behind them, wrapped in their tents, the torso of a decapitated people, which my master wants to give them.

AHASUERUS

If my knees carry me, I shall obey you. At present, I sense something like a wound from your pike in my bosom; will it still be there tomorrow?

SAINT MICHAEL

Judean wild boar, you are dragging the hunter's spear in your back.

AHASUERUS

Tell me what it is necessary to seek on my route in order to heal myself.

SAINT MICHAEL

You shall seek a balm, and find a venom; you shall seek your dream when you rise from your mat, and find your wound in your heart.

AHASUERUS

I feel a poison on my lips, which I drink at every breath. Will it be as bitter tomorrow?

SAINT MICHAEL

More bitter the next day than the day before, in the evening than the morning; more bitter in the depths of your water-skin than at the rim; more bitter in your shelter than while traveling, while traveling than on departure; more bitter in a golden cup than in the palm of your hand; more bitter in the stars than in the tempest; more bitter than in the stars and the tempest on the lips and in the eyes of your host.

AHASUERUS

My feet are heavy; I shall not be able to reach the shepherds of Arabia, the peoples of the forests.

SAINT MICHAEL

I have brought you the horse Séméhé, which has been wandering night and day since the morning of the world. On seeing you, his mane will bristle; his tears will fall upon the sand. With his silver hoof he will hollow out the threshold of your door; the Devis of the desert have bitten his flanks; in his nostrils, he summons the Wandering Jew. Take your whip in your hand, in order that his blood might trace your route.

AHASUERUS

Night has not yet fallen. Please, let me say adieu to my father, my sister and my little brothers.

SAINT MICHAEL

I will allow that. That farewell will be long. If I were human, I would mourn. Go! Before summoning you, I shall wait until David's cart has climbed above your head with its four starry wheels.

V.

Inside Ahasuerus' House.
Ahasuerus' brothers, Joel and Elia, little children, are playing
on mats

JOEL

When I am grown up I want to have silver beard that
hangs down to the ground, like my father.

ELIA

And I shall carry a patriarch's staff as long as his.

JOEL

I shall also buy a cup from the potter, which will hold an
entire water-skin; no one shall drink from it but me.

ELIA

And I shall buy a fig-wood bench from the carpenter, in
order to sit higher than everyone else at the table.

JOEL

Shut up; our father is looking at us.

NATHAN, *Ahasuerus' father*

What are you saying, children? Put on your colored
robes for today. Rejoice with me in the house. The false king
of the Jews has climbed on to his throne of Calvary. He will
not come down from it again. Who knows whether we shall
see the true Messiah one day?

JOEL

So there will be a more powerful king than the Christ,
Father?

NATHAN
So great that all the others will serve as his cupbearers.

JOEL
Will he have a palace as fine as the king of Sheba?

NATHAN
His palace will have a hundred doors, for his hundred messengers.

JOEL
What is it necessary to do to be the Messiah? I already read in your book every evening; I sing prayers in the temple with my sister.

ELIA
The priests give me the incense-burner, and it's always me who carries the pigeons to the sacrifice. Is it necessary to be the eldest to be the Messiah?

NATHAN
No, age doesn't count; it has always been predicted that an eternal child would emerge from my house. Only tell me what you see in your dreams; is it, perchance, a golden crown and a miter decked with diamonds?

JOEL
I never see anything in dreams but birds singing in silver hawthorn bushes.

ELIA
I see better than Joel; only yesterday, a lovely golden tower from which ivory horsemen were riding.

NATHAN
Do you remember whether you have ever thought that you were holding a trenchant sword such as kings wear?

JOEL AND ELIA

Father, what could we do at present with a trenchant sword, such as kings wear? Look, our hands are still too small to be able to carry one.

NATHAN

On the night of the sabbath, the fortune-tellers stop you at the crossroads; what do they say?

JOEL AND ELIA

They give us dates and blessed palms; it's always to our elder brother Ahasuerus that they speak in whispers.

NATHAN

Ahasuerus! Yes, he will be your master after me; I shall leave my field of barley, my cedar-wood stool and my place at table to him; it was him that the prophets meant. Once again, this evening, when I opened my book, I saw his name written in gold in the verses of Ezekiel; the letters sparkled like a vine-branch flame. Yes, the sixty weeks have passed; I have counted the days on my fingers; the days have also passed; my beard has grow to touch the ground, the oil in my lamp is used up, my eyes have been hollowed out by looking through the window to see whether the prince's messengers might be coming; and the towers of the city have watched with me, and their steps are worn down, and they are slippery when one climbs them. And the desert draws nearer like a horseman asking for the keys in order to enter; but the Messiah hasn't yet come, and every man seeks him in looking at his child. Will he wait, before coming, until the brambles are growing over our heads and the dogs are gnawing our bones?

No, no! The Messiah's star has risen this evening. Look at it, shining like a painted arrow launched by its archer; his messenger has already departed on a good Arabian horse; he's crossing the desert now; he's bringing, on his saddle-bow, a king's scepter and cloak. Perhaps he will enter the city tonight; I can't sleep anymore; I want to stay up this time, in order to hear him from afar. If he stops at our door, I'll be ready all the sooner to summon Ahasuerus; he's late again, and I might die tomorrow.

VI.

Enter Ahasuerus

AHASUERUS
Greetings, Father; greetings, my brothers.

JOEL
Come, my brother, and rejoice with us, since the evil
king of the Jews is dead.

ELIA
Oh. my brother, tell me who attached that crown of
darkness to your head? Jesus of Nazareth wore one of gold;
are you the true Messiah?

JOEL
And who has given you that beautiful chalice in your
hand? Our father has never had one like it at his table.

AHASUERUS
The foggy night has attached my dark crown to my hair,
and I found this beautiful chalice on the road.

NATHAN
(*To himself.*) The signs don't lie; he has taken on the appearance of the son of a king tonight. If the messenger arrives,
he will recognize his master. (*Aloud.*) Supper is ready; the
tablecloth is set out; the stools are at the table. Come and sit
down beside me, Ahasuerus, and your brothers will follow in
order of their ages.

JOEL
Look! The lamp doesn't want to shine, nor the oil to
light.

ELIA
And the moon's rays don't want to come into the house.

NATHAN
What does it matter? Drink from my cup, Ahasuerus

AHASUERUS
(*To himself.*) In his cup, his wine has become freshly-shed blood. (*Aloud.*) Thank you, Father, but I'm not thirsty; I drank at the spring of Calvary when I arrived.

NATHAN
I picked these figs from the branch; take them for your hunger on this painted clay plate.

AHASUERUS
(*To himself.*) It's hyssop that I see mixed with bile; is that the fruit of his fig-tree? (*Aloud.*) Thank you, but I'm not hungry; I've already eaten my bread in the Garden of Olives.

NATHAN
Your face is sad; your eyes are staring; your lips are trembling; tell your brothers what is needed to drive away your cares.

AHASUERUS
If my sister Martha were to sing me a song, I'd be as cheerful a guest as you.

MARTHA
Which one would you like, Brother? I'll sing it to you as I wash your feet.

AHASUERUS
One about a guest.

MARTHA

There is one that begins:

"Where have you come from, my guest? Is it from the lake-land or the forest of Carmel?"

"I have not come from the lake; I have not come from the forest; my homeland is far away."

"Who has made your cloak so blue? Who has put that hood over you to cover you in the rain?"

"It is not a woolen cloak; it is not a silken hood; they are azure wings with which to fly, when I wish, above the clouds."

"Who has put that beautiful hat on your head, which reflects the sunlight?"

"It is not a hat; it is an aureole, which is never extinguished in the wind or the rain."

"Handsome guest, show me what you're carrying in the fold of your robe."

"Look, it is a Messiah's crown, with a massive golden scepter; I have brought it for your eldest son, if his head can put it on."

AHASUERUS

No, I no longer like that song; never sing it to me again.

NATHAN

What do you mean, Ahasuerus? When you were little, like your brothers, and I gave you a new tunic or a cedar-wood cup, you sang all day on my bench. Now, where is the cedar-wood cup hollowed out by the woodcutter deep enough to contain all your desires? I have two arpents of land adjacent to Golgotha. I have a wall near the summit where storks come to nest; I have a date-palm still in flower next to the potter's field. The arpents of land, the wall and the flowering date-palm I shall give to you this evening if you shake off that black crown of cares from your head.

AHASUERUS
Thank you, Father, only let me make a short journey; I shall come back to the house more joyful.

NATHAN
Where do you want to go?

AHASUERUS
To my sister's house in Lebanon.

NATHAN
She will be coming here tomorrow by camel, for the Passover.

AHASUERUS
Or to my brother's house in Carmel.

NATHAN
When shall we expect you?

AHASUERUS
When the wheat is ripe.

NATHAN
Do you want to go right away?

AHASUERUS
This evening.

NATHAN
The night is too dark; wait until tomorrow.

AHASUERUS
I can't.

NATHAN
What's the hurry? Have you received a messenger?

AHASUERUS
Yes, Father; he's at the door.

NATHAN
A messenger from the prince?

AHASUERUS
I believe so.

NATHAN
Christ, Messiah, second Adam, walk, walk.

JOEL
Take me with you, Brother.

ELIA
I walk better than Joel; I'm the one who should go with
you.

JOEL
I've already been as far as Lebanon in two days.

ELIA
And I've already climbed up, without stopping, to the
summit of Golgotha.

AHASUERUS
I'll be walking too quickly; you'd be lost on the road.

JOEL AND ELIA
We could ride on a camel.

AHASUERUS
I'm in a hurry; I wouldn't even have time to take your
camel to the drinking-trough.

JOEL

If you go without us, at least bring us back lovely gifts from your voyage when the wheat is ripe. For myself, I'd like a robe with silken gryphons embroidered round the belt. Don't forget sea-shells, either, in which the sound of the sea when the wind blows can be heard, little amulets with a goat engraved on one side, and sandals on which the stars that enter the houses of the sun are painted in vermilion.

ELIA

For my part, bring me a linen sling, a little bronze Egyptian god with a hawk's head, an ostrich-feather and a hunter's quiver.

MARTHA

And me, a necklace of fine stones for my wedding.

AHASUERUS

When I come back, you'll already be married.

NATHAN

Until the end of your voyage, I shall not drink wine, nor shall I eat meat. Bring your staff and your sandals so that I might bless them. Here is salt for your meals in the desert; here is my full water-skin for your thirst. Go by the shortest route without stopping. Be humane to the poor, so that the lions will spare you. Be just to your guide, so that the serpents will not devour you. Have pity on the sick, so that you will have a long life. Say to your host when you go through his door: "I am Ahasuerus, son of Nathan, who lives on Calvary; give me, in his name, food and shelter for the night," and say as you leave: "Thank you my host, let me roll up the mat under the table; I shall pass this way again when the crops ripen; my father will invite you for the Passover." When you meet a shepherd, help him to find a place to drink, so that he will give you a slice of lamb. When you see a rider with a good horse, help him to find pasturage, so that he will lend you his horse for a day. As you pass by, go to kiss the beards of old man of my age sitting at the gates of cities, and the hems of the cloaks of kings. If you meet a messenger, give him news; if you meet a weaver, or a shoemaker, or a potter, or a fisherman with his net, greet him by name: "Master, where are you going? You are my father by age." If you ask a woman spinning cotton for directions, think to yourself: "Her hair is long but her wisdom short." If a soldier overtakes you, approach him without far: "Handsome soldier of Judea, how your pike shines, how sharp your arrows are, how well-embroidered your shield is! Protect me, in the desert, from dragons and robbers. My father is waiting for me on his terrace; he will give you, in recompense, a silver goblet, two leather belts and a purse of five deniers."

THE VOICE OF SAINT MICHAEL
Come out, Ahasuerus; David's cart has risen.

JOEL AND ELIA
Is that your guide, Brother, we can see from the window? He is clothed like a king's squire.

AHASUERUS
He's waiting for me. Adieu, Father; adieu, my brothers; adieu, my sister.

JOEL AND ELIA
When you come back, attach a little silver bell to your mule, so that we can come to meet you as soon as we can hear you in the distance.

NATHAN
Everywhere you go, ask the sky for light, the earth for a short path, your mount for a rapid pace, and your mat for peaceful sleep.

AHASUERUS

Sleep more peaceful than on your cedar-wood bed I shall never find.

NATHAN

Go! If you are the Messiah and if you have a messenger from the prince, will you not come back a king to lie at your ease, until mid-day, on a golden couch?

AHASUERUS, *going out*

Yes, I shall come back the king of dolor to sleep in my tears, much later than the middle of the day.

VII.

SAINT MICHAEL
The sun is about to rise. Go. Take that stony path. I shall return to heaven.

AHASUERUS, *alone*
1.
Adieu; my father's bench and door. Adieu, my mat and my childhood dreams. Adieu, my storks' nests, my Arabian fig-tree and my sycamores that grows on top of walls. Adieu, companions who tend mares by the edge of the pond. When I see them again, the wind will open the door to me, the storks' chicks will have left the nest, and the mares with their dismounted riders will be whitening beneath my feet like the stones of the road.

2.
I am not one of those travelers who go from Joppa to Galilee in a day to sell their linen cloth and their expensive jewels. They walk with their caravans; Ahasuerus has the desert for a companion; while they dress in silk and gold; Ahasuerus is clad in darkness; while they wear cloaks with silver clasps, Ahasuerus has the tempests for a roof; while they have a guide with iron-shod feet, Ahasuerus is led by the hand by the sirocco; while they go to their beds and well-furnished tables, Ahasuerus goes to an angry host; while they travel a day-long path, Ahasuerus travels a thousand-year path that is always uphill and never down.

3.
In truth, no, I'm no longer the son of Nathan. The sphinxes have sat down, the gryphons have gone to sleep; I have neither a seat nor leisure. Behind me, the cities that have served as shelter crumble to mark the border of my route. My

125

tomb is always hollowed out beneath my path, in order that my feet should resound more loudly. My tent, if I set it up, is a pyramid of granite; my hut, if I build one for a night, is a temple of fine marble; my precious jewels, which I leave behind me wherever I go, are the debris of towers and sculpted sepulchers, the bones of peoples and forgotten kingdoms.

4.

How tedious the Orient is! I know its paths too well, and its sand is burning. Its cities kneel down, without their breath being audible, beneath their temples and incense, and beneath their terraces of porphyry, as a camel does beneath the cargo of nard and fragrances, calabashes and rolled-up carpets that it has been carrying since Aleppo. The Ocean, which forms its girdle, is too small a lake into which to throw my anchor. Its desert has not taken its boundary far enough in its furrow to sow all my desires there, one after another, and the vault of its firmament, embroidered with colored stars, is not profound enough to shelter all my dreams.

5.

The Orient, at present, is accursed, like me. Its highest summit is striped barer by the wind and thieves than my highest hopes. Its cities, devoid of forts and walls, are more ruined in their valleys than the plans I made yesterday. Its goats gnaw the battens of its door all day long, more corrosively than memories gnaw at my heart. The water of its desert wells is warmer than my tears, and the absinthe it has planted on its hillsides is more bitter than the breath of my lips.

6.

Is there no other land beyond the mountains of Asia? Is there not a valley where a simple grows that might cure the wound I my soul? Further away—much further away—are there not forests without woodcutters, tall grasses without reapers, and frost on the branches all year round, where the sun of Arabia will no longer drink my sweat? Let me tell the stories of Babel and the lands of Egypt, which the stones tell as one passes by. Let me tell the names of vanished kings, patriarchs and empires a thousand years older than me. To be rid more quickly of all my memories, I shall ask the little robins on my roof to tell me their stories of yesteryear.

7.

Is there not another God somewhere better than the God of Judea? I shall go to hide myself in his heather, all the way to the foot of his tower made of stars. Adieu, my heavy amulets. Adieu my beautiful bronze hawks. Adieu my porphyry serpents. Since they cannot follow me, let my gryphons remain without their shepherds, let me unicorns browse their obelisks, let my sphinxes sleep in the sand! The only relic I shall carry in my journey is the wound in my bosom, and I shall have no idol beneath my cloak but my dolor.

8.

Now, summits lost in the mist, paths made in advance or me by errant stags and hinds; valleys, forests, marshes where buffaloes and herons stroll; peaks, rocks and isles where sea-swallows nest, sharpen your thorns for my feet. Sow far in advance your fields of hyssop for my harvest. Mix your tears in the trunks of our old oaks with the venom of serpents to answer my thirst. Night-birds, merlins with blazing eyes, vultures in search of prey, chamois that drink in brackish springs, centenarian crows, eagles that carry the crowns of kings not yet born, quit your nests at the sound of my footsteps in the foliage. Yield me by place for a night. Go before me to prepare my shelter.

VIII.

THE VALLEY OF JEHOSOPHAT

By my barest path, here, from afar, comes the traveler that my master has cursed. When all the dead sown within me call me by my name, they will not make as much noise as the nostrils of his horse. His shadow extends further over my sand than the shadow of an entire people passing. His feet, where they pause, hollow out my rock more than the feet of an empire. His soul, in my bosom, is heavier to bear than a city with heavy battlements, and the cares of his forehead sadden me more than a cloud of Taurus.

AHASUERUS

This strange valley extends beneath my feet. Its master has sown it with ashes everywhere to spare the feet of young mares. Is that the neck of a vulture piercing the clouds up there? No, it's a bare summit. Is that a she-wolf with light brown fur licking her young over there? No, it's the heather on its slope. Leaves fallen from an invisible oak-tree are pattering on the paths. Above the summit, a hawk with hundred-cubit wings is racing a circle in the sky. The silence is profound, more profound than a shadow in a ravine. I would gladly build my hut on this rock forever, if I found water here.

THE VALLEY OF JEHOSOPHAT

Traveler, handsome traveler, go on your way. I have no well or cistern. Those who inhabit my slopes are never thirsty.

AHASUERUS

Where have you planted your date-palms?

THE VALLEY OF JEHOSOPHAT

I have neither dates nor date-palms. Those who live on my summit are never hungry.

AHASUERUS
Search your brushwood to see whether you might have a simple to heal a wound in the heart, like the iron of a spear.

THE VALLEY OF JEHOSOPHAT
My simples, in my brushwood, can heal all wounds, except a wound of the heart, when the thorn remains within it.

AHASUERUS
What is the country that surrounds you called?

THE VALLEY OF JEHOSOPHAT
I am the valley to which every path leads. I am the empty sea, the road with no exit, the Ocean without waves, the desert without caravans, the Orient without sunlight. Everything hastens to sit down on my slopes. The little chamois that has just been born asks its mother: "Mother, where is the road to the great valley? The stork, when it grows old, leaves before daybreak to alight in my heather. When the leaf of an olive-tree in Andros falls, the wind brings it to me in its robe to make my litter. To render her soul, Greece piled up here, like winter leaves, beneath my Alexandrian palm-tree. Yesterday, I saw Rome landing in her galley on my Byzantine shore, stripped bare, in agony. Until now, I have had no name. Since the death of Christ, the entire Orient has been hollowed out in order to widen a bed in my side, a single tomb to which everyone will come to die. Today, my name is Jehosophat.

AHASUERUS
How do you amuse yourself during your long days?

THE VALLEY OF JEHOSOPHAT
For a lover I have the jealous hawk, which gazes as me all day long from the height of my summit. If the hawk chances to close is yellow eyelid, I also like the cloud full of hail when it brushes my granite shoulders. After the cloud has

129

passed, and it can no longer turn back, I like the roaring wind that calls to me at my door. In the first days of winter, I go to see whether the spider has woven its sheet of fine silk at the summit of my pyramids, or whether the idle worm has become bored sawing up the cadavers of old empires that the lions have brought me on their backs. From far away, I listen to the balcony of the crumbling lighthouse, the column that sinks down on its side, groaning, weary of carrying the crow on its head for such a long time, and the breathless sphinx that runs to seek shelter in the desert when the rain has demolished its lair in the temple. I also listen to the wild flower withering at the top of its stem, he old eagle that sheds its talons and beak one after another at the foot of its aerie, and the gnat that sheds its two wings in my valley.

AHASUERUS
Have you nothing else to do?

THE VALLEY OF JEHOSOPHAT
I wait until dusk for the dead to return to life. At the sound of a chamois passing by, or a tear shed in a grotto, I become anxious, wondering whether it is a people sharpening a spear-point or a reed arrow in its sepulcher. As far as the Arab well sheltered by two cypresses, I go in search of a little water to help the crop of peoples and kings sown in my furrow germinate more rapidly. My anemones, when they blossom, will be the young daughters of princes, sitting in golden veils; my great lilies will be clouds that will tie their white turbans around their heads when they wake up; my aloe-flowers will be candelabras that priests will light on my slopes; my heather will be innumerable peoples who will sigh beneath the wind and the rain.

AHASUERUS
So the dead have not yet come?

THE VALLEY OF JEHOSOPHAT
No, not yet.

AHASUERUS
Will they come tomorrow?

THE VALLEY OF JEHOSOPHAT
When the hundred-cubit hawk screeches, when he earth grows weary.

AHASUERUS
However late they come, let me wait for them on your boundary-marker. I'll help you to draw water from our spring for the hawk, to pile up dead leaves for your litter. I'm a merchant from Joppa, weary of travel; hide me under a ledge of your rock; I find you more beautiful than a city with a hundred bastions, a hundred minarets, women beneath their veils and its king under an awning.

THE VALLEY OF JEHOSOPHAT
Merchant, handsome merchant of Joppa, to be so weary, you must have come from a distant land. Show me your jewels, I beg you.

THE ECHO *continues*
Is it true that you wear for relics—yes, for relics—your wound in your bosom, and for an idol—yes, for an idol—beneath your cloak, your dolor?

AHASUERUS
I have gone to where the earth ends, to where the boundless sea begins; I have been all the way to well-built Byzantium, if you know its name. On the wall of its basilica a cross-bearer from Nazareth was painted in solid gold, with twelve companions, who were pointed out to me. What point is there in going further? Ennui has gripped me. I have seen enough towers and turrets, columns and colonnettes, and battering

131

rams beating on doors; I have seen how the world ends at its Caspian gate. Two angry lions on the steps forbid passage. After them, one of Odin's stags, with antlers that one might have thought to be a thousand years' growth like a forest on its head, blocks entry to the eternal mist. Further on, a crow croaks in its master's ear beneath the ash-tree that bears the stars of heaven on its branches every year, by way of flowers. I plunged my silver-plated cup in the seething spring; it filled with tears. I called out in the forest; I heard a sigh like that of a weeping man. Now my journey is over; my soul upon my lips is disgusted. Keep me forever in your enclosure, which no sound ever reaches.

THE VALLEY OF JEHOSOPHAT
Handsome traveler, I can see from my summit a land to which you have not yet gone.

THE ECHO
And will you ever want to give me, to amuse me, your precious jewels, your debris of towers—yes, towers—your sculpted sepulchers, your bones of peoples—yes, peoples—and forgotten kingdoms?

AHASUERUS
Help me: an archer is pursuing me to steal the jewels from my satchel.

THE VALLEY OF JEHOSOPHAT
That archer is my master. He is two cubits taller than I am; he would see you, by standing up behind my summit.

AHASUERUS
At least let me stay until tomorrow.

THE VALLEY OF JEHOSOPHAT
Adieu. Don't say anything more where the dead are asleep. I shall fall silent.

132

THE ECHO
Further on, further on: go all the way to the sea.

AHASUERUS
Give me, like the dead, a little water from the Arab well.

THE ECHO
My well is empty.

AHASUERUS
And your cup?

THE ECHO
It's broken.

AHASUERUS
At least let me sit down on your bench.

THE ECHO
It's full, and my door is bolted.

AHASUERUS
Lend me a little of your cool shade.

THE ECHO
Prophet, get out of my shade. Walk! Walk!

AHASUERUS
Truly, the voice of the mountain is an echo of the voice of Golgotha.

THE ECHO
Yes, Golgotha.

AHASUERUS
What? Go on, already, go on forever?

THE ECHO
Forever.

AHASUERUS
But no one here has cursed me.

THE ECHO
Cursed!

AHASUERUS
Oh well! Let's get up, my heart! I'll sit down further on.

THE ECHO
Further on, much further on!

IX.

THE EMPEROR DOROTHEUS[12], *standing on the walls of Rome*

From the top of my highest tower, I'm watching for the arrival of my three messengers. The first has followed the road to Ravenna; the second has taken his ironclad sandals to climb over the Alps; the third has gone to where the Danube hollows out its bed. Oh, how late they are in coming back. The shadows are growing at the foot of my towers, and the fear in my heart. Italy, what have you done that the storks are taking their young away from the roofs of Rome and Florence? I cannot, like them, take your cities away and hide them under tree-branches in the mountains and forests of Sardinia. What have your azure sky, your orange-blossom, your somnolent bays, your forests of myrtle your mountains of marble done that you are trembling like a slave fattened for the lions in the circus? If you were still asleep in the cradle of Rome, it least you could be hidden under a thatched roof, or an oak-wood; you could eat your bread in safety, like a child at his father's door. For then your sun was mild, your sea placid, your islands perfumed, when your people were born with the grass of your shores; but now your rivers respire blood, and the hyssop of Golgotha is growing everywhere on your mountains. O Italy, what have you done? The noise that woke me in the night is getting closer at every moment; one might think that the horse of the Apocalypse were running frantically over the slopes of the Apennines, his hooves striking the tombs that border the roads of the empire.

---

[12] There was no Roman emperor of this name, although there was a sixth-century jurist who helped to codify Roman law in the reign of the Eastern emperor Justinian. The last emperor of the Western Empire, when Rome fell to the barbarians in 476, was Romulus Augustus.

(*A messenger arrives at the foot of the tower.*)

THE EMPEROR DOROTHEUS
Greetings, good messenger; what have you found on your route?

THE MESSENGER
I have found eagles screeching in the forest and wolves howling in the ravines. Is that not the noise that woke you?

(*Another messenger arrives.*)

THE EMPEROR DOROTHEUS
And you, good messenger, tell me what you have heard.

THE MESSENGER
I have heard avalanches in the Alps sliding into the depths of valleys, and stags belling under the branches of ash-trees. Is that the noise that has kept you awake?

(*A third messenger arrives.*)

THE EMPEROR DOROTHEUS
And you, who wear ironclad sandals, tell me what you have seen.

THE MESSENGER
I have seen the green waters of the Danube, rumbling over granite rocks, like the voice of an angry crowd.

(*In the distance*)

CHORUS OF BARBARIAN PEOPLES
CHORUS OF GOTHS
Do you know a good signs for the man of war? It is a good sign if the clash of the blade is accompanied by the cry

of the crow and the howls of Freya's she-wolf under the ash-tree Yggdrasil. The mountain vulture knows the path where the wild horse that it shadows with its wings will die; and we too know the oak beneath which the Roman mare has fallen, which our claws will tear apart. Norns and Valkyries, mingle in your cauldrons the eagle's beak, Sleipnir's teeth and elephant's ivory that form the runs of combat and give wisdom to the teeth that touch them. By the edge of the shield, the prow of the ship, the tip of the sword, the wheel of the chariot and the foam of the sea, follow us, be propitious for us. The raven is leaning over Odin's shoulder to repeat our words in his ear; the stag is running through the forest and nourishing himself on the branches of the ash-tree that shades the gods. And we are marching, after him, over the dead leaves of the forests. We are heading southwards, like the melting snow that flows down into the valleys.

CHORUS OF HERULES
Let us take one another's hand for a war dance. The women of the Danube are raising up their swan-like bodies in the river to watch us pass by. But the north wind is our king; he is sending us to cast to the ground the leaves of orange-trees and the flowers of the vine. Oh, let us march with great strides before the figs ripen and the lemons fall of their own accord at the feet of the trees, and the grapes dry up on the vine. One more day, and we shall find the peel of the oranges swept away from around the woods.

CHORUS OF HUNS
Mount up! Mount up! Tomorrow you shall finish braiding the manes of wild stallions. Mount up in the plain and on the mountain! The fays[13] are suspended by their tangled hair;

---

[13] The French word *fée* is usually translated into English as "fairy," although its derivation from *féerie* [enchantment] implies that it can be applied to human users of magic as well as supernatural beings; its use here evidently to a kind of super-

gnomes and gnomides are biting the rumps and tails of the horses as they run. Mane upon mane, nostril against nostril, in the distance, in the open, all around, let our horde pass like a winter cloud over the Mongolian steppes; rapid as the sun sets, and more rapid when the morning begins to gleam, and more rapid still beneath the burning sun of day, and then, after the day, in the darkness of the night. Woe to him who turns his head to look back! A winged djinni that is following him will cast him to the ground and throw him to the vultures. Look! The grass is still depressed by the feet of archers who have gone ahead of us; their arrows will reach the target before ours. We shall arrive when the treasure of Italy has been pillaged, and the cup of Gaul has been drunk to the lees.

CHORUS OF FAYS

Without deception, this is a strange voyage. The grass is drying out beneath the breath of horses; magical songs can be heard in their manes. If we could die, we would be afraid. For a thousand years we have trembled beneath the turf of the mountains of Scythia. Our cheeks have wrinkled there in blowing on our hands to warm them. Every day we have found a green oak branch full of dew in the wood to nourish us, and yet we have lived better than gods fattened on the blood of oxen and horses. But today, handsome horsemen, your anger causes us to swoon. Wherever you pause, please leave some old wall standing, where we might shelter beneath the threshold of a door, a bolt of linen for us to dress ourselves, and a little dry wood to bring our cauldrons to the boil.

---

natural being, but its coupling with *gnome* and *gnomide* (a gnomide is a female gnome) deliberately mingles Gallic and Teutonic terminology, neither being appropriate to Huns; the Arabic *djinn* [djinni] is subsequently included in the set to further emphasize its syncretic quality. Here and elsewhere I have translated *fée* as "fay" in order to preserve its ambiguity and its conscious impropriety.

ONE OF ATTILA'S CHILDREN

Why can our horses not pause, Father? Why is our shadow the color of blood? Do you see that old man up there in a stone niche? His head is leaning out of the window; he is singing as we pass by; his hands are holding a book, on which his eyes are lowered. He's doubtless a wise man, Father; perhaps he knows where we're going.

ATTILA, *to the hermit*

Companion in your niche, our horses are sweating blood, and cannot stop. Do you know where this road leads? We have grazed our herds in the mountains of Scythia. If you can tell me why the wind is chasing us, why the shadows are bloody, why the horses are panicking, I will give you a golden cup full of my mare's milk.

THE HERMIT

Archers and horsemen, you are arriving very late. Yesterday, I came to meet you. I was waiting for you here, riffling through my book. The vultures have passed by, and the crows thereafter. The wolves arrived at my door last night and I showed them the way. Only you have stayed so late at the doors of your huts.

ATTILA

What has happened then, companion? Your eyes are sparkling in your niche like those of a hawk in its nest; your book is shining like the book of death.

THE HERMIT

Tell me whether you have not heard the rivers sobbing in the valleys while you were taking too long to saddle your horses and fold up your tents? Have you not encountered two stars on your route shining like the eyes of a man in agony, a cloud rolling over the mountains like a blood-stained shroud, a forest moaning like the songs of a priest beside a tomb? Those are my eyes shining in the stars, my cloak hanging in the

139

cloud, my voice moaning in the forest. It is because Christ is dead. He is dead, my son, the God of the earth, and my archangels are driving your horses past my door with whips. Don't stop to drink at my well, don't seek shade beneath my porch. Go! Run! Efface beneath your feet the blood that still stains the earth; uproot the cities before I have finished the last page of my book. In place of the peoples, make a great cemetery in which coarse grass will grow, as in the garden of my cell. Three days you shall march; you shall cross two rivers; afterwards, you will have arrived.

ATTILA
Is it you, then, in that narrow niche, who are the Eternal? I was told that you lived in a diamond tent on a mountain of gold! While we pass by, cover your hawk's eyes with your eyelids, and your flamboyant book with a flap of your robe. My quiver is yours. When an archer of our tribe dies in combat, we make him a tomb with clods of earth, with iron and the bones of horses, with amulets and the blood of thirty prisoners. Since he is dead, your son, the God of the earth, we shall make his funeral with the bones of peoples, with the ruins of cities, with the gold of crowns, until you say: "That's enough."

THE HERMIT
Dusk is approaching. The horses are whinnying. On the way back, they shall sleep in my stable.

INTERLUDE OF THE SECOND DAY

CHORUS OF OLD MEN
1.
Spectators of the mystery, bourgeois of France, merchants, citizens, on all matters, the chorus has always given, in moments of repose, the wisest advice, principally on public affairs. Thus Aeschylus and Aristophanes built their renown, those semi-divine men, great citizens as they were, and such as nature will never make again, tomorrow or thereafter, two similar individuals with as much intelligence as bold courage; to the condemnation of Euripides, who, by contrast, endeavored to flatter the public and corrupt them by means of wordy reverences and genuflections, and only obtained therefrom this smoke and a great waste of praise. Thus, I shall tell you, without waiting for this day's end, that many things displease me in your Estate: first of all, your frivolity; secondly, your vanity, and thirdly, your avidity.

2.
And truly, nothing about you pleases me entirely, except for your war-horses. When one lays a hand on them, those old chargers, who remember what bloody grass they have eaten, cry again: "Take me to graze on a field of glory." But you, without saying anything, take them by the bridle along a road where a crop of shame is growing, of which they want neither the grain nor the straw. Men of Lodi, of Castiglione, of Marengo, where are you? Emerge from the earth. You have gone to bed an hour too soon. Come and execute the task that your children have not the heart to finish. Cold as you are, pale as death has made you, it is the least that you owe your sons.

3.
For, in my opinion, your greatest mistake is this: to have twice allowed this great country to be surrounded, tormented

and foraged by your evil enemies; seeing that it would have been better to have rendered your souls to the last, men and children two months old, and all served together as prey for crows, than to have such an insult on the body. And again, I will tell you that I would prefer, personally, to see half of your cities still deserted to this day, overthrown by flame and battle, but with souls armored and barded with hope in the little that remained, than all your cities standing with strong bastions and well-aligned walls, but with all hearts sick to death, on seeing the insult posted in their squares, parading their defeat.

4.

As it is necessary, however, I want to salute the soil of France that nourishes you. Salutations to its four rivers, all full to the brim, to its cities full to the rooftops with men valiant in anger, to its furrows of wheat, of oats, well nourished for a hundred years by a hundred armies of warriors fallen thereon. Salutations to its roads, powdered by the dust of empires, to its forests of birches that still shiver on the eve of the great battle, to its houses of straw where its Emperor once set on the bench, when he said to the world, on the day when he distributed alms: "Heads or tails! The world or Saint Helena!"

5.

After the salute come the vows. To the country that I am contemplating, to the sky that I envy, to the field that I ferti-lize, I wish a bright sun to warm her, and two morning stars, one that scintillates to light her, the other that mourns to mois-ten her with its dew! In war, may her pike be trenchant, high, firm and sure; may the point of her sword cry out in the scab-bard; may her blood grease the axle and wheels of her chariot! In peace may her shuttle weave her clothing tirelessly, and may her horse draw the ploughshare on its fertile travels from Burgundy to Brittany, from where the Ain makes and un-makes its litter to where the Rhone chews on its bit. To make her enclosure more secure, may the river that flows toward Cologne give her its fresher and more beautiful bank, with the castles, balconies and turrets, and the women who bathe in it! On for your part, in your Alpine aerie, eagle of Austria, let your claws fall on thatched villages lost in the clouds, crumbling mountains, forests, snows, with which to make a nest for your eaglets.

6.

My God! France, sweet France, flower of heaven sown on earth, you have already cost me, without knowing it, tears that no one can give back to me! Beautiful boat without an oarsman, for which I have waited in the dark night until morning many a time, hoping for nothing more than to find you alone on your bank! Beautiful bird with golden claws, how often have I looked out of my window to see whether your wing was broken when the window brought a feather from your breast! As a small child, barefoot in the rain, I followed your great battalions beyond the frontier in the direction of Cologne, and your soldiers have taken me in their arms to enable me to touch, fearlessly, the mane of your war-horse. Oh, why did they give me, when I was hungry, their bread to eat, better than my father and my mother, if it was to hear, from the other side of the barrier: Hola! Are these bourgeois of the city really the people who, yesterday, trampled their blood in their vat at Rivoli, and took twenty steps without trembling on the Bridge of Arcole?

7.

For you I have made vows, for you I shall mourn. The earth is fretful; it no longer knows what to do, since your Emperor no longer remains hidden, to amuse itself beneath a flap of his glory. Since your name no longer covers the Babel of the world, every man who passes by, every worker who goes forth whistling, has a different name on his lips; if one says "empire," another replies "smoke," if "flower," "thorn," if "cup," lees," if "honey," "venom." Where one wants balm, another throws his poison, and if I cry "world" or "universe" someone takes up "mud" or "ashes, master—as your choose."

FIRST SECTION OF THE CHORUS
The past has balconies and arched windows that are crumbling. Master, rebuild its ruin.

SECOND SECTION OF THE CHORUS
The present is mud. Knead your pinnacle and your threshold from it at your leisure.

FIRST SECTION OF THE CHORUS
Don't speak, you. You don't know what I am.

SECOND SECTION OF THE CHORUS
Nor you what I am.

THE ENTIRE CHORUS
1.
Neither you, not him, what I will be. Go to your discords without troubling me; I shall make my harmony. Back, though, your vile generations, lashed in being born, in your own houses, with the foreigner's whip! From you, nor them, I only want your children, the only wealth that you have not yet soiled.

2.
France without fear, nest of courage and not cowardice, listen to me; lady of true beauty, it is getting late, so get out of bed, in order that the world might attach its strings to your shoes. At the ball, it is necessary to lead you in the dance, not the dead but the living; not bourgeois, but empires. Dust of men, dust of kings, dust of gods, dust of nothing, have no fear of trampling us; laughing, crush beneath your feet our regrets, our desires, our terrors and our hopes, fallen from their stems. The undressed Orient awaits you without moving; America too is ready; and tomorrow, and always, cause the round-dance of nations to turn around us, beneath the harmony of your sky.

3.

But you, kings coifed with rubies, the fête is not for you. What have I done to you that you have betrayed me so vilely? I have given you wine, you have returned the lees; I have given you bread, you have returned ashes; I have given you my flower, you have returned the thorn. At present your mare no longer wants a rider; you have used your spurs to excess. In her quivering mouth the bit has broken. Whinnying, she is dragging you along an ensorcelled road into her pasturage, where nothing serves to stroke her rump. There you shall learn, in your turn, how many hairs on a discrowned head can turn white overnight; you shall see whether the spur of exile was gentle, and whether the evil of countries only takes the evildoers to heart; you shall see whether it is good, foreigner, to stammer a strange language, with the result that, when you ask for oil for your wound, you are given salt and vinegar. Today your table is full; tomorrow you shall barter your crown with passers-by for a piece of barley or oat bread; and some of you shall encounter others on your path, and you shall sit down, pale, to weep together, not as kings but as serfs.

4.

That, spectators, bourgeois, merchants, citizens, is what I have to say about that which concerns you. Time is pressing; I can say no more. Do not listen to those who speak to you in a different way; remove them from your assemblies and your governments, and regard them as wicked enemies; for if you follow other advice than mine, you will regret it, and the commonweal will perish; on the contrary, if you do as I say, I will hold you up as just people, glorious and reasonable.

And now, without turning round, listen to the fourth day, you who are interested in the conclusion of this Mystery.

THE THIRD DAY

DEATH

I.

Inside a city on the banks of the Rhine

CHORUS OF WORKERS IN THE STREET
From forest to forest,
Forever I shall march
The last judgment
Will end my torment.

A WORKMAN
It's getting dark; let's go. Go to bed, Fritz. Adieu, friends. Here's the watchman coming down from his door with his iron-bound rod.

THE WATCHMAN
Go home, gentlemen; cover your fire with ashes, in order that no misfortune will occur.

CHORUS OF WORKMEN, *moving away*
The last judgment
Will end my torment.

THE WATCHMAN, *alone on the bank of the Rhine*
I've seen the Rhône when it descends from the Alps; it's a chamois that bounds over the rocks, fleeing the hunter. I've seen the Necker when it dries up in the sand; it's a work-horse dying under the whip at its master's gate. I've seen the Danube when it turns back in order to gaze at Ulm cathedral twice; it's the noble archbishop's silver crosier, gleaming and twisting in the sunlight. But neither the chamois on the rock, nor

146

the archbishop's crosier, not the horse at its master's gate gives me as much pleasure as an evening on the bank of the Rhine.

Listen, my bagpipe is ready to resonate! Midnight has chimed, thank the Lord and the Virgin Mary. The Rhine also knows me with my trumpet; it's me who sends it to sleep at the foot of towers, next to boats, around islets; it's me who wakes it up, once every ten years, when it changes its bed like a bourgeois coming home at midnight by the side door. For curtains it has a forest of chestnut-trees; for litter, it has white shells, and a mountain ready to stand on its head.

The shadow of ensorcelled towers sobs today in each of your waves, my old Rhine. Is that a phantom swimming in your dream, the sound of grass in the woods, of rain in the grottoes, or is it halting speech in the dream of the stars, like the words one hears at every door as soon as a city goes to sleep? The moon, the king of watchmen, knows better than me. Here he is, emerging from his hut with his bagpipe and his silver staff, to go and cry the hour in the city of the heavens.

KING DAGOBERT,[14] *at the window of his tower*
Kindly watchman, lower your voice. The queen is asleep at his hour in her solid gold bed. My lamp has gone out; I've put on my scarlet cloak by moonlight and my brass crown, to watch you go by. Tell me what can be seen at midnight in my kingdom.

---

[14] Initially king of Austrasia in the early seventh century, Dagobert I eventually became king of all the Franks, his realm stretching from the regions now constituting Germany and the Low Countries to Burgundy. A popular song about him "Le Bon roi Dagobert" [Good King Dagobert], which also features his chief counsellor, Eligius (subsequently caonized), was satirized in a lyric that was employed in the Revolution of 1789 as an expression of ant-monarchist sentiment.

THE WATCHMAN

On the mountain there's a castle; in the castle there are three towers; in each tower there's a phantom: in the first, Herrmann is leaning on the balcony with a blue doublet and a toque the color of fire; he's gazing at the Rhine; in the second, Dietrich is leaning out of the window like the branch of a pear-tree, looking toward the town; in the third, our lord the Emperor has been asleep for a hundred years on his elbow; his russet bead has pierced his stone table and would seven times around it; his sword is hanging from the wall like birch-twig.

THE KING

Let him sleep. Look at the foot of the castle; do you see a forester's house? There's an owl on its roof; it screeches day and night. The leaves of the trees rattle on the door in summer like the footsteps of skeletons coming back from the dance of the dead.

THE WATCHMAN

I've seen the forester's house. There are three steps leading up to the door. On the window-sill there are wallflowers growing pale and carnations going green. A stork has built its nest around the chimney. Under the roof, the walls are painted as red as a gleaner's dress.

THE KING

My kingdom is very large, its limit can't be seen from the highest stairway of the tallest church. The starlings, when their wings go gray, and the crows, when their beaks go yellow, come to tell me where it ends. Well, there aren't two woodcutters in my kingdom like the one who comes down those three steps every day. Have you encountered an old woman with a limp who goes out to collect dead wood? At midnight, when she goes home, I've seen her from my perron carrying beneath her apron a scepter of fleurs-de-lis, three archbishop's and papal crosiers. If that's the widow of a forester, tell me the name of the wood where fleur-de-lis scepters

148

grow in the earth, and where the woodcutter cuts the silver crosiers of archbishops or popes from the green branch.

THE WATCHMAN

I've encountered two women in the forester's house. The older is wrinkled; all day long she spins, with her feet in the ashes; the younger one sings with the starling. They came at Christmas in a pilgrim's boat. They're worthy women who don't neglect the sacraments. They always have a silver coin when the monk comes to make the collection. May God reward them!

SAINT ELIGIUS

Oh, my king, you have woken me up beneath my awning. Have no fear. What you have seen is a dream you had in your solid gold bed, Go up to your throne; I shall explain. The old woman who looks for dead wood in her apron is the Church, which rises from its bed to save the faithful. The gilded scepter is the soul it finds, lost beneath the dew in the undergrowth. The forester's house with three steps is heaven, where the Eternal Father is seated. The leaves that rattle are the world moaning. The owl that screeches on the roof is Christ, who calls from the height of paradise to the soul gone astray and belated in its path.

THE KING

Great saint, I know that you have more wisdom than all the long-haired kings have beneath their crowns. It was a dream, I believe, but a dream that resembled what one sees while awake. My God, what has become of the times when we hunted without a care in your goldsmith's shop for my shiny crown, my holy cope and my horse's shoes? Since then, my crown has tarnished in the mist and my bay horse has lost his golden horseshoes in the forest of Ardennes; oh, the earth has grown old, Saint Eligius, like my crumbling castle; our fleshless towers, open to the wind, are great skeletons that wear crows of crenellations on their heads. The end of the world is nigh.

Look! Our cathedrals have dressed in black one after another, like kneeling mourners clad in crepe at a graveside. The stars, weary of shining, are golden bees tarnishing on the Lord's royal cloak. While awaiting the last judgment, the dead are lifting up the grass of the cemetery with their fingernails, in order to be ready for the first blast of the trumpet. Those who have heard the watchman's bagpipe are already sitting down at the crossroads and leaning over the balconies of castles. The Angel of Death is beating his wings against the stained-glass windows of churches; he will efface with the breath of his mouth their vermilion cloaks and their purple robes.

SAINT ELIGIUS
As you have said, O King, our best days are past. The world today is a great mass for the dead. The earth is the coffin suspended in the nave. The long-haired kings lead the mourning. When the peoples have wept on the day when they are to weep, the evening stars and the waters that murmur in the night will say once again: *Miserere*. Hold firm in your hand, without weakening, your scepter and your orb, as I shall hold on to my holy palm, in order that the Angel of Death, when he cries at your door, will recognize you without delay, and lead you to the crystal niche that he has built to await you on a rock in Jehosophat.

THE KING
Let us go and see, through her silver curtains, whether the queen is still asleep. Stand guard well, Watchman. I'm going back into my nave with Saint Eligius.

(*They go.*)

150

II.

A dark house at a crossroads.
Death, under the name of Mob, an old woman, is warming
herself in the ashes. Rachel, the young woman who lives with
her is the fallen angel who was beside Christ's cradle during
the scene of the Mage-Kings.

MOB
Where's my apron, Rachel? Bring me some dead wood
to warm up my skeleton. While you're chirping there with
your starling, my knees are trembling, my teeth are chattering
and my hands are shivering. I've covered a lot of ground tonight. I watched for three hours at a pope's bedside; I've
brought his miter with a little ash. Here's a ducal crown;
here's a baron's ermine mantle. Hide them in my dresser with
this urn, in which they put their tears. I've only slept for an
hour; that was on the knees of a fiancé with brown hair; without knowing it, he filled my empty orbits with his tears, and
polished the bones of my forehead like ivory with the coals of
his lips. For your festival day, I've brought you a bouquet of
lilacs from a newly-wed I led to the ball by the hand. Oh, my
life is a party once I've gone down the three steps at our door.
My horse doesn't touch the ground with his hooves. The
leaves on the trees wither as he breathes, and fall to make his
path. The wind carried me wherever I wish. The stars twinkle,
the sea falls silent like a vulture chick in its nest; the bells
open their mouths and say to the towers: "Listen! Here she
comes, our queen, passing under the porch."

RACHEL
Is that what you call a party? Holy angels, come to my
aid.

151

MOB

Patience, daughter, I know full well that you haven't always been with old Mob. Before being an Angel of Death, placed at my door to keep me company in my ashes in the evenings, you too were an angel with diaphanous wings. What has become of the time when you got up evening and morning to bring white bread to the gryphons crouching beside the Lord? Do you remember the songs with which you were able then, with the bow of your viol, to wake the angels and souls in their niches in the cloud? Tell me, do you recall the azure meadows to which you went every year to sow blossoming words, as I sow the ashes of my apron behind me here; when you spun threads of light at your door, and your spindle, as it plunged into the abyss, wound up a blessed star that spun until morning, suspended from your golden distaff? Do you remember when the bells of heaven called you by name, and the little angels clung on to the hem of your robe, laughing, to enter the city of God with you?

RACHEL

Oh, Mob, why do you say that? I'll follow you, and obey you, I promise—but don't remind me of those times.

MOB

Do you prefer the time when I met you for the first time, on the day of Christ's death? Do you remember when all the angels—you were in the middle of them—leaned over the clouds and wept? When Christ leaned on Ahasuerus' house and cursed Ahasuerus—do you remember?

RACHEL
Did you say Ahasuerus?

MOB

And when all the angels were quivering with anger, who was it who had a tear in her eye for Ahasuerus? Who looked down on him from on high with pity? Who forgot Christ, during the flap of a vulture's wing: Christ, who was dying for the living Ahasuerus, the immortal Ahasuerus, the wandering Ahasuerus? Then, to whom did the voice of God speak, when it said: "You shall no longer be an angel of life; you shall no longer live in the Celestial City; you shall live in Mob's house; you shall be hers, to light her fire, to sing her songs, to drink the ashes that remain in the bottom of her glass?" And today, who is mine, all mine, flesh and bone? Who waters my bouquets of marigolds and scabious[15] on my windowsill, if it is not Rachel, Rachel the archangel with the blue wings, eyes the color of the sky, and tresses that shakes light around them; who learned to spell out one by one in her book, with the children of the City of God, the notes of the music of Heaven. That Rachel despises me, I know. She no longer has wings with which to fly, but the thoughts of her heart fly away from my house like a vapor rising from the mown grass in the evening. She no longer has her viol with which to sing, but she still hums tunes at the window that cause passers-by the stop. Who are you to scorn me? You had an aureole around your head; now your hair is tied up in the silver plait of a daughter of Worms. You had a blue cloak in which to dress yourself; now you have a woolen dress that the local weaver made for you. When you go into town, the old women you meet say: "What can old Mob be thinking, not to have married off that girl? Truly, does no one want her? The weaver's son is looking for a wife; the weaver's son earns a silver sou every month; he ought to marry her, out of kindness."

RACHEL
My heart hurts, Mob; let me kneel down and pray to God with all my soul.

---

[15] *Soucis* [marigolds] also means "worries" and *veuves* [scabious] also means "widows," so this phrase has a highly pertinent double meaning.

MOB

Pray with your lips alone, if you can. What has he to do with your soul? Do you not think the prayers of desiccated leaves, of the hazel when it dies, of the ash when it is sown, of the lamp when it goes out, are worth more to him than the prayer of your soul? You should have thought of your soul when you had two blue wings to carry you and the sky to fly in. Pray today? Oh, pray if you want to, as the worn paving-stones of cathedrals and stained-glass windows effaced by the mist pray; pray like a drop of rain in a cellar, a banner eaten away on its pike-staff, a worm in the damp earth. What have you to do, sitting on your wicker chair, gazing at a patch of sky through the pane of your window? You can't enter the world of dreams any more.

RACHEL

Mob, I'll kiss your hands, but don't say that it was a dream. Oh, don't say that—you'll drive me mad!

MOB

Get away! Forget those miters of light, those golden aureoles; wither in your hear those flowers of light, those flaps of vermilion cloaks. Instead of the songs of Heaven, listen to the song of the cricket on your hearth; pale in your soul, until death, the chubby faces of your Seraphim. The viol of the archangels is finished for you, I tell you. Like a young woman who throws the faded roses of the ball into her alcove when she returns home, throw away your memories; throw away your blue sky, your infinite hopes. All you know of the world is what happens above the clouds. Real life, my dear, is slightly different from those adolescent fantasies. Follow me, clinging to the hem of my dress; I'll show you what you've never seen, in all things: the dried-up spring; the desiccated bark; the broken heart; the empty cup.

RACHEL

Everyone here believes that I'm your daughter; I've never told anyone my secret, I swear. My God, if I'd only known once, in all these years, what the children with their aureoles that I cradled in Heaven are doing!

MOB

Do you really think that anyone up there still cares what your heart thinks? Oh, if you hadn't lost your wings I'd gladly refer you to others with my silk mantle, but your heart isn't what it was. Nowadays, the gaze and smiles of Heaven wouldn't mend it; it's necessary that it get drunk in its turn on the last tear hidden in the gazes of passers-by. Get away! When you've collected dead leaves in the forest for me, go and beg for a loving sigh for yourself if you want; when you've filled my glass of tears for me, go fill for yourself your glass of promises and your dreams of young men; but don't talk about angels any more. You're a woman, and your bosom trembles like a woman's; your eyes are lowered and your cheeks go pale when you go along the street. When the sound of the organ reaches your window in the evening, when the wind brings you the flowers of chestnut-trees, you weep without praying. Oh, just remember the angels of Gomorrah; I command you to forget all the rest.

III.

The prelude to a serenade is audible in the street.

A STUDENT
Yes my friends, she lives here. Go look under that window, where she has sown bouquets of mignonettes and marigolds. She's there, be sure of it, behind those leaded windows. Wait a while longer. My God, my heart's trembling like a leaf! I can't sing. Am I mad? I've been looking for her for three months without being able to talk to her. You now, now that I'm a doctor, I could marry her tomorrow—if she wanted to.

A MUSICIAN
Is it really possible, Doctor, that you've never yet spoken to her?

THE STUDENT,
Oh, never! I once sent her a bouquet of wallflowers; that's all. But her mother seems to be a worthy woman; I'm sure that she'll come to an understanding with mine to live with us in Linange. Since I've been at the university, my eyes haven't seen any other girl than Rachel. Come on, my friends; my heart can't hold still any more. Let's begin.

A MUSICIAN
Our viols are ready; our bows are folding over our strings. Courage! Sing loud!

THE STUDENT, *singing*
Tell me, my bride, what you're hiding beneath our long black hair.
Is it a snowflake that fell on your way home from Christmas mass?

Is it the foam of the Rhine chased by a storm as you walked on the bank?

Is it a newly-born white swan that has already spread its wings?

If it's the snowflake, let me drink it, on returning from a long voyage.

If it's the foam of the Rhine, let me moisten my brown hair with it.

If it's a newly-born swan, let me take it to the mountain-top.

"No, what I'm hiding in my long black hair is none of those things;

"It's the bosom of your bride, where you set your head to sleep this evening."

MOB, *at the window*

Bravo, my lords! The music is beautiful, and well-played. It's too much honor for poor folk like us. Let me come down to the street to thank you. (*She comes down.*) My lords, I've brought wine from my cellar to refresh you; here's a large cup that I've filled to the brim for you; I wish I had better; I picked it myself from my own vine, I swear to you, and pressed it I my own press. See how it sparkles! The color is perhaps a little dark, and the foam at the edge resembles the foam that moistens the bit of the horses of the night, isn't it? Just taste it and drink it; it will cure your fatigue. It cures songs as well as tears. The cup is pure ebony-wood; I sculpted it myself during the winter evenings.

A MUSICIAN
Since you offer, we won't refuse.

MOB
You're too honest, my lord. Pass the cup on to all your companions.

(*They all drink, and fall down.*)

THE STUDENT, *throwing away the empty cup*
Damnation! It's the cup and wine of death.

(*He dies.*)

MOB
Poor fools! But isn't death the intoxication of life? Let him go to sleep it off under the table of the world, until the great revelry of the last judgment.

IV.

AHASUERUS, s*itting on a bench at the city gate.*
His horse is lying beside him on the road, dying.
1.

O Christ! Release me, O Christ! If I were a boar tracked
by dogs I could escape by night to my lair. If I were a branch
of dead wood, a woodcutter would pick me up and take me to
his fire. If I were an earthworm, I'd go to sleep beneath a cool
cellar, in the tomb of a king, and I'd spin my damp web
around his damp crown. O woodcutter of Nazareth, take me,
take me on my arid road. Gravedigger of Bethlehem, bury me
in your sepulcher, where the rain and the dew trickle; take me
in your eternal shroud, in the depths of the sculpted rock in
your Calvary of Golgotha. Mercy!

2.

Who cried for mercy? Is that you, Ahasuerus? Oh, the
angels in the highest heavens will laugh. Have you forgotten
the cross-bearer who went past your door in Jerusalem? What
have you stuffed in your ears in order that his voice should no
longer ring around you? And in your eyes, in order that they
should no longer see his flamboyant eyes, and the finger of the
hand that he raised beneath his mantle? Speak, Ahasuerus;
what did you do that day? The stony path that leads to Golgotha, that dead fig-tree, that drunken crowd beneath the fig tree,
those women dragging themselves along on their knees, the
hoarse sobs on their lips, and that voice, which resonated in
the marrow of your bones: you remember that, don't you?

You'd like it to be a dream, a thousand-year dream,
wouldn't you? But it's not a dream, any more than that stork
passing over your head, which is going to seek your shelter in
the reeds, and nor are you the child of your dream. Can't you
feel your heart weighing in your bosom like a heavy stone in
the arm of a sling-wielder? And that city, too, is no phantom

formed beneath the tomb of a dead man's skull. Its cobble-stones are resounding, its battlements glistening, its bells ring-ing, and its church, to curse you, is kneeling beneath its towers like a ma dragging himself along on his hands beneath the weight of his cross.

Knock on any of those doors; at each of them there are people like you; they have eyes like you, not to devour, like you, an eternal tear, but to bathe, during their brief summer, in loving gazes; they have lips like you, but not to drink, like you, the dust of valleys and the salt of the earth, but to rink their rapid lives from the lips of heir new spouses; they have arms like you, not to hug, like you, the north wind and the sirocco, but to hug the child of their bones to their bosom.

From all the houses, choose whichever you wish. Go to the threshold with your iron-clad shoes, and the women will hide their eyes in the men's bosoms, and the little children, will slide between their father's legs in horror, crying: "It's him, Father! It's the Wandering Jew!"

3.

Oh, if only I were still a young companion of the tribe of Levi, in my father's house; if only this crenellated city were Jerusalem, Jerusalem the beautiful, Jerusalem the perfumed, like a flowering vine in the rock, I would sing a song on my return, loudly, in order to be heard by the lepers and the cam-el-drivers. And passers-by would come, and they would touch my clothes and say: "Is that you, Ahasuerus? May you be blessed, good Ahasuerus! How long your journey has been! Where have you come from? Your mother has sent us to wait for you. Here are figs for your hunger; here is wine for your thirst."

Your father, whom you thought dead, would be sitting on the bench of your house, and your little brothers will leap over their mats when they see you from afar on the road, saying "Brother, Brother, what have you brought us? Is it sea-shells that sing? Is it a colored woolen robe for the cold? Is it a new silver coin? Is it an embroidered belt, or a shiny cassolette of good Lebanon wood?"

4.

Ah, in my cassolette there is neither myrrh nor incense, nor powdered gold, nor dates; on my belt, there is nether pearls nor embroidery; and the woolen robe I wear was not woven for celebration. I have seen Jerusalem again, but it was no more Jerusalem than this place. When I returned, the bones whitening there got up to see me pass. My house was still standing. The window was open; the door bolted shut. In the garden, I saw my empty tomb; an Angel of Death covered it with his two silken wings to prevent me from resting there by day or night, like the crow who shelters his brood beneath his breast when it rains.

5.

Christ's gaze is attached to my soul as a dead man's lamp is attached by its copper bring to a sepulchral pillar, to illuminate in the night the tongues of the vipers and the mouths of the scorpions who are eating him away: a gaze devoid of tears, devoid of movement; two brazen eyes weighing upon my eyelids. For a heritage, he has transmitted to me his immortal dolor and his bloody sweat. He has dug into my bosom with his eyes; he has ignited his inferno and his limbo there, that king of the dead, but no heaven.

"Others shall have my tunic; you shall have what remains of the hyssop and the bile." But King, I'm drunk on your hyssop; my knees are bending like those of a guest leaving a full table, and since that time, I swear to you, I've walked without pause. I've seen hawks on the summit of the Vourcano flying over my head, round the monastery, and their circles extend far enough to touch the sea on the far horizon; I've seen a flock of teal bathing in the Lake of Perugia, and the water trembling beneath their wings, rippling all the way to the bank. Everywhere, I've seen, in the depths of my soul, despair born and grow and overflow, to the extent of enclosing the mud of my days and the algae of my dreams in its infinite shores.

6.

Where are you, then, king of the dead? In searching for you, I've worn away the soles of my feet; I've dug, like the vulture, beneath the ashes of cities and the mantles of the dead. The sea resembles the blue of your tunic; I've searched the hollows of the sea. Rome, which sweats blood, resembles, with its walls, your crown of thorns; I've searched in Rome. The whitening desert resembled your shroud; I've searched in the desert. I've asked women threading their distaffs, children eating their oat-bread by the door, horse-drovers braiding their hemp in the words: "Have you see him pass by?" Where are you, then, king of the dead!

7.

When I was ten years old, I watched the storks and cranes resting on the neighboring roofs on returning from their journeys. I would have liked them to tell me what was on the other side of the mountain, and tell me what they had seen beneath the foliage of the woods and the rushes of springs. When the pigeons gathered to depart, my heart rose up in my breast, and from afar I followed their flight, like the evaporating smoke of a shepherd's fire.

8.

No, the cranes and storks have not traveled as far as me, and the pigeons have not drunk from as many springs as me. The mountain springs have the taste of absinthe. The flowers in the meadows bear crosses the color of blood on their leaves. The woods moan when I pass by; grottoes weep when I go into them; the earth resonates beneath my iron-clad shoes like the stone of a tomb on Calvary. Since you have emerged from your sepulcher, Jesus of Nazareth, tell me, by means of the cry of the eagle, the vapor of grottoes and the leaves of the ash-tree, where you are; by means of the noise of the city, the watchman's bagpipe, the chains of the drawbridge, the shining lance and funeral bells.

9.

One day, I thought I had arrived at the end of my road, at the house of Christ, to find him sitting under the porch with his mother; still the road went on, through the heather; still the streams lost their breath behind me; still my heart expected to encounter him, before nightfall, with his golden aureole, with his palm-leaf. But the evening passed; after the night, the morning passed, and after the morning, the midday too; and after that, there was a time when I saw that my worn feet, without aging, were wearing away the stone of the thresholds of my hosts; beneath their tread the stairways crumbled, their valley filled with dead leaves, their well was filled in, but my life was not filled in. In the evening, I sought a placed to rest, in cities that I had left full of people, cries, songs, smoke, carts and sighs; I found them dried up on the road, like a spring from which jackals have drunk the last drops of water.

10.

And when new people came to replace the dead, I went before them, alone, to the city gates, to show them the way; their wild horses looked at my suspiciously; their long-haired kings shouted and laughed in their new tongues without ever having seen me. "Look on that stone! That's Ahasuerus! Don't draw your bows; it's the man who will never die."

11.

Not to be able to die! To wait forever, and never meet! That's it, isn't it? Always to gaze and never to see! Who said that? Is it you, long-haired kings on your wild horses? And do the stones of my path also know Christ's secret? I threw myself off a peak in the Alps; an eagle extended its wings to carry me to verdant grass. I marched into the waves of a bottomless lake in order to plunge myself into the skies reflected there; the water fled before me, leaving nothing beneath my feet but stones that it had muddied and bones that it had rubbed together.

AHASUERUS' HORSE

Master, I hear your plaint, but I can't change anything. My hair, longer than a woman's, makes my sweat rain down to the ground, a sweat of blood. In my mouth, the bit has worn away. One day, when I followed my sweetheart without you, I crossed the desert of the four rivers without wearying. But your dolor is wider than the desert of Asia and the sea of Macedonia; its borders have never been seen. Your cares are too heavy; the wound in our bosom is too heavy for me to carry; your injury pricks and spurs me too harshly. Your road stretches out beneath your paces, and no horseman has ever walked as far. The grass of your pasturage only grows in ruins. In my trough you put tears. Neither my feet nor my flanks can run any longer. If you love me, bury me in this place, beneath that leafy grass where the mares are gamboling. Braid my mane on my neck and leave me my colored coat, my stirrups and my ivory saddle too, and the worn remains of my silver bit. On my black litter, I shall dream about you. When I close my heavy eyelids, I shall weep for your pain, but not my own.

AHASUERUS
Get up! We have to go.

AHASUERUS' HORSE
I'm too tired.

AHASUERUS
One more day.

AHASUERUS' HORSE
If my feet were willing, I'd have heart enough for a thousand.

164

AHASUERUS
As far as the city; a few steps.

AHASUERUS' HORSE, *dying*
Master, my hooves are worn away, and my breath exhausted.

AHASUERUS
Me too—like you, I'm going to die. At least carry me, without your hooves resounding, as far as the place where you went to your pale mare. Without whinnying, carry me there, where the bottomless spring is hollowed out for our thirst; where the trough without limits is full, for your hunger, with gilded barley; where the landlord and his groom will wipe away your sweat forever. Of your black litter, only give me half, that I might go to sleep beneath your feet in your stable, fully-dressed with dreams.

AHASUERUS' HORSE
Look, Master, here comes my last sigh.

(*He dies.*)

AHASUERUS
And here come my death-throes. No, I'm not the trunk of a centenarian oak that the woodcutter has forgotten in the forest. This time my black cup is full; my eyes are vacillating; my heart is trembling with the fever of the dying. For me too the bells are going to ring; their beautiful bronze and shining silver voice will make the water tremble in the springs; and the hawthorn will shake its dew in the bushes in the words, and the flowers will drop their bloody crosses when they hear it. "Ahasuerus is dead! Ahasuerus is dead!" And the watchman, when he opens the city gate, will summon me with his bagpipe without waking me up.

CHORUS OF THE BURGERS OF THE CITY, *on the walls*

Master, what is stopping you? What are you waiting for, on that milestone? Come into our worthy city. We've never seen a traveler walking so slowly, nor one so weary, nor so handsome. Where have you come from? From the mount of Armenia, or Rome, the distant land? Who are you? Where is your home? We would gladly learn that, if it is not a mystery.

AHASUERUS
My journey has scarcely begun.

CHORUS OF BURGERS
1.

By that arched door, enter my house. The wine here will please you; the hop-beer in my pitcher is fresh, and verdant, and foamy. The bread here is made from new wheat, and cut on the table-cloth. Around the table, my wife will serve us in painted earthenware bowls, and my daughter, with the smooth hair, will bring more.

2.

Don't weep, traveler. If you are a master image-maker or page-maker with no work, I want to have a belfry in the town center; you can sculpt it. If you're a master tower-builder, I need a tower built on my church in order that the angels might dwell there; you can build it.

3.

Sit down here. You will certainly have news to tell us, about the countries your eyes have seen. Which, in your opinion, are the most abundant, and the best, and the most welcoming? Where does incense grow? Where does myrtle grow? Where does Syrian balm grow? We would like to know, in order to soothe your pain.

166

V.

RACHEL, *alone in her room, feeding her caged starling*
My head hurts. Since that stranger arrived, I can't think about anything else. Come on, come on, my lovely starling, amuse me, cheer me up. You're my entire joy; you have no sad secrets. I'll give you and almond-branch to peck.

THE STARLING, *in its cage*
Beware of the stranger, Rachel. Since he has come, I'm no longer hungry for almond branches; I'm no longer thirsty for well-water.

RACHEL
Did you speak? Wretched bird. No, it wasn't you, was it? It was me, sighing. Stay in your cage; I'll amuse myself better with my wallflowers. Oh, how beautiful you are, my wallflowers! I'm going to give you a little sunlight and shake you dew from the window.

THE BOUQUET OF WALLFLOWERS
Run away, Rachel. Since the stranger has come, what good is the sun to me? The sun no longer warms me. What good is the dew? The dew no longer refreshes me.

RACHEL
My God, are my ears ringing? Science the rain has already watered my flowers. I'll amuse myself better playing my mandora.

THE MANDORA
Run away, Rachel. Since the stranger has arrived I've forgotten the songs I knew. Let me be, my breath frightens me.

RACHEL

What's the matter with me? I don't know any more whether that voice came out of my mouth, or whether I really heard it.

THE STARLING

Go! Leave us. What can you do now with a starling? A starling's wing doesn't beat as fast as your poor heart beneath your dress. What can you do with a bouquet of wallflowers? A wallflower doesn't lean over on its stem as far as your head on its neck. What can you do with a mandora? A mandora doesn't moan was much as the breath in your bosom. Since your neighbor has come, I'm afraid in your house. Open the window for me, so that I can leave, to fly over the sea to build my spring nest on Christ's tomb.

THE BOUQUET OF WALLFLOWERS

And me; I'm stifling here. Let the bird carry my spring perfume on its wings, to drop it in passing on the road to Bethlehem.

THE MANDORA

And me; let it take with it my evening sighs, to drop them far from here in the foliage of the fig-trees and the old walls of the Holy Land.

RACHEL

I'm going mad! I'm afraid of my own voice. It seems to me that everything I touch murmurs like me. Oh, it's too long since I've had any fresh air; at this hour of the evening I've always been sadder than during the rest of the day.

VI.

The Esplanade of Heidelberg Castle

MOB, *dressed as an old woman of the region*
Everything promises us, for our share of pleasure, a magnificent day. At first I feared that cloud over the Heiligberg. (*To Ahasuerus.*) Permit me to entrust Rachel to you for a moment, while I collect a bouquet from the cemetery. Don't leave her alone.

AHASUERUS
I promise.

MOB
I'll be right back.

(*She leaves.*)

RACHEL
No, there's no other place that pleases we as much as this arbor. The water murmurs under the electors' balcony; the deer drink in the shade in the valley. Listen to the students' hunting-horns in the towers, and the pilgrims singing, and the sound of the organ. Here, truly, the road of the Necker resembles a serpent that has shed its coast behind it. The cherry-trees flourish, the saint is asleep in his reliquary, the Rhine in the hollow of its bed. Tell me, my lord, whether your homeland is as beautiful as mine.

AHASUERUS
In my homeland, the sea rolls over golden sand. The stars are bees that suck the flowers of heaven. My city, when it was in celebration, resounded on the mountain like the quiver

on the back of a horseman. The rivers curved like the saber at his side; the desert shone like a ring on his finger.

RACHEL
And now?

AHASUERUS
The ring is tarnished, the saber rusted, the quiver empty. In my homeland, the cypresses were verdant, the gazelles frolicked, the antelope with golden eyes grazed golden branches; stone lions dug in the sand with their claws and crowned unicorns waited for the last judgment to give them, when they awoke, the scepter and the miter.

RACHEL
And now?

AHASUERUS
The lions have shaken their manes and thrown sand at the summit of Calvary.

RACHEL
What is the name of your homeland, my lord?

AHASUERUS
You'll never see it.

RACHEL
Is it a long time since you left it?

AHASUERUS
Time does nothing to me. It only leaves wrinkles in my heart.

RACHEL
If you wanted to, you could send a message.

AHASUERUS
The cranes, when they go there, serve as my messengers.

RACHEL
When you left, did you have no little brothers?

AHASUERUS
They're grown up now.

RACHEL
And no one keeps your house?

AHASUERUS
The storks, when they are weary, and the swallows, if they perch on the roof.

RACHEL
Your sister must have wept at the window when you left. I'm sure of it.

AHASUERUS
The land wept, and the sky wailed, but it was not for me.

RACHEL
And who accompanied you?

AHASUERUS
My dog, while baying at the granite sphinxes and the stone dragons that came to crouch down by the roadside in order to watch me go past.

RACHEL
When you go home, everything will be changed. You won't recognize anything.

AHASUERUS

On the contrary; nothing changes in my homeland. Everything there is awaiting my return, to hear the news I bring. Every morning, without changing foliage, the old palm trees stand up on their trunks, and the cedars on their mountain, and look out to sea to see whether my ship is coming in. Every summer, and every winter, the torrent dries out in the same place to give me passage. Motionless, the hawks hover in the sky; the old gates in the desert remain open; the same tent hangs on the same summit; the same ibis sleeps beneath its obelisk; and when evening comes, they say to one another: "Again, again, let's wait for nightfall; let's wait until morning. We don't want to close our circles in the sky, nor rotate on our hinges, nor fold up our canvas, nor shake our wings, nor let our walls crumble before having seen him return."

RACHEL
Are you a king's son, then? I thought as much.

AHASUERUS
No, I'm not a king's son. The crown that makes me bow my head is neither silver nor gold, and the rain and the wind assail me in my palace.

RACHEL
Perhaps you're a baron coming back from the Holy Land?

AHASUERUS
Yes, child, that's the land from which I come.

RACHEL
Why have you brought back no falcon on your wrist, nor any ivory relics, sea-shells, golden sand or dates?

AHASUERUS
I've brought more memories than I wished. My burden was heavy. I wasn't able to add anything more to it.

RACHEL
Where is it, then?

AHASUERUS
In a fold of my heart.

RACHEL
Oh! You must have brought with you a piece of wood from the true cross. Memory isn't sufficient.

AHASUERUS
None of my memories can be erased; for me there is neither age not antiquity.

RACHEL
What, my lord? Your eyes have seen the summit of Calvary?

AHASUERUS
By a sky in wrath, and beneath a bloody cloud.

RACHEL
And your feet have touched the stones of Carmel?

AHASUERUS
When they rumbled as they rolled, and when only the echoes spoke.

RACHEL
And you have picked flowers in the Garden of Olives?

AHASUERUS

When they were filled with the tears of stars, when they were soiled in their dust like a torn tunic.

RACHEL

Oh, fortunate lord who has seen everything, who has kissed, with his lips, the stone of the sepulcher. Tell me, what can one hear in the foliage of the trees in the evening?

AHASUERUS

A name, always the same: the name of an eternal traveler, which every leaf repeats on its branch while groaning.

RACHEL

And in the sands of the deserts thorough which you have passed?

AHASUERUS

The voice of a man uttering a curse.

RACHEL

It's a lifelong good fortune to have seen what you have seen. Now you can die content, when the time comes. How many pilgrims would envy you!

AHASUERUS

I have left them all behind me on my road. The wind drives me; I go on without pausing.

RACHEL

At the foot of the olive-trees, were there angels on their knees, singing canticles over golden books.

AHASUERUS

No. There were vultures crying over my head and the wings of owls brushing my cheeks. (*Aside.*) Mercy! Mercy!

RACHEL
Were there not children with aureoles whose hands were joined together, and who were smiling as they said: "Father! Father!"

AHASUERUS
No. There were vipers hissing beneath my feet; they had voices that cried in the waves: "Accursed! Accursed!"

RACHEL
I understand. You're a saintly man. Let me kiss your feet. Let me adore you.

AHASUERUS, *aside*
Christ, have pity on me!

RACHEL
Don't refuse me your blessing, my lord; I'm at your knees.

AHASUERUS
Get up, Rachel! Mercy, my child!

RACHEL
Pray for me.

AHASUERUS
I can't.

RACHEL
Save me!

AHASUERUS
My heaven is full.

RACHEL
Just one of your prayers!

AHASUERUS

Rather go say to the lepers: "Give me the holy water of your leprosy."

RACHEL

Just one sign of the cross.

AHASUERUS

Rather go say to the king of the Saracens: "King, give me the salute of your hand."

RACHEL

What have I done, then? Your eyes are flashing; there are tears in your eyes.

AHASUERUS

Can't you see, when you speak to me on your knees, the violets that are filling up with blood?

RACHEL

My lord, that's the evening dew that shines when the sun sets.

AHASUERUS

Can't you see, when to tell me to pray, an eternal tear, which falls from the grotto.

RACHEL

My lord, that's a raindrop that a passing hind has caused to fall from the vault.

AHASUERUS

Can you not hear the songs of the fays who repeat my name when they blow into their cheeks?

RACHEL

Be sure that it's the sound the Necker makes against the fishermen's dikes.

AHASUERUS

Further on, further on; I must hurry. Let's go down the mountain.

VII.

CHORUS OF FAYS

1.

Turn, then, spinning-wheels around our ruby-shod feet. Turn, ensorcelled spindles of the Fates, twist in our hands. Needles of the fays, without breaking, run, jump, crawl and embed ourselves in your mesh. Yes, before midnight chimes, we shall have embroidered a hundred thousand silver stars for the realm of the evening. The snowflakes of Cornwall fall from our distaff. In Brittany, the moon's rays, finer than our hair, our pieces of thread. We card before daybreak, for the isle of Thule, the frost that hangs from the trees. When the earth it sighs, it is our spinning-wheel murmuring; when the sky moans, it is out spindle going to sleep. When the Ocean of Aquitaine turns green, it is our finger that is moistened to draw it out.

2.

At present, compared with us, all the ancient gods have become dwarfs, scarcely big enough to carry the train of our dress. Jupiter is a dwarf; his father, Time, a fire-follet that dies as soon as it appears. Do you see that genius over there, at the crossroads, anointing his head with a drop of dew? That's the old god of Chaldea, making himself small so as not to be seen by the God-Giant of the cathedrals. The one who's trembling under a dry leaf was enthroned two thousand years ago in a granite temple. And that goblin, sniggering as he brings that old man a strand of thatch, is Memnon discrowned, driven mad by his ruination. Sylphs, ghouls, gnomes and all of Olympus could fit into a hollow tree today. Dust of gods, those colossi of the pagan gaze are trembling beneath the branches, under the alders, under the woodcutter's roof, so long as our two-wheeled cart refrains from crushing them.

3.

Rome the much-lauded, where is your empire? I have broken your short sword with the back of my hand. By breathing on it, I have rusted your helmet. With my diamond hammer, I have demolished your walls, and I have carried away your dust in my silken apron. On their winged chariots, the fays climb around your triumphal column, over the gates of your chiseled cities, on your sculpted roads, through your legions of stone, with bucklers of nacre, with swords sheathed in a summer sunbeam; cutting and thrusting, they sweep away your armies. Can you hear the whips of spider-silk that they are cracking at your summit over your accumulated dwarfs.

4.

Rome has fallen. Let us celebrate; let us eat her crumbs around the round table. To the sound of the horn, in the forest, I have summoned the court of Arthus[16] here. Twelve noblemen are armed and full armored. Among the many queens that are awake, Yseult is the most cheerful, the most beautiful and the most blonde. Of the many barons who will ride, her lover is the sturdiest, the most courteous and the most silvery. His horse is a bay, his lance rigid his fur mantle crimson. Dukes, pages and golden-haired maidens were sleeping in the forest of Broceliande. All of them said when I passed by: "Awaken to the sound of the horn."

5.

To the sound of the horn, with the echo, awaken in Spain, where the figs are ripening, kings of the Moors, of Oriental Arabs and Galilee beyond the sea. Over our emerald surf the saber of the prophet is curved like a snake in the grass. On

---

[16] One of Quinet's most notable articles for the *Revue des Deux Mondes* was a study of 12th century verse romances, in which this version of the name of the legendary king Arthur occasionally crops up. It was later adapted by Ernest Chausson for the title of his opera *Le roi Arthus*.

its blade, a negro, one of our relatives, has engraved magical words. In Grenada the beautiful, the sultana is sitting at her window, which our chisels carved. Our brush tints her lashes, our file polishes her bosom. Paler than the meadow-rose, she gazes from afar at the minarets with their stone turbans tied around their heads, the agas on their foaming mares, the leaping greyhounds, and the flash of yataghans springing from their sheaths, and the plumed tents that quiver to the call of clarions, and the forests that sparkle—oh, the beautiful fire!—and the battle that howls. Go on, citrus-trees of Spain, fade; I have dispensed more perfume on her lips than on your branches. Sea of Cadiz, dry up; I have put more azure, the color of the sky, in her eyes than in your waves, more than on your banks or the mules that bathe, more than in your bay, whose galleys and three-decked sailing ships are amorous, more than in your bottomless bed, where people fish for pearls, more than in your blue-tinted abyss, as far as the port of Macedonia.

6.

Come on, then, Charlemagne and his squire! His empire is ready, like a chick in its nest. To make it, we only need three strokes of the wand. Morgande has embroidered its banner, Fleur d'épine has laced its helm.[17] Neither sabers nor sultan' scimitars can undo it. Listen! Marjoram, daises and rosemary are trampled by the soldiers; the earth is trembling beneath the armored squadrons. So many noblemen, barons, coats of mail and crests! What a pleasure for the fays, to see before evening, that beautiful empire break like a giant lance on the shield of Roncevaux!

---

[17] "Fleur d'épine" [thorn-flower] is the title of a well-known French traditional ballad, in which the female singer claims it for her name, thus identifying herself as a *femme fatale*, though not necessarily (as here) a *fée*. Morgande is a variant of Morgan le Fay.

7.

On a pavis carried by four emperors, higher than everyone else, we raise the pope. His miter will be gold, the finest that was ever sold. Our best spinners will sow his chasuble. Truly his science is greater than ours. His old book is enchanted to the very last page. So, let everyone obey him, with neither delay nor demur. In all things, let him be the first. When he wants to mount his mule, King of Germany, you will hold his stirrup. Dukes will kiss his feet, noblemen his floor-tiles, and the chain of souls, like a blessed rosary, will hang from his belt.

8.

Above all, we want, we intend, we order, for it is our pleasure, that land and sea, babbling spring, silvery star, sea of Venice, of Brabant, untied scarves, and queens' tresses, rings, stained-glass windows, embroidered, sculpted and ensorcelled arches, to murmur incessantly, without pausing by day or by night, the four letters that spell L-O-V-E. To all our genii and servants, let us prescribe the stammering of the same word under the pines, under the oaks, on balconies, under coats of mail, on the hilts of words, at the tips of lances, in the folds of banners, in the creases of the clouds, in order that heaven and earth shall have but one sound in our ears.

9.

Furthermore, we enjoin all the diviners that there are or will be, mages, dwarfs and negroes to add a pinch of venom to the bread of Ahasuerus, a pinch of hyssop to his cup. It is necessary that his penalty be redoubled. Do not spare the tears that freeze in his eyes, nor the sighs that suffocate people, nor the beating of the heart that bruises it without wearing it out. Tears cost us exactly the same as dew.

10.

Then, when the measure is full, when all the kingdoms have drunk all the gold on earth, when the bell-towers and bell-turrets mounted at their summits have placed their crowns of cloud upon their heads, when queens are clad in silver, we shall blow it all down. Kings, noblemen, cathedrals, fine empires of ash, fine empires of mud and fine nations of clay will crumble beneath the axle of our chariot. Who will laugh at their glory? The marjoram, their heir, which they trod down without crushing it, and the rosemary on the squares, on seeing our dances.

VIII.

Inside Rachel's room. Rachel is asleep in her bed. Day is breaking.

THE CHORUS

1.

Shh! Shh! At this hour, Rachel is asleep. At a less sono-rous pace, fays and aspioles,[18] holding our breath, go into her room, without saying anything, with our fingers over our lips, the better to bewitch her. Let us hide, some in a curl of her hair, some in the bouquet of wallflowers, some in those nut-crackers, some in that prayer-book, some in the folds of her sewing. Above all, whisper. Let her mistake our voices for the sound of her thoughts in her resonant soul.

2.

Are you all right? Yes. Me too. Silence. In order to see her asleep, I've passed my head under the awning of her bed. Oh, how white, and straight, and soft her neck is. Her teeth, when she breathes, seem silvery and all the gold from beyond the sea, or the distant land of Syria, could not be as golden as her blonde hair. Peace! Now she's sighing. Now she's turning on her side, and back again. Now, here's a dream passing over her forehead, and over her cheeks, and her lips; now it's in her heart. Oh, no, it's certain; never, in a tower, nor in a plenary palace have you ever seen an aristocratic girl, any sister of a king or a nobleman, as beautiful to be hold. With no lie, I could believe that she was an angel.

---

[18] *Aspiole* was a literary synonym for *fée* popular with the Romantics, used by both Victor Hugo and Théophile Gautier.

3.

Shut up, loquacious fay! One more word and I'll discrown you. In her line-curtained bed, Rachel might hear you. By kissing her eyelids an hour too soon, a ray of sunlight has half-awakened her. The cock is crowing, the bee is beating its wing against the window, and the sun, emerging in the Orient, has already spilled three drops from its cup of light over the world.

RACHEL *waking up*

How long the night has been! My God! And always the same dream! What does it mean? Berthe will have to sleep with me tomorrow. Oh, my heart is hurting. It's as if I'd been struck there. It seems to me that I have Syrian bile on my lips. No, since that stranger arrived, I'm no longer what I was. The suffering he seems to be enduring is too great, and I can no longer think about anything else. What a story that might be; there's a great mystery there. The idea keeps coming back to me; all the way to church I think about it. It's an entire week now since I said my prayers. That's why I'm so anxious. I no longer know what I'm doing. May God forgive me. (*She kneels down beside her bed and begins to pray aloud, her hands pressed together.*) Our Father, who art in heaven, hallowed be thy name, Thy will be done...

THE CHORUS

Tel me, Rachel, who is making that racket in the street? The cobblestones are resounding, the windows quivering. Is it your guest, going for an early morning ride? Lean over his reins, is it him making so many sparks fly from the hooves of his horse with the gleaming rump? His saddle is polished ivory, and its bow is wrought in fine gold. Don't you want to see him passing under your window?

RACHEL

Lead us not into temptation, but deliver us from evil. Amen.

184

THE CHORUS

There he is, drawing away. Listen, listen! Another three strides and you'll no longer be able to hear him. I've traversed many mounds and many great valleys, but I've never seen merlin or a rider fly so fast, nor one so proud or valiant. His turban is whiter than snow or frost in the sunlight. Could you roll and loosen one as well as him, without making a knot? A silver chalice is hanging from his saddle-bow. Wouldn't you like to drink an enchanted beverage?

RACHEL

Hail Mary, full of grace, the Lord be with you.

THE CHORUS

Do you remember the day when you saw him for the first time? He was leaning against a pillar in the cathedral, and you mistook him at a distance for an angel of hard stone. It was Christmas Day. All the bells were ringing. His forehead was pale, and his eyes had wept many tears in the night. When you went up the steps of the church, he looked at you dolorously; and you, without turning your head, saw him all that day, and the next day, and the day after, saying to yourself: Who is he?

RACHEL

Pray for us poor sinners, now and in the hour of our death.

THE CHORUS

Who is he? The one who made the sky and the dew knows him well. Of all men, there isn't another like him: too young to be a hermit, too sad to be the son of a prince, too pale to be a Templar, too proud to be a loving pilgrim.

RACHEL

I confess to omnipotent God and the blessed Virgin Mary.

THE CHORUS

He's not one of those young men who only think of deceiving you; he has never been seen with them. What he says, one senses that he believes; he takes everything seriously. I swear that there are a thousand resemblances between you; and without fear, you could confide to him, I'm sure, your heart and your thoughts: the thoughts of a young woman, which rise into her soul, circulate and murmur, after daybreak, before nightfall, like a sleeping spindle beginning to hum in her ear.

RACHEL, *getting to her feet*

Oh, it's certain! I'm too distracted at the moment. It's only my lips that are praying; my mind is elsewhere. My mouth pronounces words; my heart is saying others. Things can't go on like this.

THE CHORUS

Go, over golden sand, pursue your dream. Without anxiety, go where your bright hope leads you. Can't you see joyful days already, dancing around you in a circle? Can't you feel your pain evaporating with the lilac flowers and the almond-blossom? If your soul has dipped its broken wing into the bitterness of that lake, it's to soar into the sky with even greater agility. If your heart, swollen already, weighs upon your bosom, that dolor is honey; it does no harm. If a tremulous and involuntary tear moistens your lashes, it will disappear of its own accord in the warmth of the evening.

RACHEL

The odor of lilacs is going to my head, and the noise of that fountain is making me sad. A thousand ideas are tormenting me, which I can't tell anyone about, and even if I wanted to, I don't have the words to do it. My forehead is burning. I want to cry, without knowing why. Instead of staying here, I'd do better to go and get some air in Berthe's garden.

(She goes out.)

THE CHORUS

Yes, get out of here; everywhere, your harmonious soul, always with you, will murmur in a low voice: "Do you remember the firmament? One breathes the same eternal flower there, without discomfort. Do you remember the edge of heaven? One hears the same sound of falling water there. Dreams of summer, drowsy in the dawn beneath diaphanous clouds, winged desires, sighs as great as the universe, gazes that plunge into shadow, thoughts that travel a thousand leagues an hour, all would return if only someone here would love you completely, without deceiving you."

IX.

Berthe's Garden. Rachel and Ahasuerus are walking there together.

THE CHORUS
Complete love? Is that what I said? Here's the place where one finds it, when the nightingale calls in the woods in the morning, when the days are long in May, when the leaves thicken in the orchards, when the grass is green and the heather is in flower. It's the evening hour, when the rainbow shining over the Vosges brings joy and peace to men of good will. It's the even sweeter hour when the flower gets up to say to the Rhine, and the Rhine to its bank, and the bank to its boat, and the boat to the sky, and the sky to the day, and the day to the night: "Are you asleep or awake?" As for me, I'll keep quiet.

RACHEL, *collecting flowers*
Yes, flowers know secrets that we don't; I want to consult this daisy.

(*She picks the petals off a daisy.*)

THE DAISY
Are you asleep or awake? For myself, I'll keep quiet.

RACHEL
It's withered; the other, now.

THE DAISY
Personally, I can only say two words: earth, sky; earth, sky; earth...

RACHEL

And this one; it's the biggest

THE DAISY

And me, I only know one syllable: Christ, Christ, Christ...

AHASUERUS

It's you who's speaking, Rachel, isn't it? Oh, leave the flowers alone. They repeat anything that the wind makes them say. Come along. We'll be able to talk better under this bower of honeysuckle.

RACHEL

My God, is this possible? Would you believe it? When I hear you speak, it always seems that I've heard your voice before, far away from here, in a place of which I no longer know the name.

AHASUERUS

And when I look into your eyes, I seem to remember days that are no more, and could no longer be. That's what happens every time we're together.

RACHEL

It's a very distant memory. In that other place there was an odor of a flower that never fades, which I've never breathed in since.

AHASUERUS

The flowers I've seen have always faded.

RACHEL

There was a song audible there that I've never heard since. Do you remember?

AHASUERUS
I only remember the song of the desert.

RACHEL
The sun's rays there illuminated without burning.

AHASUERUS
The light of day has burned my forehead everywhere.

RACHEL
The air was more delightful to breathe there; there were neither tears nor sighs.

AHASUERUS
Never, believe me, have I passed through that country. Was it an island, a plain, a mountain-top?

RACHEL
I no longer know the place, or the road.

AHASUERUS
It might be an illusion.

RACHEL
Oh, I'm sure that I'm not mistaken. You promised to tell me your story when the warbler fell silent. Now is the time.

AHASUERUS
No, when the cricket has withdrawn too.

RACHEL
Now the cricket has withdrawn.

AHASUERUS
A little while longer, when the star appears.

RACHEL
Here's the star now.

AHASUERUS
One more day. Tomorrow, you shall know. Only show me that I'm no longer a stranger to you.

RACHEL
What do I have to do?

AHASUERUS
When we part, once, in saying farewell, when no one can hear us, angel of love, address me as *thou*.

RACHEL
Me! You're mocking me.

AHASUERUS
More quietly, if you wish, than the star seeking its golden honey, more quietly than the warbler folding its neck to go to sleep, more quietly than the cricket closing its wing.

RACHEL
I would no longer be able to raise my eyes from the ground.

AHASUERUS
Just once: the first and last time.

RACHEL
No, I would never dare.

(*She leaves.*)

X.

AHASUERUS, *alone*

1.

Don't walk any further, Ahasuerus. Your journey is over now. The hour that has just passed was an eternity. Beneath these fresh lilacs, behold your heaven. There something has said: "I love you." Not the tempest overhead, not the hyssop in the undergrowth, not the dust of your road at noon, but the lips of a woman with a human voice, with human words that your own tongue might murmur if you wished.

2.

Oh, this is it; this is what they call love: when everything gazes at you sighing, when your breath refreshes your lips, when the hawthorn gives you a perfume for your route, when the star opens its smiling eyelid over you, and also when the source sends your shadow back to you more lightly, and when the painting breeze licks your door without insults, like a bloodhound returning from the woods at dusk.

3.

In this valley shaded by walnuts, my feet will halt forever. Forever, I shall make the tour of the city without losing sight of it; without going more than a short distance away, I shall wander night and day on the summit of the mountain that shelters it. What can that swarm of suns that has cursed me bring down on my head now? A child has said to me, involuntarily: "I love you," when everything else put together is not worth as much as one of the hairs on her head. And what are the centuries of centuries that are to be lived, compared with a single breath of her heart?

4.

Yes, everything for me is attached to the possession of that delightful being; the rest of the world is empty. I realize that, I know it; the seas, the lakes, the forests, I have visited them all; but I missed a place in that heart, and that is where the universe is.

5.

The universe! You have forgotten, perhaps, that it is extinguished at every breath. That drop of water on your lips will dry up. Today or tomorrow, Rachel will die. Of the eternity that burns in your breast you would give her half, but you do not have an hour to lend her. She cannot take you with her in her death; you cannot take her with you in your life. More alone, more accursed, you will walk your blind alley. When you return to her city, the heather will bar your way, and the thorns on the bushes will ask you: "Where has she gone, the woman who said she loved you, who was worth more than the centuries and empires that have scorned you?"

XI.

MOB

Forgive me for entering without knocking; I thought I heard you sobbing; I've made you a drink that will calm your down.

AHASUERUS

You take care of me too well, truly; I'm confused by your generosity.

MOB

Is there still that same anguish in the heart? Two grains of foxglove will cure you. The specific is infallible; I know that from experience.

AHASUERUS

Such hospitality is found nowhere but here; but reassure yourself, the sobs you heard came from an excess of joy.

MOB

Joy, dolor—it's forgivable, isn't it, to confuse them? Why do they have the same cry? I've been deceived by that before, and I've often given the same remedy for the two fits.

AHASUERUS

What you say, my dear, is truer than you know; but without wanting to, you're renewing all my pain.

MOB

Forgive me; my intentions were good. Alas, all men nowadays are made like you. What has become of the iron armor of their fathers? In their bosom, they all have a wound; one can't touch them without wrenching a cry from them; lips wound them, a word kills them.

AHASUERUS

Be sure that my pain is sincere, and that you would take pity on it if you knew it.

MOB

My God! I share it in advance. I'm racking my brains to find you a remedy. Could you not try traveling? A change of air might dissipate your melancholy. It was my great resource when I was young: for every pain in the heart, a new climate; nothing but the dust on my road was already doing me good.

AHASUERUS

Sometimes, in the depths of the soul, there is a void that the dust of all the worlds would be insufficient to fill; I have experience of it. And then again, where would I go?

MOB

The Orient is very beautiful, the Occident no less so. The sun warms up the heart, but the moon chills it again. In truth, I no longer know what advice to give you.

AHASUERUS

I thought, at first, that I might find some consolation by devoting myself to poetry.

MOB

Bravo! It's the art that I would have liked to cultivate, if I'd been left free to do so. To hurl fine words into the bright light, to dress with phrases a shadow, a skeleton, less than that—a mere nothing. A hairdresser of rhymes, a hunter of adverbs, a plume-maker of adjectives, a powderer of commas: what a faculty in a man, Monsieur! And think that everything obeys him, primarily that which is not! To plunge into the transparent ocean of things in order to fish up the sky and bring back to shore a dozen polished, glittering, streaming words. Oh, that's a life of emotion of which I shall be eternally jealous.

AHASUERUS
I don't know, but I might need something more real. A vague desolation surrounds me; I've become the echo of all the melancholies of the places through which I pass. The wild grass, the winter wind and the fallen leaf all resound, everything cries with despair in my heart.

MOB
If what you say is accurate, it's a truly great inconvenience to hear that pell-mell at close range in the bony box of your brain. Instead of dreams, why not occupy yourself with the positive aspects of things? Science is made for men like you; at your age, you could still penetrate the secrets of nature. Take up alchemy, for example. Go on, to work! Stoke up the forge, crush the diamond, melt the gold, stir the crucible—go on, that's it! One more hour. In the end, a little smoke evaporates, and there's a life passed. Isn't it true?

AHASUERUS
No, science thus reduced is too dry. I've tried; it has never been able to fill my heart.

MOB
Oh, as for the heart, you see—let's not talk about that; mine is as empty as yours and I have more to complain about than anyone. You have an unfortunate constitution: the real displeases you, the ideal doesn't suit you; however, it's necessary to choose one of the two.

AHASUERUS
That necessity is one of my greatest torments.

MOB

Listen; if you can trust the advice of a friend, let exaltation alone; youth vanishes, illusion too. At your age, the world opens its arms to you, all careers are open to you; obtain a solid status and a position in the world. The most honorable profession is that of war; merely thinking about it makes the head giddy. The sword befits a gentleman; see how the sun gilds his breastplate; axes, halberds, iron gauntlets, falcon's beaks glistening at his side. He curls his lips, pronounces a word: "Battle;" and the echo responds, "Battle;" and the saber too in its sheath: "Battle." How many lances have been broken already! And swords will never cease to clash, until everything is ground down, flattened, cut to ribbons and taken apart. The horses sniff blood, the dagger, which is thirsty, slakes its thirst, and the vulture drinks its residues. Evening comes; one goes home, and one kills time.

AHASUERUS

More than one dart has already been blunted on my escutcheon; more than one double-edged sword has broken on my crest; I've ridden through many banners. I know how a standard flutters at the end of a halberd, how a bowstring resonates, how an unhorsed cavalier groans under his coat of mail . Many poisoned javelins have sought my bosom, whistling; many fletched arrows have screeched over my head: "Let the best-plumed lift the visor of his horse!"

MOB

A terrible moment! My teeth are chattering. What happened?

AHASUERUS

Hand to hand, tooth and claw, the combat trampled, foamed and panted; forwards and backwards, upstream and downstream, far and near, the axe of arms stripped the bark from the battle-tree. The eagle, passing overhead, closed his yellow eyelid, in order not to see the dew turn red at such close range.

MOB
You're making me shiver on your behalf.

AHASUERUS
Me! A cavalier followed me everywhere are parried the blows. From daybreak on, in the mêlée, he was my brother in arms. A thousand darts sought me, but not one reached me.

MOB
The brave companion! May the earth protect him. What armories did he have?

AHASUERUS
On his escutcheon he bore a death's-head; his pale horse did not whinny by day or night; he never took off his helmet; his arm was never weary when evening came.

MOB
So, thank God, this time your merit was recognized.

AHASUERUS
Until, in mid-mêlée, one day, a memory—oh, a rapid hour, passed in another clime—covered for me the racket of both armies; the chariots of war were passing by furiously, but I heard nothing rumbling but my voice in my bosom. Lances resounded on lances, but my eyes, behind my visor, saw nothing but myself: nothing but an image, I tell you; a shadow of myself, nothing more, who has been, who is no more, who can no longer be, and who was fighting a gigantic battle in my soul; yes, a battle within a battle! What sighs that cannot be heard! What wounds that cannot be seen! Memories more trenchant than two-handed broadswords; dreams more tangled than the plumed arrow of an arbalest: life, death, oblivion, regrets, doubts more reckless, more ponderous, more rapid and

more flamboyant than cavaliers leaning breathlessly over their bridles.

MOB

My word, that second war is crueler than the first. I had no idea. If, decidedly, war no longer suits you, you might launch yourself into State politics. Self-interest, of course, would be your infallible guide. The equilibrium of powers is the doctrine that I advise you to adopt to begin with. Monarchy has merit. Aristocrats have a sense of ancestry. Democrats are all bone and sinew. The mixture is my business; be positive, no compassion. Only numbers, bare, fleshless, unshod, filleted, you hear? All rights are recognized. With a stroke of the pen, you'll bury two or three peoples, and that always brings honor.

AHASUERUS

Don't go on; I've already had enough.

MOB

How terribly blasé you are, for your age, and how quickly people live these days! But enough resources still remain to you, and you'd be very wrong to lost heart. You could throw yourself into the arms of religion.

AHASUERUS

Explain yourself. I admit that more than once, on hearing the bells of an abbey, I've shivered from head to toe; at that moment, I envied the repose of a hermit in his convent.

MOB

My own sect is Methodism. Life therein proceeds on a small scale. I can introduce you to it if you so desire. Can you imagine that we have reduced all of life to half a dozen petty maxims that, carefully counted and well-calculated, could be packed into an eggshell. Earth, sky, waters, clouds: everything there is goes into the shell; that's the universe; everything that can't go in, that's nothingness. I hope the division is easy to retain, and you'll see that it's really very comfortable to possess thus, all the time, all the secrets of life, al the mysteries of the soul and heaven, all the science of the heart and nature, on a piece of paper as large, at the most, as a prescription for a headache-cure.

AHASUERUS

If you're not joking, that idea is disheartening.

MOB

Me, joking? Can you think so? A conversion like yours would make me very happy, and to bring you back to the pure spirit of the gospel, my director Paulus[19] will first inform you of dogmatics, dialectics, diplomacy and hypercriticism.

AHASUERUS

Please leave those empty words there. To render me repose, it's a new religion that I require, which no one has yet drawn upon. That's what I'm looking for. Only by that means could I slake the infinite thirst that's devouring me.

MOB

Novelty pleases me as much as you. It often happens, in fact, that a god is dead and buried in heaven, while we're still worshiping him on earth. The entire difficulty lies in knowing the exact moment of the decease, in order not to waste time before a skeleton dangling from the vault of eternity. After all, though, a clever man can always, if necessary, be his own god

---

[19] This reference is ambiguous, but probably refers to St. Paul; that might seem hardly consistent with Mob's dips into Protestantism and positivism, but she is a model of inconsistency throughout this dialogue, in which the author is clearly identifying with his character and Mob is standing in for his father, his mother and all the other conflicting voices that attempted to guide him in life.

for fifteen years or so, while waiting for heaven to declare itself.

AHASUERUS

Thus far, alas, I have only wandered from place to place, from hope to hope, from cult to cult. Tearfully, my soul has knocked on all the points of the universe, and found no echo anywhere. I would often have liked, during my insomnia, to embrace with my thought the rolling skies, to bed swallowed up in the whirlwind of worlds. Oh, often, while traveling, at the sound of an Alpine waterfall, I have waited foolishly until dusk for my soul to evaporate with the stream! How many times, while swimming in a remote bay, I have hugged the swell passionately to my breast! The waves hung, tangled, from my neck, the foam kissed my lips. Around me, embalmed sparks sprang forth. In the distance, shores, cities, villages, the shadows of citrus trees, valleys, mountains, everything was rocked and palpitated by my breath. At every exhalation I said, without speaking: "Love me, forgive me," and from the bottomless abyss there emerged in part, tremulously, a sigh.

MOB

You make the Ocean more modest than a girl. Her response is all that you could hope for.

AHASUERUS

I believed, wrongly, that I would one day be able to drown my desires in its immensity.

MOB

Who embraces too much grips poorly, you know. It is, permit me to say, a great vanity of our time to believe that nature has sympathies and antipathies, whatever they might be. Nature has atoms, and that's all; you'll admit that she would have been wrong to place herself at the disposition of anyone at all who wanted to become the confidant of her vapors. That's a sad thing to say, but true; and if you were honest, you'd recognize that all your troubles are internal.

AHASUERUS
So everything flees from me, everything falls, everything crumbles into ashes around me.

MOB
Not at all. If, at all costs, you require a religion, love, when it is pure, is one, in its fashion. You have a fortune, birth, you're independent, you can be excused a little folly.

AHASUERUS
Do you think so? To forget the universe that escapes me, to shelter myself entirely in a loving heart; to make it my heaven, my religion, my roof; to seek nothing else, to hear nothing else, to breathe nothing else, to plunge myself thereinto, annihilating myself alive; to quit, for a voice that blesses me, the worlds that curse me. Oh, yes, an obscure being, vile in the eyes of men—if there were only a tear for me!

MOB
That's not enough. The senses shouldn't be entirely sacrificed, and you'd be wrong to discount them entirely.

AHASUERUS
To challenge at her feet the wrath of the worlds!

MOB
It's necessary to say everything, though: there are some conventions that can't be infringed, some customs that can't be changed. One has a rank, a name, a position to protect, duties of fortune. Then again, you see, above all, opinion demands respect.

AHASUERUS

Yes, there's a parting; a thousand things separate you, life and death. But there's a moment when the secret that burns in your breast has passed your lips. People never see one another again—never—but the world is full; a single instant suffices to embalm an eternity of centuries.

MOB

Embalm, that's the word; but what? A mummy? Don't exaggerate. Every sentiment conceals a calculation, and deep down, all women are alike. Who says one says the other. Sooner or later, the best will deceive you; besides which, provided that you amuse them, you owe them absolutely nothing. They're there for the pleasure of men, they take that as read, and nothing is easier, you see, than to make them adore you.

AHASUERUS

Love has never been a game to me; if things are as you say, it's better to destroy that last hope within me, as soon as possible.

MOB

Don't get excited. On the contrary, you need love, and plenty of it. Without it, what does one know? What does one do? What does one see? And what is life? Nothing, nothing, nothing: that word says more than it means. One has only savored half of things, and intimacy is the most delicious of all.

AHASUERUS
You're giving me heart.

MOB

Except, let's be clear, that it's necessary not to abuse it; past thirty, it's already rather ridiculous. Sentiments run out like everything else; then again, one thing I forgot is that it's really very disagreeable to think that those eyes, before they have read the utmost depths of yours, will be filled up with

203

earth; that a spider's web will close that mouth before it has been able to finish its secret, and that tomorrow, that beauty, adored body and soul, will be one of those brazen I-don't-know-whats laughing at all comers in a niche in the catacombs.

AHASUERUS
On listening to you a mortal chill grips me, freezing my tongue beneath my palate.

MOB
I didn't know, my dear, that your illness was so serious. I thought that reason would have had more empire over you, and that our friends were right to hope that you wouldn't get carried away to that extent. Anyway, in your state of mind, one can always tell oneself that death isn't far away. If you knew how effective death is as a remedy for all dolors! No, you let yourself be too easily distracted. You don't think about her enough; you don't desire her enough; you don't love her enough; she's a woman too, though, so light, so profound, so serious, so old, so young, so flighty, so kind, so changeable, an angel, a queen, a great lady, a gypsy—anything you like; any situation, any rank, easy to live with, ready for anything, good at everything—playing the guitar, the tambourine, the harmonica, the tom-toms—a good neighbor, a good housekeeper, not prudish, not monotonous, hard-working, a trifle sarcastic, but very happy, provided that she has a piece of charcoal with which to write: Here lies...your name, if you please?

AHASUERUS
What does the name matter? She's so slow in coming.

MOB
There are, in the final analysis, extraordinary situations in which it's excusable to anticipate her by means of suicide. Morality condemns you, but heaven absolves you. It's some-

thing that remains for you to try. A wisp of straw would suffice, and you might find oblivion amusing.

AHASUERUS
And when that too is impossible, nothing remains but endless despair.

MOB
I know, like you, and better than anyone, that one is often hanging by a thread—but that thread is sacred. One has duties to fulfill, a career to carry forward, a family to raise, friends who are dear to you. Then too, it's necessary to be patient and take life as it comes. It's short—not short enough, I confess, but fifty years, at the most, isn't too exorbitant. At present, it all depends on you; think about it, reflect, and make a decision.

AHASUERUS
What to do, or what not to do? I don't know. Chaos is weighing upon my bosom.

MOB
A deplorable conclusion!

AHASUERUS
My entire heart is a wound. The slightest new pain awakes all of my past dolors. I can hardly stand up; wait, it's a passing weakness.

MOB
Don't hold it against me, at least. The truth, when it comes from a friend, will always produce that effect.

AHASUERUS
Look: my eyes are blinking; I can no longer see anything but darkness.

MOB
So much the better; night brings counsel. On that note,
I'll retire. Midnight's chiming. It's my usual hour. My duty is
summoning me elsewhere. Your most humble servant, sir.

AHASUERUS
Listen to a prayer.

MOB
An order, you mean.

AHASUERUS
One more word.

MOB
Sorry to refuse; my moments are counted.

AHASUERUS
Just a second.

MOB
Impossible; my health would suffer.

XII.

MOB, *alone*

1.

Ha ha! Mob, if your crazy laughter gets hold of you, you're lost, my dear, my favorite, my darling, bone of my bone. How dreary all these immortal spirits are! Is it conceivable? And yet, without them, how could one put a brave face on things? What a void! What tedium! What rigidity! What cold intimacy—with whom I ask you? Answer me! With less than nothing, with oneself…since you can't do any better, at least let them distract you. Tears come to the eyes…tears, did I say? Thank God, it's already too late to have any of them but the location.

2.

There, the comedy's played; now for the tragedy. It's getting late; what task before tomorrow. An empire's standing; before daylight, it's necessary that its head be bowed, that its limbs be splayed in accordance with my whim, one arm eastwards, another westwards, its heart in the sea. Let's go, beautiful angel, it's time. Spread your great black wings beneath your mantle. Put on your court clothes, your silken slippers, your long dress; your monogram embroidered on your sash would be very useful. Your blazon is indispensable too. There are grandeurs, you see, kings and kingdoms, that it's necessary to dissect with dignity.

3.

My faithful wings are bearing me away…good…cities are trembling beneath my flight. Poor little ones, my shadow passing over is heavier than your walls, isn't it? One more wing-beat, and I'll be above the clouds. From here, believe me, the view is divine. The Ocean is like a whitening sea-shell, the land like a set of knucklebones. But the veritable viewpoint is higher still: the black sky, the horror of the void and a single drop of water, evaporating.

4.

At this distance, there's joy in hearing the silence of the heavenly bodies. At closer range, the harmony of the spheres gets on my nerves. It's more pleasing to listen to the lyre of infinity when its three strings are broken. Thought rises to the secret of the skies. Everything is counted by weight and measure. Everywhere, however, emptiness is superabundant. Zero is the sacred number. Everything rests on that. Its form is mysterious. It has neither beginning nor end. It grips without grasping. Without being, it appears; and the sphere of the worlds is a great zero that traces its emptiness in empty space.

5.

To makes something out of nothing is difficult, but everything comes from nothing; therein lies the true problem. From a memory take a shadow, from a shadow a thought, from a thought a dream, from a dream less than nothing, and in a nothing of which one is unaware, there lies life. Except that, thinking about it, the head splits. At that depth, ideas are clouded. Your reasoning turns to ashes, and I too would lose heart, if, fortunately, a false relic didn't fill the place very well.

XIII.

RACHEL, *singing*
Don't weep, God of the earth
If many siroccos
And many hurricanes
Whistle at you in anger.

BERTHE, *Rachel's friend*
Where did you learn that song, Rachel? No one here knows it but you.

RACHEL
I've always known it, and I don't recall where I learned it; from time to time, a few words of it come back to me, and I search for the others, but I can't find them.

BERTHE
Yet another thing. So tell me, Rachel, has your fiancé asked for a lock of your hair?

RACHEL
Oh! Yes.

BERTHE
And have you given it to him?

RACHEL
A long time ago.

BERTHE
Then I'll cut one too, for Albert—a long tress—and I'll give him one with three strands, for I love him with all my heart, and would certainly give my life for him; but I wouldn't want to act differently than everyone else.

RACHEL
That's what you've always told me.

BERTHE
If you wanted, we could get married on the same day; yesterday, Albert was appointed professor of gymnastics. We've been waiting for that moment for five years, without expecting that it would ever arrive.

RACHEL
So you have nothing more to desire.

BERTHE
No, nothing in the world. If you knew how everything pleases me in our house, because of him, and how I find him in everything! On the roof, a stork has built its nest around the chimney, and that brings happiness. I'm attached to the little garden, and the roses he's planted there, as much as to living things. All of his old furniture seems to have something to tell me about him; when I'm alone, I talk to them about him, without saying anything. You know the beautiful engraving of Strasbourg Cathedral that he gave me; I've nailed it to the wall facing my sewing table; every time I look up, that's what I see. My crucifix is on the other side, and my room now resembles a little chapel where my life is spent thinking about God and him. Below my window there's a honeysuckle cradle in the form of a heart. My heart never goes far anymore; without getting up, I can see my entire universe through the window.

RACHEL
You deserve that happiness.

BERTHE
Oh, it's so easy to be happy, Rachel. If you only knew! Going out of the city together, across the bridge, on a sum-

mer's day, gazing at one another in the waters of the Rhine; collecting wild roses from the hedgerow, and then making garlands of them to hang on the bedroom wall; singing while sewing; listening to the organ in church and, in the evening, the watchman's trumpet; spending entire hours without saying anything; seeing a swallow building its nest by your window; preparing everything in the house when a neighbor visits you; watching over everything there, doing every day what one did the day before: that's happiness, and you could have it if you wanted to.

RACHEL
We don't ask for anything more for ourselves.

BERTHE
When you spend so long together, you and your fiancé, what do you talk about?

RACHEL
He tells me about his travels. He tells me the names of islands he has visited, how sad his heart was there; the shores of lakes, forests, heaths, battles, storms at sea, nights in the desert. I hang on his words, as on enchanted wings; when he's finished, it seems to me that the music of the angels has fallen silent; I can't help weeping, and he wipes away my tears.

BERTHE
His sentiments seem very honest, and he only has good intentions, I believe; it's astonishing, however, that he hasn't talked about marrying you.

RACHEL
Since the day when he met me with you, I've known that nothing in the world can ever separate us. We're more necessary to one another than the air we breathe. As soon as my eyes no longer behold him, I suffer, my heart becomes heavy, my head empty.

BERTHE

He ought, however, to act other than he does; a thousand rumors are running around the town on his account; he does nothing to deny them. That compromises him; if I were to believe Albert, I ought no longer to be going out in the street with you or him.

RACHEL

My dear Berthe, don't avoid me completely. What was I without him, before him? Tell me. I looked at the sky without love, and the earth without desire. On hearing the sound of bells, I dreamed that I had fallen from I don't know what abode, which I regretted without knowing it. When I passed by a stream, its water said to me: "Can you see, Rachel? I'm flowing, I'm flowing toward a land of love to which you shall never return." If I raised my eyes, I always found a cloud that whispered to me: "Can you see, Rachel? I'm flying, I'm flying in the sky, higher than you'll ever rise again." If I went into a church, I forgot my prayers at the door. On the edge of my lips I murmured empty words, and my head became exhausted searching for names I could no longer find. Now, on the contrary, I pray with delight for him; there are moments, when the organ is playing, when it's heaven that surrounds me.

BERTHE

You see? What I don't like about him is that one never sees him in church. He's reputed to be a great heretic.

RACHEL

But I've seen him hide his eyes in his hands and sob on the day when, by chance, we were walking toward the large crucifix at the entrance to the city. His pain was so great that he was obliged to lean on me, and he didn't say another word to me that evening.

BERTHE

Also consider that his status is above yours. Often, these sons of princes amuse themselves with us, with fine words that make us cry; they're playing, but for us it's death.

RACHEL

He's not playing, be sure of that. If you heard how he can put his entire life into a single sentence...my God! It seems to me that I've always known him; it's so easy to distinguish the voices of a person who loves us and one who's deceiving us. No, he's not playing. When he's with me, it seems that he, who has seen so much, only has eyes for me, in the entire world. An infant could not be more submissive, nor easier to please.

BERTHE

What an inconceivable man! Certainly, I believe that he loves you, but his love doesn't resemble anyone else's. When he speaks, there's as much pain as joy in what he says. He's too ardent, too violent and too passionate for everyday life. He doesn't say anything or do anything like other people. There! I'm afraid that he won't make you happy, and I can't see anything good in your future.

XIV.

Rachel's Room

AHASUERUS
Yes, my angel, my heaven is in this room. I don't ask for any other.

RACHEL
Call me all the names you wish, but don't call me your angel.

AHASUERUS
Everything to be seen here does me good. Everything in this humble retreat is enchanted to me. It's here that I'd like to spend thousands of years. How many times you've sighed at that window in the evening! How many times, beneath these curtains as transparent as your soul, you've dreamed by night! There's the lamp that illuminates your footsteps when you shelter its light from the wind with your hand. There's your mandolin, which I heard before knowing the sound of your voice, while walking in the street. The acacia planted opposite has cast its flowers on the floor, and a perfume of spring is breathable in everything here. One might think that voices of enchantment were resonating in the air, and that the radiance of the stars might come in trembling with love to ask whether you're awake.

RACHEL
There's no other enchantment here than your voice, when you speak.

AHASUERUS
Leave your tresses unbound, falling over your shoulders, my love, as it was when I came in. Into every curl, all the way

to the ground, I have put a thought of my heart, a year of my life. It's my soul that evaporates when you shake their perfume over your feet.

RACHEL
Often, before you, they served to wipe away my tears.

AHASUERUS
Now they envelop you like two wings closing.

RACHEL
My God, how good we are together, are we not? A single hour spent like this can cause all ills to be forgotten. I desire nothing else in the world. Do you?

AHASUERUS
Nor me, since your shadow refreshes my brow. My eyes are drowning in yours. All is silence, all is happiness. I should like to adore you here, without taking a single step, throughout eternity.

RACHEL
In the early days, I had a scruple about loving you as much as God. I've suffered from that combat for a long time. I wanted no longer to find any one in my heart but you, in church, here, everywhere. A thousand voices cried out to me during the day: You'll doom yourself. Now, however, by contrast, I'm sure that my love is holy and that it has the blessing of heaven.

AHASUERUS
Don't worry, dear heart. The true heaven is in you; it's in your eyes, when they smile; it's in your name, when you pronounce it. Above your head, there's only the cloud that leans over; there's only the abyss that opens its blue-tinted eyelid to look at you; there's only the eternal Void that listens to you, in order to repeat indefinitely the words that it has heard from

your mouth. You are everything, and everything that is not you is nothing. It's from your lips that the wild roses have taken their perfume. It's for you that the evening star rises. On a single thought palpitating in your bosom, the entire universe is suspended.

RACHEL
Once before, Joseph, you said the same thing to me, and I thought it impious. Today, I can see that it was me who didn't understand well enough. Fundamentally, you have more religion than me, and you have a much greater idea of love.

AHASUERUS
You'll see that your other doubts will also dissipate with time.

RACHEL
There's one thing to which I'll never become accustomed, and that's the thought of your death.

AHASUERUS
Chase away that idea, my darling.

RACHEL
To die with you, here, at the same moment, I can understand—but for you to die alone, oh, who could imagine that?

AHASUERUS
If you cease to love me, that will be death, from that moment on; until then, in one of your glances, there will always be an eternity of life for me.

RACHEL
That idea comes back to me incessantly, tormenting me; tell me, at least, do you not believe that you will be resuscitated, and that we'll live together forever in paradise?

AHASUERUS

Who can swear, dear heart, that death won't chill his bosom after a thousand years, and that he won't wipe the soil from his eyes only to see, beside him, the image that he adored? Who can swear that, so long a dream won't numb his tongue, and that phantoms won't amuse themselves in the tomb, after the moment of awakening? Life, death, oblivion, who knows the difference? And without the beating of our hearts, who can reply to the universe when it asks, breathlessly: "What time is it?" Yesterday, without you, there was death; today there's life; in one breath of your bosom, centuries of centuries respire; in one tear from your eyes, in one sigh from your lips, in one incomplete word, in the footprints that the wind has raised, there is all of immortality. To feel anything other than you, not to desire you, not to attain you, not to see you coming, not to dream about you now and forever, not to think about you, not to live for you, that's the horrible inferno full of burning vipers. Paradise is you, it's the road where you have walked, the flower that you have touched, the blush that passes over your cheeks; it's here, where you are.

RACHEL

Certainly, I'm happy with you, when I listen to you; but paradise must be something more perfect. There, I shall understand you in all things; here, it often happens that I don't think like you; that troubles me, and my head spins.

AHASUERUS

Don't stop at the words; always see into the depths of my heart, which speaks to you.

RACHEL

I'm only afraid of one thing; that's that you don't love me sufficiently because of my soul.

AHASUERUS

Isn't your soul, Rachel, you, in everything you are? Woe to the day when I could say: This is her, and these are her ashes. Do you think that there's no invisible spirit in your hair, which makes it glisten in the sunlight? Do you believe that there isn't one that is leaning toward your eyelid, at this very moment, to stop your tears in your lashes? Do you think that there is no divine breath that makes your lips tremble and bows your head beneath a burden of love? Do even you know whether you're anything but a spirit for which my spirit is thirsty, a shadow to refresh a shadow, a thought to swallow my thought in a void punctuated by perfumes and sighs?

RACHEL

My God, my ears are ringing; my head is aching; everything around me is spinning…it seems to me, when you speak to me, that the crucifix around my neck is weeping. Look at it—is that blood?

AHASUERUS
No, no.

RACHEL
Yes, it's blood; I can see it...

AHASUERUS
It's a tear fallen from your eye. Let me wipe it away.

RACHEL
Mercy! The more you wipe, the larger the stain becomes!

AHASUERUS
Indeed? My kisses will erase it completely.

RACHEL

Your kisses are as bitter as absinthe. Oh, angels of heaven, the stain is spreading beneath his lips. Leave it!

AHASUERUS
My breath will drink it.

RACHEL
No. Your breath is a flame that tarnishes it further. Lord in Heaven, have pity on me!

AHASUERUS
Christ! Christ! I recognize you there. Yes, it's you; what do you want with me? You've pursued me all the way to the heart that beats for me. You're challenging me, aren't you? You're laughing at me from my own beard; you're over-whelming me, crushing me, amusing yourself, great Master, with this long dream that you call my life—you, a dream if ever there was one, a dream become a god for a world of dreams. Well, to entertain you better, come and see my happiness at closer range; be jealous of it and die again. Tears, delirious despair, desire, envenomed delights, palpitating anguish, doubt and remorse, drowned in a tear, adulterer of earth and heaven, how much life, how much death, how much everything you drag with her, with me, in my joy of the damned!

RACHEL
What are you saying? My knees are trembling. I can't bear it any more. Open the window, that I might breathe.

AHASUERUS
Christ, it's you who willed it.

RACHEL
I'm at your feet; I'm embracing your knees. Have pity on me.

AHASUERUS
And him—does he have pity?

RACHEL
Christ! Help me, Christ!"

AHASUERUS
Don't call upon Christ. All his blood will flow into the ground, before my lips ever quit yours.

XV.

CHORUS OF FAYS

1.

Speak, Sodom and Gomorrah,
Where shall I find now
In the vale before evening,
Bitumen black enough
And soot and sulfur
To reseal your gulf
Before this evening?

2.

Handsome prince of fays
Among the clouds,
Who sits so high to see even higher
Don't you hear the voice,
Which displeases me,
Of Rachel weeping?

(*The chorus draws away.*)

3.

Adieu, world that gets worse every day. Adieu, dew of
the woods, now too impure to bathe our invisible mounts
there. Adieu, women, our rivals, with light bodies, presently
too wasteful of your plaintive hearts, for us to extract our
heavenly beverage from our lips. You've wept too much. Your
beautiful eyes are weary. Your cheeks are paler than the pale
flowers of lilies picked in the Val de Clarençon. Adieu, too,
stars of David and the shepherd, who, without closing your
eyelids forever, half-hidden in your clouds, too curious, have
seen too many sly adulteries. In this great universe, there is no
longer, by omnipotent God, a corner of the Earth where my

chariot would not be muddied to the axles overnight. Shame!
Let us launch a kick before departing.

4.

As we depart, sister Brigitte, do you know what has become of the love that I love? There's the man with the long
gaze, the clear brow, the tilted head, who never—morn or
night—said: "Enough," whose thirst was slaked for a year by a
drop of May rain, whom a kiss from a kind friend might kill.
There's a word spoken on a moonlit evening that one would
like to remember, and then another, and then a third, each
more secret than the last, and better and quieter, and longer,
which make one forget, on listening to them, that the day is
dying and that the distant bell is ringing the *Ave*. When the
dawn has brightened slightly, there's a meadow-daisy that a
queen to be married comes to consult, sighing, in her garden,
about an amorous dream she has had. There's also, if you must
know, a Prince of Thule, handsome, well-built, of great renown, who is courting, on his knees, a fay on her coral sofa, in
an orchard rose.

5.

O for an orchard rose! Oh, Morgande, the earth is too
old. In its thatch, nothing germinates but grains that die. The
eye deceives, the mouth too. To tarnish two lips only requires
one breath. Already, in this ugly universe, the hem of my dress
is soiled. I'd like to wash my memories in a lake of light. Yes,
let's go, and promptly. If, perchance, by lingering too long, we
lost our pure innocence in his place, what would we do? Every
star would point a finger at us: "Look! There's the ill-famed
fay that a gnome, her friend, seduced and abandoned on an
emerald rock in an island of the sea."

6.

In the islands of the sea, women, women with bright faces and fresh complexions, the only honey I regret in your dark
vale, think of me. Oh, it costs me more than a sigh to leave

you! So, I shall no longer braid your hair over your neck, whiter than snow or crystal. I shall no longer rock myself on one of your golden hairs, to amuse myself for a whole day, listening to the wind singing: "How beautiful your mistress is!" At present, your distress is too great for my balm to heal you. Men are too harsh; impure worms that gnaw your heart, once they ask you for a trifle, and afterwards, a breath, and then a whole life; and then, for your wedding, they dress you in a robe of cares. Go! Weep! Weep! One tear that you hide between your fingers will always be more beautiful than the turquoise of rings or ringlets, rarer, more precious and more cherished by heaven than the colossi of dust where the handsome dwarfs strut.

7.

Besides which, in departing, I read this on your white hands: "Everything will be better in the future." From here, standing on my chariot, I can see other, bluer skies that are swarming; in this direction, a new sea that has not yet kissed its sand is waiting for me to betroth it to its shore. There, no boat will ever need a mast in open water, and my breath will inflate the veil of over-anxious desires until it arrives. Regrets will only last an hour, at the most, or two. For queens you shall be, and all your lovers will be kings. Over a bridge made of a single hair your soul will pass lightly, without shaking it; in looking down, leaning over the edge, its last tear will fall, and drown in the great river where every tear arrives.

XVI.

Rachel's Room

RACHEL, *her eyes wild*

Horror, horror! Begone, demon of Hell. You're not him! You're not the man I love; you've taken his face in order to deceive a poor girl. Oh, begone, begone, I implore you. I'll tell him everything; he'll no longer love me—oh, that's certain. But begone, spirit of the dead! Go, spread your black serpent's wings. What do you want with me? I'm not dead, oh no!—only my heart is hurting, and my head too; but I'm still alive. Look!

AHASUERUS

My dear life, don't frighten me any longer. Don't you understand?

RACHEL, *bursting out laughing*

Yes, indeed I understand. Shut the window! Oh, we're happy, aren't we? Very happy, as happy as Berthe. You'll never leave me again, since we're married; never, you hear? We'll never leave this room again. (*After a moment's reflection.*) My God! You counterfeit the voice of Heaven. Once, do you know, I lived in Heaven; but today, Heaven is a long way off, and Hell is close at hand. Your eyes shine, but it's the flame of the damned. Whatever you do, you won't deceive me. His hair curls beneath my fingers, and yours bristles beneath a crown of darkness. You say the same things as him, but his voice was soft and yours resembles the sniggering of spirits in the night. If you're the king of demons, in the name of the Father, the Son and the Holy Spirit, begone!

AHASUERUS

What can I do, if you no longer know me? I've sought Heaven; I've found Hell.

RACHEL

Why do you say Hell? Are we already there? Ah yes, it's here; here where one stifles. And him, my fiancé, where is he? Is he among the living? Is he dead too? Tell me, give me news of him. Is it really true that I shall never see him again?

AHASUERUS

Can't you feel this cold water that I'm pouring over your temples? The evening air is refreshing your breath. Don't you recognize it? If you love me, please, don't parade your wild eyes around you like that; look into mine, again, again.

RACHEL

My feet no longer want to carry me.

AHASUERUS

Try to walk, my love, on your own, as far as me. (*He holds out his arms to her and retreats as she advances.*) One more step, one more step.

RACHEL

Yes, now it's you. Your hand, oh, how hot it is! But who was here just now? Did you see him? Listen, I want to tell you a dream.

XVII

MOB, *opening the door with a burst of laughter.*

She is only dressed in a fold of a cloak, which leaves her skeleton visible.

You, my lord, at this hour, in that angel's room! A marvel! A thousand pardons for disturbing you. It's your own fault if you see me undressed this time.

AHASUERUS

What! It's you: frightful, mocking death that I have sought so long. Insect, dwarf, colossus! Lame, winged, crawling, with mute steps, it's you! Let me see at my ease how you're made.

MOB

Go on! Don't speak too ill of me, at this moment. It's me who gives a meaning to human beings, and who often obliges them to make a minute eternal.

AHASUERUS

What should I call you, then?

MOB

Take your choice. I have many names, from which one can make a litany:

If one speaks of the sky,
My name is the void;
Of the sea, the tempest;
Of the earth, the abyss:
Of trees, I'm the cypress;
Of birds, the vulture;
Of fire, the ashes;
Of the cup, the lees;
Of the church, the crypt:

Of the lance, I'm the point;
Of the sword, the edge;
Of love, the moment of adieu;
Of hope, the smoke
Of desire, the regret;
Of the crown, the thorn
Of the bell, the knell:
Of colors, I'm the black;
Of Arabia, the desert;
Ruins, if one speaks of empire;
If of fruit, I'm the worm;
If of the world, nothingness;
If of kings, the dust;
If of humans, the sigh;
And finally, of all things, I'm the ABSENCE.

AHASUERUS

Why did you not come when I sought you in the old
trunks of forest trees? I've often thought I saw you beckoning
to me with your finger, through the window of a basilica; I
went up to the tower, but found nothing but a blind man,
sounding a knell of agony.

MOB

At that moment, I was in the world. It's there that I find
myself at ease, and have a better understanding with everything that surrounds me. No, there's a moment then, when the
lamps are lit, that nothing can replace: after dinner, in a circle,
everyone in his seat, when the clock chime my hour; when
hands, in clasping one another, become icy; when hearts, in
touching one another, break; when every woman, on her chair,
weaves around her, with her ivory shuttle, despair in silken
thread; and when the nothingness on which I live circulates,
honeyed, in a crystal glass borne by my liveried page. Besides
which, on that occasion, a single memorized tune, a line of
verse learned by heart, and a cloak of sable fur disguises me
marvelously.

AHASUERUS

Another time, it seemed to me that I met you in the morning mist, on a bare mountain-top; you were fighting hand-to-hand with the cross-bearer of Nazareth. His brandished steel blade blazed on your escutcheon, and your strike-weapon fell without restraint upon his aureole. When I came closer I could only see the dew trodden by the feet of two jousters.

MOB

Your senses deceived you again. I never strike more than one blow; and then again, if I remember correctly, I was amusing myself that day by attaching a crown to a king's head and whispering in his ear the sacred liturgy: *Rex in aeternum*.

AHASUERUS

What has been has been. Now take us wherever you wish. Hide us, drag us, bury us in one of your tombs—but seal the stone well over my head, so that I can never emerge therefrom.

MOB

Very good, Master. If you were a snail that the rain finds on the road far from its shelter, or a viper in the undergrowth, or a poor man in the street, I'd be able to drag you off unceremoniously to where you say. But that this moment—can you imagine it?—I honestly have a scruple. This young woman is interested in you. You have the appearance of having been created for one another. Such a union touches me, and I'm certainly not the one who'll break it. All that morality demands is that it ends with marriage, and I'm the one who'll arrange the betrothal.

RACHEL

Her, the betrothal! Oh, flee, flee! All is lost, and for eternity!

MOB

Excitement is making you unjust, my dear. I don't know you with that fake cherubic tone.

RACHEL, *to Ahasuerus*

Come into my arms, that I might cover you with my body. She'll be unable to do anything to harm you.

MOB

Truly, passion embellishes you, Rachel, and that kind of coquetry suits you marvelously. You know, however, that I have very irritable nerves, and you ought to be wary of me.

RACHEL

Oh, don't kill him, Mob, in the name of Heaven, let him live as long as me. If I've offended you, forgive me. Everything you command, I'll do. Tell me, what do you want? Why don't you know what it is to say: "I love you?" You wouldn't want to torture me more than the damned.

MOB, *to Ahasuerus*

The girl has the physiognomy, you know, and I congratulate you on the choice you've made. So much religion and poetry. I can't wait to see you married.

AHASUERUS

Have pity on her; now she's fainted.

MOB

How delightfully that befits her! Her blonde hair, hanging loosely over her pale lips! Admit it, she's almost as beautiful as death, and I can understand your inclination better than anyone.

AHASUERUS

Curse you! Will you let her die?

MOB

I'm very tempted—but fear not; I'll answer for her on my honor.

AHASUERUS
You swear?

MOB
Yes. Here, take this pinch of dust as a pledge.

AHASUERUS
What do you intend to do, then?

MOB
This. I don't doubt that your love is as pure as the day; however, my scruples demand that you and Rachel receive the nuptial blessing as soon as possible; otherwise, I won't sleep tranquil.

AHASUERUS
You mock when you command; but this time, whatever it is, your order isn't hard.

MOB
It's a veritable angel that I'm going to give you, you understand. However, if I have any advice to give you, it's that when she's in your possession and you'll be the law for her, you treat her as a simple slave.

AHASUERUS
You can kill her, but you can't disenchant that utterly celestial being.

MOB
Let me be. For a long time your situation has touched me. It would, in fact, be infinitely regrettable if your name

were to perish, and no offspring remained to collect the advantage that life has given you. Your isolation pained me, and I felt it only too keenly myself—for you see before you a poor widow.

AHASUERUS
Whose widow?

MOB
Oblivion's. You need a companion. Without that, the meaning of your life would be incomplete. In future, all your impressions will be doubled. When you dream of haven, your companion will darn your socks and count her stitches; that's how you'll arrive at the mirror of reality, in which I never tire of looking at my face.

AHASUERUS
Will you be at our wedding?

MOB
Almost always, nowadays, I make arrangements to be between two spouses in their nuptial bed.

AHASUERUS
And when you want to leave?

MOB
I die of impatience. Of all the sacraments of the living, a rational marriage is the one that suits me best.

AHASUERUS
Your power ties my tongue. I no longer feel either joy or dolor.

MOB
We shan't invite anyone, shall we? And yet, there'll be no lack of witnesses.

AHASUERUS
You're dragging me; I'll follow you anywhere.

MOB
Can you hear my horse pawing the ground in the court-yard? Let's go, handsome spouse! It's time for the dance of the dead. Go buckle his saddle. Load your fiancée on to his rump, and hold hard with her to the saddle-bows.

AHASUERUS
I'll obey you, but I can't help shivering.

MOB
That's good. Hold the bridle high and firm; otherwise he'll go to lick the bloody dew of Pharsalia or Roncevaux.

AHASUERUS
I'm ready.

MOB
Just one minute more; I've forgotten my hour-glass. There—let's depart together.

AHASUERUS
Which direction?

MOB
This way.

AHASUERUS
How dark it is!

MOB
That's the shadow of my wings.

RACHEL, *semi-conscious*
Oh, how cold it is!

MOB
That's the cloud that carries me.

RACHEL
Where am I? What's making that noise that woke me up?

MOB
The great bell of Strasbourg.

XVIII.

The organ and bells of Strasbourg Cathedral resound and respond alternately.

THE CATHEDRAL
1.
Can you hear my voice, which rumbles, my voice, which booms? I sleep curled up beneath my stone mantle. Organ with pipes made in the sky, beautiful organ, what do you want with me? Why are you intoxicating me with your cries, like a cup of Rhine wine? My bells and belfries are trembling, my windows quivering, my feet tottering beneath the hail and wind of your songs.

Get up, my stone saints, get up, my colored saints, drowsy in my windows, on your feet! Can you hear? Get up, my granite virgins, sing in your niches while turning your spindles. Get up too, my gryphons, which bear my pillars on your heads, open your mouths. Get up, my serpents, my marble doves, which hang from the branches of my vaults! Get up, my long-haired kings, who are dreaming along my galleries on your caparisoned horses in Vosges rock! Cut, wound, spur their flanks, lacerate their rumps, break your granite scepters on their granite breasts and manes, so that the stone whinnies, so that at length, in the vicinity, the mares of the Vosges will ask their masters in the stable: "Master, master, where are the whinnying stone horses going? Where are the stone cavaliers going, who are mounted at the gallop from the towers to the edge of the clouds?"

Get up, dwarfs, angels, serpentine dragons, salamanders and gorgons incrusted in the pleats of my pillars, inflate your cheeks, open your mouths, shout, sing with your tongues and your voices of porphyry; howl in the arcades of the vault, in the paving-stones, in the tip of the spire, in the dust of the crypt, in the niches of the nave, in the hollows of the bells.

Give me all your songs in the folds of my mantle, as I rise into the sky with my highest tower.

More! More! Oh, I want to rise higher. One more step, one more wall, one more turret, one more corroded shaft that would enlarge me enough for me to hurl their voices with my own voice to the highest cloud of all, on which the Lord is seated!

2.

Who traced, a thousand years ago, on a scroll of parchment, the plan on my indented towers, of my gilded nave? Was it a master from Cologne, or a master from Reims? Who traced in vermilion the plan of my agile columns, my roaring doors? Was it a master from Vienna, or a master from Rouen? No, no. It was the Devil who sold it to the workman for the price of his soul; so rise up, my turret; disheveled, dressed in mourning, slip and slide into the cloud like a soul knocking with its silken wing on the vault of heaven, without being able to open it.

3.

My head, ah, my head has pierced the autumnal cloud. It has pierced the highest of the clouds. Why do the trees not want to rise higher than the ferns? Why do the hawks not want to rise higher than my belt? It is because the hawks' wings are weary; it is because the hawks' eyes are troubled. Already my towers have vertigo. What will they do to come down their steps again?

4.

Look! My little black chapels are lying around me like black heifers at the foot of a mountain. Have no fear, my little chapels. Stone trefoils and vines are growing my valleys; the reaper will not scythe them, the grape-gatherers shall not uproot them from my vineyard. The trunks and branches of fir-trees are sprouting on my summits. The woodcutters shall not fell fire-trees in my forest, shall cut neither trunks nor branches on my hillsides.

5.

Kings and popes are enthroned in my valleys; for castles they have niches chiseled by good workmen. If the falling rain discrowns them drop by drop, after a thousand years, they have above their heads an awning of rock festooned in three days by a fay's needle. The sun's rays salute them as soon as it rises; the hawks build nests on their diadems; the ivy remakes their mantles every autumn. Day and night, for a thousand years, they hold up their scepters over the frosts and massed storms that kneel at their feet.

6.

Listen! Listen! Without lying, I'll tell you my secret, in order not to crumble. Numbers are sacred to me; on their harmony I support myself fearlessly. My two towers and my nave make the number three and the Trinity. My seven chapels, bound to my side, are my seven mysteries that hug my flanks. Oh, how dark and mute and profound their shadow is! My twelve columns in the choir of African stone are my twelve apostles, who help me bear my cross; and I'm a great lapidary figure that Eternity has traced on its wall with its wrinkled hand in order to count its age.

7.

Courage, my saints, my dragons, my virgins incrusted in my pillars! You've replied to me in the dust of the crypt, the niche of the nave, the hollow of the bell. Your voices are magnified, my doors are howling, my towers are resonating like a hurricane; my columns and colonnettes are vibrating like the string of a viol.

8.

The sheer mountains have no voice to reveal their secrets; the rocks have none in their grottoes, nor the forests of

236

fir-trees in their graying crowns. I speak for them; from my summit, I listen night and day to their stray genii, their mute spirits, in order to lend them my voice of brass, and to roll their idle soul in the winter clouds, on my bounding words and my songs with wheels of bronze.

9.

When the young workers with their trowels had climbed up, singing, to the foot of my tower, they said to their master: "Master, will we be finished soon? The work is long, and life is short."

The master made no reply.

When the young workers, who had become men, had reached the window of my tower, they said to the master: "Master, will we be finished soon? Look, our hair is turning white, our hands are too old, we are going to die tomorrow."

The master replied: "Tomorrow your sons will come, and then your grandsons after them, in a hundred years, with brand new trowels; and then your descendants; and no one, master or worker, will ever see the tower close beneath the sky, nor its last stone. That's God's secret."

10.

In the folds of my robe I draw eternal peoples; in my belt I knot chiseled centuries around my waist, to make myself more beautiful. For a thousand years, I sought in the city a place to sit down. Who knows, who knows where in the city is the busiest crossroads at all hours, in order that I might see from my windows where the kings, peoples, years, empires and generations of debauchees, monks, thieves and dyers who pass days and night over my paving stones, without ever re- turning, are going with their muddy feet, as the she-wolf hud- dles with her cubs to watch the snow fall from her fissure in the rock?

11.

Do you know who my master is? Ah, do you know his name? He has reddened my windows with the blood of his tunic. He is the one who attached my nave to the shore of the sky by a rope of stone, like a Galilean boat to the trunk of a fig-tree, in order to sail when it pleases him. Get up, my nave, sail, sail, with your rigging, with your granite mast, over the mist. Sail with your handsome pilot, with your marble sails furled into spindles, high and low, over the sea of the centuries, as far as the city of the angels.

CHRIST, *on one of the cathedral's stained-glass windows*
That's enough, my cathedral.

THE CATHEDRAL
Lord, I'll say no more.

SAINT MARK, *on one of the windows*
And me, Lord, I beg you, let me remove my crystal mantle from my eyes in order to gaze, through my azure eyelids, at the people who are entering the church. It's time for the dance of the dead. All the dead have heard the cathedral's voice. Here they are. They're coming, they're coming for the dance. They're coming with a light tread, noiselessly, along the galleries, noiselessly, into the chapels, noiselessly, behind the rood-screen, like snow falling in flakes in an orchard on Christmas Eve. Can you see them?

They all have their best clothes on; now they're leaning over the balconies like little waterfalls over their rocks. Oh, how sad their expressions are for coming to the dance! When the oak-leaves swirl in the wind in the crossroads of the heather, they don't regret the crowns of the trees, or the hollow of the grotto, more profoundly. My tears are raining down one after another beneath my aureole. But what are they thinking, turning their empty eyes toward the clock?

Now they're hanging with their teeth on the grilles of the choir; they're clinging with their fingernails to the dragons of the pillars; they're huddling in the niches; they're bumping into one another, crushing one another under the vaults, on the steps of the main altar.

Now the doors are shut; the church is full. What are the popes and archbishops doing? They're keeping their miters on their heads; after them come the kings, who are wearing their crowns on their skeletal heads; after the kings, six thousand peers covering the napes of their necks with their cloaks. Look at them! The ranks are tightening to make room for them.

Now they're holding hands. They're forming a great circle in the nave, and they're beginning to sing. What are they going to say? Their feet make no sound on the paving-stones. Their sheathed swords are clashing at their sides. Their unsteady heads are colliding; the cathedral is prancing with them like a boat in a tempest on the sea of Galilee.

CHORUS OF DEAD KINGS

Let's go back into our crypts. Our eyelids are too heavy; our hair is shaking too damp a dust around us; our dangling hands are too cold. O Christ, O Christ, why have your deceived us? O Christ, why have you lied to us? For a thousand years we've been rolling in our crypts, beneath our sculpted stones, seeking the door to your heaven. We've only found the webs that the spiders wove over our heads. Where, then, are the sounds of viols and your angels? We only hear the sharp saw of the worm that eats away our tombs. Where is the bread that ought to nourish us? All we have to drink is the tears that are hollowing out our cheeks. Where is your father's house? Where is his canopy of stars? Is this a dried-up spring that we're excavating with our fingernails? Is this a polished slab that we're striking with our heads, day and night? Where is the flower of your vine, which ought to cure the wound in our hearts? We've found nothing but vipers crawling over our slabs; we've seen nothing but snakes vomiting their venom over our lips. O Christ, why have you deceived us?

239

CHORUS OF WOMEN

O Virgin Mary, why have you deceived us? On waking up, we've searched at our sides for our children, our grandchildren and our beloved, who ought to be smiling at us in the morning, in niches of azure. We've found nothing but brambles, faded mallow and nettles, which are plunging their roots into our heads.

CHORUS OF CHILDREN

Oh, how dark it is in my cradle of stone! Oh, how hard my crib is! Where is my mother to lift me up? Where is my father to rock me? Where are the angels to give me my robe, my beautiful robe of light? Father, mother where are you? I'm frightened, I'm frightened in my cradle of stone.

THE CATHEDRAL, *to the sound of bells and the organ*

Dance, dance, kings and queens, children and women; this is no time to weep. Eternity is laughing at you, like the wind, when it amuses itself through the crossroads with the haymakers' grass that it has heaped up in the clearings.

KING ATTILA

Is this my kingdom? Six feet long for its king to lie down? A curse on my amulets! A curse on the sorcerers' wands! My mare has gone astray in Christ's forest. Look! She's unhorsed her rider beneath her black breast. Tell me, then, my amulets, where the crowned vultures and the gray crows who follow them have gone? Tell me, my beautiful black mare, where my people have gone, who grew beneath the hooves of your ebony feet like the shadows of evening in autumn? The shadows have remained. My brothers have gone. My tent, the color of your coat, is hanging over my head from the branch of the tree of battles by the ring of death. Take me to them in the steppes of the sky, my beautiful black mare. I shall bathe you one day, up to your breathless rump, in the spring from which the stars drink.

KING SIGEFROY[20]

Is this Valhalla? No, this is not Valhalla. Is this the ash-tree of the Aesir, becoming verdant over the world? Is this the charger of the seas whinnying on the waves with the men off war? And that howling voice, is it the raven prophesying on Revil's[21] shoulder? She-wolves harnessed to vipers; magical horns that the oxherd fills to intoxicate the lips of heroes; antlers of stags that distil the rivers drop by drop; runes engraved on the sword-blade, on the oar-blade, on the shield's rim, on the vessel's prow, on the chariot's wheel, on the cloud's tip; all of Revil's stormy sky, how has that changed above my head into vaults of rock? Why do the valkyries have beds of stone? And why have the nebulous Norns put granite girdles around their waists? Woe, woe! The gods are dead; their twilight has arrived. Let us sing the funeral chant.

KING ARTHUS, to his court

No, no, Lancelot, Tristan, Perceval, my honest men, don't say that this is the forest of Broceliande. For more than a hundred years I have been listening, my ear to the ground, for the enchanted horn of Clingsor.[22] For more than a hundred years, I've only heard the chariot of a fay bumping my crown with its axle. Why have we left our cups half full on our round table? If we had stayed in our places, the dwarfs of Brittany would have filled them until the end of the world. But Christ has nothing to give us. He has neither bread, nor wine, nor pantler, nor cupbearer, nor courteous squire. Look! His table is empty and hollow. It can only accommodate one guest at a

---

[20] Probably the Danish King Sigifrid mentioned in the Frankish Annals as having sent an emissary to Charlemagne.

[21] Quinet is obviously using "revil" as an alternative name for Odin, but it appears o be an extremely esoteric substitution.

[22] Clingsor is an evil magician mentioned in some versions of the grail legend as one of Perceval's adversaries.

time. His cup is only ever filled by raindrops sweated by the flag-stones, one by one, every year.

THE EMPEROR CHARLEMAGNE

Lower your voice, Arthus. If you take one step more on my flag-stones with your resonant spurs, my gleaming white beard, my imperial orb, my scarlet doublet, the twelve peers by my side, my heart of an Alpine eagle and my fleurs-de-lis scepter cut from a forest of Roncevaux, will fall into dust on a flap of your royal mantle; and you will say, as you shake the earth from the flap of your tarnished mantle: "Where is Charlemagne, my kinsman? Which way did our emperor go, with neither heralds nor pages, who was holding his orb in his hand just now, like a sleeping falcon?" (*Joining in the dance.*) Christ! Christ! Since you have deceived me, give me back my hundred monasteries hidden in the Ardennes; give me back my gilded bells, baptized in my name, my reliquaries and my chapels, my banners spun by Berthe's[23] wheel, my silver-plated ciboria, and people kneeling all the way from Roncevaux to the Black Forest.

THE CATHEDRAL

In the shady valley that leads to Italy, I know a grotto more hidden than your hundred monasteries; I know a peak in the mountains higher than your belfries; the clouds, in summer, float higher than your banners spun by Berthe's wheel; the dew is fresher on a Linange daisy than in your silver-plated ciboria, and the Ocean waves are bowed down to the earth more deeply than your people extended from Roncevaux to the Black Forest.

CHORUS OF WOMEN
Give us back our sighs and tears!

---

[23] This Berthe is Bertrada of Laon, Charlemagne's mother.

THE CATHEDRAL
The winds also sigh when evening comes; ask the winds for your sighs. The grottoes weep as they distil, drop by drop; ask the grottoes for your tears.

CHORUS OF CHILDREN
Give back to us our crowns of flowers; give back our baskets of roses, which we have thrown into the path of priests at Corpus Christi.

THE CATHEDRAL
There are stone roses on my stem; there are stone garlands around my head. Children, if you wish, discrown my head and take back your roses from my stem.

POPE GREGORY
And me, what shall I do henceforth with my double cross and triple crown? The dead are assembling around me in order that I give each of them the portion of nothingness due to them. Woe! Paradise, Hell and Purgatory were only in my soul; the hilts and blades of the Archangels' swords were only flamboyant in my bosom; there were no infinite heavens but those my genius folded and unfolded itself to shelter its desert... But perhaps the hour will sound when Christ's door will grate on its hinges... No, no! Gregory of Soana,[24] you have waited long enough! Your feet have dried up tramping the flag-stones; your eyes have melted in their orbits gazing at the dust of your crypt; your tongue has worn itself out in your mouth calling "Christ! Christ!" and you hands have remained empty; yes, they are empty still, always empty, as before! Look, look, my good lords; it's the truth: look! let all the dead hide their wounds from me! let all the martyrs put their wounds in shadow! I can't cure any of them. I bring in return a

---

[24] This reference suggests that the particular Pope Gregory referenced here is Gregory VII, formerly Hildebrand of Soana, who was pope from 1073-1085

243

web spun by a spider to those who have given their crowns to Christ; I bring, in the palm of my hand, a pinch of ashes to those who were expecting a kingdom of stars in the ocean of the firmament.

CHORUS OF ALL THE DEAD KINGS
Woe! Woe! What will become of us?

THE CATHEDRAL
Ha! What would all of you do with an eternal kingdom if I were to give you one? Believe me, your arms are too thin, your hands too cold, to bear once again a scepter, an orb or a crown. Two or three days of life, standing in the sun, have dried out the marrow in your bones. What would you say if it were necessary to bear upon your head, like me, summer and winter, beneath snow and rain, without flinching, a diadem of rock? Come on! When the clock has chimed beneath my arcades, the tremulous hour did not say to Eternity: "Stop me on the rim of the bell; I want to last, I want to vibrate forever!" And me, I am Eternity visible on earth. You are the errant hour that has put on its resounding mantle in the world, on the run. Now, let me enjoy with you, if you please, my crowned hours, oh, so fragile!—is it possible?—oh, so capricious! oh, so noisy! Come on! amuse me, cheer me up, smooth my brow. My beautiful reddened hours! Sound a carillon, make your papal miters, your archbishops' crosiers, your kings' scepters, your nodding heads, your dangling hands, your captains' swords, your hermits' chaplets, your cavaliers' spurs, your blazons, your names and your crowns vibrate in the air, one against another, like a bell-ringer marking my day! I'm sad; you're my playthings; dance and dance, kings and queens, children and women, until dawn!

244

XIX.

Three raps are heard at the cathedral door.

THE CATHEDRAL
Who's knocking at the door?

MOB
An old acquaintance. Open up.

THE CATHEDRAL
Your name?

MOB
Mob.

(*The doors of the cathedral open, turning on their hinges of their own accord.*

Mob enters, giving her arm to Ahasuerus and her hand to Rachel.)

CHORUS OF THE DEAD
Behold our queen! Salutations to our queen! Let us bow down, if we can, to the ground, and strew our ashes beneath her feet with our own hands. Her horse is slaking its thirst under the porch from the baptismal font of porphyry. She is laughing sardonically while leaning on the arms of hr two companions. She has attached a new bouquet of scabious to her robe. But never has her horse been so pale beneath the porch; never has her own face been so white; never have the soles of her feet clicked so loudly on the flag-stones. How is the fête going to end?

MOB, *to Ahasuerus*

We've arrived a little belatedly, as you can see. The company is brilliant and numerous. Let's mingle with the crowd, my handsome lord, and return the salutes of those who salute us. Come on, Rachel, my arm is weary of dragging you. (*She advances toward a circle of the dead.*) Bonjour, Queen Berthe! Bonjour, Yseult the Blonde, my beautiful queen of love! My God, what's happened to you since the day when I attached your crown to your head? Wrap yourself up in your incarnadine Spanish mantlet, my dear! If your Cornish lover could see you now! What have you done with the golden tresses smoothed over your temples, which went so well with your long gaze, your rosy complexion, your bracelets and gauntlets? Go and see whether you haven't left them in the bottom of your cassolette at vespers...

Your servant, my Holy Father the Pope. Your sanctity recognizes me, I hope. I'm the one who carried the golden miter, with my herald's sash, limping, on the stairs of the conclave. If your papal head isn't too unsteady, come and open the dance with me; your indulgences don't dispense you of that. I'll whistle my old tune between my teeth, which I learned from the wind in the crevices of your Italian towers...

You too, my noble King Robert![25] So naked, so white with age so bearded! Who cut your hazel-wood scepter in the Black Forest, if not me? Who carved the throne of quince-wood in your court, with the blade of her ax, if not me? Now the hazel-tree has been pruned, the quince-trees has shaken off its nightingales' nests. Reign, my noble vassal, eyes hollow, head empty, in my nameless barony, devoid of banner and drawbridge, which I have enfeoffed to you eternally.

But if you love me, my lords, don't bump into the pommel of my cavalier's sword, I beg you. Just think—what if you were to fall into dust? How would I be able to say, while

---

[25] Surely Robert II, nicknamed *le Pieux* [the Pious] or *le Sage* [the Wise], King of the Franks from 996-1031, rather than Robert I, king of West Francia from 922-3.

throwing a handful of your dust into the face of the Lord, without mistaking either the century of the climate: "Lord, this powder in my hand is the army of Attila, or Alexander the Great; this is thirty centuries of kings of Syria and Chaldea; this is Rome, with its emperors and popes; this is a thousand years of the real of Brittany, with its peers, with its squires, who tarnish as they fall the golden clasps of your shoes, as one of your footsteps does when you walk out of the gate of your eternal city."

AHASUERUS
Oh, my good lords, tell me, for pity's sake, whether one of you has heard Christ passing over your paving-stones with his cross.

CHORUS OF THE DEAD
No, no, we haven't heard him.

AHASUERUS
Tell me, oh, honestly, whether you have seen Jesus of Nazareth, with eyes ablaze, through the spiders' webs that veil your eyelids.

CHORUS OF THE DEAD
No, no, we haven't seen him.

AHASUERUS
Tell me, my good lords, I beg you, whether he has asked you where a traveler from the Holy Land has passed by.

CHORUS OF THE DEAD
No, no, he hasn't asked us anything; we're the ones who've sought him without finding him. Don't you know him? There is no Christ, nor Jesus of Nazareth. Go on, go away, if you please, to mock the living. Neither the cricket nor the worm has announced to us for today the coming of a trav-

eler or a guest from the Holy Land. Our table is full. Go elsewhere, further on, further on, all the way to oblivion.

AHASUERUS

Repeat what you have said, and when you have said it, repeat it again. Have your mouths not opened once to say: "There is no Christ?" Have your tongues not loosened once to say: "There is no Jesus of Nazareth?" Oh, if I lie, my lords, if my ears lie, if my eyes lie, only give me a sign. Am I blaspheming? Forgive me; I'm a poor traveler who has no thought of insulting his hosts.

CHORUS OF THE DEAD

Believe us if you wish; but Christ is not resuscitated; he is no longer with us; once again, passers-by, leave us be; there is no Christ.

AHASUERUS

And no more Hell for me, not so, my lords? No more path of mourning that my feet, like a weaver, ravel and unravel endlessly around his realm. Did you hear, Rachel? Shake away with your breath the centuries amassed on my hair, like the dew from a new almond-branch. My day of celebration has arrived. Let's go, let's attach our iron spurs to our feet. Let's saddle our black horses. Now, I shall be the good messenger, from city to city.

Leaning over my saddle-bow, I shall say to the grass of Arabia: "Withered grass, why have you dried out underfoot? gather your spring foliage around you once again, and your joyful colors;" to the stream of Palestine: "Why have you dried up? bring back the spring to your bed, and your robe of foam to your bank;" to the mountains of Judea and the summit of Golgotha: "Why have you rent yourselves to the rock? why have you sown brambles, hyssop and eternal dolor on your flanks? bring back your vines and gather your grapes on your hills;" to the Orient: "Why have you burned your face under the sun? why have you uprooted your fields? why have you donned a tunic of ashes in your ruins? bathe yourself again in the dew of the first day of the world, and sit down, laughing, at your door, that the sun might gild your hair again. Do you not know the news that my horse brings, when he strikes your threshold so swiftly with his hooves?"

I shall say to Rome, on passing over its roads: "Beauty! Beauty! why do you weep and cry evening and morn? Caesar! Caesar! why do you go down the steps, every year, into your catacombs, like a young woman going into a cellar, bending her head, in search of a cup of foaming wine for her guest? go back up your stairs; go up to your highest window to see the joyous messenger pass by who is no longer thirsty for wine or spring-water."

To the cathedrals, to the churches and chapels of Germany and Brabant, I shall say: "Hola! why are you veiled, from tower to toe, in black lace, crepes of granite and widows' mantles? bring out your virgins' clothes from your trunks, your steeples the color of marble and your gilded turrets; do you not know that you have neither been betrothed nor married, and that you spent your wedding night standing at the crossroads waiting a thousand years for your espousal, in the rain."

To everything that my eyes behold I shall say: "Why are you sad? mown grass, spring rain, falling star, trembling leaf, thick cloud, moaning wind, howling bell, don't you know that there is no Christ? have you not heard? There is no Jesus of Nazareth; there is no Lord of the Last Judgment; no more mourning, he is not dead; no more fear, he is not alive; rejoice in the ear of wheat, the radiance of the stars, the drop of dew, the crown of the tree, as you did in the first day of the world, before having learned his name."

RACHEL
Joseph! Say, if you will, that heaven is here, and I will believe it; say too that these cold stones are the carpet of the light of the firmament, and I will believe it; but don't say that it's necessary to rejoice.

249

AHASUERUS

Come on, my love, leave your Lord there; what use is he to you? Your eyes are bluer than his tunic; our gaze shines brighter than his aureole.

RACHEL

Don't believe the chorus of the dead. Their voices are so cold when they speak; one doesn't know whether they're mocking or complaining. Their hearts aren't beating in their breasts. When they look at you, it seems that nothing about you interests them, and that you're dead, like them. Don't believe them; they're mistaken, I'm sure, and you'll lose your soul. Come, let's go back to Worms; I'll sing my songs that please you the most; I'll wait for you all day by my window; oh, you'll be happy—you'll see!

AHASUERUS

I am now, my love. Let's go wherever you wish; my chain is broken.

RACHEL

Every word from your mouth breaks my heart. What have you done that you should be so afraid of Christ?

AHASUERUS

Nothing, nothing, I swear to you: one of those slight sins that one commits in the morning and has forgotten by nightfall.

RACHEL

Your eyes are burning me. God! What have you done? Tell me.

AHASUERUS

Once again, almost nothing, my child; don't think about it anymore. Where is the man who can say to his life, when it is full: there is not one drop too many in your cup?

RACHEL

Your lips are pale. It seems that they are saying one thing and your heart another. Have you been cursed? Admit it: tell me. I'll embrace your feet.

AHASUERUS

My love, is there a man who hasn't been cursed, at least once, before birth? cursed in his heart, or cursed in his head? cursed on his doorstep or cursed on his bench? cursed in his love, or cursed in his hatred? cursed in his desire or cursed in his regret? Is there a flower on its stem that hasn't been cursed, before blooming, by a passer-by? a bramble by a ram? an oar by the sea? a bridle by a mare? a bank by a river? a star by the sky? Cursed? Is there, tell me, an ear of wheat that hasn't been by the wind? a burrow by an eagle? a path by a traveler? a threshold by the north wind? a roof by the rain? a pebble by a torrent? What does the curse of a pebble in the sand, the threshold, the burrow, the ear of wheat in the field, mean now, since there's no Lord any more to judge? Don't worry about it, any more than they do, my love.

RACHEL

But my God, if there's no Christ, who'll bless us? Who'll marry us? Who'll save us?

MOB, *to Rachel*

Don't worry about that either. The blessing is always facile; heaven makes of it thereafter what it will. We have no lack of bishops or cardinals, and Pope Gregory has already put his triple crown on his head; he's waiting for you at the main altar. Aren't you, my lord?

POPE GREGORY

I am indeed. Have your two fiancés approach. It's you who shall hold the linen stole over them. Now, let them tell me their names.

RACHEL
Rachel.

POPE GREGORY, *to Ahasuerus*
And you?

AHASUERUS
My name? I can't say it. My tongue can't pronounce it.

(*The dead form a great circle around Ahasuerus, holding hands.*)

CHORUS OF THE DEAD
Your name? Your name? So that everyone can see him, let's turn our circle around him, like a water-snake swaying in a meadow spring. Look how pale he is! His head seems bowed down by an invisible weight. What's the matter?

A KING
He's a king who has left his crown in his tent.

A BISHOP
He's a false god who has lost his heaven.

A SOLDIER
He's a good squire whose enchanted shield has been stolen,

THE CATHEDRAL, *to Ahasuerus*
Your name, so that I can hurl it to the passing cloud.

AHASUERUS
I lack the breath to say it.

MOB

What does a name matter to all of you, my lords? You've collected enough of those leaves from my tree; you've trampled enough of them marching through my forests. What would you do with one name more?

POPE GREGORY, *to Ahasuerus*

I consent to that. Only tell me where you come from?

CHORUS OF THE DEAD

Yes, where do you come from? Who are you? He isn't answering, or the windows, shivering, are drowning out his murmur. Once again: who are you? Speak louder, if you speak.

CHRIST, *on one of the stained-glass windows*

He's Ahasuerus, the Wandering Jew; and I'm the Christ, for whom you've searched in your tombs. All night, I've seen you through the windows of my church. Go back under your tombstones until the day of the Last Judgment.

SAINT MARK, *on one of the windows*

Lord, I beg you, don't say another word; your voice has already caused a section of my crystal tunic to fall out of my window. The dead have gone up in smoke like a grain of incense burned by a child in the nave; the cathedral is bounding like a horse under the spur; Ahasuerus has fallen down the steps of the main altar, and the demons carved on the pillars have come down from their columns to tear the young bride with lashes.

THE VOICES OF THE DEAD, *vanishing*

Be accursed, Ahasuerus!

THE CATHEDRAL

Be accursed, Ahasuerus!

RACHEL

Be blessed, Ahasuerus. Have mercy on him, Lord; open your Heaven to him. (*The demons whip her with thongs of flame.*) Are their angels on watch at the gate of Paradise? Angels, angels, open the gate for me; there will also be a place for Ahasuerus, will there not? Oh, how your swords blaze! Oh, how heavy your bolts are! Come on, come on, Ahasuerus; the stars of Paradise are rising on the other side of the threshold.

MOB

Poor fool! It's the dawn beginning to break. Don't be afraid, I'll envelop you with the night of my royal wings. Come on; the door is creaking on its hinges. Let's go. Our horse will trample your Ahasuerus on the paving-stones as it passes by.

THE CATHEDRAL

And you, my colored saints, my virgins in your stone niches, my dragons incrusted in my pillars; come on, shout, sing, howl, in the arcade of the vault, in the stalls of the nave, in the dust of the crypt, in the hollows of the bells; hurl this story loudly, during the night, with my voice, over the spring cloud, over the hawk's wing, over the pine-tree's branch, over the sleeping baron's bed-head, over the crest of the cavalier delayed in the mist, over the watchman's trumpet, over the foam of the Rhine.

INTERLUDE OF THE THIRD DAY

THE CHORUS

1.

Since the sun has been shining upon my head, I've seen more than one church. I've seen San Marco with its five cupolas like the inflated sails of a ship coming back from Palestine, in the port of Venice; I've seen the dome of Cologne emerging from the Rhine like a water-flower that puts forth new foliage every century. I've seen in the land of Andalusia, where the citrus trees grow, cathedrals for my lord like a white linen mantle suspended from a nail in his hostelry. I've seen your nave, little chapel of Brou, like wooden clasp carved by Alpine shepherds for the shepherd of Heaven.

2.

In France, in Germany, and in the lands from which the citrus fruits come, when a church is finished, when the workmen have departed with their wages, the master who has built it hollows out a jasper niche in a corner. From there, he watches over his work night and day; until Eternity, he watches to see what it lacks. And if, by chance, one evening, the March wind, or the hail, or the rain, or the snow, or a passing soldier, or some spirit resuscitated from his tomb, breaks a tile, tarnishes a stain-glass window or brushes a rose-window, he comes down from his place in order to repair, with his stone trowel, the crumbling colonnette or the tottering window.

3.

And you, poet, already your roof is crumbling, your colonnette shaking, the hinges of your door are worn down; and nowhere do I find you beneath the broken arches of your words. More than one section is missing from your work; already the goats are gnawing the clay pillars of your prose as they pass. Your voice has dried up on my lips; I have expended the last wave emerging from your spring on my bank. I have repeated the last line that you taught me. Mouth closed, within an hour, if you do not come, it will be necessary for me to retire from your resonant ruin with the brambles. In its chaos, everything is confused. The cedar grows there without bowing down. Where are you, then, blade of grass?

THE POET
Here I am.

THE CHORUS
In which direction?

THE POET
From the nave of Brou,[26] where Marguerite of Savoy sleeps in her marriage bed on her mattress of fine stone, without ever any longer turning her head toward her husband lying by her side, a path leads into the forest. In the forest, if you go into it, the snakes of my undergrowth will go as far as the crossroads to meet you. The herons will wait for you on the edges of ponds. My wild mares will lift up heir streaming tresses from the marsh to see who is passing by, and the wild boar digging in my field will say from afar: "Let's go; it's our master who is coming." In the distance, nearby, the earth is bare, as worn as a mendicant's mantle, with neither salt nor dew; and at the hour when the sun carries its blond wheatsheaf into the wood of Dombes, on its shoulder, the fever is as cold there in summer as it is in Maremme. Beneath a flowering cherry you will find my roof, which shelters many dolors. On the doorstep my mother is reading Luther's Bible; my sister, whom I love, has gone to pick ripe mulberries from the bushes for her child. My house is small, my bed is hard and often

---

[26] The royal monastery of Brou in Quinet's home town of Bourg-en-Bresse, is a Gothic masterpiece, commissioned by Margaret of Austria, Duchess of Savoy, to house the tomb of her husband Philibert II, Duke of Savoy from 1497-1504.

soaked in tears. There is room at my table for a stray traveler and for a robin prevented by the Christmas frost from gleaning in the clearing.

THE CHORUS
What do you do there?

THE POET
1.
Everywhere, my heart in my bosom pricks me like my horse's spur. Everywhere, I have devoured the dew that I have found on my path. I have drunk more of my tears than the wine of my valley in Burgundy. I have eaten, crumb by crumb, more of the bread of my regrets than the rye of my furrow in Bresse. At this moment, I am coming to draw a drop of water from the well of my heritage to wash the sweat from my soul.

2.
Here my life is a tower that I am building in mystery. I have climbed half way up the steps of my days. I see nothing appear but the shadow of my ruin, which lies in my brambles, the peel rejected from my table-cloth, the accumulated years that cannot follow me, and my spring, which has no more water to knead the mud of tomorrow. A little higher up, shall I see anything else? Well then, let me go back down to my threshold, toward my young years, in order to take them in my arms, like an Alpine goat-kid knocking on the door with its horn, unable to climb the ladder.

THE CHORUS
The sky is not as far away as the door to your life; and dolor, once you have entered it, is a path that goes ever upwards and never down. Drown your pain, like a willow leaf, in eternal poetry, into which all pain flows, and which will give you in return, to put you to sleep, a plaint from its shore.

THE POET

1.

Many times I have opened my mouth to speak, but words failed me. My voice was in my heart; my heart is broken. When a tear, falling on to my bosom, gradually hollowed out a dwelling there, my thoughts, in order better to heal that wound, often went wandering through the world, begging the sea for a little of its water, a star for one of its rays, a vessel emerging from the gulf for a scrap of its sail. I asked the boat for the gold of its wake, the river-bank for the murmur of its grass, the fisherman for a broken thread from his net, the desert for the lake of its burning ands. Oh, what could the Ocean do, what could the star do, what could the grass of the river-bank do, what could the Syrian desert do in this dusk, to fill the abyss and the ennui of my soul?

2.

Instead of making my ears ring with sonorous words any longer, I would rather nourish my thoughts henceforth with the heads of poppies, so that when I wake up, on searching in my bosom, I would not find them anymore. I would rather the cold wind of my path, as it flowed, took them from my lips, where they remained frozen, in the evening, with my breath on the panes of my window. For it's an hour that I hate; and always, winter or summer, my thoughts are standing by my beside, in order to grind the poison of that hour in secret, and mix it with all my days into the crucible of my years.

THE CHORUS

If you can do it without weeping—for your tears, in falling to the ground, would become mud—you must tell me, then, what hour it is that does you harm, and how that came about.

THE POET

1.

I would rather have hidden it forever; and if my strength had not failed me once, no one would ever have heard it from my mouth. To you, however, I shall speak, although the memory weighs me down, and every morning it wakes me up too soon in my bed. It is a word that my mouth does not want to pronounce, that my land never wants to write in my book; it is the one that all things pronounce with a sigh, that queens covet under their awnings, that two souls stammer on seeing one another, that women know how to say, that the palpitating stars write in their summer vigils with their golden ink, and which has broken my heart since the morning of the May day when I read it.

2.

That day, on the road, the one whose honeyed name my mouth is too coarse to pronounce said to me: "Go! Take this flower of May; before it has withered we shall see one another again, tomorrow. But the flower faded, the next day passed, and the one after that; and after that day another night; and our eyes have not seen one another again, from afar or at close range, in the plain or on the mountain. We have made a thousand detours, without ever finding one another; we have climbed a thousand steps without ever encountering one another; we have knocked on a thousand doors, and a stranger had always opened them. Life had separated us and death did likewise. A harsh destiny did not want to give our bones the same earth. We shall turn over eternally in our half-empty, half-empty tombs, each crying: "Is that you?" Eternally we shall search for one another in the place where everything is reborn, without ever recognizing one another.

3.

To distract myself, I have seen more than one sky, more than one spring, more than one city full of people. No sky is as pure as her eyes, no spring as profound as her heart, no city, on a day of festival, as full as the stairway that she climbed every day.

4.

It is seven years since that tear was shed; and, if you want to know, an impure world, for which nothing is sacred, was the cause of it. Never was it able to believe that I adored a thought, as it adores its mud; nor that my eyes, on the hill where the vines ripen, were only seeking an image of the heavens. Well, are you content, world that I do not know? Oh, what have I done to you that you should kill me so quickly? Calumny, black calumny, which grew up around me, where my feet trod; damned lie, which has lived in my shadow, are you content? No tears in my eyes, nor breath in my soul, nor chimera to nourish, nor thought to cradle, not heaven, nor earth, nor me, nor her—I no longer have anything. Nothing! And that word, you have written in your venom everywhere I look.

5.

Poetry, poetry—a fine word that resonates so loudly!— when I search the entire sea of my thoughts, to the depths where its waves roll its pearls, I no longer find anything now but sand and marsh grass. She, she was poetry, at all times, in all places, and her lips without speaking, told tales of heaven when she sought the shepherd's star from her terrace, after dawn, in order to show it to her child; and when she heard her great poplar trembling in her garden and she said: "Here's the dusk;" and along the canal, when she saw the water pause and quiver; and when she opened her door to the odor of vines in April and May; and in her courtyard, when the nightingale sang to her on a currant bush until midnight, to amuse her and its own young; and when, sitting, without saying anything, on her bench, she held my soul in her hand all day like a partly-open book through whose pages one is turning without ever getting to the end.

6.

Oh, the book is finished, and more than one page is missing. The wind has snatched them from her hands one by one and has not returned them. The grass in her garden sees her all the time; it is only me who will not see her again. The bird on her roof can hear her, if it wishes; it is only me who will hear her again. The errant leaf can ask for news at her door; but only death will give it to me. Too great for the world, the world will not know her; her pure secret, the most beautiful on earth, will perish on her lips without anyone ever knowing it— except for the person who cannot say anything about it.

7.

Nonchalant, in the midst of her needlework, her gentle genius rose up, and up, without knowing it, to where the stars do not go. As others, without wearying, night and day, spin cotton or silk on her threshold, she, in her house, making all sorts of things for her task, without wanting to, dropped enough wool and silk of thoughts steeped in tears from the furthest regions of her soul to dress a world. In the city and the fête, at the first breath, her heart, effortlessly, went up to heaven, as a boat with a lateen sail, at the first gust of wind, soundlessly, with neither oarsmen or adieux, quits the coast and the harbor-wall, and the heavy vessels of the port, and the streets of merchants, to go all alone to dream and bathe in the great Ocean. Then, afterwards, she said that the rumor of the earth was not worth a sigh, and that nothing can be said except the end of what a soul would like to say. And I believed in her God; and I remained mute, and I lowered my eyes; and never thought of descending again from that living poem to the shabby work that my regretful hand was making at that time.

8.

It is done. There was no adieu; there will be no point of return. Why write? Why speak? Why remain silent? Why touch words that are no longer anything but needles? What heaven has taught me does not guide my pen and will not bring me back to the place of my fault. All is finished. There is no more poetry here; there is nothing more than the string still vibrating to the bow of calumny.

9.

For whoever looks and passes by, the wound scars; but the worm, to hide itself, crawls further forward every day. Every evening, it says: "One more step," and the fruit of your life falls from your branch, on a beautiful summer's day, just when it was thought to be ripening. That is the cause of my pain, and how I learned how hard it is to shed the tears that you see. I cannot say any more.

THE CHORUS

Involuntarily, your pain causes me to bow my head toward the earth, and draws one of those bitter tears from me. If the one who played her part therein, in the time of cruel sighs, has forgotten it, I shall not ask it of you, nor how that azure flower came to be born of the impure furrow of our days. But your lips have closed too quickly; rather than die alive, like you, I would have wanted to knead my blood and my dolor in a poem; and the stars, on seeing me, and the rumor of the waters, the rumor of people, the rumor of bells, and he changing sky, would all have murmured around me in the evening, to lull my hear, as a woman, in a low voice, sends her child to sleep on the road.

THE POET

1.

Yes, if my pen were a skylark that had never touched the earth, if my ink were gold, if my book were parchment, then, perhaps, without speaking, I would have liked, one again, to write the names of all the things I love, in order to prolong their life until nightfall, Land of Burgundy, which has given me, instead of your wine, my tears to drink beneath your press, I would fill your vat to the brim with grapes from Cyprus and Candia, so well that you would cry in the end: "I have had enough!"

Little town of Charles the Bold, where my sister lives, who cut my bread on the table when I was a child, seated on your two rivers, near Cluny and of which Elvire speaks so highly;[27] you who hide travelers and shepherds in the hollow of your valley, ashamed of seeing yourself so weather-beaten beneath your old postern, instead of your walls and your decrepit tower, I would make you three blue-painted walls, three sculpted towers and three ivory roofs to shelter, with your starlings' nests the memory of my young years. And you, village with neither belfry nor bell, who has banished me, watch, watch night and day without getting drunk on your grapes, over the one you have stolen from me.

Oh, I would have given for her all the mosques of Syria, with their white minarets, their fresh cisterns, all the arched palaces of Venice, with the gondolas moored on their steps, and all the old castles of Germany with their balconies over the Rhine. Even now, if you only told me that you have seen her pass, that she went to the fête, that her mouth was smiling, that you have planted balm in your hedge to soothe her dolor, I would go to seek, in the depths of my thoughts, I another climate, for golden sand for your stream. I would tell, when I passed by, the waves of the bay of Zea, and the lemon-trees of the villa I love, to send their breezes untiringly, each by a different path, to your crossroads.

2.

But to you, land of Germany, I would say with no lie that you have returned my love for you in bile, in black insomnias,

---

[27] The "little town of Charles the Bold" is Charolles, from which Quinet's family originated. The Elvire to which the poet refers is presumably the childhood sweetheart of Alphonse de Lamartine, who hailed from nearby Mâcon, and whom he remembered very fondly in his verses, as lachrymose poets tend to do,

in dolorous days. Do you even remember when I lay by the edge of your road, fainted in my dolor? In the depths of our science, ah, how black the night was then! In your whitened church, how cold it was, alone, on the flag-stones, with no priest and no God! Above all, how harsh your women are, a thousand times harsher than your sky! Their smile is made of winter flowers; why have I tasted its honey? The Danube pauses to gaze at their blonde tresses; a mystery closes their mouths.

Whiter than almond-blossom, timid they are born, timid they die; one thought brought once by the wind, murmurs without dolor in their ear all their life; like a spring in the Black Forest their footsteps undulate languidly, but their overly pale blood scarcely tints their cheeks with a memory. For whoever comes from the land where olives and oranges ripen, their hearts beat too slowly; beneath the sky of passions, it melts in a day like snow; their silence is gently, more gentle than their speech, but its meaning is harsh. Their lips are too cold to heal the wounds that they have made. Their tears remain frozen in their bosoms; and the hearts that they have broken once never heal.

3.

No, I no longer like, in Germany or anywhere else where the mist thickens north of this side of the Alps, the paths beneath the fir-trees that all lead to regret, not the tall linden trees too full of shadows and memories, nor the Gothic ruin that one sees at Linange, too similar to a desire on its slope, nor the long waves of the Rhine, toward Baden, which make me dream too much and sigh like them, nor its vaporous isles, nor those supercilious cathedrals, nor its amber, nor its excessively deep valley, nor its excessively plaintive wave, which says to me as I pass: "Remember me."

4.

At present I like the region near Salerno in Calabria, or even further on, toward old Navarin and Tinos, when the sun that comes from Asia, as soon as it rises, scintillates in my night and cuts my insomnia in half. Evening and morning, I like to drink its myrrh-scented radiance with every breath, for my remedy. It is cold and somber at that hour in my heart. I like to dry the wound that another has given me, also too bitter, in the light of August, when the fishermen of Capri extend their nets on the shore at midday, as I extend my memories; when the lonely seagull in the bay of Lepanto seeks its shadow under its wing, or when the lightning on the Albanian shore say to you: "I want to glisten, and gaze, into the depths of your bosom, at what has caused your pain."

THE CHORUS

Indeed! Tortuous as it is, the path of your poem is better than that of life. There your wound can be its balm; and, without going as far as Albania, the sun that is setting on your hill can aspire the tears in your bosom like dew. Enough love! Enough suffering! Too much hope! Don't expect any longer that your oft-deflected desire can be fulfilled before death, or that you can retain more than one drop of the Ocean in your hand. Ask no more of the universe than two rays of daylight in order to see, and see again, beneath the vaults, the gilded paintings of old Florentine masters, and the narrow path that your thought leaves as it marches. After love, after faith, art is beautiful, art is holy. It isn't Heaven, but it's no longer earth.

THE POET

1.

If you can, I'd like that; bring me back in my mind to the place at which my feet went astray; and I'll follow the example of the man whose feet follow his guide, and whose overly heavy heart remains behind with his burden. As for you, world, in quitting you, I know you; you have broken me, but you haven't vanquished me; it's you who have killed me, but it's me who is scornful of you. So you're mocking, beautiful mask? An hour before death, I've perceived that: an hour, oh, that's enough!

2.

Oh, how my heart is beating me, after having shut me up before speaking! Everything irritates me, everything annoys me; I've finished too soon what I wanted to say.

3.

Oh how my heart is weighing upon me; I don't know how I can finish my task this evening. My ink isn't gold; it's made of tears. My pen isn't a quill from a bird of Heaven; it's ripped from the wing of my dreams. My book isn't parchment; it's the fabric of my soul, yes, my soul and my despair.

4.

Oh how my heart is squeezing me, how my heart is bleeding me; I no longer know anything but that phrase, and I need, in order to finish my book, more than a thousand. Since my bosom is bloody, why am I not a bullfinch? Evening and morning, moaning, in the garden, I always repeat the same phrase on a branch in the currant bush. Since my voice is sobbing, why am I not a stream? Without advancing or retreating, but snaking, all my life I bathe the threshold where my thoughts, too poorly healed, want to remain sitting, night and day.

THE FOURTH DAY

THE LAST JUDGMENT

I.

THE OCEAN, *to Ahasuerus*

Stop on my shore, Ahasuerus, I beg you, until nightfall. Once, hosts of people passed with the noise of their cities over the sand of my shores. On approaching their walls by night, in the mist, I heard their secrets escaping in whispers, waves of love, anger, sighs, priestly hymns and wedding songs, which I allowed to mingle with my waves. Often, I reached as far as their balconies, sad, wearied by my journey, having found nothing in my path but rushes and uprooted seaweed; and I carried back, an hour later, a golden crown, a diamond-encrusted miter or some old ruined empire that a passer-by had thrown to me in handfuls from his triumphal chariot, to amuse me at night in my abyss. Their towers climbed to the summit of my rocks in order to see me from afar; the stair-ways of their places descended into my waves in order to help me climb up when I needed to do so. To court my all-too-amorous waves the merchant ships and flag-bearing frigates leaned over my bed, listening to my breath. Merely to touch me with the tip of wing, they went tirelessly to carry my messages to my howling capes, my gulf and my scattered islands.

The shadow of cities and bell-towers that rolled their humid voices in the depths of my waves served me as shelter beneath vaults of foam. Often, a soul that chanced to gaze at my quivering skies has held me in suspense in order to respire his secret, or his troubles, or his joy, better than a myrtle in my bay of Naples, or an incense tree in my Arabian gulf. I loved those human crowds, those cries, those resonant tongues, the eternal sigh that emerges from the human species like the breath from my nostrils when I arrive at a beach. Tell me, where is it? what is it doing? what has it become, that monster with a thousand feet of marble and granite, which had gilded walls for scales, crenellated towers to march over the sand, cities for teats, and which girded all my shores with peoples and empires, like a giant serpent going to sleep in my sunlight?

AHASUERUS

I'm seeking it, as you are. The flowers in the woods don't remember that it ever existed; the dust of the road hasn't retained the traces of its feet. The meadow daisies have been better able to defend the crowns on their heads than the iron-clad kings. The rushes you have sown have lasted longer on their stems than the bastioned towers that climbed to their summits to call to you from further away.

I've seen the crowd dissipate gradually around me, as on a feast day when evening comes. People sat down on the boundary-markers and searched in the heather for their hearts, which had ceased to beat. Their souls were dead in their bosoms, but they waited, still standing, for a thought, a hope, some name, some forgotten god to come and reanimate the life in their breast.

The children looked into their mothers' eyes, and found them empty, devoid of tears and thoughts, and cried out in terror: "Let me go, Mother, Return me to the unknown virgin who cradled me, before birth, sighing more profoundly than you. Her eyes were softer, her veil was longer, the stories she knew gave me more joy than yours."

The peoples went away too, their eyes empty, searching, groping over the flowers and the stones for a name they could no longer read. If, by chance, they encountered me, I heard them saying, with their hands joined: "Ahasuerus, good Ahasuerus, you whose eyes still see, tell us the name for which we're searching, which we've lost, which would have saved us." But when I replied. "Do you mean Christ?" or "Do you mean his Father?" they laughed and continued: "Christ?

Oh yes, of course, Jesus of Nazareth. He's too old for us. The earth's furrow no longer produces new gods for or hunger. Jehovah, Christ, Mohammed we sowed their ashes in our fields a long time ago. Now we're gleaning nothingness. Our souls have dried up in our breasts, like a cistern that lacks rainwater. How can we obtain the rain of the firmament? The thirst of our hearts can no longer be cured. You, remain after us to sing our funeral hymns. We leave you as a heritage the tears that we still have to shed, and all the bile that we have not drunk."

THE OCEAN
So, day and night, when I implore my shore to send me, from the crossroads, the songs of love that lulled me yesterday, I'd do better to hide myself in my bed. So the kings will no longer throw me their cups full of Cyprus wine, and the Doge of Venice, who was my fiancé, will no longer pass his necklace of pearls around my neck.

AHASUERUS
No. Don't wait any longer. The *Bucentaur* will no longer go forth with her gilded keel to rock in your waves. The bells of Venice will no longer ring for your marriage. The Doge, with his embroidered ermine mantle, will no longer go on to the poop to place the ring of espousal on your finger.

Oh, go your own way now, if you wish; give your sighs to your azure grottoes, your kisses to the sands of the Lido, and your amorous caresses to your sleeping gulfs. Rock in your arms an old derelict boat, fully laden with your mud. Crown, if you wish, with the flowers of your lagoons, the rusty anchor of a galley turning to dust. Wash, like a woman in her laundry, a soiled veil, holed by the tempest, which your breeze now hesitates to touch. Ask, evening and morning, murmuring beneath the balconies of the city, like a poor man begging in the street, for the embalmed serenades for which your waves are avid, your share of the flowers and perfumes of the royal feast, your women's veils, your madonna with her lighted lamps, the banderoles that played in your bosom, and the blessed sword that your fiancé buckled by his side.

Go now to search your shores; you will no longer find anything for your thirst but sand and rushes. You shall no longer rise up on to the flag-stones of the ducal palace for your wedding. You shall only have for lovers the weary star that goes to its repose in the evening, the iron ring suspended from the rock, the broken oar, the tattered mesh of a fragment of a net, the moss of the reef, the grass uprooted from your mud, and my soul, shipwrecked in the ocean of your dolor.

THE OCEAN

If there are no more festival banners for me; if the cities will no longer throw me shadows or incense or songs of love; if the boats I love have all folded their wings under the wind of death, what have I to do henceforth in appealing with my tempestuous voice to the shores that no longer reasons? What have I to do in bounding with my streaming rump, if I no longer have any merchant ship with embroidered robes to carry, nor any frigate with silken veils? If there is no more spouse or fiancé for me, I would rather be an obscure spring, hidden in the forest of Ardennes, known in the universe solely to the bullfinch who comes to its bank to bathe his coral throat in secret.

AHASUERUS

Do you not fear, on the contrary, that your waves will dry up, one after another, in your bed, as the souls of peoples have dried up in their bosom?

THE OCEAN

For some time, truly, the rivers have no longer been descending to my valley; they are sleeping in their lakes, giving no further thought to their work. I have raised my voice in vain; they are amusing themselves on the way on their golden sands. Doubtless they have gone astray in some bushy wood, since the guide who showed them the way every day no longer

270

climbs the stairway of the lighthouse on my promontory with his beacon.

AHASUERUS
Now that your piers are destroyed and your harbors have crumbled, where will you come ashore?

THE OCEAN
Nowhere.

RACHEL, *to the Ocean*
And you too, do you not believe that your master can return all your waves with his urn, when you ask him for them?

THE OCEAN
Yes, when my foam was born with the world, when the grass of my shores brushed my shoulders for the first time, yes, then I believed. Without looking back, I marched to my master and each of my waves called "Lord! Lord!" But you, Rachel, are younger than the youngest of my waves. My grass, which I tore up this morning, has lived more than you; and my white foam is more soiled by the years than your heart in your bosom. If, like me, you had sounded all my abysms; if, like me, you had waited in the hollow of the rock, during the hail and the tempest; if, like me, you had spent your days wearing away the sand of my shores, you would say, like me: "God is dead; let us celebrate his funeral rites."

RACHEL
Be careful that they are not your own.

II.

AHASUERUS, *to Rachel*

Angel who follows me go, return to your abode if you can find it again. The closer the dusk of the world approaches, the more the aguish of my soul increases. When humans lived, I walked with them, in their crowd, in the evening. I knocked on the gates of cities and the guards opened them to me. Now that the cities are closed and the guards can no longer get up to draw the bolts, even the Ocean is going to hide in the hollow of its bed. Have you not seen the spring from which I had drunk dry up beneath my feet, the star on which I had rested my eyes fade, the forest that had lent me its shade wither? Flee, if you don't want to end up like them. Soon, I shall have no other companion in the universe but a single sprig of heather upright on its stem. The earth will be empty around me, but I shall still be marching on my path; even my shadow will leave me; and the last night, the immense night, will come, without my having yet found with my iron-tipped staff a fragment of wall on which to sit down, or a host to lend me his lamp.

RACHEL

Let the flowers die on their stems, if their day is done; let the star fade; let the heather dry up on its rock; I shall always find a mountain spring in order to bring you water to drink, and a path to guide you. Ah, what do the cities and the doors on which we knock matter to me? Human voices were so harsh when we passed by! Their stairways we so sad to climb! Always, when they looked at us, they seemed to be cursing us. I'd rather climb this hard path than climb the steps of their threshold.

AHASUERUS
But their traces are being effaced, and our path is fading away.

RACHEL
Have no fear. Keep walking. The more their traces are effaced, the better I shall be able to recognize in the valleys the footprints of my Lord, with his large sandals, before the cities and the towers and the walls have collapsed.

AHASUERUS
Did you not hear the Ocean? There is no longer anyone but you who believes in your Lord. Do you think you know better than the banks of rivers and the sand of the sea?

RACHEL
The more the Ocean sinks to seek its drop of water, the more the forest is desiccated above my head, the more the star hides away, the more clearly I see his eyes shining in the forest, and his mantle in the firmament.

AHASUERUS
For me the night only gets darker.

RACHEL
Don't you remember when you saw him on the stained-glass window of the cathedral, and he said: "That's Ahasuerus?"

AHASUERUS
How many years have gone by!

RACHEL
They have not made us a day older.

AHASUERUS

Look. That sun going pale, is it not his aureole dimming on his head? That blue sky behind the cloud is it not the remains of his tunic, torn apart by the tempest? That bed which the sea has just quit, is it not his sepulcher, excavated for him in the rock?

RACHEL

Ahasuerus, you who will live forever, don't talk as the dead talk.

AHASUERUS

If I had been born in the first days of the world, when the star as it rose, the spring as it saw the sand of its bed, the flower gazing at the sky for the first time, and the bird shaking its down over the abyss said: "Master, here we are; what have we to do to earn our daily wage?" I too, my soul in my bosom, would have sung with them. I would have sat down to repeat, within myself, the canticles they had commenced. But all that the things my eyes can see, the grotto, the star, the flower on its stem, no longer have a voice, nor a sigh. There is no longer anything but you that prays.

RACHEL

Let me pause to pray once again for you.

AHASUERUS

Yes, pray again. Oh, if I could believe!

1.

Everything dies, everything is effaced. Stars and skies, everything falls apart; islands, capes, distant seas, everything disappears, save for this plaint in my bosom, save for these tears in my eyes, save for this cup upon my lips. The daylight fades. Like a breath of Oblivion, the firmament evaporates. Like migrating teal, the worlds pass rapidly through the mist, and do not return. After them, in their shadow, nothing remains but dolor.

2.

Nameless dolor, voiceless dolor, formless dolor, which infinity exhales as the censer exhales incense, what are you waiting for before you vanish? The last star has shone, the skies are extinct; so extinguish too that glimmer in my heart, and don't forget, this evening, to dissipate the vapor of my thought with a breath.

3.

Agonizing lamp, why must I gleam, alone in the night, by the death-bed of the human race? since it is dead in its bed, and its great eyelid will never reopen to shed a tear, nor its mouth to say "Are you keeping vigil? Anoint my moribund forehead with Christ's oil."

4.

Further on! Let's go! When the world has passed, a bitter drop still remains in its glass; when it has fallen silent, one can still hear quivering in its place a word that calls itself Despair. Its branches have shed its names, its feast-days, its calumnies and its bloody flowers; like dead leaves in November, my feet stir them up. When will it be my turn for my season of November to come?

5.

Further on! Further on! Here, perhaps, I shall be better off. No more road, no more undergrowth; no more deafening water, no more verdant grass; no plain, no valley; no thatch, no heather: it's the crossroads at which everything is lost. Over its door is written: ABSENCE. Hola! Without knocking, enter here as a guest. Neither my dolor nor my soul can follow me there.

6.

Ah, further on! Still further on! Yet further on! Until the end, will eternity amuse itself with you? Beneath its weight the skies have crumbled, and in my bosom a memory remains upstanding, without tottering. The universe has dissipated, and my utterly sickened heart is not yet worn away! The storm has carried away a world; on my lips it has left my soul and my breath, and a name lighter than a leaf.

Everything has withered, everything is empty—save for my chalice, which is still full of lees.

RACHEL
Give it to me; I will drink half.

(*She takes the chalice and drinks.*)

III.

The four evangelists in Heaven;
at their feet, the lion of St. Mark and the eagle of St. John.

SAINT MARK

If I were on the lake of Nazareth now, the two oars attached to my boat wouldn't save me. Look! What a tempest the four winds are amassing on the lake of humankind! Is not the faithless creation coming apart, bit by bit, in the hands of the Creator, and falling into the abyss, as the chaplet of an Armenian priest falls at his feet, bead by bead, on the threshold of a church, when the copper clasp and knot have broken? The rain is even reaching us; it's tarnishing our aureoles. The wind is plunging into my niche and tonight the mist of Oblivion has moistened the panes of my window. For more than a thousand years, I've read my golden book to the end without raising my eyes. Since it's finished and its clasp is shut, take it in your claw, my lion; keep it under my feet, without wearing away the binding, in order that I can look down there, beneath the clouds, where Ahasuerus is passing.

THE LION

Great saint, I beg you, let me return to my land of Nubia. My claws are weary of carrying your book and striking the air with the flat of your sword. The centuries have eaten away my mane. Tel me, what good has it done me to hold your bronze escutcheons, your stone bible, your trophies of victory, your thunderbolts, your clouds and the globe of the world that emperors have given me above my head, day and night, winter and summer? If I had only been able, one day, instead of your treasures, to carry in my claws a little desert sand, or a blade of grass uprooted by the wind, I would have fewer dead leaves now, and a little dust on my road to make my litter.

SAINT MARK

Oh well! Go to the earth, if you wish, for an hour. In three bounds you'll have seen it all. Look at your cave in Palestine and the white bones you heaped up there; come back afterwards and tell us what you've found.

SAINT JOHN

Saint Mark, do you hear my eagle screeching on my shoulder? Its beak has devoured the golden radiance around my head; its wing is shaking the curls of my hair down my back; its thirsty tongue is licking the edge of my cup, which it has emptied. Why are you screeching so loudly on my shoulder, eagle of Christ?

THE EAGLE

Master, I beg you, let me return to the hollows of my ravine on my Syrian mountain. Shall I never see again, with my diamond eye, the sea beating her wings in her aerie, over the brood of waves that she has suspended beneath my crag? Shall I no longer see beneath my yellow-tinted eyelid the sun building his open nest over my head, to make me a fiery prey in my old age? Take the ring off my feet. My eyes are weary of spelling out the future on your parchment scroll; my claws are worn away supporting your soul at the summit of heaven. Find someone other than me to drink the beverage of flame drop by drop from your cup and to tear apart the bloody lamb of Eternity with his talons. Tell me, what good has it done me to war a diadem of emeralds and gold sequins on my head? What good has it done me to grip in my claws the scepters of emperors, the crowns of kings, the miters of popes, the flags of pashas and the necklaces of queens? If I had once pecked at a warbler's nest, the stubble of heather, a white shell on the shore, or verbena on a rock, I would at least have a scrap of bark, an empty shell and a marsh reed now, to make an aerie for my little ones.

SAINT JOHN

Take flight, if you wish, and skim the summit of the earth in passing. Go alight momentarily on the sand of my isle of Patmos; when you have gone twice around the world, come back and tell us what you've seen.

THE LION

Am I late, Master? Here I am, back from the source of the Euphrates.

SAINT MARK

No, What have you found on your journey?

THE LION

I've swept the dust of a hundred cities with my tail. My mane is thoroughly soiled by the ashes of kings and the cobwebs of the tombs of their peoples. I've sniffed harsh noises. When I went by, the flowers in the hedges, the streams in their beds and the summits of the mountains were saying: "No, no, there is no God. Look! The lion of St. Mark has lost his master. His flanks are thin. In all his sky, he has not found what he requires to staunch the thirst of his palate. He has not had a wage for his eternal servitude. What good will it do us to wait, like him, for our master? He will not come to our summits, nor our banks, to see whether our flowers have bloomed in their seasons; whether we are drawing our brimming waves from our urns; whether we are rising up for our hour in the sun; and whether we are keeping alight, for his arrival, the heaths of our volcanoes. That's enough perfumes lavished in their air; that's enough waves on our banks; that's enough rays shed from our clouds. Let's rest, without doing any more, since our master isn't coming to inspect our work."

Great saint, that's what they were saying, I swear; and the more their faith has flowed away from their hearts, the more their steps are lacking in life. I've seen rivers that, doubting whether the valley still awaits them to take them to their lake, are stopping on the way and drying up their waves; I've seen seas that, no longer knowing what name to pronounce on the night breezes, are hollowing out a mortal silence within themselves, and dispersing their waves in secret; I've seen beautiful vagabond stars that, doubting tomorrow, are stopping in the night and drowning themselves in the Ocean; I've seen great deserts shaking their sandy manes around them over the world, weary of waiting, crouching down at the doors of temples, which the temples have opened.

The flowers no longer believe in the dawn, and the faded flowers no longer lift themselves up to drink the dew; the shadows no longer believe in bodies, nor the waves in their source, nor the wine in its cup, nor the bench in its threshold, nor the boat in its oar, nor the valley in its ridge, nor the universe in its Lord. The young forests, which doubt their sap, wrinkled their lianas over my forehead; and the earth, at hazard, rolled beneath my claw, empty, without any more concern for its route, like the brass ball that the kings gave me, with which to amuse myself, on their gold-langued escutcheons.

SAINT MATTHEW
Did you still find my land of Galilee and its fig trees?

SAINT LUKE
And my olive garden, to which I went down every morning to pray?

THE LION
I no longer recognized the roads of Judea. All the cities were deserted. The evening wind was tearing their gates from their hinges, and I heard them singing: "Since our inhabitants are no longer holding celebrations, what good are our heavy walls to us? Since God is dead in the heavens, and the saints have attended his funeral, what good are our bells and basilicas, and the naves above our heads? Since neither kings nor lovers are any longer to be seen passing through our streets, let us throw down our balconies and terraces." With every word they sang, a stone fell.

Laughing, the cities of the Orient were sitting down on the damp earth. On a muddy wave I saw Venice pass by in its black gondola, half-submerged; it was no longer the Venice that gave me its flag to carry while descending the stairway of its ducal palace. It was Venice dead on its silken cushion, which a gondolier was talking to Jehosophat through the tempest. Unmuzzled cattle were grazing on the tomb of Rome, and wild horses were digging the earth with their hooves. "Hola! Where are you, our riders? Come and comb our long hair, which is falling over our foreheads as the rushes of the Tiber marshes accumulate on the waves that snatch them from the shores."

But what hurt me the most was this: Outside the walls, on the road that leads to Maremme, the great church of St. Paul was broken. Here and there, its columns were lying, having taken their stumps for bed-heads, no longer able to get up. Serpents of masonry, grass-snakes and vipers, came to lick the ciboria and carry away the white host in their fangs, for their offspring. In the enclosure of the monastery, a single brother was kneeling, in tears. It was the Christ-Giant, counting the blades of grass on the altar. Day and night, two tears streamed from his great eyes on to the stone slab, which they were wearing away. Bent double in order to sustain the crumbling nave on his shoulder, heavier than his cross, he was sighing: "I can do no more." In consequence, my mane turned white on my back, and my tongue, with its darts, roared more loudly than in the desert: "Master, let it fall; I will lick your wounds."

Italy was seated like Sodom on its shore. The waves of its volcano were an army roaring as it rose to attack its battlements—and finding no one, they sought their path through the ventilation-shafts, though the crossroads, through the marble ramps; they lay down in its bed, still warm, and murmured at its gate: "Ah, my gulf, take me in your abyss. My grotto, hide me in your hollow in the rocks of Pausilippo. My Ischian boat, bring me in your sail a sigh from my islands, to refresh my bosom, devoured by the bitumen of heaven.

Master, I have also traversed the salty sea, without mois-
tening my claws; beneath the algae that embrace it, I found
Albion with my talons, collapsed on its side like an old trireme
abandoned by its pilot. In the lands whose thirst the Rhine
slakes, and which the Danube, weary of eating away its fields
of hops, leaves behind its waves to go and ask the Bosphorus
for its share of sun and sand, the cathedrals were howling:
"Martin Luther of Wittenburg, what have you done? Why
have you prevented us from raising out towers to the firmament? Now we could rise without fear, making mock of our
ruins."

Further on, where the sobbing Seine retraces its steps and
makes more than one detour to search its mud for the city it
watered and which still kept it company yesterday, the bank
was weeping, and the waves said, lamenting to the sea, further
away than it could see: "Sea, return to me, to help me save
myself, what remains of my emperor of Saint-Helena." In the
same place, a people had decapitated a king, the son of an ancient race. That giant torso, which still lay without a sepulcher,
was still on his knees, searching for his head and moaning.
Scarcely had those around him, who were weeping, given him
another, than he dropped it at his feet, like a burden that a man
can no longer carry. Three times that happened; three times
the head fell; three times the old torso demanded a royal head
with which to crown his wound, which was bleeding on his
shoulders. That sight was hard to bear, and it drew a lion's
tears from my eyes.

SAINT MARK
Did you find nothing but that in honored France?

THE LION
I stirred the sand of the abyss; I swept the beach. France
has left no gold, nor vases, nor precious bracelets, nor beautiful ear-rings, nor painted mosaics, nor marble stairways. I
found nothing of her but this oak-branch trampled in combats,
this beak of a bronze eagle, and this stainless sword-hilt,

which I have brought you to keep with your escutcheon. Everywhere around, in the heather of the human race, as when hounds run over hills when the horn sounds, mouths agape, following the wild boar into the thicket, one falls silent and listens, the other sniffs the undergrowth and bays, and the pack follows, with the hunter behind, bent over his horse, and after him, silence falls again, thus a pack of empires that Oblivion leads on a leash goes by thousands upon thousands of paths, ears pricked, heads bowed, seeking their God, who flees further on, and, always losing the track, one searches the abyss, another passes by, and then looks, becomes vexed, turns back, uttering a cry that makes the earth tremble; and they all resume the quest, each wanting to howl in turn, and to devour before nightfall his share of a shadow.

SAINT MARK
Tell me what passers-by you encountered after the Holy Land.

THE LION
When I came back, all the empires were finished, all the cities were deserted. I only encountered Time, who was descending to the shore to fill his hour-glass with the ashes of the dead, and Mob, on her pale horse, who was asking the heather whether any blade of living grass still remained. I only heard Ahasuerus, who was sighing when I passed by, and drinking his tears from the palm of his hand.

SAINT MARK
That's enough. Go back now, if you wish, to your Nubian homeland.

THE LION
Master, what would I do now in Nubia or in Palestine? The paths have been effaced. No travelers pass in the night. Let me lie here at your feet forever. Better than the empty sky that hangs over my head, I like my golden-sequined awning.

Better than that immense sea, which no longer has any pilot and murmurs without God, I like the hem of your blessed cloak. Better than the sun that is going out in the vault of humankind, I like your oil-filled lamp. Better that that desolate soul dragging himself along on my road, I like the shred of my banner and your worm-eaten niche. Better that the sobbing of the universe, which is audible from here, I like your bronze escutcheon, your stone bible, your thunderbolts, your clouds, and the globe of the world that the emperors have given me.

SAINT MARK
Now, St. John, here comes your eagle.

SAINT JOHN, *to the eagle*
Where have you come from?

THE EAGLE
From the summit of Golgotha.

SAINT JOHN
Why so late?

THE EAGLE
The birds of Oblivion, which, from the rim of their nests, are falling with their vultures' necks upon the cadaver of the world, blocked my passage. The earth was like the aerie of an eagle of Taurus when a man has taken away its eaglets to amuse his children. The shadow of my wings bloodied the summits over which I passed. Already, the resuscitated dead were sprouting everywhere through the grass. The kings, like ears or wheat, were piercing the grassy turf over their tombs as they rose with the points of their crowns. Their beards were falling to their feet and winding seven times around their stone tables. They were singing, fearlessly: "We have germinated during the winter of our furrow. Now our summer will commence. We have found, in seeing the light, our diadems blooming on our heads and our scepters verdant on our stems.

We have only to await the morning dew to drink our happiness from the cups of our spring."

By the roadsides, the peoples were raising themselves up, supporting their heads on their elbows. The tears they were weeping are flowing from the hollows of their eyes down their shrouds to the ground. They were extending their worm-eaten mantles over their skeletal feet. Their hair had continued to grow in their tombs, partly covering them. When I passed by, their tongues, swollen by the sand, stammered: "If I had the brazen wings of that passing eagle, if I had his claws and his diamond beak, I would quit the glebe of my field forever and carry away the wicker door of my hut. I would fly to the summit of heaven, in order no longer to see the harsh furrow in which I have mingled my sweat with the water from my pitcher. But my arms are weary; I already have difficulty stretching out my hand on the Lord's road to beg every day for my new life, as for an obol."

On the summit of the world three children were sitting, in tears, crying: "We no longer have a father or a mother; take us under your wings." From a distance, I said to the first: "Who are you?" and he, without getting up or wiping his cheeks, said: "Who am I? Perhaps he will remember, he who has so often woken me up in the night on my pillow, that at this hour, I am still sleep and my eyes can no longer open. I am Louis Capet.[28] I have wept many tears; I was born on a throne and died in a harsh prison. My hands, which ought to be attaching my crown to my head, have clung on more than one to the shoelaces of passers by. Like my master in his shop, Eternity has said to me too soon in my tomb: 'Are you asleep, Louis Capet?' I'm awake, and now I'm weeping, because my

_____

[28] The younger son of Louis XVI, who survived the death of his older brother before the Revolution and the execution of his patents, but died in 1795 at the age of ten (although myths of his survival gave rise to numerous pretenders). Royalists continued to recognize him as Louis XVII, so the Bourbon king of the Restoration became Louis XVIII.

father and my mother are already half-resuscitated, and they both lack a head on their shoulders."

And I said to the second: "Who are you?" And he said: "I was, when I was alive, Henri de France, descendant of a hundred kings, Prince of Navarre, heir to Sicily and Naples, Duc de Bordeaux.[29] At present, I no longer have a name. In my glass, I was given honey at first, but bitterness is at the bottom; I don't want to drink it. The bread of exile is ashen; I don't want to eat it. That's why I'm weeping."

The third was leaning over toward the sand, like an eaglet, and I asked him: "What are you looking for?" "My heritage," he said. "I am the one who was named King of Rome but never wore a crown.[30] Later, I had another name, but my pain was still the same. France has had my heart, Germany my bones, the world knew my father; he only held me on his knees one evening, to teach me to spell his giant name. Go seek him out so that he can take me to my kingdom."

One bound and I crossed the land; another and I crossed the Ocean. On an island in the sea, under a willow, am emperor was standing like an eagle. I said to him: "What is your name?" and he said: "The universe knows it well."

"The universe only knows one name; are you the man named Napoléon?"

---

[29] Henri d'Artois, Duc de Bordeaux, better known by his alternative title of Comte de Chambord, was briefly proclaimed as king by some Royalists in August 1830, when he was still short of his tenth birthday; long after *Ahasvérus* was published he remained a pretender to the throne, and very nearly got it back after 1870, allegedly failing to reach an agreement with the Third Republic because he refused to let the tricolour remain the French flag.

[30] Napoléon Bonaparte junior, the son of Napoléon I and his second wife, Marie-Louise of Austria, known to Bonapartists as Napoléon II, nicknamed "L'Aiglon" [the Eaglet] and known subsequent to Waterloo as Franz, Duke of Reichstadt (1811-1832).

And when, without speaking, he had said yes, I was afraid of more than one arrow launched, and I wanted to run away, but smiling, he said: "Have no fear; the eagles know me. If you have come from France, give me news. What are my soldiers doing?"

"They're reawakening."

"And my son?"

"He's crying: Where is my father?"

"And my marshals? Kléber? Desaix? Lannes? Duroc? Ney? Murat? Rapp? Bertrand? and Montholon?"

"They're waiting for you."

"And my throne?"

"Is broken."

"And my column?"

"That's standing."

"And my glory?"

"It's wearing out my eyelids. Let me leave."

Master, that's what I've seen. When I came back up, the angels had already put their trumpets to their mouths.

THE FOUR EVANGELISTS

We can hear them from here. Our entire bodies are trembling. Our awnings are about to collapse.

THE EAGLE

Look! Just now, Ahasuerus' horse reared up when the trumpets turned in his direction.

THE FOUR EVANGELISTS

Now they're resonating in the direction of the ruins of cities to awaken them more rapidly. Listen!

IV.

THE CHORUS OF THE ANGELS OF THE LAST JUDGMENT
1.
Sanctus, sanctus, sanctus, Dominus, Deus Sabaoth. Now is the hour, now is the hour. World, if you are asleep, get up! Let the withered flower gather its crown around it in the mud and replace it on its head. Let the Ocean pass, trembling like a brook, so that its judge might count its waves. Let the dead stars, one by one, spring forth from oblivion, like a procession of candlesticks, in order that their master might look, beneath the crimson of the sky, to see whether their faces are pale!

2.
Humankind too, get up! Gather around you, in your oblivion, your memories, your desires, your hopes, your re-grets and your long grief, in order to remake your own clay. Knead it in your tears, dress yourselves in despair. In the Campo-Santo, and there, where many naves pour darkness upon their tombstones with full hands, and in the cemeteries where the bullfinches whistle in the hedges, and there, where nobles sleep in African marble, and there, beneath the strand where the sea manipulates what was a people between its fin-gers, as a child does, get up, get up, get up! If your soul, which remembers your dolor, and falls half-sleep again, murmuring "It's too soon," my redoubled cry will awaken it.

3.
Cities, too, of the Levant and the Ponent, of marble or fire-baked bricks, remount your stairways. Collect your great bones that are whitening in the wilderness. Insect-giants, regird your loins with your long aqueducts that serve you as antennae to drink from distant springs. Coif your foreheads with your cupolas; comb your tresses of blonde columns with

a golden comb, over your shoulders. High and low, as before, you are already brim-full of sighs and wailing. You are shaking your heavy heads and sobbing. In your street, your crowds are returning to life. Another hour, and you will only have to go up on to your roofs to see the coming of your Christ.

ATHENS
I'm ready, Lord; the sun has spun my gilded tunic around my column every year, and dressed my chiseled marble every morning. I have only to bend down to pick up the robe my sculptor has made from my steps. Come on, lovely Pallichares,[31] bring me the basket of beautiful wedding-gifts that the master has given me; my acanthi plucked in the heart of the rock, my funerary urns that accumulate so rapidly in the potter's house, my centuries of genius, and my entire history, once emptied in full into my alabaster cup. To make me more beautiful than the others, pick three anemones from my bush and put them in my hair. Now, untie my ship, raise the anchor of my floating mountains, my marble summits, my islands swaying in the wind, my battlefields, my citrus woods, my blazing rivers, my paths worn by my chariot, and all my memories, in order that I might overflow with hem in the valley of Jehosophat. Now, bring, bring the veil! My boat is so small, and the sea is so vast!

THE ANGEL OF JUDGMENT
Wake up, wake up!

ROME
One more day, I beg you. I'm searching my dust for my clothes, in order to get dressed, without being able to find them. Beautiful angel, tell me, what robe should I put on to

---

[31] An esoteric term referring to an ancient Greek region or tribe, which Quinet had previously resurrected in his book about modern Greece; he used again in future works, although no one else followed his example.

please the Lord best? Should it be my Sabine tunic, from when I was a girl, and I spun the cloth of my days to come on my doorstep? Should I take my priestess' book in my hand, my Etrurian mantle, or my bloody crown, from when I was a queen seated on a sheaf of ripe wheat? Should I draw my sword, rusted for ten years in my Thrasymene lake, or buckle around my waist my belt of freedom, or put out to dry at my window my mantle, reddened all the way to the neck with the blood of my emperors?

THE ANGEL
Have you nothing better to wear for the fête?

ROME
Do you prefer my old man's miter and crosier, and the blessed cupola with which they have charged my head? Do you prefer my hundred ringing bells, my marble chasuble that the world has made me with all the gold in the world and the debris of the past that ornaments my mantle, as a Lateran pilgrim wears the seashells of his shipwreck on his shoulders? Would it not be better, to reenter the crowd without being recognized, to retain my harvester's sickle in my hand, which I now carry every summer to my mountains of Abruzzi? At present, my feet are bare. Look at them! My eyes are dark, my robe is white linen. I have two steel needles in my hair; in my basket I carry, for the passing traveler, figs from Velletri and strawberries from Umbria. If I hold my basket and my sickle, the Eternal himself will no longer recognize Rome. Instead of my past, my hundred emperors, the peoples fallen in my path and my gigantic years, he will only put into his balance the days of a suntanned girl of Perugia or Terni, her harvested grain, her blessed rosary, her songs of springtime and the Madonna suspended from her velvet collar.

THE ANGEL
He would recognize anywhere the bloodstain that you have not been able to wash off in Pilate's ewer.

ROME

What if, in order to save myself, I go up into my tomb, which is my fortress; if I draw my bolt, you'll never see me again.

THE ANGEL

The Eternal has a ladder, which he would lean on your wall; he would pluck out from your battlements like an eaglet of Terracina from its nest.

ROME

What if, in order to hide, I sit down on the ground in the shadow of my Coliseum; he might believe that I'm a beggar begging a horse-stabler for my barley-bread.

THE ANGEL

He would give you his bread of vengeance in your hand for your hunger.

ROME

What if I were to descend into one of the extinct volcanoes in my region; he might believe that I'm cooled lava, calcinated foam or a little ash vomited from its crater.

THE ANGEL

He would collect you in his apron like a laborer, to sow you in his field of wrath.

ROME

Are you sure, then, that all my centuries of life have passed already, one after another, through my triumphal gate, and that not one of my people remains behind, and not one of my stray years, which might arrive this evening to rescue me, and might still save me?

THE ANGEL

All your years have passed, all your peoples have reentered in their time, when their sun set. Now, go present the key to our postern to the master who lent it to you.

ROME

Tell me people, then, who are riding in marble along my imperial column, that they should turn the bridle on their triumphs, and that it is time to go down, with their habits of stone, to march ahead of me; tell my seven hills, half-effaced beneath my footsteps, my toppled walls, the circuses I rounded out with my trowel, and my rusty weapons that have drunk from my river for a thousand years, that they must come together to make me a vast breastplate against the wrath of my judge.

THE ANGEL

Come along, then. You shall have, to defend you, the crickets that sing in your thistles and the long reeds of the Tiber.

ROME

What! Not one hour more? Twice living, twice dead, and that's all! What, not a single hour to drink once more the water jetting from my cornelian fountains, to comb the mane of my stallions after a race, to throw the spoils of the hunt to my dogs howling in the night? What, not a single hour to disinter with my spade half of the days buried beneath my steps, to take my herds of goats to pasture in the courtyards of my palaces, to light my lamp in the crypt of my popes, to draw the curtain over my virgins, whom I'm abandoning all alone, asleep at their weaving, to take my bread and salt from my guest-less table?

THE ANGEL
No, not one hour!

ROME

Oh well, my God, I'll go! My towers are already far away. I can no longer see the cypresses of Monte Mario on my hills, nor the pines that served me as an awning, nor my oak of Saint Onuphrius, which extended its shadow over my bench. My sun, in setting, is braiding forever a crown of rushes and the mown grass of my countryside, like a guest who goes away carrying away the pomegranate flowers and roses that were lying on the tablecloth. My road is very hard. Who's that down there on my path, traveling ahead of me? the black eagles of Abruzzi, the vultures of the Apennines with their bruised necks and the she-wolves of Calabria with their thirsty tongues? Go along my road, my black eagles, my vultures and my wolves, I no longer have anything to give you to drink. My streams have no more blood, my sword is no longer trenchant. Seek another companion for the voyage. Who's that coming after me? the popes, the children that I nourished in my Church, my young virgins who are coming down from their canvases to see where I'm going? Go on, my popes; I have no more miters or censers to give you. My little children, retrace your steps; I have no more oranges, lemons or figs to give you. My beautiful virgins, return to your blessed canvases and go to sleep along my walls; my palette is exhausted, I can no longer paints your robes every day in Foligno vermilion. Let me go down alone to the utmost depths of the valley that leads to Jehosophat.

THE ANGEL, *turning eastwards*

Oh, how slow you are in Chaldea, in Arabia and the Orient! Must I saddle your mares and attach your water-skins to your camels?

BABYLON, *to the Euphrates*

Don't murmur so loudly, my river. It's you who woke me with a start. I was dreaming of banquets and fêtes in my valley.

THE RIVER
I wish to God that I was the one who spoke!

THE ANGEL
Are you ready, Babylon? Or must I come down to rap on your window?

BABYLON
My dream was so beautiful! My unicorn, my crowned lion and my sphinx, why are you speaking so loudly on my terrace?

THE SPHINX
It wasn't me who spoke.

THE UNICORN
Me neither.

THE LION
Nor me.

BABYLON
What time is it?

THE ANGEL
The last hour of the world.

BABYLON
It you want me to believe you, come and sit by my bedside.

THE ANGEL
Here I am! Do you know me?

BABYLON, *to the angel*
Oh, yes, you're so beautiful! You wings have bathed so often in my naphtha wells by night! How the sweat runs down

your brow! Come, I'll wipe you with my hand, and give you my wine in my Alexandrian cup. Leave your tiresome sword on my bed. You're so young! Stay with me. I love you; I'll lock my door; no one will see you; you shall have my bracelets and my phials of perfume. You shall have all my kisses; you shall drink the tears from my eyes, drop by drop, and I'll draw my curtain over your sleep while the empty universe rolls around us, like a palm leaf in the desert wind.

THE ANGEL
What good are your bracelets to me? They've been rusted for more than a thousand years; your phials are cracked; they've lost their scent. It's too late now; I've already found the madonna I love in a chapel in Perugia, and she's more beautiful than you.

BABYLON
Are my sisters also coming to your fête? Shall I send a messenger to Bactra, my elder, to Nineveh, who's sitting in her garden, to Thebes, who dwells in the desert, to Memphis, who's betrothed beyond the mountain, and—to serve as our slave—Jerusalem, who can fill our hookahs with Arabian scents, who can lay our cushions on the ground to sit us down, and extend our canvas awning against the sun? I'll send my sphinxes, my alabaster gryphons and my granite lions on ahead so that they can sweep the path along which we'll pass. The gryphons will carry our skins of Idumean wine on their backs, the sphinxes our tents and the lions our crowns, which would weigh us down on the road.

THE ANGEL
Your table is already laid.

BABYLON
So we have nothing to carry but our gods?

THE ANGEL
They're waiting for you.

BABYLON
Where?

THE ANGEL
There, in your shady valley.

BABYLON
And who is our host?

THE ANGEL
Prop yourself up and you'll see him at your door. (*He turns to the Occident.*) And you too, city of the evening, hiding your head in the mist, hear me.

PARIS
Where now is my roof of wicker and holly, which Geneviève[32] the shepherdess made for me against the arrows and darts, while spinning my regal swaddling-cloths, dressed in dawn and the dew on my abundant mountain? Not a woodcutter to show me the stone where I sat for so many centuries. It was there, on that bed of chalk. My passions have eaten it away, as the Red Sea has its dunes; my waves have deposited neither seashells nor algae there. Sometimes I find the bronze beak of my eagle, which drowned in my tempest, sometimes a soldier's sword with a bronze hilt, sometimes a golden crown, sometimes a wedding-ring. Around me, I can only see, to help me, an enchanted bird the color of time, which is bathing its wings before leaving, in the wave that I've dried up by wash-

---

[32] The patron saint of Paris, who allegedly saved the city from the Huns by means of a "prayer marathon" in 451, and subsequently pleaded for the people of the city when it fell to the Franks.

ing the arches of my bridges, the cables of my boats and the shadow of my cathedral there, every day.

THE ENCHANTED BIRD

Tell me, poor city without walls, wasn't it you who once built, in this arid vale, towers with battlements so high that the little magical birds of Normandy came to nest there without fear? Wasn't it you who built here, in this leafy wood, triumphal arches and a bronze column, so that the starlings and wagtails could rest there when they were tired? Tel me, wasn't it you who threw to the wind, in that field of hemp, flowers and mint, so much gilded wheat, so much dust of ruins and so many royal festivals, and shook your winnowing-basket so hard that the wheat flew away with the tares, to better nourish our broods around you?

PARIS

Yes, that was me.

THE ENCHANTED BIRD

Well then, have no fear; come with us to your judge.

PARIS

But I have swept his name away as well, and thrown it to your chicks.

THE ENCHANTED BIRD

It is not lost; we have picked it up and carried it beneath our wings to the woods of heaven.

PARIS

But the judge will remember.

THE ENCHANTED BIRD

Don't be afraid; we'll speak for you.

PARIS

In that case, land of France, let's get up! The angel's trumpet resembles the clarion of battles. All of you get up, my soldiers, with your worm-eaten clothes! I've only given you, to cover ourselves, the dust of battles, in order that your tomb might be lighter and the sleep of your eyelids easier to shake off. Hola! Pick up the remains of your halberds and you blunted arrows, serfs of Bouvines and Azincourt.[33] Lace up your steel corset, which the rain has rusted, my maid of Orléans; pass your resuscitated archers before you, like your white flocks of Vaucouleurs.[34] Cavaliers and infantrymen, dig up the stumps of your rifles and the blades of our broken swords; put your Marengo boots on your feet, and deploy, before the sun perishes, the flag that the spider has just oven for you. My emperor, who has come from Saint-Helena, is already mounted on his horse, and is running at a gallop. Death has not changed the sword by his side, nor soiled his spurs, not toppled the hat from his head. In his hand he carries the names of all our years, and he is the one who will arrange all our centuries in battle order on the hill. Let us go and see, with him, whether we were mistaken when we drank our blood like water, when we drove the wheels of our war-chariot, and when we stood for a thousand years as the sentinel on the edge of the high tower that the human race has built.

---

[33] The Battle of Bouvines, in 1214, established French sovereignty over Brittany and Normandy. Azincourt is the French spelling of the place (known in English as Agincourt) where the battle of 1415 took place in which the English king Henry V won a crucial victory in the Hundred Years War.

[34] Jeanne d'Arc stayed in Vaucouleurs for several months seeking permission to visit the court of Charles VII before going on to play her own part in the Hundred Years War, which became a powerful national myth, elaborately developed in Jules Michelet's *History of France*, in which an entire volume is dedicated to her.

V.

DOCTOR ALBERTUS MAGNUS

(*Locked in his laboratory, apparently emerging from a profound reverie during which he has not noticed the world ending. Open books and scientific instruments are heaped up before him pell-mell.*)

1.

Yes, in my palpitating bosom, the uncreated light is pumping life. I had a presentiment of it. It's the hour when the truth will be revealed to me. The mystery of things is beginning to appear, and my eyes will see clearly to the very bottom of my abyss. The last day of science has arrived; my meditation will bear its fruit. Logic is ripe, and criticism too. Metaphysics has bestrode its diamond circle *a priori*, and has revealed itself in the enchanted forest of dogmatics, combing its golden hair. Everything is ready. Six thousand years for the preface of human science is not too many. On the elements the conclusion depends; a single broken step in the ladder the rises into the sky, and I would fail eternally in my eternal problem. Since yesterday, the method has been found; let's begin.

2.

What am I? Body and soul? the whole together, or one without the other? Am I a dream? a soap-bubble? a word? or perhaps a God? or perhaps nothing at all? Fatal question! When you think you're passing before it, barefoot, without waking up, it always starts howling in your ear, like Cerberus at the gate of Elysium, and it's necessary to stop before its triple maw and stay there until evening in that desolate region. Come on! It's done! There's another day wasted. That's certain; I shan't do anything more this week.

3.

Whose fault is it? Entirely mine! The formula was clear. It's in the heavens that it was necessary to begin. The letters there are wider and taller, spelling out the name of infinity, and in that equation of stars, the great unknown stands out more clearly. (*He looks up at the sky.*) Horror! Nothing! The sky is empty. An infinite zero is floating over my head. The worlds have died. While my genius got ready to follow them, they hastened the flutter of their wings, like frightened birds before a good fowler. I've arrived one day too late to know everything.

4.

Insensate! I was wrong just now; the first road was the better one; let's go back to that one. Let the worlds go out; their real hearth is within me. The rationale of the universe is written in my soul, and in the sky of my heart the risen stars are not setting. A second Prometheus, if life succumbs, exhausting that in my bosom, which too much love stirs up day and night, I'll reignite it. Let's see; the thing is worth the trouble; without trembling, this time, let's descend again further than my thought, by way of analysis.

5.

Here I am, touching the bottom. Already, in my darkness, I can feel a wound there, and another there, and there a source of tears that have not yet flowed. Hola! In that place, here once again, *in fundo cogitationis*, is a memory that bleeds. In faith, I'm like an old arsenal full of envenomed rags, swords broken on my threshold, armor dented on my paving-stones, weapons that wound when touched, and darts suspended from my wall that will kill anyone who disturbs them. Beneath its sobbing debris, beneath those moaning regrets, something's shining. Yes. No. A God, perhaps? Certainly not. It's another tear falling from my vault.

6.

At the noise which my thought makes marching through my ruin, a thousand images resuscitate, standing up in my soul. The slingshots of the pale, beneath their shroud, hurl a thousand half-dead, half-alive hopes, looming up in my heart. Go back to sleep, my hopes. Oh, all my desires, go back to sleep, for a long, long time. In the ashes that I'm raking, there's no gold. All is dust, cooling down.

7.

There's no doubt about it; I've begun badly. One human heart on its own is impotent to draw much from science. Too many well-sharpened darts have pierced it and holed it like a sieve. The truth passes through it, without stopping. Human-kind would certainly be a better study.

8.

How to get a grip on it? Its racket is already effaced. In its book, the worm has eaten away its image, and the page that bore its name falls to dust under my cold breath. It's too late now to decipher the names of its empires and peoples. My lamp's running out; it's growing pale. Oh, let it cast darkness over my science!

9.

World that is closing your eyelid over my soul without weeping, infinite void, black nothingness, tell me, at least, what you are. At the last moment, exhale a word of truth like a sigh. Before engulfing itself in the Ocean, a river looks back and yields up its secret to the sprig of oats whose thirst it slakes. Mysterious torrent, do you want to sink without even uttering your name to the reed you're uprooting?

THE DOCTOR'S SERVANT

Doctor, a stranger who has come a long way is asking to speak to you.

THE DOCTOR
If it's my respectable master of dogmatics, Dr. Thomas of Heidelberg, or my good friend Sylvio, show him in.[35]

(*The angel of the last judgment enters.*)

THE ANGEL
Throw your books and your renown at your feet and follow me.

THE DOCTOR
Leave me alone; I only need one more day to discover the secret of life.

THE ANGEL
Come and learn the secret of death.

THE DOCTOR
In an hour, before dusk, I'll have found the final word of science.

THE ANGEL
There are no more hours, nor days. That's the first word. Ask the question of the resuscitated child.

---

[35] These two references are puzzling; Thomas Aquinas was Albertus Magnus' pupil, not his tutor, and had no connection with Heidelberg, and no one names Sylvio or Silvio was prominently associated with his biography.

VI.

THE POET, *semi-resuscitated, in his coffin*
1.

My heart alone is reanimated in my bones. It's already beating in my breast, but my breast is still cold; my eyes can already see the one I adored, when I was something; but my wyes are still full of the earth of the cemetery. Why, my heart, have you come back to life so quickly, without even waiting for the light to reheat my place? Oh, what would you do now, if I were to take a step back into eternal death?

2.

A thousand images I dreamed, when I lived on earth, are reappearing around me. There is, however, one that still, dead as I am, makes me palpitate and weep.

CHORUS OF RESUSCITATED WOMEN
1.

How will you recognize the one you seek? We all bear the same wound in our hearts; it is, if you know it, the harm that nothing cures, neither simples, nor balm, nor the plain, nor the mountain, nor desire, nor regret, and which continues to grow in death, like a flower in its vase.

2.

Our stories are different; so are our words; but they all have the same meaning. We have lived far from one another, in many places, connected with one another without being aware of it, by dolor. In our tears, in our songs, in our sighs, we are, one after another, the ever-repeated echo of the great love that makes the heavens beautiful enough to endure, and the world sad enough to die.

THE POET

Pass by and weep. By means of these more divine tears, I shall learn more about the one who can resuscitate.

(*One after another, the souls of the resuscitated emerge from the earth and pass by.*)

SAPPHO

I was Sappho of Lesbos, when Phaon was on earth.[36]

The sea, the vast sea into which I threw myself, has not drowned my desire in its abyss. With my lyre, the Ocean has cradled me throughout Eternity on its finest shores. Just one tear, in its bosom, from the one who caused me to shed so many, would have sated me more than all the waves of Leucadia and Asia that have kissed my lips and have wearied of it without slaking my thirst.

HÉLOISE

I was Héloise, when he was named Abailard.

The skies, the vast skies, greater than the sea of Asia, are not great enough for the love of my soul. The pillars of the cloister have not chilled my bosom; my hope has been incubated in death. More than one, beneath my tombstones, I raised myself up on my elbow to embrace my Abailard. In his heart, my seven heavens radiated. Him, that my God; he is my faith, he is my Christ. I am his mystical bride, and our tomb is our paradise. Let us not emerge therefrom. Our bones are mingled, our ashes too; no, I do not want to be resuscitated.

---

[36] It was for love of the ferryman Phaon, according to Menippus, the Sappho jumped off the Leucadian cliffs; the story is nowadays discredited and Sappho has a very different reputation, but Quinet would have credited it, as did the painter Jacques-Louis David, who produced a famous image of the couple in 1809, which is now in the Hermitage.

QUEEN BERTHE THE BLONDE[37]

On a throne decked out with oriflammes, I have often wept when I had to smile. Ten nations kissed my robe if I passed by on my ambling horse; if I threaded my distaff, a great empire said: *Shh!* in order to hear my spindle purr. But beneath the awning and in my gilded chamber, and in my innumerable peoples, more than one empire was lacking. Without bargaining, I would have given away of my decorated throne for less than a sigh, my cities and domains for one sweet breath, and my three kingdoms, filed with barons, squires, tournaments and long war-cries for the three word "I love you" said, and heard and repeated in the evening, in whisper, in the forest, on a bench, in an arbor of branches.

GABRIELLE DE VERGY[38]

Listen to me, queen of love, and tell me whether I'm right to turn my mouth away from bread and life, and to want neither crumb nor leaven. The last meal that I had on earth is still bitter on my palate. It was in the tower of Vergy. It was a bright day in May; a bullfinch was singing in the bush. The one that I cannot name was at table with me, so close that his spur touched my dress many times, and I still tremble mortally at the thought. We were alone, not speaking. After grace, my eyes gazed at the tablecloth, but my heart as far away, on the road to the Holy Land, in expectation of a new pain. The cruel

---

[37] Bertha of Holland (1055-1093), the first wife of Philip I, who suddenly had three children after nine barren years, given rise to some speculation about their parentage, and was subsequently repudiated by the king and imprisoned, dying soon afterwards.

[38] A legendary member of a famous noble family, also known as la Dame de Fayel; the relevant tale, summarized in her speech here, formed the basis of a 1777 tragedy by Pierre de Belloy and an 1826 opera by Donizetti, although Quinet, an expert on twelfth-century romance, would been familiar with the original Breton version, *Le Chastelain de Couci*.

lord said to me: "What are you thinking about, my love? You're not eating; take this." And when I had put my lips to it: "Oh, how bitter it is! I shall die of it, I see. What have I eaten?" "You have eaten, Madame, the heart of your lover, the Sire de Coucy."

That is how I ate my last meal, and why the taste of my poison is still in my mouth, so insistently that all the bread of the angels can never take it away.

BEATRICE

On my lips, life has left neither sweetness or bitterness. Its taste is past; I no longer know what it was. The one who put in verse the Paradise, the Inferno and the Purgatory, and who met me near Florence while going up to San Miniato, knows it in my stead. Without seeing him, I went on my way. Was I a dream in his heart? was I a sigh in his mouth? or a phantom in his night? or a flower picked too soon? or a Florentine too soon betrothed? or a wave in the moaning Arno? or nothing but a name? or nothing but a shadow that he dressed from head to toe in his deep desire? I am not the one who can say. Sigh or dream, wave passing by, flower losing its petals, or shadow, or girl, that which I want to call eternity of love with the one who dreamed me.

MADEMOISELLE AISSÉ[39]

For myself, I remember only too well that it was on earth that I lived; if I ever forgot, this wound in my heart, here,

---

[39] Charlotte Aissé (1694-1733) was the daughter of a Circassian chief captured by the Turks and sold to the French Ambasador to Constantinople, who brought her to Paris, where she allegedly rejected the future Louis XV's regent, Philip II, Duc d'Orléans but formed a romantic liaison with one of his courtiers, by whom she bore a child. Her letters to her friend Madame Cadandrini were edited for publication by Voltaire—Quinet's first literary hero—and became an important historical source of Regency gossip.

would remind me. In the world I lived, in the world I suffered. The fête glittered around me, and at the ball I played. To amuse myself, like the others, I pulled the petals from my crown. My mouth was still smiling, although the worm had already eaten away my joy. During the day, I lived on desires, during the night, on remorse. Once only, tremulously, the word that was the sweetest for me to say passed my lips; and that word, heard all too clearly, brought me where I am.

THE CONTESSA DI GUICCIOLI[40]

The one for whom I left the Conte, after my marriage, all the others called Byron, when I alone called him Noël. He, whose ennui neither the Thames nor the Rhine, nor the Tagus nor Venice, nor all the minarets beyond the Dardanelles had been able to dispel, remained seated beside me throughout the long summer months, counting my golden hairs. For one day of absence, his tears began to flow again in the garden of Ravenna, and his lips to pale. At Mira, Bologna and Genoa, but especially at Pisa, near the Arno and the Strada Lunga, in the Palazzo Lanfranchi, what hours, my God! all seeing one another, listening to one another, then falling silent, and always seeing one another again, whose skies will never return, nor anything so beautiful, so warm with soft sighs! Under an Italian pine, I cured with a smile the wound of Lara, of the Corsair, of Manfred, of Harold. With the star of Tuscany, ever ruby-red, with the breath of the sea, always half-asleep, with the balm of villas, I too appeased, for one evening, the harsh

---

[40] Teresa, Contessa di Guiccioli, was Lord Byron's mistress from 1819-22 while he was in Ravenna writing the first part of Don Juan, and subsequently wrote an account of his life there. She was nineteen when they met, married to a man twenty years her senior; Byron apparently lived in fear that the latter would hire assassins to kill him. He eventually left her behind when he went off to join the fight for Greek independence; whether he would have gone back to her had he not been killed remains a matter of speculation.

pain of an immortal spirit. That is the reason for which I was put on earth, and I do not repent of it, even if the Conte finds out about it.

CHORUS OF DESDEMONA, JULIET, CLARISSA HARLOWE, MIGNON, WOLDEMAR'S JULIE, VIRGINIE, ATALA[41]

Between the earth and heaven we float indefinitely, without ever an hour's repose. Never have we had face or form, meaning or shelter, except in the dreams that made us. We are images from above, living tears, eternal tears without eyelids, infinite sighs without voices, impalpable caresses, naked thoughts, souls searching for a body as pure as ourselves, without being able to find one in the mud of the universe.

Reply, dead man, in your coffin; is it us that you expect to resuscitate you?

THE POET

No, it isn't you. The one for whom I'm waiting has an even softer voice; her aspect is even more celestial; with a glance she would already have drawn me from the depths of my dust like Lazarus. Keep moving, and tell me what caused you to die.

---

[41] And, presumably, all the other tragic heroines of English, French and German literature. Mignon, from Goethe's *Wilhem Meisters Lehrjahre* (1795-6; tr. as *Wilhelm Meister's Apprenticeship*), became particularly famous in France as a subject for popular prints and engravings; she was also the subject of a French comic opera by Ambroise Thomas (1866). Julie is from Friedrich Schiller's Sturm und Drang classic *Kabale und Liebe* (1784; tr. as *Intrigue and Love*). Bernardin de Saint-Pierre's *Paul et Virginie* (1787) and René de Chateaubriand's *Atala* (1801) were both regarded, rightly, as classics by the French Romantics.

A VOICE

My face was as pure as the face of an angel, but my heart as empty. My eyes were as profound as the sky, but like a sky devoid of stars. The world called me its divinity; for myself, I did not believe in any God. I did not love anything. *That is why I am dead.*

SECOND VOICE

1.

Beneath a linden-tree my name is written at the place where the Vosges gazes at Spire. When the Rhine flowed, it is him that I saw, on feast-days, when emerging from my city. In the vines, there, at the foot of Mont-Tonnerre, under the walnut-trees facing the church, there was a path on which my heart as broken of its own accord. I thought to collect a balm in death; but on awakening, my pain begins again too soon. Hope wearies me as much as a blade of grass to sustain. Oh, Father, where are you, to bring me something to drink? I have a fever. Where are you, my little brother, to relieve my bedside? If you want me to revive, go tell the Lord to efface in my soul, with his finger, the vine, the mountain, the walnut-tree, the path, and my name too, as he has effaced them without difficulty from the earth.

2.

Neither tomorrow, nor afterwards, the one who knows who I am will never come again. It is not into his arms that I have thrown myself, but it is his heart that I have broken. It is not his voice that I have followed, but it is his bosom that I have wounded. It is not at his door that I have knocked, but it is his hope that I have trampled. I wanted to love everything. *That is why I, personally, am dead.*

THIRD VOICE

1.

My name means Wisdom and sounds like Love. In the land where Gabrielle de Vergy's tower crumbled, I lived

309

without counting the months or the tears. Town or country, all was indifferent to me. I desired nothing, evening, morning or the following day. Sitting at my half-closed window, I scarcely raised my eyes to see who was coming up my steps. But one word that I heard awakened me with a sob. Since that moment, heavens and dolors have opened up to me. That is why I was born.

2.

For seven years, while doing my needlework, I waited on my balcony, overlooking the canal, for the one who had kissed the flower that fell from my hand one day on my fête in May to pass by. I had retained my breath in my heart, as much as I could, merely to hear his horse whinnying under my window; but the wind carried the sound away. The world went by in his stead. In my hearth, morning and evening, I covered my memory with my ashes. Without weeping, I did my work as before. As before, I smiled. *That is why I am dead.*

3.

In my bosom, I have kept in silence the faith of times that were no longer. When everything said: "It is a dream," I alone believed in hope prolonged. A thought, a dream, chimera were sacred to me. Behind my blinding tears, I glimpsed better skies. I lived in a dream that no one else has had. For my fête, I ornamented myself, but my fête was beyond the earth. The world called to me, and without saying anything, I replied in a whisper to the sky: Here I am. *That is why I am alive again.*

THE POET
1.

One voice, one voice has pierced my bones. Two tears falling on my ashes have remade the clay of my heart; I am resuscitated.

2.

By this path, let me follow the one who has caused me to be reborn. My days, when I as on earth, were too short to pour my entire life at leisure on her footsteps, like a perfumed oil. Many unfinished secrets that she ought to have known, many half-pronounced words, remained on my lips. It is the very least, my God! that I can see that bodiless soul passing here, as a blind man sees a flower in its perfume.

3.

Of all the world, nothing remains to me but this ring on my finger, and on my heart, this letter, which death has not effaced, scarcely read, scarcely closed, in an ink paler than tears, the response to which must be sought in heaven. Heaven, yield me the one who wrote it. Just one hour, that her light might illuminate me! Then I will become dust again; ah! yes, dust, to dry in my book these final words, which you will show her.

VII.

A desert country. In the distance, the empty sea, and a ruin, which represents that of the world.

RACHEL
Yes, if that is what you want, Joseph, it is what I want; we shall stay here in this nameless valley; this jasmine shall be our cradle. While the worlds finish dying, you and I, here, without separating for an hour, will begin to live again, as we did in Linange. All the love of the earth will be enclosed between these two rocks. With you, without God, without Christ, without sunlight, I swear to you that I shall have no need of anything. The souls are rising up to heaven again, but we shall never go beyond this flowering heather. I shall see nothing but you; you shall see nothing but me. No one star shall say to me again: "This is dusk," when I would rather it were daylight. My hand in your hand, my eyes in your eyes, we shall spend eternity here, beneath this linden tree.

AHASUERUS
We could be happy here, I think. But that happiness is too easy; tomorrow, or the day after, we can find it again, whenever we wish. Let's go further on, all the way to the end of the world; it's there, it's there, that I should like to be.

RACHEL
We are there; after this comes the heavens.

AHASUERUS
What! That's all? This is our barrier already! It's too close. I'm weary of the earth; in the heavens, I think, I'll feel better.

RACHEL

Once, when I gave you a flower, you desired nothing more. Now that I'm all yours, I'm no longer anything to you—tell the truth.

AHASUERUS

Forgive me, my heart. It's only the moments passing. There are some, as you know, in which a blade of grass makes me weep for joy, and others in which all the heavens are insufficient for me.

RACHEL

This world, which is ending, does not make me weep; but I am no longer for you what I once was; that is what is killing me.

AHASUERUS

The evil does not come from me, be sure of that; but here, I can't be healed. When I mean the most to you, and I feel my heart breathing in your heart, it's precisely then that my ears ring, and there is a voice that cries out to me: "Further on! Further on! Go all the way to my sea of love."

RACHEL

What! When I hold you in my arms, I'm not sufficient for you?

AHASUERUS

It's the sickness of my soul. When my lips have drunk your breath, I'm still thirsty, and the same voice cries out to me: "Further on! Further on! Go all the way to my source," and when I hug you to my bosom, my bosom says to me: "Why is this not the infinite virgin who dwells in heaven?"

RACHEL

Oh, Ahasuerus, don't make me jealous of Mary. For a smile from you, I would damn myself a thousand times.

AHASUERUS

I would never have spoken to you about it first, but in all my joys there is a fundamental pain, and that pain is so bitter, so bitter that your kisses can never take the taste of it away; I thought that it would pass, but it has only increased!

RACHEL

Your desires are too immense; it's my fault for having been unable to fulfill them.

AHASUERUS

No, it's not your fault. To provide myself with an illusion, I wanted to adore you in all things. If I heard a passing stream, I said to myself: "That's her sigh;" if I saw a bottomless abyss, I thought: "That's her heart." From the vapor of islands, and clouds, and the stars, and the heavy breath of the evening, I made myself an eternal Rachel who was you, and you again, and always you, and you everywhere, you a thousand times repeated. Forgive me: I'm telling you the truth; my despair lies therein. That whole world has passed; it has dried up my heart.

RACHEL

So I can no longer be anything to you? Yes! That's Hell! Me, who wanted to be your entire Heaven and your entire Paradise.

AHASUERUS

Listen to me! If, for just one hour, I knew what it was to be loved by Heaven, I would be more tranquil, I'm certain of it. I have made a thousand chimeras of divine love; if I were to taste it, they would surely dissipate, for it's a madness more powerful than me that drives me to love more than love, and to adore I don't know what, of which I don't even know the name. This evening, to finish it, I would like to drown myself in the infinite sea that I've never seen. To dive into it with you! To die there with you! Yes, that's what I want. Guide me to its shore.

RACHEL

But my Christ is that sea; come, come damn yourself there with me.

AHASUERUS

Is its rock high? its strand steep? is its water deep enough to drown two souls?

RACHEL

Yes, and all their memories too.

AHASUERUS

Tell me, are you quite sure that I'll no longer feel this disgust, not this desire that everything stirs up, and that my heart will stop in the end?

RACHEL

I'm sure of it.

AHASUERUS

And that your God, in that abyss, will always be suffi- cient for me, and that I shall not need a greater one tomorrow, for a greater desire?

RACHEL

No, come; you will never want any other.

AHASUERUS

Never any other? That's the only thing I doubt.

RACHEL

Well, come on, then! My God! The earth has no more water, but my tears will baptize you. Get down on your knees, as in the time when you adored me.

AHASUERUS, *kneeling down while Rachel baptizes him with her tears*

More tears! Yours are too warm. Rather weep upon my heart; there, yes, there; it's there that I'm thirsty.

RACHEL, *to herself*

And me, it's also there, without wanting to, that you're causing me to die, never again to be resuscitated.

VIII.

Mob is audible in the distance, pursuing the dead emerged from the ground.

MOB
1.

Resuscitate! The thing's worn out, and the word too. Who is that, whispering it so quietly? The echo, I suppose. The dead have heard; the dead are repeating it. Here they come; there they go; here they stroll; there they run. But above all, they're yawning and whispering: "I'm still asleep."

2.

Courage! Bravo! Raise yourselves up on your limbs, my lords, as if my horse hadn't trampled you as thoroughly as the vintner treads his wine in his vat. Courage, accursed! Germinate in my furrow, as if I had not harvested you with my sickle and beaten you on my threshing-floor. Without laughing, kings and queens, put back on your heads the crowns that I had taken under my roof. The key to tombs and crypts hung jangling from my bunch; who has taken it from me to open the lock? I laid every man under his slab myself, whistling my tune to send him to sleep; who has come to wake them up at my door? Hey, accursed flock, do you hear my bagpipe? Return to my fold before the master sees you. What shall I do now to fill all my empty tombs, if, by chance, they trip over them in passing by?

AHASUERUS, *to Rachel*
Do you hear that shepherd?

RACHEL
It's not a shepherd; it's Mob pursuing the dead with her whip. There she is, coming down our path.

317

MOB, *to Ahasuerus.*

Still here, Ahasuerus! Still wandering! I thought you were asleep in some tomb. Do you want me to make your bed, now, like a king sculpted in stone? If you want, I'll give you the mausoleum of an emperor or the crypt of a doge in beautiful Candian marble. If you want, I'll heap up for you, in a single tomb, all the tombs that the kings have left me. They'll rise up higher than the highest hill. You can sleep easy on its slope.

AHASUERUS
I can no longer sleep.

MOB
Who has robbed you of it?

AHASUERUS
Hope.

MOB
Bah! That's the word I give the dead to press between their lips, with their dust, to amuse them; a soothing empty word, only made for them—leave that plaything to them. What are you hoping for?

AHASUERUS
Another life.

MOB
That's too modest, my dear. What else?

AHASUERUS
Forgiveness.

MOB
I'll give you that.

AHASUERUS
Not from you, but from your master.

MOB
If he's pursuing you, I'll hide you in my shadow.

AHASUERUS
And my soul? Where will you hide that?

MOB
Soul, spirit, love, hope—big words that I carved myself, I tell you, like my five great pyramids in the desert, into which I only put three grains of sand and a bench on which to sit down.

AHASUERUS
You're returning the burden I had on my breast.

MOB
Will you continue to take it seriously until the last day? Life isn't possible with those crazy dreams. You have but a minute, and it's only the positive that lasts.

AHASUERUS
What you call the positive is what I have before my eyes?

MOB
Of course.

AHASUERUS
But look—the sun is getting fainter, the Ocean is withdrawing, the forest is dying; this evening, they won't be here anymore.

MOB

But I'll always be here. Truly, what would I become if I were like you? Fortunately, my wings are broad enough to cover the universe, and my ideas go no further than the shaft of my scythe.

AHASUERUS

Judgment is nigh; don't your knees tremble when you think about it?

MOB

The awestruck imagination exaggerates everything, my dear. It will be a day like any other, a little smoky, especially with ashes, and that will be all.

AHASUERUS

At every word from your mouth, my heart becomes heavier.

MOB

It is indeed a very inconvenient organ on rising paths. I suffered a great deal from it in my youth, and I still have hiccups now, as you can see.

AHASUERUS

Leave me alone; you're giving me a chill, but you can't kill me.

MOB

Oh well! Hang on to the dreams that angel brought you as a dowry, then. Handsome couple, let them follow you to Jehosophat; you'll see there how they'll be repaid. But take the short cut—this way, stay to the left. The firmament is cracked from top to bottom. Within an hour, it's going to collapse. I can already hear the eternal swarm of my bats, whistling in the vault of the heavens, and down there, the last drop of water weeping and gurgling, lamenting and sinking for the last time in the pond of the world.

IX.

The valley of Jehosophat gradually fills with the dead during the following choruses. The saints sing the litanies and prayers of the Virgin.

THE VIRGIN MARY
The withered flowers on the tombs are the first resuscitated; I see them here, standing up again on their stems.

CHORUS OF FLOWERS
If this is the Day of Judgment, we shall raise ourselves higher on our stems, in order that our gardener might pick us. We have nothing to fear from the gardener of Golgotha. We have carried out the task he gave us. Every morning we have washed our sashes and tunics in the dew, in order that the kiss of the bee would leave no traces there. Every evening we have threaded our spindle, perfumed by our fingers, on to our distaff. Not once has the sun, on rising, blossoming in the highest foliage of the sky, found us sleeping in our beds. Nor once has the sea, in setting in its corolla of rocks, called to us quietly in its last murmur, without out letting fall thereinto our basket full of the leaves of lemon-trees and wild roses. In winter, we have put our mantles of snow on our shoulders. In summer, we have taken our girdles from our trunk, which the radiance of the stars has woven for us. If a woman's tear chanced to fall upon the ground, we have always collected it on the edge of our calyx. If Ahasuerus passed close by, we have always bathed our crown in the blood of Golgotha.

ROSA MYSTICA
I have put all perfumes in my cassolette; have no fear, they are not lost; I shall render them for eternity.

CHORUS OF FLOWERS

Without ever wearying, we have climbed by the paths of the chamois to the very summit of the Alps, to see Our Lord at closer range. Without ever bending our knees, we have descended, fresh and matinal, into the depths of grottoes, to ask whether our master might be sleeping there. From our summits we have seen, without being afraid, the lava of volcanoes knock on the door of cities and sit down, like a crowd, on the thresholds of house and the benches of theaters. From the rim of our caverns, smiling, we have seen armies, chariots of war, and horses with bounding rumps, bathing in their dew of blood, crests stand tall, shields glisten and swords reap their ripe fruit from the branch of the tree of battles. When the scepters of kings dried out in their hands, when the peoples, one after another, withered in their autumn, we came in their place to sprout in their valleys, and to anoint our crowns in the rain of their crypts. Of our past, we don't regret a single hour; what will become of us now?

MATER SANCTISSIMA

Have no fear; I shall pick you in your hedge to make myself a garland, like a young gardener.

CHORUS OF BIRDS

And we too have done what our fowler has commanded; in the depths of the woods we have dipped our wings in the silver steams that ran drop by drop, and that no one but us ever knew. We have sharpened our eagle's beaks on the edges of blazing clouds and reddened our warbler's throats at the heath-fires of laborers. Oh, how small the cities were when we passed with the clouds, necks extended, over their brushwood! With their bridges and their walls with seven rings, with their ships in harbor, with their bells that sang at daybreak, how many times have we said on seeing them beneath the shadow of our wings: "Come on! Let's go down to them; it's the brood of a warbler, leaning out of its nest to fill its beak." Without ever worrying in our travels, we have been, every year, to seek the golden grain that our fowler held out to us in the palm of his hand, across the Ocean and the desert. Now, our wings are weary; we are about to fall into the abyss, if a finger does not retain us. All the masts have returned to port; all the cities are closed. We have begged the kings of the earth: "Kings of the earth, give us a tuft of grass on which to rest. Give us in your kingdoms a branch of dry wood on which we might perch for an hour." Not one of them was able to find, in his land, either a tuft of grass or a dry branch. The valleys are trembling, the summits quivering like autumn leaves.

MATER CASTISSIMA
Have no fear any longer; in the Tower of Heaven I shall make you a silken nest in the corner of my window.

CHORUS OF MOUNTAINS
Like a herd of wild mares that wake up one day and lift up the hair from their foreheads if they hear a noise, our rumps and our flanks have reared up beneath the whip of the tempest. Our mane is made of forests, the hooves on our feet are made of white marble; our saddle-bows and bits are made of gilded clouds; our foam is a river that blanches our bits; and our nostrils, when the spur pricks us, vomit their lava into the Ocean. All the gods, one after another, have passed over our summits. Of their treasures, Lord, we have only kept your cross to cover our peaks with storms. By our narrow paths, we have risen up day and night to catch the rivers and springs in our cups. Every evening, we have enclosed the embalmed breezes and perfumes of summer that we have collected during the day in the depths of our grottoes. To please you, every winter, we have wound our accumulated snow around our heads; and we have groaned, in the depths of our volcanoes, like a man whose sleep is troubled, in his bed, by the weight of your name.

THE VOICE OF MONT BLANC
I have driven my white heifers to pasture before me; the mountains of the Alps are my white heifers; their horns are of

snow; they shake the clouds of winter above their heads like a sheaf of mown grass. To patch their flanks they have three forests of dark firs; their udders are crystal; their tails sweep my path. When they bellow in the wind and the squalls they wash the hooves of their feet in the basins of lakes. Towns and villages are suspended from their necks, with the voices of people and crumbling states, like fine steel cowbells, that they may be heard from afar in the pasturage of the Lord.

CHORUS OF THE ALPS

Search where you will for your white heifers; we no longer recognize your bagpipe. We are now a round-dance of maidens, ready to give our hands in marriage. Lord, please exchange, for a garment of celebration, our old robe of vapors. For a lover, we have only ever had at our door the eagle who kissed us with his black wing, for a fiancé, the chamois, and for a husband, the torrent falling beneath our feet. Sinless, every day we have carried the rivers in our bowls, like a milkmaid descending from her chalet; but summer is over; the winter of the world is nigh. Let us, too, descend from our summits to see in the valley, in our turn, travelers, merchants, monks and pipers passing over our open threshold.

THE ETERNAL FATHER

You have doubted for an hour in the depths of your grottoes. Go on, I shall make of all your summits, put together one atop the other, a stone bench on which to sit down at my door.

THE OCEAN

Do you remember, Lord, the day when you led me to pasture for the first time? Do you remember the time when I was alone, under your eyes, in your immensity? Your hand caressed me then like a faithful dog; you took me in your arms then to teach me to bound on my rock like a little chamois taken for the first time by its father to the Alpine meadow. You loved me then; my breeze was so fresh, my sand so new! I saw myself azured and my limbs limpid all the way to my bed, like a young woman beneath hr bridal curtains. What have I done since then, Lord? I have kissed my shores; is it of them that you are jealous? I have rocked passing shades in my waves. When you left me for another, more beautiful than me, I cast my sighs upon the wind that woke me up, on the stones of my pier, on the rocky strand, in the fisherman's net, in the sail that dressed me with linen. Are you jealous of the sail, or the fisherman's net, or the rocky strand, or he stones of the pier? I can no longer see anything in my abyss but the carcasses of wrecked ships; my waves no longer flow free of weed wrenched from my shores; my sand is made of the dust of the dead, so many crowns and broken scepters, so many prows of vessels, so many drowned cities, so many shields and rusty sabers, colliding in my waves, that they prevent my voice reaching you!

THE ETERNAL FATHER
You have doubted in the depths of your waves. Go on! I shall take all your water in the palm of my hand to wash my son's wound and his chalice.

CHORUS OF STARS
As a pilgrim from Palestine wears on his habit the shells of the shore, so we have attached ourselves to the edge of morning's mantle. As the mules of an archbishop going to Toledo shake gilded bells beneath their manes, so our silvery voices hang down and resonate beneath the manes of the mules of the night. To cut short our journey, it only required a drop of dew in which we could be reflected as we passed. Until daylight came to shine, we related our dreams; and if any cloud moistened our tresses, we asked for directions, smiling, to the road to the desert. But now, the storm wind is chasing us, with the leaves of the forest, to Jehosophat.

STELLA MATUTINA

You did not weep enough in the eastern night of the Passion, when I held my dead son in my arms on Calvary, and you smiled the next day!

CHORUS OF STARS

Forgive us, Mary! What other crime have we committed? Is it having brushed in the night the closed lips and eyelids of a Turkish woman, having lowered her turban, her poniard with her tresses and then untied her girdle under her tent? Is it having been too slow to rise in the bay of Naples or too lazy to cradle myself in the climbing vines or her islands? Is it having forgotten the time in the gondolas of Venice, at the doors of deserted palaces, or having taken the poet's message too frequently from his window, to carry it to the ends of infinity?

THE ETERNAL FATHER

That's enough! You too have doubted, in your time, beneath your tent of light. Render me all your brilliants, that I might make an ear-ring of them. From dawn to sunset, from afar to nearby, from the folds of the firmament, from the summit of the wave, from the treetops where you awaken, render me all your sparkling jewels that I might make a ring for my finger.

CHORUS OF WOMEN

1.

The earthly road that we follow, weeping, is too rugged for our feet. It wounds without thorns, bruises without stones. When it is weary, the flower leans on its stem; the tired star rests on a cloud; but our breathless hearts can no longer lean on a cloud or a stem.

2.

Many sighs, which no one has heard, have consumed our breath on our lips; an everyday evil, with no name and no scar, has worn away the hope in our breasts like a rasp. I would rather count the hairs on my head than the invisible tears that have flowed in my soul. Without complaint, in my house, I have done my work, I have spun my wheel, I have suffered in my ashes; my embers are extinct. Too many tears have fallen there, one after another; and the spindle on which my murmurous desires wound and unwound their fabric during the vigil has broken in my fingers.

MATER DOLOROSA
Pity! Pity! *Miserere!*

CHORUS OF WOMEN
1.
I did nothing but sigh and dream. Before my heart as full, all my days had flown; my life was worn away between my fingers, and my soul has stayed in the middle of its task of love, as a piece of needlework, set aside when scarcely commenced, falls back on your knee when the needle and the thread are broken. I would like another life, and would render an entire glance tomorrow to anyone who would give it to me.

2.
Yes, an entire glance! Nothing but a glance! And no heaven, inevitably! No God! No Christ! Nothing but a sigh, nothing but a breath, nothing but a flower that he has touched. And afterwards, the abyss, the night without tomorrow on my empty head, oblivion beneath my feet.

THE ETERNAL FATHER
In that love so long, you alone have kept me memory without knowing it. The earth has been your time of betrothal. Your wedding will be in the heavens. Here, for your dowry, is the ring I have made from the gold of the stars.

X.

The Valley of Jehosophat, where all the dead are assembled.

TIME, *to the Eternal Father*

Lord, I have managed my hour-glass as best I could. Grain by grain, slowly, I have allowed my dust to fall back on the footsteps of the human race. If some more rapid year, lightened by its happiness, chanced to escape my fingers, I rendered all the others after it heavier than a century. Hour by hour, I have poured the life of the poor into their ulcerated hearts, like drops of oil in the leaden lamps that no longer illuminate their tables. Like a devouring tear that burns the gaze and cannot run away, I have suspended in the thoughts of the poet, beneath his sleepless eyelid, memories of the sweat of his years. I have given to Ahasuerus, drop by drop, the venom of his innumerable years wherever he paused. And yet, in the end, my hour-glass has run out. Forgive me; I have been unable to conserve my sand or my oil as a soul does its life and a spirit its breath.

MOB

Here is my scythe, Lord. When you gave it to me, its glittered in the sunlight, and I could mirror my face with it; but it has been necessary for me to mow down in your pasturage so many towers and posterns, so many lighthouses on the strand, so many pyramids in the sand, that its trenchant blade is chipped. Give me another, I beg you.

THE ETERNAL FATHER

My meadow is mown, and the haymakers have carried the fodder beneath the roof of my stable, for my mares. Now, take your scythe to the entrance. Have all the dead pass before me, in order that I know what work you have done and what wages are owed to you.

MOB

As an Easter procession emerges from the doors of San Marco in Venice or San Pietro in Rome, a mitered swarm that buzzes your name in quitting your hive, my peoples and my swarms of empires will emerge from my black cathedral, by means of a door that stands ajar, into the light. At the head, I shall carry the banner; lounging Absence will lie down beneath the awning. From their baskets, the nations will allow many faded flowers to fall as they pass, many hopes plucked too late. Into their hands, the censer shall throw only ashes, and the cracked bell in my tower will howl to call their names. My finest dead are the gods; it is with their Eternities that I commence, singing with them Psalm 99, verse 3.[42]

CHORUS OF THE DEAD GODS
Amen.

1.

For humans, it is hard to die; but for gods the agony is a hundred times worse. The knell tolls for a thousand years; our breath, in fading away, causes an entire world to sigh. On our invisible tomb, the lamp, without knowing it, illuminates our oblivion; and the worm that has eaten away or eternity, is enthroned and sibyllizes in our stead, clad in our names.

2.

Our funerals are sadder than the funerals of kings or doges; our life is everywhere, our death as well; our cadavers lie in everything that is breathed, in the air, in the night, in the star, in the flower, and in sound, and in hatred, and in love, and in the heart that we have made. To dig our grave requires nothing more than a name greater than ours. That name falls upon us like the earth that one throws on the dead; and the

---

[42] "Let them praise thy great and terrible name, for it is holy."

330

great gravedigger, who carries is in his barrow to the abyss, writes above our heads: *Here lies a god*; and that is all.

3.

Who are we? Either all or nothing; either the universe or less than a word; perhaps a shadow, but a shadow of what? of infinity, which comes and goes, and climbs and descends all day in its tower? tell us: smoke or ash, what are we in the censer?

THE ETERNAL FATHER

You have been dust and dust you are. Titans and hundred-cubit giants, Brahma, Jupiter, Mohammed, eternities of a week, you shall be my squires, my cavaliers, my court fools and crowned dwarfs, to amuse me, when I wish, in my empty infinity.

MOB
Approach, cities, towers and colossi of the Orient.

BABYLON, *with the cities of the Orient*
Woe! We are the first.

THE ETERNAL FATHER
Who are you?

BABYLON
Babylon.

THE ETERNAL FATHER
And those peoples crowding in your wake, more numerous than the flakes of my beard on my breast?

BABYLON
They are all of the orient. This is Nineveh, this is Bactra, this is Thebes,

THE ETERNAL FATHER
What have you done?

ALL THE CITIES OF THE ORIENT
Lord, Babylon is our elder sister. When we were all little, sitting on our thresholds, she it was who taught us to climb our steps to the highest of our towers; she it is who will speak for us.

THE ETERNAL FATHER
I approve of that.

BABYLON
The desert that you had made around us was naked and voiceless. To populate it, we sent the sphinxes, porphyry goats and golden-winged gryphons cast in our crucibles to graze the sand. Not one bird raised its brood there; we fattened hawks with human breasts by hand on our obelisks, sculpted ibises in the rock and storks of granite. Going up every evening to our terraces, we looked at the vault of heaven to see whether you had written some new line on your tablet, with the gold of the stars.

When the desert, in the night, rose up with a start, awakened by the wind of the sirocco, and said while propping itself up: "Where has my master gone?" we replied: "He is there, in the clouds."

When the sea, shaking its shore, said to the tempest: "Do you know where my pilot has gone?" we replied: "Look, he is there, on the Erythrean sand."

When the horses of Arabia said, whinnying: "Where is our divine rider, with his diamond bit and azure spurs?" we said: "Look, there he is, on the summit of Horeb, having tied to his whip the spikes of the storms."

It was us who sang you canticles, in the morning of the world, while kneeling on our steps; it was us who wore miters of crenellated rock on our heads, and took upon our shoulders, like a priest, our alb of walls; it was us who, for forty centuries, without raising our heads, prostrating the sand and dust of our ruins beneath our crumbled doors, like a Chaldean slave when he has brought his master his full cup and embroidered sandals.

And Master, we have given you our religions and our faith: India beneath its mountains shook its censer; Persia lit its candle in the fire of the desert; Memphis leaned over the Nile to was the sacrificial plate there; Judea drank, without drawing breath, the chalice of blood, at the height of the altar; and all of us, hands joined, lost in the crowd, Nineveh, Thebes with the ivory teeth, Bactra with the eye of an antelope, Ecbatana with the golden girdle, Tyr with the teats swollen with love, marched toward the altar, taking one step every thousand years, beneath the nave of the firmament that you had built with beautiful azure bricks.

THE ETERNAL FATHER
I remember. But why did you build your tower of Babel so high that I was obliged, with my angels, to descend to the perron to send away the workers and break their towers?

BABYLON
Lord, everything in the Orient surpassed our heads by more than ten cubits. The mountain of Kashmir was a wall that closed the sky to us; the palms you had planted rose high enough to touch the clouds; the rivers ran so rapidly on the evening of the day when you had filled their urns that we could not bestride their banks; the sea was so large that we could not follow its course to its source with our eyes. When we raised our towers higher than your palms and your mount of Kashmir, we wanted thus to climb by the art of our hands higher than your creation, to see you passing beyond your work, like a man whose children look from his courtyard behind the enclosure of his inherited field. Now let us be reborn; let us turn backwards, toward the cistern from which we drank. If you wish, we shall load our camels once again to pass over the desert of death in caravans. This time, Lord, our

vases will be made of a purer gold; our walls will be better painted, and we shall polish our new pyramids with our own hands.

ALL THE CITIES OF THE ORIENT

Yes, Lord, let us live again; we shall make you more obelisks of porphyry and subterranean temples to rest in the shade thereof for more than a thousand years. We shall send forth our armies of cavaliers, archers, infantrymen as messengers by the same road, we shall count the same centuries on our fingers, tirelessly, as a woman counts the pearls in her necklace after she has finished it; we shall throw the same names, I swear, into our sand and our tombs, as the goat of Iran, in retracing its steps, throws the same dust after it. We still know our old hymns and our poems, of which you were the hero; suspending our harps from the same willows, we shall recite them at the same times; and when we lean over the wells of our deserts, the crocodile, in seeing us again, will believe, in our absence, that we have gone to carry water in our pitchers to water our flocks in our camps.

THE ETERNAL FATHER

I cannot go back myself to my garden of Eden. How can you recross your threshold through the door that I have closed? My son and I are marching forwards in our infinity, driving before us our flock of stars and worlds. But you, you think you can find by yourselves, in the darkness that falls behind us, the bench where you might sit down? What you have been, you shall not be again. I know your obelisks, and the weight of your temples. I have held your walls and crenellated towers in my hand, with the daisies and ferns of the meadows. To fill my eternity, I now need names that have never been, noises that have never resounded, swords that have never shone outside the scabbard.

To build the city that I am making I need towers that have never resonated to footfalls. Give me back the walls, red and gold-tinted by the sun, that I have given you. Go, if you wish to sit down, to the gate of my new city, like mendicant queens, to show the way to those who ask for directions. For your resuscitated peoples, I have planted a thousand tents outside my walls in that part of the sky over there, on the edge of my Milky Way, which whitens beneath my footsteps more than the road of Assyria. The kings shall be clad in emeralds there; the princes silver, and the slaves in fine linen woven by my angels.

ATHENS

From my shore, Master, I heard as I was born the noise they were making in the Orient on the rim of their walls. To listen to them, I leaned over the sea, and, to make myself more beautiful, I looked at myself in the mirror of its waves. The bandlets of their priestesses hindered them; I untied my long hair over my marble forehead, which shook the aurora over the world from my hill. With my chisel, I sculpted in my Pentelic rock the blocks that you had sketched with your hand in the workshop of the universe. If an errant idea, image or thought had remained inadvertently incomplete beneath your hand, on the waves, the mountains, or the air that surrounded me, it was me who finished the creation with my chisel, and who sent it forth lightly, in marble, to ask at your door for it to live every day, with the stars, the springs, the sea, to which you gave existence day and night, without ever refusing. If you are making a new world, Lord, take me into your service. I shall knead in my fingers, with my Corinthian clay, the urns in which to store the tears of the new human race. In your courtyard, I shall carve in advance cornelian tombs into which to pour the ashes of peoples to come; and I shall raise, if you wish, a funerary column of the fine marble of my islands over the world that is to die.

THE ETERNAL FATHER

You have never thought of anything but your beauty. Life, for you, has been but one grace more, an ornamentation for your void, a glittering sash to veil my star. Even now, with

335

the alabaster dust that you trample underfoot, with the acanthus leaves of corroded marble with which you crown your
head, with the odor of hyacinth that you sow after you, with
your paving-stones that the horses of voivodes have worn
away, with your columns extended in the wheat like white
crops resting in the shadow, your charms are greater than in
your pagan feasts.

ATHENS

Do you remember, Lord, the work of your hands? Your
mountains were made of marble. If I raised my eyes, the stars
germinated in my nights of spring. Their embalmed flowers
turned their azure stems toward me to say: "Can you see, pour
city of reeds? I am more beautiful than you." If I lowered them
toward the sea, your islands, in their blue-tinted mist, floating
like a flock of swans, seemed to say: "Can you see? Our rocky
wings, which skim your shores, are whiter than your walls;
and your amorous gulf likes us better than you in your ship of
misery." Lord. I was jealous of stars and islands, of the shade
of your olive-woods, the crystal tears of your grottoes. To
please you as much as they did, I collected from the marble
my garlands of acanthus; I poured out my rapid glory and im-
patient days with full hands. As far as the summits where the
olive groves stopped, which the chamois never reach, where
the hawks have vertigo, to which the heather is afraid to climb,
I have carried my burden of columns on my shoulders, in order to see you, on my own, unrivaled, at close range.

THE ETERNAL FATHER

Go! Leave your burden of pagan columns at your feet
now. Their stumps are too broken to serve for my work. Put
on the new habit of a Klepht that Botsaris[43] and your arch-

---

[43] Markos Botsaris (1788-1823) was a hero of the Greek War
of Independence, a leader of the insurgents who adopted the
term klepht—which had formerly meant "brigand"—as a
badge of pride.

bishop have given you. Attach your pasha's saber and silver pistols to your belt; put your amulet around your neck. In my new city, at the foot of my diamond walls, I shall make you a hut of reeds to sing your sings of war, to your guzla, better than a Romelian bird with golden wings.

MOB
Here's Rome, Lord!

ALL THE DEAD AT THE SAME TIME
Condemn her! Curse her! She it was who led us, with our hands tied behind our backs, to give us to her Abyssinian lions in her circus. She it was who made this cold wound in our breast with her gladiator's sword.

ROME
Don't believe them, Lord; I was working my field tranquilly on my hillside. Leaning on the heads of my oxen, I was watching my wheat grow, and my grapes ripen on my trellis, when all your peoples, escaped from your hands, like wild horses that had broken out of their enclosure, passed close by, dispersed at hazard throughout the world, running from your lash. Each one was going by a different path, each one following the spur on another god than you. The Orient had broken its ring; Greece, disheveled, went crying through its islands: "The god Pan died last night." Then, on my furrow, I took my sword in my hand, as a shepherd of Albano takes his knotty staff to herd his cattle in the paths of my marshes. In Asia, in Africa, and where the Rhine turns back in its bed, I went to search for their flock. All the way to the enclosure of my walls I drove their crowd before me whinnying furiously. For three centuries, I muzzled their anger at my ease, and when my circus enclosed them all, sitting on the ground on their elbows, no longer in tears, and crying with infantile voices: "Thank you! Thank you!" I went of my own accord to seek Byzantium, with my emperor, in order to give you the key to your stable.

337

Oh, how much easier it would have been for me to lead my two obedient oxen along my furrow, to train my vine on my trellis, and to make a path for my goats instead of my triumphal road!

THE ETERNAL FATHER
It was you who killed my son on Golgotha.

CHORUS OF SAINTS, SAINT BERTHE, SAINT HUBERT, SAINT BONAVENTURE
Let her be chastised and condemned, and let her tower collapse with her battlements! If you believe us, Lord, no pardon! Her sin is too great; she would repeat it tomorrow. *Ite, maledicti!*

ROME
The Vatican expiates Golgotha. To efface my crime, it was me who first cried from my walls: "Christ is my king." To pay for the tunic that my soldiers tore, it was me who gave your son the house of my emperors with their heritage; and to wipe away the blood from his side, it was me who extended to him, on the tip of my sword, the shroud of the old world. Within my walls there are two Romes: one kneeling in the squares, amid incense and sighs, begging you, day and night, to forgive the other. The pope redeems the emperor, the Vatican the Capitol; the church prays for the temple, the cross prays for the sword, the miter for the crown, the monk's habit for the purple, the ruin for the triumph, the lamp of the madonna for the torch of the gods. And every evening, the bell that the saints have given to me goes to trample with its silvery feet the steps of the Coliseum, and the stones of my gates, and the battlements of Belisarius' wall search my surrounding from afar for some relic of a resonant vault, in order to weep there, like a night-bird, over my crumbled sins.

CHORUS OF SAINTS, SAINT BERTHE, SAINT HUBERT, SAINT BONAVENTURE

Her words have touched me; I'm shaken by what she has just said, and no longer know what to advise. She, once so great, is now so small, that my heart wants to weep. Should he have pity, have pity on Rome? put a little honey on her bitter lips? For myself, I forgive her. *Miserere! Miserere!*

THE ETERNAL FATHER, *to Rome*

Give me your sword, your javelins, your bronze breast-plate, your golden cross and your miter. I shall make a trophy of them, which I shall attach to the banister of the stairway of my new city. I shall take away your walls and your entire his-tory, as a picture engraved on my shield, which I shall hang, during my eternal night, above my bed-head. This very even-ing, four bloody comets will be harnessed, to drag your weep-ing souls day and night around my circus on your triumphal chariot; and the world will tremble when they shake their tresses over their shoulders, soiled with your dust.

PEOPLES OF THE MIDDLE AGES

As a child lowers his head toward the ground when his master summons him to read from his book, so, under our arches and battlements, we tremble at this hour. To make our-selves a beverage for heroes, we have mixed in our witch's cauldron the claws of the gryphons of Persia, the myrrh of Arabia, the seashells of the bays of Greece, the honey of the golden bees of our long-haired kings, all the names, all the gods and all the tears at the same time. On the dust of the hu-man race we have climbed up, as on our hill. That summit surpassed, we built our tower in order to see the coming of the messenger of the last judgment from a distance. If a birch tree trembled in our courtyard, if the visor of a helmet came down, if Ahasuerus knocked on our door, we thought to ourselves: here is the messenger coming with his iron-clad shoes; we must go.

Our pale years have germinated in the shadow of our stained-glass windows, without our having thought to bend down to pick the fruit. Beneath the real world we have searched, groping, for your invisible spirit, as, for want of a breastplate, one searches with a lance for the warm heart of a knight. Beneath our windows, Lord, we have made our colonnettes so frail as only to last until evening. Today, Babylon has the debris of her terraces; Rome has the steps of her circus on which to sit down; Athens has her marble bench at her gate; but my steps are worm-eaten, my towers, turrets and fragile cells are hidden beneath the brambles. What shall become of me, poor naked soul that faith clad, a people of spirits without bodies, a crowd without cities and without walls, who never thought of making any other shelter than my heart against the night and tempest of your eternity?

THE ETERNAL FATHER
The dreams of the hearts that you covered with their wings are worth more than the brick terraces of Babylon and the circus of Rome. Enter into my city. All your dreams are built there in diamond stones. Illuminate with your diaphanous souls, which I have kneaded in vermilion and gold, the windows of my porch; and if the morning wind ever strikes your resounding eyelids, fill the city and the crossroads with sighs and mysteries, like the murmur of a world that is no more and which asks to live again. Look! I have built your dwelling at the crossroads of the empyrean, up there where my evening stars are heaped up one atop another, and my suns, like bricks that are still hot, built in turrets and blazoned towers, in gleaming arches of onyx and opals, and in cathedrals of light. (*To Mob*.) Who are these peoples over here that I do not know?

MOB
They come from the land where incense grows on trees.

340

CHORUS OF ARABS

A saber sculpted in Damascus, when one draws it from its scabbard, shines more brightly than a torch in the night; and I, my Master, have drawn myself from my darkness, like a sculpted saber, to make myself sparkle at the saddle-bow in the hour of battle. My cutting edge has been whetted on the stone of the sepulcher of Calvary, and my blade has resounded upon the breastplates of Cordova and Grenada the Beautiful. When your son died and Carmel trembled, I departed to sow sand and salt before me everywhere that my prophet of wrath took me. On my illuminated shield I bore for a motto: *Fire and Blood.*

I have raised my minarets in the desert, like lighthouses over the sea. And if any stray city, thinking itself alone, raised itself up on its elbow to look in the direction of Golgotha, I decapitated it, and I buried its heavy head in my cisterns, with its tresses of columns that I loosened over its shoulders. I have led the wind of Arabia by the bridle and spurred it along the road as far as the valley of Roncevaux, under the banner of Charlemagne. I have bound in the Alhambra, by my iron ring, two shores that sought one another murmuring aloud, the Atlas and Spain, the Orient and the Occident, which you had forgotten to attach to one another.

When my desert had thus increased to surround your son's tomb, I sat down to keep watch on his rock, for fear that a gazelle, or a stork, or a wild chamois might take shelter there. Now I have finished my day's work, where are the virgins that the prophet promised me? In what ship have you been able to bring them without its sail leaning over to catch their breath? In what star have they been sold to you, without the star dreaming of kissing them with its rays? Have you painted their eyelids yourself with the brush with which you made the nights of winter? Have you wound a turban of light about their heads as for the wives of emirs? Have you whitened their shoulders, as the source of the Guadalquivir does its foam? And have you taught them to spin their cotton on their mats, until their master, on arriving, shakes the sand of death from his feet at their door?

PEOPLES OF THE MIDDLE AGES

Back, Moors and Saracens! On hearing your voice the sword rattles in the scabbard; the iron mouth of the halberd cries out beneath the crest; and Babieca, the worthy horse of the Cid, Rodrigo de Bivar, weeps beneath the iron caparison that Valencia forged for him. Our helmets are fastened. If you wish, Lord, we shall all return, with our gilded shields, our swords of furbished steel and our colored banners, to help you unseat them.

CHORUS OF ARABS

We are ready for combat, and our chestnut horses too; our arrows are strung.

CHORUS OF SAINTS

Another battle! What will happen? There they run; there they cry. The east and the west, crossing lances! Two open tombs! Which will be filled? Everyone carries the same number of feathered arrows in his quiver. I tremble that a poisoned dart might reach this far, unwittingly to inflict an eternal wound on a divine spirit.

SAINT CHRISTOPHER

I am the strongest; on my shoulder, far from the battle, one after another, I shall carry Christ, the Virgin, his mother, and his Father too, like hurried travelers who pass without paying the toll.

SAINT MICHAEL

The Father is too old to quit his accustomed heavens henceforth. Before him, in the battle, I shall extend my wing like a shield.

SAINT GEORGE
Beneath my azure escutcheon, I shall shelter the firmament, as a hen shelters her brood, and the heavens beneath the iron of my lance.

THE HEAVENS
The bow is drawn. Before the arrow, I too want to flee.

THE ETERNAL FATHER
Heavens, do not tremble or flee; remain here. Saints, fold up my banner. I have seen jousting for a long time between east and west without turning a hair. From the tower of the Bosphorus to the jetty where the lemon-trees of Andalusia bathe, the two worlds have risen every day with their shores, to overflow and collide with one another. All their promontories have extended their arms, armored with cities and battlements like gauntlets, to seek one another out and attack one another in their eternal struggle. Strip off your gauntlets on the road, Moors and Saracens; I have made you azured spurs in advance; saddle your Arabian horses; race forward off the bridle, far from here, for a thousand years, to discover where the edge of my immensity is. Say to Oblivion, as you pass by: "Get up; emerge from your tent; my master is following me."

To my left, I hear other people buzzing. Their kings have neither scepters nor names nor crowns; they are recognizable on by the blindfolds I have placed over their eyes. No heart beats within their breast; they go barefoot, before the crowd, like a woman being stoned.

MOB
They are the peoples of France, Germany and England. I have wounded them so deeply in the soul that they do not recognize you, and pass by without seeing you. Listen to their songs.

CHORUS OF SAINTS
1.

Don't listen to them. Their songs are drunken, your eyes with weep harsh giant tears. Over your thousand-year beard, Lord, that eternal weeping will flow; and tomorrow, and forever, it will make a sea, yes, a bottomless sea, in which every hull will drown, with its mast, its sail inflated with love and its anchor of hope.

2.

Close, close your great eyelid in order no longer to see the universe passing, upright, over your paving-stones, without bending the knee. Like a little bird that has woken up too early in its nest, and, saying nothing, half-fledged, has quit the wing of its father or mother, it will go, for its sin, to be caught in your fowler's net, and nested in Oblivion. Our voices sing more softly without it; only listen to our chorus.

THE ETERNAL FATHER
Nothing makes me weep, and it is necessary for me to know everything.

MODERN PEOPLES
Beneath the wind of the tempest, in the heather and the brambles, we are going to seek our God, whom we have lost. He is not in life; let us search all the crannies of death. (*To the Eternal Father.*) Hola, Old Man, looking at us from the top of your wall, what are you doing there? Can't you see that our feet are bruised and that our lips are drying out in our breath? Tell us, then, if you know, which way our God has gone?

THE ETERNAL FATHER
Until the end, without turning your head, continue on your road, which descends into the abyss; when you reach the bottom, you'll find a path that I've made to climb back up toward him.

THE PEOPLES
Adieu, Old Man! Sleep well! The night is drawing in; we can no longer see anything but your beard, which is whitening on your bosom, like an Alpine torrent.

THE ETERNAL FATHER
March! March!

THE PEOPLES
Now we can no longer see anything but the belt of your robe, which shines around you like a river of lava around the waist of a mountain.

THE ETERNAL FATHER
March! March!

THE PEOPLES
Now I can no longer see anything but the edge of the sword by your side; oh, raise it against our kings!

CHORUS OF KINGS
Lord, we are the ones who, until the end, have filled your lamp with oil. Show us the road to our future thrones.

THE ETERNAL FATHER
The oil that I wanted lights up in souls, not in the lamp.

CHORUS OF KINGS
We are the ones who have written your name in letters of gold on our crowns of brass.

THE ETERNAL FATHER

Back, go away! You have eaten away the skull of my peoples, like Count Ugolin,[44] for long enough. Disappear, accursed ones! I want none of you in my new city.

THE VOID

Master, give me their mantles in which to dress myself, and to pasture their bitter tears.

THE ETERNAL FATHER

Also take their fleur-de-lis scepters from their hands. (*To Mob.*) Have I seen everything now? Is the world finished?

MOB

Not yet, my God! Here's America emerging from its canoe.

AMERICA

What, already, Lord? The water of the deluge has scarcely wetted my shoulders. I don't yet know my shores, nor the paths of my forests, nor the springs of my pampas. I've only looked at myself once, in passing, in the lakes of my savannahs. In a day, I moored my islands in my gulfs, like brand new canoes. I have thrown my rope-bridges, which I haven't yet crossed, over my torrents. Why have you made the shadow so dense in my valley as not to let me rest there for one night?

Like an infant whose mother cradles him beneath a palm-branch, the Ocean rocked me in its waves, and I listened to the plaint of the old world on the breeze, which as dying. Oh, if it's weary of its long years and its memories, if its towers and heavy walls are too burdensome to keep, carry it up to your summit as the royal vulture carries away in its claws the rattle-snake that it has found dead on the beach; but a for me, Lord,

---

[44] Ugolino della Gherardesca (1220-1289), whose posthumous fame was greatly boosted by his prominent role in Dante's Inferno, where he is depicted gnawing on any enemy's skull.

my towers are light, and the memory of my years is as easy to carry as the lianas of my forests. A single Mexican flower opening in the morning contains all my tears in its calyx. My kings are young date-palms standing on their mountains; my nations are wild pineapples leaning over their shadow, which no one has picked.

Lord, when the condor has made its nest on my summit, with the scales of the crocodile, the wool of the cotton-plant and the cane of the reed, it lays its eggs there; and your aerie is made of the sides of my mountains, the trunks of my forests, the water-drop of my lake, the blades of grass of my field and the shores of my islands. Why don't you want to hatch out your peoples there beneath your breast at leisure, until they can follow you, wings extended, into your eternity?

THE ETERNAL FATHER

I had made for you, in hollowing out your profound valley, a mold in which to pour your thought and your soul. I had sent your rivers on ahead to show your cities the way. As a master spells out for his pupil the word that he must repeat, I had filled your forests and shores with the voices of my cataracts, in order that you might learn in good time to echo in the voices of your cities, to rumble in the hosts of your peoples, as loudly as they with their waves. I had built the summit of your Cordilleras stone by stone, in order that you might see how high your pride and your towers ought to rise. But while my peoples where working for more than a thousand years, you, nonchalant on your elbow, playing with your sea-shells, had not yet turned your head toward the giant-world that sent you so many sighs.

Now that it is at rest, raise your genius around me as high as the Andes. Give me, in order to riffle through them, more names in one day than a palm tree has flowers in spring. Unfurl in my ears the poem of your years, better than a forest liana runs from one trunk to another, from one bank to another. As the cotton-plant waves its cotton on its bench, weave the future for me henceforth, every day.

If you make me a banner, I want it to be embroidered better than the girdle of your shores; if you make me a church, I want the arches under its vault to be denser than my virgin forests, and the pillars to expand there at the summit better than my aloes n their stem; I want the organ there to have more pipes than there are voices in the swaying of date-palms, the whistling of pampas grass, the serpent's rattle, the lowing of bison, the jaws of caimans, and the Ocean that lashes you with its rods without awakening you.

ISLANDS OF THE PACIFIC SEA
And we, whom you have led so far, to the end of the world, to close the chain around your neck, have learned to polish our diamond flowers. We can make you, if you wish, a Babylon with ebony-wood towers, and another town of Bethlehem with a sapphire manger for a new Christ, if he is ever to be reborn.

THE ETERNAL FATHER
I consent to that. Work. Here are ten centuries, which I'll give you in our hour-glass. Now, in the earth, the foam of the wave, the cloud of the sky, does any secret still remain that no voice has pronounced?

MOB
Not one more. If some excessively timid flower in its hedge, some excessively modest spring on its sand, has not dared to tell its mystery, the great voices of cities and peoples have told it to you in their stead to the sound of trumpets.

THE ETERNAL FATHER
1.
Now my city is complete and populated, full to the brim with souls. All the world makes up but one closed city with battlements and walls of azure. Every star is the house in which a soul dwells. From its terrace it gazes, smiling, beneath its painted eyelid, at my streets full of people, my gilded

bridges over the bottomless abyss, my palaces built with the stones of the firmament, the glittering stairway that my squire, fearlessly, goes up and down, and the stars that spring forth beneath the hoof of my horse. My outskirts extend to the ends of the universe, without fear of getting lost; and nothing knocks on my door but the waves of the sky when it is angry.

2.

Waves on the sky, hear me. No longer break my boat. It is full, now, of resuscitated spirits that your foam will salt. Mares with golden manes, no longer flinch at my threshold. You all draw immortal thoughts in your chariot now, which your saliva would soil.

3.

In my city of souls, the same language will be spoken everywhere, the name of which is poetry. Made, without letters and without words, of the sighs of receding water, the last plaint of a bird falling asleep, the voice of a primerain flower in its silvery bell, the murmur of a sea-shell of its shore and desire in its decline, it will be understood without having been learned. Everyone weary of being awake, who would like to stop, need only say, when a star arrives in the morning, in the house of Sagittarius or Gemini: "Open up, beautiful Sagittarius; open up to shelter me"—and the heavens will understand.

4.

Gathered more carefully in my hand, my peoples will be better able to listen to me henceforth. Of a hundred kingdoms, I shall no longer make but one kingdom, greater, more beautiful and more powerful. Of a thousand laws, I shall make just one, easier to obey. Written on my vault every day, with a ray of sunlight, it will only be necessary to look up to see it. Following their golden orbits in their profound groves, my empires shall rotate their fiery wheels around me every year, in my carousel. Look! they have set forth again! Behind them the firmament totters. Courage! Faster! Let's go! Faster" I shall await them to watch them pass. Disheveled, out of breath, let them lean forward over their constellations, with their flaming whips. The first that touches my barrier without falling, I shall crown.

5.

As in Holy Rome, when it is time for the *Ave*, the Byzantine bell-towers shall quiver and cry: *Kyrie eleison*, and the bell-turrets reply lower down, in chorus: *eleison*; and all the people shall emerge from their houses and go to church, and the sound rises up to me on its bronze wheels; thus the worlds in my azure campanile bound, shiver and hum. For my celebration, they shall ring easily, as a bird flaps its wing. If I wish, they shall toll; if I prefer, it shall be the baptism of a new universe. Vibrant under their golden hammers, the sun shall bellow and rumble eternally.

For the day that is dying the evening stars are silvery plaints; those of the morning are an aubade and a crystalline chant for the day that is lighting up again. The earth has a murmur that never stops, day or night; and all those voices of worlds make up one voice, all the sighs make up one brazen sigh, which summons from the void, to kneel down barefoot in my nave, days to come, future empires, half-born hopes and regrets already commencing.

6.

It's getting late; from my mound I see, like a shepherd, my flocks returning to the fold. On the grass of my hill, my Taurus, who has hollowed out, all alone, under my goad, the furrow on my zodiac, has lain down, and is thinking, while ruminating: *I have done my work.* Since dawn, my Aries, walking at random, has left his fleecy wool hanging in vapor on the hedge of the firmament. Bounding, my Capricorn, browsing the heather of the clouds, is already butting the red threshold of tomorrow with his forehead. I his blue quiver, the color of time, my Sagittarius has replaced his feathered arrow; and there my Scorpio, with his feet of stars, is scuttling hideously on his golden abdomen through the ruins of the old world.

7.

That's enough. The earth has listened, the earth has wept, the earth has uttered a sigh to the distance heavens. Like an echo, the heavens have understood the venomous plaint, and have thrown it back; yes, the heavens in their empty abyss. And now, everything is silent. Have I nothing else to forgive?

THE UNIVERSE
No, Lord.

THE ETERNAL FATHER
Nor anything else to curse?

MOB
There is still one man who marches day and night. His beard falls to his feet. He remains in my shadow in order that your eyes might not see him. He has folded his head over his knees in order that you might not hear his breath. His name is Ahasuerus.

THE ETERNAL FATHER
Where is he?

MOB
There, in the bottom of my valley. To climb out, he will traverse all the dead.

THE ETERNAL FATHER
Have him approach, Saint Michael.

XI

ROME, *to Ahasuerus*
Go away! I don't know you. Don't climb my steps.

BABYLON, *to Ahasuerus*
Further on, accused! Don't cross my threshold.

ATHENS, *to Ahasuerus*
Further on! Further on! Don't touch my marble.

THE PATH
March elsewhere than on my trail.

THE MOUNTAIN
I was your lord, Ahasuerus; I shall make your Calvary at the summit of all my worlds, in order that you will be climbing for longer.

THE FORESTS
And I, for the cross you are to bear, will choose all the heaviest cedars I can find in a wood in Carmel.

THE RIVERS
And I shall change all my waters to hyssop, to give to you to drink.

MOB, *to Ahasuerus*
Let them speak; I'm with you. They envy you my company. See here, in the crowd, your aged parents, who are looking at you, and your brothers, who are talking to you. Listen.

JOEL, *Ahasuerus' brother*
O, my brother, where have you come from, with no tribe, all alone, after the dead? Oh, how long your beard is, and how

worn your sandals are. A woman is following you, as a spirit follows every man in life. What have you done? The forest of Carmel was large and dense; is that where you got lost? The grotto of Calvary was dark, the rock was carved for Jesus' sepulcher; is that where you went to sleep in your dream? We've brought nothing from our life except out desert pitchers. Take this and drink, to give you courage.

AHASUERUS
Thank you, my brothers. Tell me, who is the old man asleep on that stone bench, whom I went past and to whom I cannot go back?

JOEL
On that bench? That's our father Nathan, who's asleep. Once every hundred years he wakes up to ask where you are; then he closes his eyes again and leans his head on his elbow. The angels of judgment weren't able to wake him. But look—he's raising his head now.

NATHAN, *shaking his head*
Has Ahasuerus come?

ROME
Go back to sleep, old man; why did you send him to Calvary this morning?

NATHAN
Has Ahasuerus come? Tell me where he is.

ATHENS
Are you mad, old man? Why didn't you look after him better in your house?

NATHAN
And you, do you know when he'll come?

353

PEOPLE OF THE MIDDLE AGES

Get up, blind old man, if you want to; you can see him judged.

AHASUERUS, *to Rachel*

We've gone past all the dead; we only have the bare mountain to climb. Oh, their voices are harsh to hear! Stay with them. They don't know you; you'll find some fragment of a wall to hide you.

RACHEL

No, it's beneath your cloak that I want to hide.

AHASUERUS

Their eyes, which are cursing us, are visible from here.

RACHEL

Don't look down; look up higher, higher still! Can you see the angels weeping? They feel pity for us!

AHASUERUS

When I look up, I can see the hem of a blue tunic, like the one the soldiers tore up at my door. I can't go any higher; let me go back down.

RACHEL

Keep going! Keep going! Lean on my shoulder. Oh, look up! Can't you see the spirits and angels fluttering their wings? Tell him, tell him—my God, can't you see them?

AHASUERUS

No! I can't see anything on the summit but a wooden cross with bronze nails, awaiting a damned man. If there's a path here, let's take it to retrace our steps.

RACHEL

Have the tears blinded you, that you still don't recognize the patriarchs on the summit, who are already pointing at us? and the Virgin Mary imploring forgiveness for us with her hands joined—can't you see her robe beneath the cloud?

AHASUERUS

A burden is weighing upon my head; my heart is too heavy in my breast; it's bending me toward the ground.

RACHEL

Let me wipe away your bloody tears with the veil of Saint Veronica, still moist with Christ's tears. You're nearing the summit. Little angels, whom I once led by the hand in the city of Heaven, don't you know me? Stars that I sowed, rays of light that I spun, dragons that I fed every morning on your clouds, have you nothing to say for him? You haven't met him, as I have: Oh, you'd take pity on him; you'd shout, with me: *Forgive! Forgive!*

XII.

Heaven and Hell

HELL, *to Heaven*
Heaven, bend down. I can't do any more. A moment to draw breath; let's chat.

HEAVEN
I'm touching your gulf; I can hear you.

HELL
Before passing sentence on me, look into your plain. Who can you see coming to my rescue?

HEAVEN
I can see my suns shining again; I can see my abyss hollowing out.

HELL
And now?

HEAVEN
I can see my waves massing, and a star drowning.

HELL
And now? Hurry up.

HEAVEN
I can see the dust stirred up on the road of infinity, as if by a horseman.

HELL
It's a new God coming.

HEAVEN
I believe so.

HELL
I'm saved. Later, the last judgment will be set aside, and the judge will be judged.

XIII.

CHRIST, *the judge*
Can you hear me, Ahasuerus?

AHASUERUS
I've heard that voice before.

CHRIST
Look. Do you recognize me?

AHASUERUS
I've seen those blazing eyes before, and those lips, which said to me: "Be accursed!"

CHRIST
Where did you encounter me?

AHASUERUS
On Calvary, by my bench, in front of my door.

CHRIST
And who am I?

AHASUERUS
You're my Lord.

CHRIST
Who has told you that?

AHASUERUS
My bench before my door, my tongue beneath my palate, my tears on my mat, and Rachel by my side.

CHRIST

What have you done since you left your house?

AHASUERUS

I've sought repose, and found the storm; I've sought shade, and found the sun; I've sought the road to my youth, and found the road to eternal dolor.

CHRIST

When you encountered a passer-by, what did you say to him?

AHASUERUS

If I encountered a passer-by, I said to him, while walking along my path: "I'm a traveler who walks days and night through the city of humankind, without finding any bench or table at which to sit down. The peoples are at their windows; the kings are on their balconies; the street stretches beneath my footsteps. On the river of tears, the boatmen carry the years away in black gondolas. Blazoned lions roar in the night at the crossroads; crowned eagles screech on their escutcheons. God no longer lights the lamp hung on the wall. I'm lost. Tell me which way to go, and the best hostelry, in order to find a table for my hunger, and a silken bed in which to go to sleep."

CHRIST

And when you found a city, what did you say?

AHASUERUS

I said to the guards on the towers: "I've seen too many towers and castles and balconies suspended from windows. I know only too well, on coming in, how bitter the bread here is, how hard the bed, and that my heart will drink its wine of tears and bile from my glass here. Open the door for me, if the bolt has been shot; if the drawbridge has been raised, lower it, I beg you. This is not the city I seek. The city in which I want to

359

dwell has eternal walls. The wheels of chariots trace infinite circles there. The blacksmiths strike eternal stars from their anvils there. The angels are leaning over their golden crenellations there. The bridges there are made of clouds. No, this is not its drawbridge there, nor its watchman, nor its turrets. Another day to arrive before nightfall beneath its walls."

CHRIST
And when you went into a hostelry, what did you say to the landlord?

AHASUERUS
I said to him: "My host, take your wine back to your cellar. It's salty on my palate, as if I were drinking tears. The wine I seek doesn't dry up in its skin, and its glass has no rim; look further in the depths of your cellar. Take back your bed, too, and your fine silk curtains. One can't sleep here. On the bed that I seek in my hostelry, all the dreams are true, the dreams are life; and the curtains that my bed requires will dress me in their darkness, until the new morning of the world.

CHRIST
I have sent you to Calvary after me to collect, in every place, what remains of dolor in the world. Are you quite sure that you have drunk it all?

AHASUERUS
With one glance, you have filled my eyes with eternal tears. I have already shed my tears in the night that I have lived. You had left me as a heritage a cup always full of bile. Rachel, drinking her share, emptied it with me this morning. If you want me to recommence my path, oh, give me more tears in my eyes and ore bile in my cup. With your hands you have attached an aureole to my head, not of light but of mourning, darkness and obscure cares. That is my diadem; when kings encountered me, they made way for me, murmuring to one another: "Have you seen him? Truly, our crowns, of diamond

and sapphire, are not as heavy, nor so firmly attached to our heads as his black crown. When the waves cursed me in my boat, the storm on my path, the sword in its sheath, the lightning above my head, they said to one another, in a whisper: "Be careful not to touch him, sine Christ's fingers have touched him before us."

CHRIST
The world will tell me whether you have left any pain behind. Valleys, peoples, mountains, is it true that no pain remains in the abyss that has not been collected?

THE UNIVERSE
All the dolor you have sown in my furrow has been harvested in due course. There was always someone beside me to drink my hemlock. Always, if my waves were livid, if my sky was veiled, if my flowers faded, there was a soul in the vicinity who faded and was veiled more so than my flowers or my sky. In the morning, I dipped my sponge in bile and vinegar; always someone pressed it to his lips by night to dry it out. When my dusk approached, I filled my table with poisoned fruit with deceitful rinds, and my glass with tears, to the brim. On seeing the feast, the gods went away; then the kings; and the people thereafter. Ahasuerus alone remained at the end of my empty table, like an insatiable companion who does not leave until morning.

CHRIST
Since you have finished the task I gave you, I shall give you back your house in the Orient. Do you want to go back there?

AHASUERUS
Oh! No, Lord.

CHRIST
What would you like?

361

AHASUERUS

Neither here nor there can I sit down any longer. I ask for life, not rest. Instead of the steps of my house on Calvary, I should like to climb the steps of the universe, without pausing, to reach you. Without drawing breath, I should like to whiten my shoes with the dust of stars, climbing, always climbing, from world to world, from heaven to heaven, without ever coming down again, in order to see the source from which you brought forth the centuries and the years. I should like, as I knocked on the thresholds of hostelries in Spain and Germany, always knock at unknown stars, at a new life, on thresholds standing ajar to the end of Infinity and better skies.

CHRIST

Are you not exhausted by your first voyage?

AHASUERUS

Your hand, in rising over me, has already dried my sweat. Bless me, and I shall depart this evening toward the future worlds that you already inhabit.

CHRIST

But who would you like to go with you?

VOICES IN THE UNIVERSE

Not us. If you wish, we'll trace our steps, but we can't go any higher. Our waves, our wild mares and our tempests are weary.

RACHEL

Me, I will go with him; my heart is not weary.

THE UNIVERSE

A woman doomed me; a woman has saved me.

CHRIST
Yes, that voice has saved you, Ahasuerus. I bless you, pilgrim of worlds to come and second Adam, Give me back the burden of the earth's dolors. Let your tread be light; the heavens will bless you, if the earth curses you. Carry in your hand, instead of your traveler's staff, a palm of stars. The dew of the firmament shall nourish you better than a desert cistern. You shall clear the path for the universe that follows you. The angel who accompanies you shall not leave you. If you are tired, you shall sit down on my clouds. Go forth, from life to life, from world to world, from one divine city to another city; and when, after eternity, you arrive from circle to circle at the infinite summit to which all things go, to which souls, years, peoples and stars climb, you shall cry to the stars, the people and the universe, if they want to stop: "Climb, keep climbing, here it is."

MOB
And me, Lord, must I also go with him? What shall I have for a wage?

CHRIST
You no longer have a scythe or a goad to hasten your horse. With one bound, go back down to earth. Draw in your wings there, and brood your oblivion for Eternity.

THE PEOPLES
Listen to the song of Ahasuerus, who is continuing his march.

AHASUERUS
1.
Adieu, Father; adieu, my brothers. Did you hear? The Lord has pardoned me. My journey is recommencing. How far away from me our paradise is, already! The road is paved with clouds. Oh, won't you ever come here? The stars blossoming on their stems here are more beautiful than in your new city.

Here the flower grows that embalms their route on its own. On its leaf is written: THE FUTURE. Will you never come after me to pick it? When I am at the summit of the world, I shall make a hermitage to watch for your arrival. My chapel will be painted the color of the sun, His roof will be azure; and I shall ring my bell, like thunder, to call to you from afar, if you go astray.

2.

Like the spire of a nave, when a church is finished, my song rises, in a point, to lick the skies. An eternal delirium flagellates my heart. I want to see what no eye has ever seen; I want to touch what no hand has touched; until death I want to love that which has no name. Beneath the underslung vault of the clouds, everything vexes me, everything embarrasses me. Against a passer-by, against a word, a memory, less than a sigh, my thought is bruised at every step. Beyond the universe, I shall go to seek a path on which to draw breath in my abyss.

3.

On my road the dust of suns rises up; on the wing, they catch their breath in the great shadow of tomorrow, which flees incessantly. The breathless universe is a sigh of infinity; it is a moment that comes and goes, staggering between two eternities. Every empire fills a world. The heavens pile up; their flood overflows in the immensity like wine in a cup. Every disinhabited emptiness is repopulated; every void is filled in, except for one single place, here in my heart, narrow, dark and imperceptible, scarcely big enough to hide a tear. Neither God, nor son of God, nor Christ, nor Angel, nor Creator, nor worlds are enough to fill it. Tomorrow, perhaps! That's the whole of the mystery.

4.

All is ended; everything begins again. New skies unfurl. The may-tree of the universe has reflowered beneath the breath of a spring that has kissed neither coast nor bank.

Mounted on carts that have not worn out their drivers not the feet of their horses, my hopes and my desires move a day ahead of me everywhere. Beneath their steps the road grows: further on, further on it's necessary to go. The host who has laid a full table and a banquet for them dwells beyond eternity.

5.

An errant world beneath my feet is already crying out to me: Master, my traveling belt is worn out. The firmament knotted around me has come loose, and the void that dresses me is torn. Wait for me." Further on, further on! I'm in a hurry. Nothing stops me. Nothing amuses me. When one star has broken its axle, another has set up its chariot for me. When my excessively fast mare dies, another, even faster, has already put on its bit and saddle of light for me. Time passes, but tomorrow never arrives; and my feet will only rest, crossed one over the other, on the bench of infinity.

THE ETERNAL FATHER, to Christ

Ahasuerus is the eternal man. All the others resemble him.[45] Your judgment of him will serve for them all. Now, our

---

[45] This opinion has been endorsed, perhaps correctly, by most of the commentators on the text, even though it is voiced by a God whose Last Judgment has just been reversed, and in spite of the fact that a substantial fraction of the rest of the human race might, if offered a vote, have opted to stay in God's paradisal new city. Perhaps it is worth considering the hypothesis that Ahasuerus is not symbolic of all men at all, but only of those highly exceptional men committed to the idea of progress: to the idea of an infinite march into an unknown future, with no further assistance from the idea of an Eternal Father. If so, the Eternal Father's decision to pull the plug on his planned new city, leaving Ahasuerus to play the role of Messiah as well as that of a new Adam, leading humankind into a God-free future, might be interpreted by the faithful as rather unfair.

work is finished, and the mystery also. Our city is closed. To-morrow, we shall create other worlds. Until that time, let's both go and rest under a tree in our forest, in our eternity.

XIV.

A choir and orchestra of Archangels, sitting in a circle on the clouds

THE ARCHANGELS

Inflating our cheeks, let us finish this day with the universal harmony of our viols, our clarions, the organ, the lyre and all our other instruments. On high and down below, great and small, every star that scintillates is a note in our divine symphony, and the world is a scale that begins with Earth and Tears and ends with Heaven and Joy. Let us sound our trumpets.

THE TRUMPETS

With my powerful breath, my task is the most beautiful and the easiest. Always the same note, always the same sound, always the same word: *Sanctus, Sanctus, Sanctus.* Merely by repeating it as it is written, I make so much noise that the void quivers and reverberates, and the heavens love me more than the viols, the mandoras and the clarions.

THE VIOLS

1.

Beneath a golden bow that harasses, stabs and tears me, I palpitate, shiver and moan. Like a virgin beneath her veil, I sob. My voice propels tears. I should like to sing; and my vibrant weeping streams over my strings, already taut. Still crawling at the foot of our edifice of sound, I exhaust myself climbing the resounding steps to the summit, where vertigo forces me to descend. Dolor! Dolor! Dolor! that's the word I know best, and Love, which pleases me the most, and Infinity, the one that makes me sigh so much.

2.

Alone I sing, alone I listen, alone I descend to the bottom of my well of harmony. In the distant heavens, no one understands me, no one replies to me, no one loves me. Oh, how sad my soul is! I am a poet but I have no words, I only have my sobs. And now, golden bow, let me be; it's the clarions' turn to resonate.

THE CLARIONS

Over your vibrant souls, over your murmurs, over your sparkling silver-threaded sighs I extend, like a princely mantle, my songs of gold and crimson. I whinny better than a horse. My voice is more resplendent than a sunlit sword. In battle I have resonated. On the lips of the heralds-at-arms I have published, in tournaments, the commands of kings and queens. Just now I am publishing, on the lips of angels, new heavens.

THE ORGAN

Beautiful golden clarions, shut up. I've inflated my lungs with air; it's my turn to sing.

Storms, hail, tempests are amassed in my giant bellows; it's me who makes the thunder. All that resonates beneath the vault of the sky—forests that growl, nations that fall, cities that buzz, names that resound—emerges from a thousand divine pipes. I am the voice that speaks and shouts in realms and ruins. When I raise my diamond key, a people rises to its feet and resounds; when I let it fall again, the people falls, and falls silent. And the plaint of empires, crumbling one after another, is the song with which I amuse myself with my bellowing notes in my golden case.

For the moment, however, there's one word that I can't say; my voice is insufficiently mixed with incense. The lyre can do it better than me.

THE LYRE

1.

Future! Future! Future! is that the winged word that your thousand pipes lack? Only the breath of morning, touching me, makes it resonate. It vibrates by itself, without a bow. To listen to it, the heaven pause. Like a flower, they open their calices to receive its dew.

2.

Suspended from the vault, my three strings are as large as the world. Under the finger of my player, who goes back and forth and never tires, the first, spun from the tresses of stars, is the voice of the universe. The second, of pure gold, is the voice of an empire. The third, which I like the best, the smallest, the softest, always warm with sighs, is the voice of a young woman as virginal as me; and the word they all know together, with no deception, is Harmony.

3.

You who are passing through the crossroads of infinity, pause; form a circle around me. Although old, my melody is always new. The one who made it is the master to whom I belong. Beneath his hardened fingers, a thousand centuries ago, I learned it in order to make the round-dance of the stars, worlds, skies, people and hours who link hands circulate and sway around him. Again, again! let the round begin again! let the suns rotate more rapidly! Let the waltz of the spheres and their satellites pass and pass again, whirling, until they are dizzy, until they say, staggering: "Satellites, where are we? Let the amorous stars, lifting their veils, drop the bouquets from their bosom."

4.

When I play more softly, nodding her head, Eternity sings her song: "When I was born, in what place, I do not know. Without worrying about it, in my turn, I spin, spin on my wheel heavens and news stars to embroider my robe.

5.

"Many gods, one after another, have come to my door to espouse me without further ado, all clad in rubies, all borne on clouds, all holding golden globes in their hands, saying: 'Choose me for your husband; I shall live more than a thousand years.

6.

"But the one who pleased me had neither rubies nor gold. His tunic was torn. I wanted to mend it for him. His side, bleeding from a spear-wound, I wanted to heal. His crows was made of Judean thorns; I wanted to wear it.

7.

"His father was too poor to dress him in glory; I was rich enough for two. With my mantle I dried his harsh tears. But thousands upon thousands of years have chanced my fancy. Find me another, younger god, my messengers, whom I love more. Without deceit, this time, I shall be faithful."

THE VIOLS

Enough, I can stand no more. If we must keen like disheveled sisters, we'll weep our tears spun from virgin silk and silver together.

THE TRUMPETS

I'm too bored in silence. The dead are dead. If it's necessary to awaken them, I resound better than the lyre.

THE CLARIONS

If it's necessary to fight, I'll whinny with my brazen mouth.

THE LYRE
1.
Alleluia! Alleluia! No more death! no more war! no more tears! all dolor is consoled, when I resonate.

2.
Look! Two amorous souls that have long wept, and about whom a poet spoke to me, are living here in one bosom, in one heart, and no longer form more than one angel. Like the brood of a swallow in spring, they seem themselves to be assembled in a single being, beneath the same transparent wing. In a single breast, two joys, two memories and two worlds are quivering. Half-man, half-woman, for two lives there is but one breath. And when they brush my strings, they have but one mouth to say: "Is that your voice? Is it mine? I don't know."

3.
Thus, henceforth, earth and heaven are betrothed. It's at the end of the universe that they will marry. Together they will be an infinite archangel, who will hide every bitter valley beneath its flight. The earth will be the baser and heavier body, in order to crawl. The heavens will be the azure-tinted wings, deployed and more sublime, in order to soar. The cortege that will follow them will be rich and populous, consisting of the most diligent stars of the morning, then the most silvery stars of the evening, and then the most ornate stars of the night. Let's go and see them on the road, before they've all passed by.

FINAL CHORUS
Everything concludes in accord. The mystery is over. Taking away their seats, the gods have already left. Spectators, go home too, quietly, as before, each in your trouble commenced, in which your life will inevitably be worn away. Across mountains and valleys, high and low, like a cavalier laden with messages, our fearless harmony has risen and de-

scended, passed and rebounded. In front, it has collided with the abyss; the abyss echoes it; and then the sky, and lower down the star, and lower still the earth, over its broken string. While going home, continue to listen to the murmur of Infinity that rumbles around us, and that sigh, and that silence, and that sound afloat, and, in time, no longer anything—no, nothing at all, I said—and in that sonorous nothing, one word still, down there, which vibrates eternally...and eternally fades away.

EPILOGUE

CHRIST, *alone, in the vault of the firmament*

1.

Since the moment when Ahasuerus returned my chalice to me, the wound in my side has reopened; my tears are flowing into the abyss. The four winds are drawing lots, dividing up my tunic of clouds. The breath of my bosom is causing the lamp of the world, which is going out, to flicker. Around my steps, my feet drag as snakes once did over the stones of Golgotha, and my long hair is massing on my heart, like a storm swollen with the tears of the earth.

2.

Universe, ruined basilica, which had a stairway of stars to climb to your infinite tower, and which has attached me to your vault, why have you let the hour pause on your clock? Why have you let the nave of your firmament fall in fragments on to your pavement? Why have you broken, in anger, the sky-blue panes in your window? Why have you told the nettles to rise up as far as my seat, the worms to gnaw away the feet of my bench, and the silver stars to sound their knell in the heavens, as on the eve of the feast of the dead?

3.

Ah! It's because the sky is empty; it's because I'm alone in the firmament. One after another, all the angels have folded their wings, like the eagle when it grows old. My mother Mary is dead; and my father Jehovah has said to me at his bedside: "Christ, my age has passed. I have lived enough centuries of centuries; the worlds are weighing me down. My diamond eyelid has worn away gazing at my lighted suns. My bald head has been battered too long by the inexorable tempest; I'm cold. My feet have made their eternal circuit too often; I'm weary. My tongue in my mouth has summoned too many worlds, one after another, to oblivion; I'm thirsty. My old age is too great; I can no longer see your aureole shining. There— your father is dead!"

4.

The firmament has shaken its god from its branch as the fig-tree shakes off its leaves. My roof has been removed and death is raining on my face. As far as the worlds swarm, I can longer hear anything but my heart beating; as far as my eyes can see, I can no longer see anything but my blood trickling from my wound. Yes, flow, my blood; flow from the furthest corner of my heart; this time Judean linen will no longer staunch you, Syrian balm will no longer dry you up; and spring water will no longer wash you away.

5.

Where are my fisherman's nets in my house at Nazareth? Where are the gifts that the mage-kings gave me in my cradle? Where is my agony in the Garden of Olives? Then, the sun made my aureole, the lions of the desert and the gryphons licked my wound and wept. Now, the suns gaze at me, and no longer arm my bosom; the wind passes by without asking who I am; the void, at its door, is winding my shroud, and for my aureole, places its empty crown on my head.

6.

Adieu, worlds, stars, morning and evening dew that greeted me by name when I was a little child. Adieu, mountain lakes whose cups I filled, clouds that I bore on my shoulders like a blessed palm. Sea, oh, who will take care tomorrow of all your waves while you're asleep? Birds of the woods, who will make your little suits of down when you go to the fields? Desert of Arabia, who will give you something to drink at the edge of your cistern when you are thirsty? Poor voyaging star, who will warm you up in his hands when you go astray in the cold night? Flood of suns, infinite tide, who will say to you tomorrow, at any hour, in any language, in any place: "I love you," when you sigh so sadly as you lick your shores?

7.

Worlds, stars, morning and evening dew, is it true, then? In the night, in the day, far away, nearby, is there no longer anyone at all?

THE ECHO
No one.

CHRIST

1.

Blacker than Pilate's bile, doubt fills my cup and moistens my lips. If I didn't put my finger in my wound, my mouth would no longer know my name, and Christ would no longer believe in Christ.

2.

What have I been? Who am I? What shall I be tomorrow: a word without life or a life without a word; a world without God or a God without a world? Perhaps nothing.

3.

Father, mother, my church with the incense of so many souls, was that all a dream, then? oh, nothing but a divine dream on my eternal couch? and the cry of the universe, punctuated by such a long sigh—was that my voice, all by itself, thoughtlessly, stammering in my sleep?

4.

My banner of heaven, was that nothing but my shroud? and that infinite rain that rained everything, was that, then, my tears falling from my eyelids, too heavy to feel them flowing?

5.

Life, truth, lies, love, hate, bile and vinegar mixed together in my ciborium; yes, the universe: that was me. And me, I'm a shadow; I'm the shadow that always passes; I'm the tears that always flow; I'm the sigh that is always repeated; I'm the death that is always agonizing; I'm the thing that always doubts its doubt, and the oblivion that always denies itself.

What! no one after me in the night? no one in the day? no one in the well of the abyss?

ETERNITY
Me, I'm still in the well of the abyss. My bosom is a woman's, but I'm not your mother Mary; my forehead is that of a seer, but I'm not your father Jehovah.

CHRIST
Help me to weep.

ETERNITY
I have no tears to weep in my great eyelid.

CHRIST
Where have you shed them?

ETERNITY
My eyes are dry.

CHRIST
The worlds are orphans. Love them in my stead, when I am no more.

ETERNITY
In my bosom I have neither love nor hate.

CHRIST
Were you nursed by a virgin, as I was?

ETERNITY

No one nursed me. I have neither a father nor a mother.

CHRIST

Who will bury you, then, when you too climb your Calvary?

ETERNITY

I neither climb not descend; I have neither summit nor valley, neither joy, nor dolor.

CHRIST

It's me who has dried up your dolor in your well; it's me who got up before you to sate myself on the tears of everything; it's me who drunk all the bitterness in the cup of day and the cup of night; it's me who cried, as soon as dawn broke: "Give me your sadness," to the passing wind, the declining day, the flowing wave, the drowning sun, and the firmament that turned aside to sigh. My chalice was hollowed out slowly in my hand, as profound as the world; take it in my stead.

ETERNITY

Now it's broken in my brazen fingers; it's fallen into the gulf.

CHRIST

And me too; you've broken me; my life was in my chalice; you've emptied it too soon.

ETERNITY

1.

No, it was time. On the Golgotha of Heaven, recommence your passion. In the potter's field where I dry out the clay of my vases, sow yourself for a second time, like an ear of wheat that you will reap yourself. The firmament, hence-

377

forth, will be your cross; the golden stars will be the nails in your feet; many clouds, passing by, will give you're their absinthe. Time has run out. Descend into death again, like a landlord to his cellar, to bring back life; and go search once again for a pinch of your dust in our new sepulcher, to knead a new world, a new heaven and a new Adam.

2.

Around your sepulcher, carved in the rock, lying there on their elbows, are sleeping peoples, like your guards on Calvary on the night of your passion. One has unlaced his hauberk, another his breastplate, another his shiny coat of mail; and the blade of faith that was hanging along each thigh has fallen from every hand. Nothing visits your summit any longer but the hungry eagle that searches on your cross for is prey and his divine pasture. Everything is asleep. Lift up your heavy stone, therefore; resuscitate for a second time. Magnified by death, by more than twenty cubits, come and march side by side, celestial revenant, with the universe, your strayed disciple, who is going forth on his road to Emmaus, without recognizing you;[46] break with him, on his table, a second loaf of more gilded wheat. With your deeper wound in your side, your feet in Hell and your head in the firmament, reappear—ah, reappear on my roof in the assembly of worlds, a finger over your lips, as you did at the assembly of your apostles, in the house of the Magdalen.

3.

To transfigure yourself a second time, go forth into a new Bethany, to a new Tabor made of al summits set atop one another. Like your apostles, in the dust, while the universe swoons at the foot of your hill, God-Giant, rise, rise up higher than an entire Heaven. Arms extended to embrace all things, take the spheres and clouds away with you, to my last still-disinhabited summit.

---

[46] The reference is to the episode described in *Luke* 24:13-30.

CHRIST
It's all over. Lay me down in my father's sepulcher. So
be it.

ETERNITY
For the Father and the Son I have hollowed out a grave
with my hand in a frozen star, which rotates without company
and without light. The night, on seeing it so pale, will say:
"That's the tomb of some god."
And then, I shall be alone for the second time. No, not
yet alone enough. I'm weary of these worlds that wake me up
with a sigh every day. Crumble, worlds! Hide away!

THE WORLDS
Where?

ETERNITY
There in that crease of my robe.

THE FIRMAMENT
Should I take away all my stars, as a reaper takes away
the flowering grass that he has sown?

ETERNITY
Yes, I want them all to be harvested; it's their season.

THE SPHINX
When you whistled to summon me as a messenger, I followed you everywhere; and I hollowed out your black abyss
with my claw; let me lie down at your feet again.

ETERNITY
Go away, like them. I've already thrown my serpent,
which was biting its tail in despair, into my abyss.

THE VOID
You'll keep me, at least; I don't take up much room.

ETERNITY
But you make too much noise. No being, no nothingness;
I don't want anything but me.

THE VOID
Who, then, will guard you in your desert?

ETERNITY
ME!

THE VOID
And if not me, who will wear your crown in your stead?

ETERNITY
ME!

Here ends the mystery of Ahasuerus.
Pray for the man who wrote it.

SF & FANTASY

Henri Allorge. *The Great Cataclysm*
Guy d'Armen. *Doc Ardan: The City of Gold and Lepers*
G.-J. Arnaud. *The Ice Company*
Charles Asselineau. *The Double Life*
Cyprien Bérard. *The Vampire Lord Ruthwen*
Aloysius Bertrand. *Gaspard de la Nuit*
Richard Bessière. *The Gardens of the Apocalypse*
Albert Bleunard. *Ever Smaller*
Félix Bodin. *The Novel of the Future*
Louis Boussenard. *Monsieur Synthesis*
Alphonse Brown. *City of Glass; The Conquest of the Air*
Emile Calvet. *In a Thousand Years*
André Caroff. *The Terror of Madame Atomos; Miss Atomos; The Return of Madame Atomos; The Mistake of Madame Atomos; The Monsters of Madame Atomos; The Revenge of Madame Atomos; The Resurrection of Madame Atomos*
Félicien Champsaur. *The Human Arrow; Ouha, King of the Apes; Pharaoh's Wife*
Didier de Chousy. *Ignis*
Jules Clarétie. *Obsession*
Michel Corday. *The Eternal Flame*
Captain Danrit. *Undersea Odyssey*
C. I. Defontenay. *Star (Psi Cassiopeia)*
Charles Derennes. *The People of the Pole*
Georges Dodds (anthologist). *The Missing Link*
Harry Dickson. *The Heir of Dracula*
Jules Dornay. *Lord Ruthven Begins*
Alfred Driou. *The Adventures of a Parisian Aeronaut*
Sâr Dubnotal *vs. Jack the Ripper*
Alexandre Dumas. *The Return of Lord Ruthven*
Renée Dunan. *Baal*
J.-C. Dunyach. *The Night Orchid; The Thieves of Silence*
Henri Duvernois. *The Man Who Found Himself*
Achille Eyraud. *Voyage to Venus*
Henri Falk. *The Age of Lead*
Paul Féval. *Anne of the Isles; Knightshade; Revenants; Vampire City; The Vampire Countess; The Wandering Jew's Daughter*
Paul Féval, *fils. Felifax, the Tiger-Man*
Charles de Fieux. *Lamékis*

Arnould Galopin. *Doctor Omega*; *Doctor Omega and the Shadowmen* (anthology)

Judith Gautier. *Isoline and the Serpent-Flower*

Léon Gozlan. *The Vampire of the Val-de-Grâce*

G.L. Gick. *Harry Dickson and the Werewolf of Rutherford Grange*

Edmond Haraucourt. *Illusions of Immortality*

Nathalie Henneberg. *The Green Gods*

V. Hugo, P. Foucher & P. Meurice. *The Hunchback of Notre-Dame*

Romain d'Huissier. *Hexagon: Dark Matter*

Michel Jeury. *Chronolysis*

Gustave Kahn. *The Tale of Gold and Silence*

Gérard Klein. *The Mote in Time's Eye*

Fernand Kolney. *Love in 5000 Years*

Paul Lacroix. *Danse Macabre*

Louis-Guillaume de La Follie. *The Unpretentious Philosopher*

Jean de La Hire. *Enter the Nyctalope; The Nyctalope on Mars; The Nyctalope vs. Lucifer; The Nyctalope Steps In; Night of the Nyctalope*

Etienne-Léon de Lamothe-Langon. *The Virgin Vampire*

André Laurie. *Spiridon*

Gabriel de Lautrec. *The Vengeance of the Oval Portrait*

Alain le Drimeur. *The Future City*

Georges Le Faure & Henri de Graffigny. *The Extraordinary Adventures of a Russian Scientist Across the Solar System* (2 vols.)

Gustave Le Rouge. *The Vampires of Mars; The Dominion of the World* (w/Gustave Guitton) (4 vols.)

Jules Lermina. *Mysteryville; Panic in Paris; To-Ho and the Gold Destroyers; The Secret of Zippelius*

André Lichtenberger. *The Centaurs; The Children of the Crab*

Jean-Marc & Randy Lofficier. *Edgar Allan Poe on Mars; The Katrina Protocol; Pacifica; Robonocchio; Tales of the Shadowmen 1-9*

Xavier Mauméjean. *The League of Heroes*

Joseph Méry. *The Tower of Destiny*

Hippolyte Mettais. *The Year 5865*

Louise Michel. *The Human Microbes; The New World*

Tony Moilin. *Paris in the Year 2000*

José Moselli. *Illa's End*

John-Antoine Nau. *Enemy Force*

Marie Nizet. *Captain Vampire*

C. Nodier, A. Beraud & Toussaint-Merle. *Frankenstein*

Henri de Parville. *An Inhabitant of the Planet Mars*

Gaston de Pawlowski. *Journey to the Land of the 4th Dimension*

Georges Pellerin. *The World in 2000 Years*

Ernest Pérochon. *The Frenetic People*

Pierre Pelot. *The Child Who Walked on the Sky*

J. Polidori, C. Nodier, E. Scribe. *Lord Ruthven the Vampire*

P.-A. Ponson du Terrail. *The Vampire and the Devil's Son; The Immortal Woman*

Edgar Quinet. *Ahasuerus*

Henri de Régnier. *A Surfeit of Mirrors*

Maurice Renard. *The Blue Peril; Doctor Lerne; The Doctored Man; A Man Among the Microbes; The Master of Light*

Jean Richepin. *The Wing; The Crazy Corner*

Albert Robida. *The Adventures of Saturnin Farandoul; The Clock of the Centuries; Chalet in the Sky; The Electric Life*

J.-H. Rosny Aîné. *Helgvor of the Blue River; The Givreuse Enigma; The Mysterious Force; The Navigators of Space; Vamireh; The World of the Variants; The Young Vampire*

Marcel Rouff. *Journey to the Inverted World*

Han Ryner. *The Superhumans*

Brian Stableford. *The New Faust at the Tragicomique;The Empire of the Necromancers (The Shadow of Frankenstein; Frankenstein and the Vampire Countess; Frankenstein in London); Sherlock Holmes & The Vampires of Eternity; The Stones of Camelot; The Wayward Muse.* (anthologist) *The Germans on Venus; News from the Moon; The Supreme Progress; The World Above the World; Nemoville; Investigations of the Future*

Jacques Spitz. *The Eye of Purgatory*

Kurt Steiner. *Ortog*

Eugène Thébault. *Radio-Terror*

C.-F. Tiphaigne de La Roche. *Amilec*

Théo Varlet. *The Golden Rock. The Xenobiotic Invasion; The Castaways of Eros; Timeslip Troopers* (w/André Blandin); *The Martian Epic* (w/Octave Joncquel)

Paul Vibert. *The Mysterious Fluid*

Villiers de l'Isle-Adam. *The Scaffold; The Vampire Soul*

Philippe Ward. *Artahe*

Philippe Ward & Sylvie Miller. *The Song of Montségur*